# ❧ THE VISITOR ❧

Elik turned.

She heard it again: a run of words that she almost understood, deep now, and laughing. A whale could make that sound, but whales rarely came so near to the shore. A seal could be nearby, but seals had different voices, not given to sounds like these.

Then she saw it. A loon, huge and beautiful, not yet faded to its winter brown. White spots on black, striped necklace around its throat. Had it lost its mate? It was coming directly toward her, laughing in that way loons had, its inner spirit, its *inua*, smiling as it floated toward shore.

Then, at the last moment, the loon stopped. The great wings, the great long ruffling wings, drew back.

Elik's heart beat wildly.

There was a man inside. A man was stepping out. As simply as if he'd turned his feathers to a coat. Dark and tall, his face smooth, his cheekbones high.

He opened his mouth. He was going to speak to her— to her, the child who was now a woman, daughter of Chevak and Gull.

# SUMMER LIGHT

## ~ LIGHT ~

ELYSE
GUTTENBERG

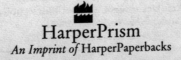

HarperPrism
*An Imprint of HarperPaperbacks*

This is a work of fiction. The characters, incidents, and dialogues are products of the author's imagination and are not to be construed as real. Any resemblance to actual events or persons, living or dead, is entirely coincidental.

HarperPaperbacks  *A Division of* HarperCollins*Publishers*
10 East 53rd Street, New York, N.Y. 10022

Cover illustration by Martin Andrews

First printing: January 1995

Printed in the United States of America

HarperPrism is an imprint of HarperPaperbacks.
HarperPaperbacks, HarperPrism, and colophon are trademarks of HarperCollins*Publishers*

❖ 10 9 8 7 6 5 4 3 2 1

∽

*To my brothers David and
Richard, who first drove
the highway north.*

And I think over again
My small adventures
When with a shore wind I drifted out
In my kayak
And thought I was in danger.
My fears,
Those small ones
That I thought so big,
For all the vital things
I had to get and to reach.
And yet there is only
One great thing,
The only thing:
To live to see in huts and on journeys
The great day that dawns
And the light that fills the world.

TRANSLATED FROM THE ESKIMO
BY KNUD RASMUSSEN
REPORT OF THE FIFTH THULE EXPEDITION

꒰꒱

# ALASKA, 100 B.C.

# Prologue

~

They came in the twilight hours before dawn: four men,
their faces streaked red with ochre, red as the color of
blood.

With the constant sound of waves lapping and the wind
to shield their steps, they crept toward the sod-roofed
house. The wood shafts of their flint-tipped spears were
held low, their parka hoods pulled back, the better to hear,
to see if the old shaman was awake inside with his curses
and his mask, if his son was already hiding with a blade
beside the door.

Red Fox, the younger shaman, towered behind his four
cousins. The sound of his breath was thick, distorted
through the curved wood of the spirit mask he'd finished so
recently, the black of the paint still shone. He had promised
them that the old shaman's strength had been subdued, that
it was Red Fox's spirit helpers who were stronger now—but
how could they be certain? How could anyone understand
or truly control the spirits of sea or land or sky?

Red Fox gestured and his mask seemed to come alive,
encouraging them, giving them strength. The men started
forward, two of them making their way to the mounded
roof, the others creeping toward the entry, slowly, so the
village dogs would not set up a cry.

Inside the house, Qajak woke with a start.
Quickly he sat up, pushing aside his blankets. The

caribou hides had twisted beneath his shoulder and he was overheated. His chest felt clammy and his heart was pounding and though he tried, he could not remember any dream that might have troubled him so.

From the smoke hole in the roof overhead, the autumn predawn light filtered down and lent enough of a shadowed touch for Qajak to see by. The fire in the center hearth had been banked; all that remained were a few white coals beneath a dusting of ash. On the sleeping platform along the wall opposite his, Qajak could see his father and, behind him, the rounder shape of the woman, Nuliaq, his father's new wife, the one the lean-faced, ambitious Red Fox had used to fuel this argument with his father.

There on a peg was her long-tailed woman's parka, and there her sewing kit and a bobbin for twisting sinew. On the floor beside the hearth sat the birch bark cooking pots she had brought into the house and there the two scooped-out wooden bowls his father had carved as part of her bridal gift—possessions that should have spoken of a settled, wealthy family, of food and guests and laughter.

Except that this season in the Seal People's village, with the rivalry that had grown between the two shamans, no one thought of laughter. From the day his father, Anguta, had decided he would not let Red Fox have a woman he had chosen first, there had been no peace, no single moment that had not been vigilant or wary or disturbed.

Their lives had changed. No longer were they a father and his son, a shaman and a hunter. They were like two kit foxes separated from their den, sometimes hunting, more often being hunted. This time it was the woman Red Fox had used as bait. Next time it might be a dream, or an argument over meat, an insult.

Anguta rolled over, shifted his weight to his arm. "You are awake?"

"It must have been the fire. It grew too hot."

Anguta didn't answer. He turned an ear, waited. His

tightly lined face and narrowed eyes—every part of his body—were listening for something.

Qajak looked again: his father was lying there fully dressed. *He knows, doesn't he? Father knows it will come tonight, which is why he wanted me to sleep. To save my strength—*

Carefully, Qajak started to rise. Each scraping hide, each foot he moved across the planked wood floor seemed close and terribly loud.

"Have you a knife?" Anguta whispered.

Qajak reached beside the bedding to where he'd set his parka and boots, not in their usual place, above the fire to dry, but closer, so he could find them in the night. He ran a finger along the edge of his flaked side blade, felt the four rib lines he'd etched in the handle. The strength lines, for speed, for life.

Nuliaq sat up. "What is it?" she asked, and there was fear in her voice but it was clear, not thick with sleep, as if she, too, had lain awake, waiting.

"Get dressed," Anguta hushed her. "Quickly."

There was a dull sound, then a scratching, as if a loose dog were sniffing about their roof. Qajak forced his hands to hold steady as he pulled on his parka with its string of amulets, his boots.

"Is he here?" Nuliaq crept with her blanket behind one of the house posts. Her long hair wrapped her face and shoulders in a hood as dark as the fur of a seal. She was beautiful, it was true. But not so beautiful that two men—one young and newly initiated in the ways of a shaman, the other no longer so feared as he once had been—should raise a battle over her.

The noise overhead was no longer faint, nor was it alone. A cry rose, the mournful notes of a loon's voice, surrounding them, outside the flap of the white bear hide door, above them near the smoke hole entry.

Qajak looked to his father. Anguta had taken down his amulet-covered shaman's rattle and he stepped toward the entry, but he seemed thoughtful and too quiet. He was singing. Qajak had to hold still to hear him, so light were the words, so rhythmic. For one moment Qajak wondered why his father didn't shake the rattle or cry out for his spirit helpers to come.

Then, suddenly, there was no chance to wonder.

The rocks that held the seal gut window on the roof crashed downward. Two men dropped through the opening.

With a shout Qajak jumped between his father and the men, drawing an arc with the tip of his knife. The men fell back and caught their balance, then two more men rushed through the entry. Qajak swerved to see who they were, but their faces were hidden behind masks of carved wood and willow strands, feather and bone—Red Fox's masks. He knew them from the tiny circles of the eyeholes, the red paint darkening one side.

Again Qajak swept the air with his blade, but there were four men to fight now and little room to maneuver and his father's chanting was soft and so plaintive that Qajak hesitated, uncertain how Anguta's spirit helpers would know which direction to come.

The men held back, two on his right, the others blocking the entry. Did they think he would run and leave his father? Or was that what Red Fox wanted?

One of the men carelessly lowered his arm and Qajak jabbed for his shoulder, but the man was quick. He raised his spear, caught the swing. Qajak's hands shook with the impact and the man reeled back. His wooden mask slipped, then fell away, but Qajak would have known Samik and his brothers no matter whose masks they hid behind. Hadn't they grown up shooting at snow targets together, learning to bring down ptarmigan with a rock?

Qajak looked to his father. He had been waiting for direction, for a signal, but something in the way his father leaned so heavily on the long-handled rattle told him it wasn't going to come. And yet—if Samik had been sent to kill them, wouldn't he have done it already, quick and sharp, with none of this dancing?

The four men were fanned out in front of them now. Each of them carried both a long-handled spear and a shorter knife. Qajak planted his feet, jabbed with his point, and circled, testing, trying to think.

The man he was closest to pulled back, but only for a moment. The heavier one on his left—it would be Bird's Mouth, Samik's older brother—pointed a spear tentatively at Anguta, then waited to see what happened. The shaman went on singing, but nothing had changed. Nothing happened. Emboldened, Bird's Mouth caught Anguta's loon skull necklace on the point of his spear, held it, then let it fall back to his chest.

Qajak glanced to where Nuliaq huddled against a wall. She hugged her blanket to her mouth, but she was watching. She would be safe. These men had no interest in her. No matter which of them walked out of the house alive when the fighting was done, she would be walking behind.

Too late, Qajak caught the hand sign passing between the men. The one on his right circled in closer. Qajak veered but there was nowhere to go and in a rush of hands and arms and heaving shoulders, they stole his knife, muscled him to the floor, and bound his hands behind his back with a braided thong and a kick to his chest that held him choking and helpless for a breath.

His father's droning kept on—*ayeii, ayeii aa ee*—magic words, words that only another shaman could understand.

Roughly now the four men prodded Qajak and, more carefully, his father, out of the house.

Outside, under a thin show of salmon-colored clouds, Red Fox stood waiting. His knees were bent, his shoulders set. His mittened hands worked a constant beat on his flat, walrus gut drum.

The mask he wore was so dreadful, so beautiful, that for a moment, Qajak could not look away. There were two faces on it, the full one with a twisted mouth that echoed the drumming beat, the other no larger than the cavity around the eye it circled. As soon as Anguta stepped outside the door, Red Fox heightened the beat, built it louder, more insistent, almost gleeful as he drowned out the older shaman's song.

One full turn of the seasons back and not a man among them would have dared steal into Anguta's house this way; not a family but would have thought first of the many children he had sung back from death, of the herds of caribou his spirit helpers revealed for them. One season back and the people would not have sided with so young a shaman over an elder, nor would they have bought peace at such a price as this.

But Qajak had already learned that a village's memory is fickle, that a long winter followed by a spring without meat can sometimes reshape a memory. Early in the month Before Birds Come a raven had whispered to Red Fox while he was in a trance. One vision and Red Fox led the hunters to a lead of open water in the shifting pack ice where the raven had shown him the dead whale. One whale that came to Red Fox while Anguta found none. One whale and now, when Red Fox spoke, the people hid inside the dark and pretended not to see the way Anguta's house was torn open, his shaman song defied.

Boldly Red Fox reached out and cut the line of loon skulls that circled Anguta's neck. The necklace hit the ground with a sharp, frightened sound. Anguta quit his singing, steadied his gaze beyond the shore, to a point on the shifting sea.

From inside his sleeve Red Fox pulled out a hollow bone sucking tube. With a high-pitched cry he jumped toward Anguta, raised the tube to the mouth of his mask, and started sucking. As if Anguta were sick with disease, as if the animal head carved in the end of the tube could magically inhale the disease and make it disappear. Red Fox circled and sucked in great, gulping drafts of air. All about Anguta's chest, his stomach, his mouth. Near every joint he sucked, and then finally, suddenly, he was done. The world seemed terribly quiet.

Red Fox stood with his chest heaving, puffed out and

proud. He gestured and the men jumped to tug Anguta's parka over his head. Even more quickly they passed it back across.

Qajak's heart caught but he choked back any show of emotion. His father had not brought him up to show fear, to cry out. He would not allow Red Fox the pleasure of seeing Anguta's son cower. Perhaps he would be dead soon, but death came to a man at any time—on the ice, in a storm. He had no children to leave without a father. No wife to worry which relatives would take her in. He would not show fear.

The crooked mouth on Red Fox's mask seemed to smile as he took a knife to Anguta's finely stitched parka, slashed the cord that tied the inside amulets to the hem and inner seams. He cut from the neckhole down the belly of the parka, as if the fur were an animal's flesh and Anguta was the animal, gutted improperly, without respect, without regard to the next life or the next.

Red Fox led the way from the Seal People's houses down to the shoreline. Behind them, faces peered from behind door flaps, but no one jeered. No one sang.

Two skin boats waited in the shallow water. Both were the open, double-ended umiaks that were built for distance, for hauling weight. One was already outfitted with drinking water and a basketful of food, a bow with an arrow case—the kind that could be used against a man. The second boat, the smaller of the two, sat empty in the lapping waves.

Qajak understood. He and his father had not been killed because Red Fox had ordered it so. He had calculated the risks: if any taboos were to be broken in the days following a shaman's death, however small or unintentional, then Anguta's ghost would become an evil spirit, wandering near the Seal People's village, bringing harm. Illness. Revenge. Red Fox was no fool to take such a risk. He would not kill them and he was not going to drown them. He would let the ocean do it for him.

It was Samik who checked the knots that bound Qajak's

hands and the youngest brother, No Bird, who pushed him roughly into the boat. Anguta was led to the other end, made to sit. The ruined parka was thrown to his lap but instead of holding still, Anguta stood and balanced against the tilted gunwale. His eyes studied Red Fox's mask and for the first time in a long while, Qajak watched a smile rise to his father's face.

Defiantly Anguta began to sing—not the mournful notes he'd chanted in the house but loud, a song of pride, an answer to Red Fox's assuredness: *Victory!* he sang. *You will not see me buried now. You who are living—will you recognize me when I return? This is my victory. Beware! You will not see me safely dead.*

Red Fox flinched and stepped back. He listened, waiting to see if the words could strike out and reach him, but the moment passed and he felt no different. No weather gathered in the sky. No storm. The boat leaned and Anguta fell to the seat. Nothing happened. It was true then. Red Fox's magic had proved stronger than the old shaman's. Anguta's spirit helpers had deserted him.

Red Fox pointed and two of the men waded knee-deep into the water, checked the line that secured the umiaks together. Not daring to meet the eyes of people they had hunted with, shared food with, they held the lead boat while Samik and Bird's Mouth traded their masks for visors to block the glare, climbed in, and took up their paddles. The water was rippled and ice-free. The boat lurched through the first line of breakers. The towline caught, then went slack, then caught again.

Qajak stared inside the umiak at the rows of exposed ribs. *No food. There was no food inside. And only a single, small bladder of water.* "Father?" he whispered, but Anguta did not answer.

Qajak turned to watch the houses, the village, the beach and rolling tundra fade to a thin, undifferentiated line of hazy coast. His stomach felt hollow, his thoughts surprisingly clear. He stretched his fingers behind his back, tested the knots, wondered how anyone's hands could be so empty. His tool kit was in that house—gone, his bone hammer for working flint, his flaker, his prized engraving tools, and his people—gone, his relatives, all of them gone. As if Red Fox had already changed him and his father into ghosts, as if they were invisible, as if they had never been born.

The lead umiak towed them on. The only sound was the keen of the wind, the low-pitched call of migrating eider ducks, the sticking sound his dry tongue made whenever Qajak swallowed. He carefully marked each turn the boatmen made, the number of times Bird's Mouth reached for a drink to wet his mouth, how often Samik peered and studied the sea. If he lived, he swore, he would kill them and find a way home. He would fight Red Fox. He and his father would have revenge.

For the first while the sun was at his back and the waves a steady roll. He planned routes and schemes that would bring them home again and forced into memory each point and bay in the coastline, how long the low-lying beaches stretched and whether there were inlets or hills or any chance of fresh water flowing to the sea.

The waves rose. The sun rose. Now and again a ringed seal peeked at them from the dark of the sea. He watched the way his father slept, with his chin sunk between his chest and one shoulder. He wondered if a loon would appear inside his father's dream and guide them home and prove to the people that Red Fox's magic was only as great as the strength of his four cousins carrying spears.

The sun climbed to a point in the sky, moved behind his left shoulder, and suddenly, in a way Qajak had not allowed himself to consider, Bird's Mouth and Samik leaned their heads in toward each other, spoke, and then turned sharply about. Qajak watched as Samik cut the towline that joined the boats and Bird's Mouth, without once glancing back, coiled the line inside. The two men dug their paddles into the water, drew them in, and steered their umiak back the way they had come.

In all this time Anguta had scarcely moved. He was awake now but his shoulders were slumped, his face expressionless. "Father?" Qajak called. "We're no more than half a day south of Woman Head Rock. The place we hunted walrus. You remember?"

No answer.

"If tomorrow we put the sun on our right, we could find our way—"

Again, no answer.

A different kind of fear stuck in Qajak's throat. If any other man had kept so silent, he would have worried differently. Ordinary men could be sick; they could be hurt. But Anguta was a shaman and shamans were not the same as other people. Never in all the years he could remember had his father been ill, never quiet when advice was needed.

Perhaps Anguta's spirit was even now wrestling with Red Fox, in which case Qajak could do great harm if he tried to rouse him. Or he might be watching in a trance, his eyes seeing into places Qajak had no desire to see.

Qajak's throat was dry with salt air, the helplessness like a bone he could not swallow. There was no land in sight and his father would not speak. There was no land, but he could not sit there and wait for death.

He let out a long breath, then slid to the gunwale. Red Fox had been careful to remove his father's powerful amulets but he had not troubled to check what a mere flintknapper carried.

He rubbed against the wood until he felt the amulet he wanted—a miniature-sized flaked jasper blade, pressing against his skin. By holding his parka firmly against the gunwale he was able to slip his bound hands underneath, then up and inside along the hem. Moving was awkward and the ties bit into his wrist until his skin was raw and scraped, but all he could think of was the way a wolverine or a fox or a hare caught in a snare would chew through muscle and bone in order to escape. The way a man was no different than an animal and he, too, would do what he had to—anything to save his life.

The moment his fingers closed around the amulet, he snapped and the blade came free.

Gently then, so as not to upset the boat, he crawled to where his father sat near the bow. Qajak turned so they were back-to-back, then worked the blade behind him. The leverage was poor and his father gave little help though he did, at least, seem to understand. Qajak's arm cramped and he had to slow, monotonously sawing back and forth, until finally the ties fell open.

Anguta rubbed his wrists and Qajak edged about, holding out the blade until, finally, his father's icy fingers grazed his and the sawing began again.

"It's done," Anguta said, and then went quiet.

Qajak reached for the one small water bladder they'd been given and helped his father to drink. The skin on his father's face was dry, his fingers cold as bones.

When he was ready to speak, Anguta would tell him what his vision had shown. Until then, it was little use troubling him. He pulled his father in to lean against his chest, took the parka Red Fox had ruined, and spread it over them as best he was able.

There were no weapons and no food. No hooks. No lines. No harpoons. There were no paddles and no way to reach driftwood unless it floated up to meet them. Yet the double-lapped seams on the boat skins were all intact. Someone had taken care to grease them with a layer of fat for waterproofing. Red Fox wanted them to travel far. To die so far away that their ghosts would never find a way home.

His single abiding thought was how much he hated Red Fox. Not Nuliaq; her only fault was in losing a first husband just as the two shamans needed something to fight over. It was Red Fox he blamed for wanting more than other men. For his pride, his temper. For learning too well the lessons Anguta generously taught.

If he ever saw the shaman again, he would kill him. He would humiliate him, rob him of any amulet that gave him strength, teach him that among the Seal People, no one survived by wasting another's blood. No one.

That was dusk, the end of the first day. Then night

came and a driving wind pushed them steadily under the dome of a starless sky. The next morning Qajak woke to the greeting of gulls, low-flying ducks, and a stretch of coast that must have followed them through the night. He waited: the tide was with them and luck and perhaps some spirit in the distant hills who, hearing his father's song, had decided to allow them to live one day more.

When they were close enough to shore, he slipped over the side of the boat and walked it in to a sandy strip of beach, then carried his father's listless weight to shore. He dragged the umiak to a patch of brown grass, set his father in its shade, then took his own clothes off to dry. For the rest of that day Qajak searched for signs of people—there were none. Nor rocks to show the ring where a fire might have burned, or a circle of tent anchors. He found no streams, only saltwater catches, no fresh water. A few clams he dug out with his fingers then licked down raw—Anguta showed no sign of hunger, no interest.

The one good thing, Qajak told himself, was that at least the umiak would have a chance to dry—in the sea a walrus-hide boat could last two days, three at the most, before the skins slipped loose from the frame and the stitches stretched to holes that let the sea come in.

But without a freshwater pond or lake or stream, without someone to help with his father—he couldn't stay. If there were mountains behind the hills or rivers inland, he couldn't see them through the haze and clouds. They spent one night; then, when the tide turned, Qajak hefted his father into the boat and pushed off with the only long pole he'd found. And then drifted. Away from his Seal People's home. That was the one thing he knew for sure.

It was thirst that next brought Qajak awake, whispered his name, told him he was still alive. The rest of the world was gone, swallowed in a dense, obliterating fog.

He passed the hours trying to nurse his father with water, until the water ran down Anguta's chin. He sang to him until his throat was too dry to remember how to sing.

He struggled to stay alert but all he could think of was the endless fog and the slap of waves against the skin boat and his hands, how empty they felt, how a man without tools might survive if he had family. How a man without family might survive if he had tools. How a man without either was already dead.

All through the night the fog held thick and dense and cold. The wind rushed them on. South, he thought, though he saw no land to tell how far. Or south and east, that too was possible, though he slept so much he wasn't certain what was dream and what was real.

The next time Qajak woke the sun was a white ball shrouded in a grey-white sky. He pulled his arm out from under his father's shoulder, where it had become wedged during the restless night. His father's weight seemed heavier, his legs and arms unyielding. Heavy.

In a sudden fear, he shrank away, stared, waited, and then crept back. He reached out to touch his father's face but nothing was there. No warmth. No breath. No sight.

A cry stole from inside Qajak's chest.

His father was gone. And he was alone in the boat with a dead man—what could he do? When a shaman died in his house, the home was destroyed, but this was a boat, not a house—not to be destroyed unless he wanted to drown himself with it.

He could use his fingers, dig out his father's dead eyes so his ghost would not come through, make the body walk again. But without ivory and jet to carve new eyes for his father to find his way to the Land Above the Sky—what use would it be? If he had a needle, he could pull threads from his parka, sew closed the mouth and nostrils, try to prevent the ghost from entering back in. But even if he could, if he did and the ghost brought no harm now, how could he give his father proper burial in a planked coffin beneath the ground?

And yet he was his father's son. Obligated. Responsible.

It was for him to bury his father, before it was too late,

before he was forever dead. With no hope but to be tied near the dead body. No way to be born again later.

He was alone with the body of dead man. And soon his father's ghost might find him dead too.

1

There was a place along the beach where the wind had bent a row of sea grass into hoops and a trail of flecked white boulders pointed out a line between the tundra and the sea.

It was down below the bluff where the sod-roofed houses of the Bent Point village stood, but farther east than Elik usually walked for wood, and close against the water's edge.

She marked it carefully that morning when she woke to find that the autumn fog had finally lifted and her mother sent her out for a load of the weathered driftwood that always blew in with a storm.

The air was sharp though the wind had settled and it was early—the sun had not yet warmed enough to melt the morning frost, but Elik tugged her boots off just the same. She started to wade along the curving line of foam—not far, she told herself, and only for a moment. But she stopped because she heard the sound of voices calling her name.

Elik turned, wondering if another of the young women had also woken early and thought to gather sea grass or search for razor clams, but no one was there.

To one side lay the endless sea, dark water, white-tipped waves showing where the fog had rolled itself away. Away from the point, the way she'd come, lay clumps of grass, taller drying racks beside the dug-out houses, and, only in the distant haze, a rise of round-topped hills to break the view.

Seabirds fighting to catch the wind. A glaze of frost on the pebbled beach; no ice—though winter could not be far. Nowhere, as far as she could see, was anyone else out walking.

Curious now, she stepped back, turned, and stood so the wind no longer whistled in her ear.

There were sounds—yes. Almost like voices. She could hear them in between the hum of wind and breaking waves, the ravens who had come up now, teasing at her back. This time the sound was layered, distant and then near. Part of the sound was a mournful, high-pitched cry, part a rhythmic breath. Was that her name she heard? Had someone called her name?

Elik squinted back toward the houses, searched among the wavering lines of morning fires till she picked out the large roof of the *qasgi*, the village ceremonial house. It was possible one of the men had taken up a drum and was beating out a verse. But no—a drum's sound would have been deeper and more regular and most of the men had been gone these last two days, following the caribou herd to their crossing place inland.

It wouldn't be Naiya—her sister seldom woke so early when their father and older brother weren't waiting for their food. And not her grandmother; Alu's profile beneath her caribou blankets had been quiet as a string of hills when Elik left to gather wood. And besides—these sounds were not from the village—they were from the sea.

Elik turned. She heard it again: a run of words she almost understood, deep now, and laughing. Maybe a woman's voice, but maybe not a person after all.

Half in excitement, half in fear, Elik stood there listening. A white beluga whale could make that sound, like a whistle or a high-pitched keening. Clicking with its tongue. Not breaching—that would have been different, with the slap of a tail and the wake moving out. If it was a whale, and if it blew, she might yet spot a cloud of moisture or the color of its back as it sliced the waves. But larger whales seldom came so near their shore and the season was wrong. Not enough of an ice pack for walrus. A seal could easily be nearby, tucked in between the waves, watching her as it bobbed for air. But seals had different voices, not given to sounds like these.

And then she saw it. A loon, a huge and beautiful loon, not yet faded to its winter brown. White spots on black, striped necklace around its throat. Had it lost its mate? She'd seen no others along the shore.

It was floating through the waves now, directly toward her, laughing in that way loons had, like no other sound she knew, so close the thought of it made her dizzy.

The loon slowed, dipped its pointed bill, its entire head beneath the water. A moment later it was up again, the smallest silver-blue herring clutched inside its bill. The fish wiggled. The loon tilted its head back. Below its neck, hidden in the downy feathers of its chest, she saw the face, the loon's inner spirit, smiling as it floated in toward shore.

Only at the last moment, just as it would have reached dry ground, the loon held still. There in the shallows—something more was happening. The wings, the great long ruffling wings drew back.

Elik's heart beat wildly. There was a man inside. A man was stepping out. As simply as if he'd turned his feathers to a coat. Dark and tall, his face was smooth, nose sharp, his cheekbones high. He opened his mouth. He was going to speak. He was going to tell her something but he coughed instead and she couldn't understand. He coughed and shook his head and could not speak and his arms—his arms changed into wings again. Wings beating the air with a sound as if the wind were coughing.

And then he was gone. The sounds all faded.

Elik stood absolutely still.

What had it been? The loon's spirit soul? Its *inua*? Was it possible? A loon's spirit had noticed her, one young girl—no, not just a girl, not a child, but a person who was a woman now. Daughter of Chevak and Gull. Daughter of the Real People living in the Bent Point village, where the land pushed itself toward the sea.

With a feeling of awe, Elik looked farther out to where the thin line of clouds chased and caught each other in their morning game. But then another thought, a different question, made her stomach go suddenly light and, quickly, she lowered her gaze and stepped back from the breaking waves.

Elik had heard tales—everyone in the Bent Point village knew of such things—of how the spirit inside a person or an animal or even a rock could change its shape at will. A seal could shed his outer flesh as quickly as if it were a jacket and slip into a different coat of feathers or skin, and whether that person who stepped out was truly a man or an animal or something in between, no one could be certain. Ever since she had been a child peering out from her mother's hood she'd been taught that this is the way things were. Since the earliest times, when a girl cut her breast and ran bleeding into the sky and became the Sun and her brother the Moon chased after her, this is the way things were.

With a guarded motion, she felt along the front tail of her parka for the lump where her amulets were stitched. A wolverine bone her mother had given her at birth, for keen eyesight. A patch of salmonskin so the stitches she sewed would always be fine as a pattern of scales. And one wooden raven for endurance the same as that dark bird carried, its luck in finding food. They were good amulets, old ones, filled with the strengths of the animals they came from and yet, she wished they had been more.

Carefully now, slowly, hoping she had not unintentionally angered those who could not be seen, Elik retraced the oval prints of her sealskin boots back away from shore.

A shaman would understand these things but what could one girl know? She listened in the qasgi, repeated the stories her grandmother taught—but these were not things to be spoken of lightly. Not for all the troublesome questions her grandmother laughed at, then never answered. Not for all the warning, frightened glances her mother had sent her earlier that year when her falling spells began.

The first time she'd fallen had been during the cold Moon of Crusted Snow, only days after she'd first become a woman. Fainting spells, brief and frightening, that continued through the Hawk Moon, then into the Moon When Geese Return—the first few months of her woman's time—and then no more.

That odd wave of fainting, the way the world had closed in around the edges of her vision and she'd felt as if she were falling inside a dream—those were things shamans did, not new women.

The Bent Point place already had two shamans: Seal Talker and the old widow, Malluar, and those two were cousins, strong with the power of their family line. Elik's family on both sides were hunters. Other Real People were shamans, but not in their village, and only shamans had the use of magical songs and the strength to call on spirits, calm them. Only shamans could turn a spirit's anger into help.

She should hurry, go home now, before a worse spirit saw her standing there, heard the thoughts as loud as voices in her head.

The path Elik had taken cut gradually back along the beach ridge to where the houses stood, but not until it traced its way beside the village graveyard. She hesitated when she realized where she was, but unless she circled far to the other side, there was no better way.

Beneath the closest mound of stones Inoqtuk's empty body lay. His was the most recent death in the village—a man of forty summers, from Fish River, not in her family line, though his young wife had been a cousin. He'd gone to sleep one night and never woken—a fit way for a stranger to die, her grandmother said, when most men were killed in hunting accidents or simply never returned from a kayak trip to an open lead out on the ice.

Elik tried to understand, but there was so much in the world that a person could hardly begin to comprehend. Inoqtuk was dead. The part of his soul which brought life to his body had gone to the Land of the Dead. All customs, all rituals had been properly kept and already a baby had been given his name. His breath soul had found its way to life again.

So it was with people, so it was with the animals in the sea and on the land and with the birds who flew; life as unending as the summer grass. The thought of it filled her with joy and yet—there were dangers everywhere.

With everything a woman did—the way she walked while her father hunted, how loudly she spoke, the way she cut her meat—all must be done with care. Someday, when she became a wife and a family depended on her, she would show the animals how gentle she could be. She would never forget to offer a sip of fresh water to each newly killed seal and they would see how generously she shared her food. The fish, the caribou, the seals, they would see her and come willingly to her husband's harpoon, to the traps she set. The laws were many. They were sometimes difficult, but how else could a person hope to have an effect on a world so beautiful and so dangerous, both?

It was autumn now, the season when crust ice begins to form along the shore and the salmon run would reach its highest level since spring. It was the time when caribou moved about and already the shaman Seal Talker had called a dance in the *qasgi* and announced that no stone must be worked or the caribou would run away. No knives must be shaped, no harpoon points. No food from a sea mammal must be eaten. No sealskin worked.

Perhaps in the earliest days, when people first walked on dry land, such care hadn't been necessary. In those times, it was said, people hadn't needed the meat of animals to survive. But those times—when animals and humans exchanged forms and more people than only the strongest shamans knew how to fly—those times were not the same as now. Now, it was only by keeping their many customs that a person could hope for a long life, without hunger.

Once more before she neared the clutter of houses, Elik stopped to listen. It was quieter here than it had been at the shore; she didn't think the loon spirit had followed and yet—what if she were wrong?

Looking ahead she surveyed the braided strings of herring drying in the wind, the thin, tall scaffolding poles waiting for new hides to be lashed on and split, the kayaks lined along the shore.

Sometimes, she remembered, when a stranger entered the village, her mother would call her to come and join the young girls and women as they formed a circle around the houses. That way, if one of the dangerous, wandering spirits had secretly followed the man, the women's circle had the power to block the evil from entering.

It was true she was only one person, but what if the loon had been evil? Wouldn't it be better to try something, anything, rather than risk bringing a wandering spirit into her house?

Perhaps, though she had no spirit helpers of her own, she could use words the way Malluar and Seal Talker did—not the same words of course, but something. What?

She waited, listened to the flapping hides of the few summer tents that had not yet been taken down, the occasional bark of a hungry, meddlesome dog.

Perhaps if she borrowed the names of each household, she could shape the names into a kind of song, a charm to block whatever spirit might have followed?

Silently—because there could be power in a name spoken aloud—Elik began a listing of the houses as she walked.

Nagi's house first, because it was closest after the graveyard. Nagi was uncle on her mother's side—Gull's younger brother. With him was his wife, Sipsip, one of the tall Forest People, whose own mother had been stolen in a raid when Sipsip was a child. And just this season her son had been given his first chipped stone point for an arrow. And there was her new baby, born within the same month Inoqtuk had died. The new girl had been given his name and already there were signs that the new Inoqtuk had the same smile as the one who had died, the same cautious eyes.

Elik looked over her shoulder toward the sea. Safe. The world seemed safe still, though the illness and bad fortune spirits could bring had a way of lingering unseen. She kept on walking.

From her own lineage then—two who had died in Nagi's house, for both her mother's parents had died in the house of their youngest son. And a third death because Nagi's first wife had died in childbirth. And four living. Sipsip, being a Forest woman, brought no relatives of her own.

Next the family of Sila and her husband, Blue-Shadow, who was known for his weather forecasting, in a house that was much the same as Nagi's, the same as all Real People along the coast built their houses—dry and weatherproof as long as winter held, moist and too waterlogged for summer.

The large rectangular floors were started partway down inside the earth as if the trick of building them had been borrowed from the lemmings, tunneled underground to hold the heat. The inside walls were lined with driftwood, framed with cornerposts that were chosen from the straightest, the longest of the smooth greyed trunks. Inside, there were smaller logs to shape the roof and hold the sod, while moss and grass were pushed inside the cracks to help keep out the wind. To enter there was a passageway to trap cold air and inside the single room, a window made of clear gut opened like a birth canal toward the sky, and smoke could leave and light from the sun could find its way inside.

It was Sila and Blue-Shadow's daughter, Kimik, who would soon be married to Elik's older brother, Iluperaq, perhaps this season if Iluperaq brought enough skins for a bridal gift, certainly by the time another winter gave way to spring. Already Kimik's younger brother had taken to carrying Iluperaq's ice-testing stick about as if he already had a new uncle, someone to take him and a dog along to sniff out a seal's breathing hole, show him how to hold a core of flint so a flake could be struck just so.

Elik used her hand to keep the count. Also in that

crowded, noisy house was Singmiut, the eldest son, and with him the first hand's count of five was finished.

Then his wife, Salmonberry, who some people said was prettiest of the women, though for all her dancing smiles her own little boy, Taku, had eyes that watched in two directions and some said he would have bad luck and others said he would have no luck at all but that his parents must carefully choose a wife to bring him luck. And so Salmonberry was the second hand's count which was ten, and one more.

Though she would never be so ill-mannered as to boast, Elik prided herself on her memory, the way she could name each person in a house, whose names they carried, and who their relations were, both here and in the trading villages east and west along the coast.

It was Saami's house she passed next, the second lineage Elik counted as her own. Saami was elder brother to her own father, Chevak, though the two brothers seldom hunted together, for some reason Elik didn't know. Saami's first wife was dead, but Saami had been fortunate to find two new wives, sisters from the next village beyond the Bent Point, though it was only the older of the sisters who had any children. Two children, four years apart. The younger sister had given birth once but a proper name had not been found; the child refused to nurse and so it died.

Saami's grown son from his first wife was also in the house. Again one hand, and two more if she named the wife who had died, one if she named only the living. Elik had never seen the infant who died before his mother left the birthing hut, but without a name it need not be counted.

Next came the large wealthy house that Seal Talker, the shaman, shared with his wife, the grey-haired, soft-spoken Ema.

And Malluar, his cousin, the other shaman, alone in a house no one else would have lived in, set back as it was from the others and perched atop a hump of ground so old that people said a race of dwarf-people had once lived underneath.

Last of all, Elik neared her own house. For all she could see, her father and her brother were not yet home. It was too soon; no one expected word of caribou this quickly. Hadn't Iluperaq boasted he would not come home until he found so many caribou, he could offer Kimik skins for a hundred blankets, for tents and leggings and outer parkas and everything a wife could want?

Elik took a breath then slowly let it out. Someone had started a morning fire; the skyhole in the roof was open and a cloud of fog white smoke caught the wind, then drifted on its way.

She had come up on the house from the inland side, nearest to the small, curtained-off room her mother had hurriedly sent her to that day last winter when Elik first became a woman.

She didn't like to think about that room anymore, the way it seemed to separate itself from the rest of the house as if it were an infant partway stuck between its mother's thighs. And though the curtain had already been pulled down and the bedding and bowls she had used were gone now—burned—still, memories had a way of tricking her, grabbing hold of her thoughts and taking her where she did not want to go.

The month of Elik's first confinement had begun with pride. She was a woman, healthy and strong, perhaps even pretty. Her nose was small and close against her face, her cheekbones wide, her thick hair gleaming. She was a woman with a body that made blood out of its own blood and someday would make a child's blood with a spirit and name to call its own. And there would be children, sons and daughters to grow up drinking at her breast. There would be labor and childbirth. There would be a husband and more than once her sister Naiya had drawn her into giggling over the names of the few young, marriageable men. How Saami's son was the most handsome but was too closely related and people would talk; how Arveq, who was Seal Talker's only son, spoke too loudly and had a temper and, besides, he had only come home once since the year he left for Fish River. How all the best, most skill-ful hunters had first wives and who was there for them, unless they shared?

Elik had been surprised that first day to realize the bleeding did not hurt and relieved to realize she would be able to endure it. That was the first day. With the second, it grew harder.

For five days, while the atmosphere of her menstruation surrounded her, she'd been required to remain on one side of the house, to sit on a single mat of woven grass, legs folded under, no companions to visit, nothing but a regi-men of restrictions that must be endured. To be an adult a boy was taught endurance and hardship, to bear the cold without complaint, to go without food, to run fast, to sur-vive. A girl's confinement was meant to teach her stitch-work, to make her lovely, to keep her and the village safe while unseen spirits watched her from afar.

She'd heard other girls whispering of the loneliness, the torment of listening to muffled voices filtering from the house, from outside in the *qasgi*, but never were they allowed to leave their confinement lest the power of their first blood interfere with a hunter's skill, or his weapon, or the powers that shamans called on with their songs.

But none of the gossip Naiya whispered had mentioned the worst part, how the walls made scratching sounds inside the layers of sod and wood. How there were shad-ows that would rise and try to grab her. How the loneliness of those first few days pounded inside her ears.

*Try not to be afraid,* her mother had whispered. *Try not to think so much. To worry. It isn't good. It brings trouble . . .*

Elik had wanted to be strong, to make her mother proud. Naiya had been required to do this. And Kimik. And Sipsip and every woman who had ever been a girl. But the walls leaned closer than they had warned her, and the voices in her thoughts spoke louder. What if the blood that soaked the moss toweling began to raise a smell? What if the smell attracted an evil spirit? What if something hap-pened and she didn't know what to do?

There was only the one shallow stone oil lamp with its wick and trail of soot, and the sewing she was allowed. And only her mother was permitted to come with water to drink, and gentle words of how much meat a husband would catch. And Grandmother Alu, who taught her how a woman transforms the colorless strips of a seal's intestine into a warm and waterproof coat. And old Malluar, who came on the third day and instructed her.

Elik had been leaning in toward the light of the seal oil lamp, not sitting in the usual way with her legs straight out in front but tucked under her and barefoot.

Earlier, her mother had brought her a fistful of beach grass to coil into a basket. Any other time the work would have brought satisfaction, watching the bottom turn up into sides, the outer curve take on shape. She'd have soaked alder chips in a bowl with urine to dye one portion of the grass a shade of red. She'd have planned the outline of a bird rising up on two sides of the basket. But not this time. This time it was all she could do to make her hands keep moving, to keep her thoughts on her work instead of the walls. Split a blade. Thread a blade. Take a stitch. Take a stitch. Take a stitch.

Three days and still two more to wait. She laid down her work and wondered at how empty the plank flooring became without its normal clutter of firewood, skins, and cooking gear. The way the timbers held dark shapes that kept staring at her: the tangle of moss chinking that had twisted to a bear's profile, the knot of wood with two gaping eyes and the open line of a beak. A face.

Elik ran her thumb and fingers down the unworked coil, then stopped. The hide curtain separating her room from the rest of the house had moved. Someone was standing on the other side. Quickly she moistened the grass so Gull would see she had been working.

A moment later her mother pushed aside the door flap. Gull peered inside but instead of her usual reassuring smile she glanced quickly about the room, took in the tangle of unworked grass, the startled look on her daughter's face.

She put her finger to her mouth. "Hush," she whispered. "Mind what you say." Then she stepped to the side.

Behind her, Malluar climbed to the platform with difficulty, shoulders stooped, one leg following stiffly behind the other. Nor had Malluar come dressed in her everyday parka but in her ceremonial shaman's finery. Her face was partly hidden behind a row of porcupine quill tassels that hung from a brow-band. Even in the still air, the wrapped quills set up a windlike sound, shushing and deliberate.

Elik had known Malluar would come but the truth was, the seclusion left her confused and more than a little frightened. All too easily she remembered the way Malluar looked when she worked herself into a trance, her eyes turning inward. The way her voice changed and the muscles in her face contorted.

Shamans controlled spirits that ordinary people lacked the ability to see—spirits of animals, of rocks and lakes and cliffs, spirits that helped but sometimes fought with them also. Was Malluar going to do that here? Go into a trance and then leave when she was done? Simply walk out and leave her alone?

Even her mother's face showed strain. Gull fussed with the stiff door hide till it scraped firmly against the wall. On the floor, the wooden bowl she set down tipped precariously to one side, the liquid spilling over. Elik watched the bowl rock. For the first few days she had been permitted to drink water but no tea, to eat, but only the slightest bits of old meat, never fresh.

Malluar wheezed, then cleared her throat, and Gull rushed to unroll a fur for her to sit on—closer than another person would have thought polite.

Elik tried to meet her eyes. She wanted Malluar to see how brave she could be, to know that if a shaman didn't fear the light behind a person's eyes, neither would she. She smiled, tightened her jaw, and returned the older woman's stare. But the shaman wasn't staring only; she was searching, widening then narrowing her gaze, peering inside one eye, watching behind the other.

Elik broke away. Malluar chuckled at the game. "You know why I'm here?" she asked.

Elik started to answer, then stopped, her thoughts all a tangle. Had her mother mentioned a proper response? Quickly, she tried recalling everything she had been told in the last few days, but she had hardly slept. And she was so hungry. Foolishly, all she could remember was her grandmother telling the story of the girl who was made to marry a dog because she wouldn't obey her father, and all her children were dog children and the people chased them away because they barked so loudly at night.

Rather than give a wrong answer, Elik studied the belt tied around Malluar's thick waist. It was a shaman's belt, made of the soft white fur of a caribou's stomach—beautiful and very old, like nothing she or any woman in her line had ever owned. The belt was decorated in rows of amulets: miniature snow goggles, the narrowest flake of glassy obsidian, the shriveled head of a loon, its living eyes replaced with eyes of jade. On her hands Malluar wore mittens of rich, black cormorant feathers. At the curved hem of her parka hung the skinned-out feet and claws of a wolverine—weapons that could be used in battle against either a spirit or a human.

Malluar waited, then turned to Gull. "They're always like this, one time trying to climb back in a mother's parka, the next time so busy sewing they pretend they don't even notice a man is watching. Has she eaten?"

"No meat. Nothing fresh." Gull held her hands together. "Was that right?"

"Fine," Malluar said. "You did well."

"She's a difficult child," Gull apologized. "Always talking, always asking questions without watching."

Elik flushed to hear herself discussed as if she weren't there, as if she was a child too young to understand.

"Naiya is the same age as Elik, though she's been a woman since spring, a full year back."

Malluar nodded. Mothers always came and talked to her this way. In the end, most things she heard were the same.

She looked down at the girl's lowered head, the two dark braids pulled back no differently than another girl's. And yet—this was a difficult time for new women. They needed to be guarded and watched, both for themselves and for the well-being of the village as a whole. And yet, now that she thought of it, this one had somehow escaped her attention.

The father she knew of course—a cranky, some said a stingy, man. Perhaps it was because of his reputation that she'd paid less attention to this girl than to others. There was the brother also, Iluperaq. He was married to Kimik. Or would be soon—there was some gossip she couldn't quite remember. It was lucky for the girl she had uncles on both her parents' sides. She could turn to them if she needed help. Then again, it might not come to that: another year and Gull would find a husband for her. A year after that and she would have children. One year. Another. Malluar felt too old to name so many years.

She smiled at the mother. "So. Your Naiya was adopted in?"

Gull nodded, pleased that Malluar remembered. "From a cousin in the Long Coast village, yes. They had children already and they were traveling. Naiya was in the middle, old enough to leave her mother, too young to walk so far."

"And now you ask how can two girls be so different? Yet they are and one can have the spirit of an eagle, another may be crafty as a raven."

"With Naiya, I always knew what to do, what she needed."

"And this daughter will also be strong enough, and pretty. Her eyes are red though, from the lamp. See how they burn?" Malluar reached up, pulled Elik closer by the chin, and quickly spit a puff of air in one eye and then the other. "Feed her porcupine meat for the eyes, but later. Not yet."

Slowly, trying not to draw attention, Elik drew back from Malluar's grip.

"At first they're afraid. Sometimes they try to sneak out—but you wouldn't do that?" Malluar caught her by the shoulder this time, more firmly than before. "Sometimes fear can be a useful thing—you wouldn't go out alone, in the dark, would you? Not while the smell and the touch of your blood shines like a lamp in the night?"

Elik shook her head. Her grandmother had said this confinement was a trial, a test to be met with pride. She would never run. She wasn't afraid. She had promised herself she would not be afraid.

"Bring me the bowl," Malluar said. And to Elik: "Remove your hood." Gull lifted the scooped-out bowl and carefully passed it to Malluar.

"What is it?" Elik asked.

"Ah—the girl has a tongue! It's fish oil. Salmon. You need to drink. Afterward you'll be allowed to eat."

Elik looked to her mother but Gull's eyes were carefully impassive. She took the bowl, lifted it. Through the oil, the two caribou painted on the bottom seemed to move toward each other, the erect male dancing toward the female. She drank it down; the oil was thick and pungent and satisfying. When she lowered the bowl her mother was smiling. Elik shifted to a more comfortable position.

"You're tired?"

"Only my legs—"

"A man's legs also grow tired," Malluar said, more sharply than before. "When he waits beside the cupped dome of the seal's breathing hole, waits to learn if the seal will return for a taste of air. So a woman must wait at home and walk softly or the seal will hear her steps and swim away."

Elik winced. She hadn't meant to complain. It was the hunger kicking at her, the long hours of sitting, and the sounds, all churning inside of her. Of course a man had to wait by the breathing hole. Everyone knew that. Of course it was dangerous to travel on the ice pack.

"But a man is outside in the air," she said, trying to explain. "At least he hears the wind and sees the sun. These walls are too dark."

"And winter is kind? And it is pleasant to wait out a storm praying that when it clears the ice won't have stolen your way home?"

"But there is something inside the walls here." Elik pointed. "Speaking to me . . ."

Gull's eyes went wide. "Hush!" she cried, and she reached for Elik's arm. "What's the matter that you don't know the scratching sound a lemming makes?"

"She's still half a child," Malluar said, "that's all. Not an adult to be listened to."

Gull locked her arms around her knees, trying not to interfere.

Elik looked back toward the door. Aside from her shaman's belt and gloves, Malluar had brought no carved spirit masks, none of the flat dance drums she used inside the *qasgi*. "Aren't you going to sing? Or drum?" she asked.

Malluar laughed. "Tomorrow, I will come again tomorrow and draw your tattoos."

"I meant with the voices. I thought you came to send the spirits away?"

Malluar leaned back. The mother was right. This one did have a mouth for questions. "There are no spirits here. Wouldn't I hear them calling? Wouldn't a shaman see the places in the dark? If you keep to your confinement, if you stay inside and break no taboo, then you have no need to fear." Malluar pulled off the ceremonial mittens she'd worn, then, with an effort, pushed herself toward the curtain. "Untie her hair," she said, and she crossed to the men's urine tub.

Gull moved quickly, nervously. Naiya had never been this way. So many questions. So much talk. Didn't Elik know how much trouble a shaman could make if she was annoyed? Malluar could find broken taboos that were difficult to mend. She could demand payments. Spread gossip. Remember things no one else remembered. Gull's fingers snagged on a knot of hair.

"Mother?" Elik started.

"A girl talks too much," Gull said tightly.

"Mother, if Malluar won't chase away the spirits, do you think she would tell me . . ."

Malluar looked over her shoulder.

"Nothing. No!" Gull warned through her whisper. This time Elik held her tongue.

The room grew quiet. Malluar returned with a dipper full of the urine and gathered up as much of Elik's waist-length hair as she could hold. Gull turned Elik's head so she faced the floor and Malluar poured the urine from the dipper, let it run down the length of hair. This was house-hold urine—not Elik's, but clean and without feces—the kind that was saved for softening raw antler and ivory, for curing hides and cleaning lice from hair. Malluar used it now for a soap, working it through Elik's hair from the roots to the ends. The urine loosened the dirt from her hair, washed the oils away to the floor.

More at ease now, Elik turned her thoughts to the way Malluar's touch felt strong against her scalp, tugging, mas-saging. Different from the way Naiya's or her mother's hands felt when they took turns washing each other's hair, different from her grandmother's hands.

Elik pulled a clinging strand from her cheek, then opened her eyes. Malluar's belt dangled in front of her, swaying and clacking each time the old woman moved. She'd never been so close to a shaman's belt before. Wolverine. Ivory. The white bone of a loon's skull. Somewhere a loon spirit dived from the surface down to the Land Below the Sea. She wondered if it slept near its amulet, or if it came only when Malluar worked herself into a trance, called to the other world.

The hands stopped tugging. Elik straighted. Gull carried over a second bowl, this one filled with meltwater from the snow outside. Malluar poured the clear water through Elik's hair, one bowl and then another.

Finally, it was done. "Now you are clean," Malluar said, "and you must keep yourself clean. Once every fifth day—count it on your hand, or cut marks in a stick. Your moth-er will teach you to remember. You must bathe and tie your hair and go gently in all things you say and do, even to your thoughts, for the animals will hear them. You understand?"

Elik nodded, listening carefully. She wanted to hear this. Anything Malluar would tell her, she wanted to learn.

"And you understand why this matters? When the caribou chooses a route. When the fish swim past our lines and our nets drag the bottoms of the river."

"I understand."

"Women have strong spirits. But the very things that make us strong are the same things that make us susceptible. The hardships of giving birth, the time each month when we make blood—these are times when we must go carefully. Our blood brings us closer to the spirits, but we anger them also, for they know we would hunt them for our food. The animals have souls, as we have souls. The hunter raises his harpoon. He aims. He throws with care. But if his wife has not shown the animals respect, they will never allow themselves to be caught."

"I understand."

"Until the time your blood has weakened and the atmosphere of your menstruation no longer surrounds you, only your mother and grandmother may bring you food and the food must always be dried or cooked, never fresh or raw, never prepared in another person's bowl. Porcupine you may eat, for the porcupine is a wise animal with keen smell and strong eyes. But no berries, because the berry is a pretty thing until it's picked, then quickly it shrivels and grows old. What is given comes back."

"I understand."

"Do you?" Malluar surprised Elik with a smile. "Gull—your daughter looks as serious as if I were a demon. What have you told her?"

"Nothing, Malluar. Only that you were coming. That you'd talk to her."

"They're all a little afraid at first. It's not bad. Fear tightens your stomach, teaches your ear to listen."

Elik lowered her eyes. *Fear is good?* she wondered. Perhaps certain fears, the kind that teach you to respect hunger, to test new ice to see if it can be trusted. But there was already so much fear. Wasn't it curiosity that was also needed? Ears to listen with, to learn, rather than to be afraid?

She looked up. She wanted to ask Malluar about this thought, but Malluar was at the door, already leaving. But there was more she wanted to ask—

The hide curtain swayed and then held still. She was alone and suddenly the small room seemed darker than before, more shadowed. Elik strained to hear the talking in the outer room. Her mother's high voice was joined by her father's deeper laughter and then the sound of something heavy being moved and then laughter again, Malluar's this time, and now her father's.

They were paying Malluar with a gift. She was a widow and lived alone and people always shared meat and skins in trade for her services. But Elik also knew her father was the kind of man who kept an eye on the count of his pelts, the size of his catch. "Be generous, this time," she whispered, "so Malluar will think kindly." And then, so she wouldn't miss hearing anything, Elik tried to stand.

She caught her mother's voice, apologetic and small. "She's a willful child."

Then Malluar: "Your daughter is a good girl, no different than another."

"Am I?" Elik said, then, surprised to hear she'd spoken aloud, she took a step backward. Somehow, the floor was not in the right place. She twisted, reaching for balance. The ceiling loomed closer, leering at her. The floor tilted at an angle and her ears were ringing now, so shrill it seemed the wind had found its way inside her skull. Dizzy. She was too dizzy to stand . . . To walk . . . Too dizzy—

And then there was nothing but her heart beating and faces in the dark. Calling her. In the light behind her eyes . . . Watching . . . And something Malluar had said that kept repeating itself: *There is an atmosphere surrounding you.* . . . But she wasn't sure what that meant.

And then silence. Darkness narrow as a tunnel.

An animal's call, but from so far away, she couldn't recognize what kind it was.

Until, somehow, she opened her eyes, found herself in the same lamplit room, her shoulders and head cradled in her mother's arms, her legs stretched at an odd angle. Her father, who should not have been there, stood in the doorway, the hide pushed open with his hand. His eyes were narrowed in annoyance. His mouth was closed too tight.

"I fainted," she said and her voice surprised her, the way it came from far away. "I heard—"

"Nothing," her father insisted. "You fell. Gull—tell her she fell."

"You fell. It's true. Your foot slipped on the flooring—"

Chevak studied his daughter's crumpled posture, her mother's protective arms. "Are you a child with no awareness? Speaking that way when a shaman is near? What if she thought you were making fun? She could do something. Make us give her something so she wouldn't tell stories. You stay away from her." Chevak didn't wait for an answer. He turned, let go of the hide.

"Is she gone?" Elik whispered.

"Yes." Gull sounded relieved. "And it's true—you must not tell people you had a falling spell because you did not. No one in our family does that. We're fishing people and hunters, not shamans like Seal Talker and Malluar to faint and cry and frighten everyone. You understand?"

"Is that what happened? I fell?"

"You fell because you were weak from hunger. That's all that happened. You fell."

Elik stepped down into the winter passage, then up again through the second entry into the house. The morning air gave way to the closeness of woodsmoke, the sound of Grandmother Alu's ever-present singing. Elik blinked, waited for her eyes to adjust to the dimmer light.

Her mother and Naiya stood to one side of the floor's center hearth. Both held woven grass carrying baskets over their shoulders and wore their white-soled wet-weather boots and single-layer parkas with the fur turned out for lighter weight.

"Did you bring dry wood?" Naiya asked. "The fire's been green and smoky all morning."

Somehow the question seemed wrong. "Wood?" Elik repeated.

"Mother sent you for firewood."

Elik looked to the rising trail of smoke. She remembered gathering an armload of wood, but what had she done with it?

"Did you go somewhere?" her mother asked.

"Only to the beach."

The corners of Naiya's mouth tucked into her cheeks. "Only to the beach," she giggled, "but not for wood?"

Elik lowered her eyes. Naiya was teasing, but then—Naiya often teased. She claimed it as the right of the older sister—older because, though they were born during the same winter, Naiya never forgot she was the one who had become a woman first.

"And maybe," Naiya added, "we should ask the ground squirrels which man has seen your boots?"

Gull looked with surprise at her daughter's bare feet, at her braids to see if the ties had been loosened. But no, here was Naiya brimming with her joke and Elik seemed more confused than embarrassed. Her daughter had been with no man. Elik was young, not the kind of girl to notice she was looked at, that her father had already told several men she was needed here at home.

Gull shook her head. "Maybe next time both my girls should wake early. Maybe two girls working together could bring a larger load and not get lost?"

Alu had been listening; she laughed to show she agreed with her son's wife, and then went back to her song. Her high-pitched, familiar voice filled the house, calmed the air. The song told of the woman who changed herself into a man, put on a man's clothing, took up his harpoon and went hunting, then changed back into a woman again.

Naiya buried her laughter behind her hands as she knelt to the hearth, resettled a flat-bottomed clay bowl against the stones.

Elik pulled off her outside clothes, hung her damp parka on the drying rack above the fire. Absentmindedly, she reached in the storage area below her sleeping place, took up a handful of basket grass and a shredding comb.

She had stood at the shore while the loon's spirit came and called to her. Maybe. Or maybe she had heard only the wind and Naiya was right to think she had a foolish, wandering mind. She looked up. Her mother was watching her.

Gull was a quiet woman, not given to talking more than necessary. But the men were gone from the house and the fog had sat thick for so many days and something in Elik's manner made her set down her gathering basket and cross to her daughter's side. She took hold of Elik's chin and turned her face to see her color, to feel if she was flushed or too cold. "You're well?" she asked. "You have no fever?"

"I went walking. I'm sorry. I forgot the wood."

Gull picked at a strand of grass Naiya had seen in Elik's hair and waited to hear if her daughter wanted a chance to speak.

But Elik didn't know how to answer. She would have spoken if she knew how, but how could she tell of a voice she wasn't certain she had heard? Or describe an idea without knowing the words that would tell it? What sound would its name have? What shape? And who was there with the patience to wait till she found such words?

Not her mother, who meant only kindness but whose ears and eyes looked only to the work that sat in her lap. Not Naiya, who knew exactly which words made Elik's face burn and her tongue stumble. Not even her grandmother, who was wise, but wise in the way of everyday things—where to search for marsh eggs in the spring and how to hold the curved wooden handle of a tool for the best way to scrape the flesh off a hide. Good things, important things, but not the kind that would answer Elik's questions.

Nor would she go to the shamans, Malluar or Seal Talker, though they would know better than anyone else what she had seen. Seal Talker she was afraid of, with his one eye narrower than the other, that way he had of looking at people as though he could hear the very thoughts inside their heads. And Malluar was so old, she had no patience for Elik's endless questions.

And if the questions themselves sounded prideful, or too foolish, or she went to one of them but not the other, they would argue and find fault and ridicule her for asking.

"Wait." Gull turned, lifted her ear toward the skylight. "Listen . . ."

For a moment no one moved. Then, "It's my grandson." Alu brightened. "Go quietly, like good wives, not to chase the animals away."

"So soon?" Naiya asked. "Isn't it early?"

"No." Alu shook her head. "This time an old woman knows. There's a smell of meat and feasting in the air."

The knot in Elik's stomach loosened. Naiya left off playing with the cooking stones and went for the door. Gull hurried to take hold of Alu's arm, to help her climb from the sleeping platform to the floor.

Elik slipped her parka back on. Her grandmother was right—she could hear more people outside, calling, spreading the word. An early herd of caribou had come their way. Nearby. In numbers large enough to celebrate. And if her grandmother was right and the caribou had come, then what if . . . ?

What if the loon spirit she had seen was the same one hurrying Iluperaq home with the news? Hushing Naiya's questions? Chasing them from the house so she wouldn't have to tell?

Barefooted, she ran out behind the others. Already the village dogs had raised a howl and the women and the few, mostly older, men who had not gone along on the hunt were standing about, waiting to hear word.

From the north in the flats beyond their village, the shapes of two men grew sharper against the fading brown of the low-lying brush. The parka on the taller man was edged in a pattern of mixed black-and-white fur—Gull's work—announcing Iluperaq's name even before his face was near enough to recognize. Kimik's brother, Singmiut, was the other man, also long-legged, also young—which meant they had been chosen for their speed, to carry word.

Elik made her way to where Kimik already stood, near the front of the women's line, hoping to catch Iluperaq's glance. Naiya came up beside them, saw the bright look in Kimik's face. With a smile, Naiya teased, "My brother won't see you first."

Kimik pushed Naiya, teasing her back. "Who will he see? Two hungry sisters eating twice as much as one new wife?"

"He'll say his catch is small and meek."

"But it isn't," Kimik boasted. "See the size of his pack, how weighted down it is."

Elik peered ahead. Both men carried narrow bundles sideways behind their backs: sinew-wrapped bows and flint-tipped arrow sets, and the longer, barbed thrusting-spears no man would be without. Both carried the rolled-up skins of newly killed caribou but little bulk—another sign that they'd packed to travel quickly, carrying news.

From behind them near the *qasgi*, a drumming beat grew louder. Elik glanced up to see Seal Talker begin his shaman's song, welcoming the hunters home. His face was masked inside the wooden figure of an animal spirit. The outside of the mask, with its antlers and pointed ears, was meant to greet the caribou, to ease their fears.

But the mask revealed more than simply a caribou's face. As Seal Talker danced toward them he reached for a string secreted inside his clothes. Hinges behind the mask's jaw moved and then clacked open. Inside was a deeper face: the true face of the caribou's spirit, with eyes, lips, and teeth no different than a human's—flesh and soul together.

The song was meant for the caribou, but another thought came to Elik—a fear of just how deeply Seal Talker's shaman-sight could travel. With small, quiet steps she moved behind Kimik's other shoulder, farther out of the shaman's line of sight.

Kimik took Elik's arm and squeezed and for a moment

Elik was surprised, thinking Kimik, too, was troubled by the double beat of the drum. But no—Elik knew Kimik's face, the look in her narrow, lidded eyes, and in her brother's also: the small things they did to catch each other's attention. The way Kimik purposefully lowered her glance whenever Iluperaq watched. How he, in turn, followed her as she hauled water, cleaned fish, carried driftwood. It left Elik with an odd and lonely feeling, that she could stand beside her friend and yet their thoughts could be so different.

Elik sighed, shook the thought away. Even for Kimik and her brother life held complications.

Iluperaq was no boy waiting to celebrate his first catch. Nor would this be the first time Kimik blushed and hid her smile. And wasn't it true they would already have been living together as husband and wife but that Iluperaq still listened to their father's rule? And what Chevak said was that a son's catch belonged to his family first, to his mother, not to a wife.

It was not for an unmarried man to say who owned the meat, the hide, the antlers. And more than once Chevak had prevented Iluperaq from handing his catch to Kimik's mother. *Doesn't your own mother need skins for our winter clothes?* He would say. *A covering for the kayak?*

And though Kimik's mother was agreeable, there was still the matter of five more caribou skins Iluperaq had promised to give along with the sealskins. One hand's count. Not a difficult amount, if only Chevak would give permission.

The two men were near enough to talk now. Singmiut's round face was flushed from the journey out of the hills. Iluperaq quickly picked Kimik from the line, smiled, and made a face, as if to show how heavy was his load.

One of the men helped Singmiut with his pack and then, suddenly, it was impossible to think about anything else. "It was caribou!" Singmiut called. "When?" someone asked. "Yesterday, at midday, along the route that led to the drives. The first one came to Iluperaq—a dark male, huge and blustery." Elik watched Kimik listen. "He brought it down with a heart shot, aiming from his knee."

Iluperaq and Singmiut took turns finishing the tale: Singmiut's short-handled spear caught one of the smaller females in the flank as she took fright. He finished her in a stream before she could limp away. Up near the portage on a trail, where the mouth of the Niukluk River blended into the Fish. But these were only the first. More followed behind. A river of caribou. So many, they couldn't be counted.

Elik listened with growing excitement. What if all of this was a good sign and the spirit who called the caribou was the same spirit who called to her? What if she had pleased it, enough so it saw fit to send the caribou? To bring her brother safely home?

All around her, people began to rush. A caribou drive meant work for the entire village—the first scouts listening for the weight of hooves, women shouting after, breaking from blinds, leaping to scare the animals along the drive. Heavy-antlered males leading their herds for the caribou crossing, the men in their boats with their arrows and spears, women with their butchering knives.

Except that while Naiya and Gull, Kimik and Iluperaq hurried to gather their gear, Elik used the bustling confusion to steal away back to the beach—for her boots, she would tell them if they asked. Only for her boots.

The work of a caribou drive would take days, the skinning, and butchering. It was a duty sacred to the caribou that nothing be wasted: antlers must be turned into tools, sinew into thread, the long bones cracked for marrow. The heads themselves must be properly treated, severed or frozen upright, so the caribou would not suffer when they died, so they would come again. There wouldn't be a chance to wander the beach, not before snow fell. Elik started to run.

She found the place, but the tide had come in. She circled the rocks and paced the shore and searched, and then repeated every step, every move her hands had made. She tried standing with driftwood in her arms again. She whispered words she thought a shaman might have used. A song. A motion.

She found nothing. No loon. No voices calling.

Nothing.

The thin layer of frost that had glazed the gravel beach was gone. There was no sign of the fog that had covered the seas. The morning clouds had lifted to a cool and reaching blue.

From the houses above the beach, people were calling. Dogs answered with yelping barks.

After the caribou drive, more work would follow. Skinning. Days of scraping hides until all the fatty tissue, the scraps of blood and meat were cleaned.

The young ice that formed out in the sea would move back in to shore. The caribou would be put away and the time for seal hunting would begin. The seasons would go on, from the Moon When Water Freezes to the Shortest Ice Moon. There would be no chance to come again, not quickly.

There was only time to pile stones into a small cairn to mark the place, then race for home.

When next she came the rocks were buried under a fall of fresh powder snow. The first thin pans of ice had crusted against the shore. There were no voices, not that time nor the next. By then, winter had come and locked the sea in ice and there wasn't any reason to search again.

# 2

Grey Owl kept the motion of his double-ended paddle to a steady, even rhythm as he steered his kayak through the waves. His back was straight, his legs extended comfortably beneath the covered sealskin deck.

He could travel distant stretches this way, paddling, marking the shore, the wind, the water for any sign of a seal or otter willing enough to come his way.

It felt good to be on the water, moving again. For three days there'd been a fog and a wind so angry it kept him and all the Real People of the Long Coast village inside the *qasgi* or up on the rooftops watching for a sign of the storm's lifting. And it had—eased off the way weather always did if a person waited long enough, if the Spirit Inside the Wind found no cause to bring more trouble.

Now, with a new day, the waves were holding to a steady roll. The kayak flexed as it passed each wave, riding with the lift, bending in the trough. Grey Owl gave thanks that the light offshore wind wasn't angrier today. Not that his kayak couldn't handle more. It was a good boat and it talked to him, to his back, to his legs as it twisted underneath. He had framed it with driftwood it had taken more than a year to collect: to find a driftwood root large enough for a stern post, smooth and steam the wood to shape, to fit the spreaders and ribs to the size of his body, exactly as a boat was meant to be. One arm bent plus another arm extended for the length from stem to hatch. The hatch equal to the size from his elbow to fingertips plus another hand's length as far as he could stretch.

Except that he couldn't help but notice how a few of the seams his wife had stitched had loosened over the season, how the weight of the one seal he'd already caught and lashed to the cross straps on the deck strained at the widening, greased seams.

Grey Owl rested his paddle against the ivory harpoon guards on the ridgeline, close in, so as not to trouble the dead animal. With his hands free he cinched in the waterproof suit Nua had sewn, emptied the puddle of water that had formed from his dripping paddle.

It was a good kayak and he trusted it. Few boats had ever given him trouble. But stitching five large bearded seal skins together head to tail in an overlapped waterproof stitch was a full season's work. And though he wouldn't say it aloud, he would have felt safer if his wife were able to keep her thoughts on her work, the way she used to before their son had died.

He scanned the horizon: somewhere to his left was the place where Allanaq had drowned. It had been late winter then; ice, not water, lived in the world. A lead had opened, a narrow, devious crack in the ice—somewhere. He craned his neck, tried lining up a point in the hazy, distant landscape, then stopped.

He had to make himself quit, stop worrying about the world beyond his control. It would be better if he took his one seal, taught his thoughts to be more quiet, his eyes content. Perhaps, with luck, if the animals did not notice how poor and cold he was, how several of the puffin beaks decorating Nua's seams were missing—if they didn't see these things, perhaps they would continue coming.

Carefully he marked the wind, angled his paddle, and readjusted his course so the colder air moved from his left. The remainder of the fog was ahead of him, also on the left, thinner than it had been but white still, as if it were a sun-bleached caribou hide standing upright on the water.

If he had chosen the other direction, away from the fog, he would have stayed closer in to shore. He would have visited the Bent Point village where his brother and his sister Gull lived with her family. He'd almost done it, too, but for the storm, and that it would have taken another day's paddling. Still, he'd considered it, not for himself so much as for his wife, because a sister-in-law's company would have brought Nua comfort, lighter talk, a woman to sit with.

Grey Owl shook the thought away before it grew, then steered for Ayak Island, where Olanna, their shaman, had dreamed of walrus come in to feed on clams. He'd take a look since he was already nearby, then come back tomorrow with more men. It took whole crews working together with their umiaks and harpoons to hunt walrus—one of the few sea mammals the men butchered where they hunted, rather than attempting to float them home first as they did with seals.

Ayak Island was tall and jagged, with shoulders and a neck that rose abruptly out of the sea. He paddled more slowly as he neared the shoals, careful not to be pulled into the breaking water that crashed in a foam about the rocks. Everywhere there were kittiwakes clinging to the cliffs, auklets, cormorants, noisy gulls—they would all be leaving soon. The sky would quiet. Winter would settle in.

Once around the far side, that's all it would take to spot any walrus, then still leave enough daylight to try for another seal if he saw one, time enough to reach the Long Coast without having to camp along the way.

The kayak carried him around to the point where the rocks flattened to a lower shelf and he saw them—walrus—basking on the level ridge. A few of the males raised their heads in complaint, quarrelsome and loud. Carefully Grey Owl stayed downwind to avoid the blustering young males who set themselves up as watchers for the herd. There was a press of females, moving back with their young ahead of the winter ice pack. He could hear their grunting, their heavy breaths. He stopped his paddling to admire them, to listen to the way they talked among themselves, the way they shifted, trying to decide whether he was a walrus or something else.

Grey Owl smiled, gave a nod of greeting. People said walrus were quick-witted as any man, and just as careless. A walrus would make a show as long as the kayak approached quietly. He didn't want to see them fight among themselves, or find out what would happen if he were loud. What was important was to be humble, to have the walrus see that he was not the kind of man who was arrogant, who went home bragging.

It must have been the fog that brought them, one last time before the ice returned. It was a good sign. He would come back later, with more men.

Qajak lay in the bottom of the umiak, too tired, too lost to think about moving.

It was possible that he was alive. But his father's body was dead and his father's spirit was somewhere—hovering nearby? Would it be angry? That, too, was possible. Would it remember it wasn't Qajak who had killed him, that there was another man who deserved to be hated? But that man was far away now . . . Too far to reach.

Qajak tried guessing at the expression on his father's face. He had seen dead people before, though never in his own family. Not his mother, who had died when he was too young to remember. Not his uncles, who had died away from home.

This stiff, white-lipped mouth of his father—what was it trying to say? That weapons and burial amulets for his journey to the Land of the Dead must be found? That death was one of the many things a man must do during his life. He must eat and give thanks that he's able, he must piss, and he must marry and make children and he must die.

Qajak rolled into the boat's curved ribs. Was he hungry? He couldn't remember. He thought about tasting the salt water, but his hand was too wise to obey. He thought about catching a fish, but he had no line, and when he tried to swallow, his mouth caught and hurt. Better to sleep, he thought, and he started to close his eyes.

That was when he realized he could see again, that the fog had thinned. There was water, everywhere, the ocean. But was it his Seal People's ocean or someone else's? And no land. But yes, wait, there was land behind him. A rocky island, tall and jagged, wide but not large. No place he had ever seen before.

Unless he was dead? And the thirst and hunger and the fog were all part of the same land his father was in.

And a kayak? Was that a kayak? Was that water sparkling off an upturned bow? So narrow? Or was it his own eyes that had forgotten how to see? And why was the man using a barbed dart-headed harpoon, instead of a better toggling point? Did he think so little of the seals to imagine they would come to him like that? What was he doing?

The glare off the water was so bright. Without a visor he couldn't be certain. A dim grey hovered around the edges of his vision.

Qajak tried to move. The bones in his shoulders cracked and complained. He had little strength, but he dragged himself forward in the umiak.

He called, but his thirst was like a cord around his throat. No sound came out.

Why was the bow of the kayak split, instead of raised higher? Did dead people hunt in this land? Did they eat?

And why was the current carrying him toward the man, directly in a line? Why not someplace safe?

Grey Owl turned his kayak through the moody water back toward the Long Coast shore. He sang as he paddled, a glad-hearted song he liked so well, he thought about saving it, practicing when he was home so he could dance and tell the people of the walrus he had seen.

He hadn't paddled far, hadn't even considered that something else might have heard his song, when a head bobbed up from out of the waves, its dark hair slick with water. It was a seal and it smiled as it looked at him. Its nostril slits opened for a breath. Its whiskered mouth turned up. It was coming closer to his harpoon—it had heard his song. . . .

He watched a moment longer before he moved. The seal's head was small, with a pointed nose almost like a dog's—a spotted seal with its dark circles and lighter rings—but that was good. He had luck with spotted seals though, sometimes, they frightened more easily than others. On the other hand, small could also be better. He was only one man. It would be difficult if he had to load anything larger into the kayak.

With a quiet motion he freed a harpoon, checked for his club inside beneath the deck, a second lance if he needed it. He felt as if he and the kayak were not man and boat, but one animal, a human seal. He smiled at the thought of it, wondering what the seal saw when it swam below, looking up at him.

It didn't say. The seal slipped beneath the dark water, disappeared instantly. Quickly, while it wasn't watching, Grey Owl reached for his harpoon with the best dart head, checked that the line was tied and carefully coiled. Before the seal surfaced again, he took up his throwing board, held it so the end of the harpoon shaft was set in the board's long groove, and readied his hand so the spear would travel level across the water's surface, not upward.

Then he waited. Patiently. If there was anything the years had taught Grey Owl, it was to be patient.

The seal's head emerged from under the waves.

Now! Grey Owl heaved the throwing board just as the seal dived. The harpoon followed. The kayak leaned. The point hit, struck the seal below its neck. Through the skin, the blubber, catching into the layer of muscle below. The shaft came away from the point, just as it was made to do, separated and dragged in the water behind a widening trail of blood.

The seal would surface rather than drown. It would have to come up for a breath of air and he would have to be ready, watching for a sign of bubbles, the tiniest wake.

His point must have bitten deep because the seal surfaced again, sooner than he'd expected, weak more than angered, close enough this time for his killing lance to reach. Grey Owl raised his arm, pulled back his wrist, then, while the sea held him steady, heaved the harpoon at the seal, once, then again, till the animal quieted and then hung there, dead.

Grey Owl let out his breath. Open water hunting was not the easiest way to find a seal and now that it was closer, he saw it was larger than he had thought—with a layer of blubber in spite of the long summer sun. Too heavy to load alongside the other seal on the kayak's deck, too much weight to risk the seams' tearing at the stress points. He'd have to tow this one home. It would drag and paddling would be harder, but it was the safest way to go.

Perhaps, Grey Owl thought, with this new catch Nua would feel well enough to help him repair the kayak. He hoped so. It had been one thing to lose a son. But afterward, to watch a wife's soul drift away . . .

Grey Owl checked the weather. The fog continued to thin, but it was there still. Ayak Island was distant and hazy enough that he couldn't accurately make out the shapes of the walrus anymore, whether they'd lumbered back into the water or still sat where they'd hauled out.

He spooled in the dripping line until the seal's body came up alongside the kayak. Ignoring the cold, he lashed the flippers together with a cord, gave a sharp tug so they pulled in against the body, so the knot would later slip without ruining the line. Next he reached for the seal's face, cut a gash in the lip, then used an ivory probe to pass the line from the tail up through this new hole, securing the seal firmly to his line.

"Calm seas," he asked the water. "Bring me home safe . . ."

He thought about lashing the seal directly to the side of the kayak, then decided the weight would throw his balance off. He let it out a little way, tested the way it bobbed and floated. When he was satisfied that all would go well, he settled back in the hatch and started for home.

The day had gone well. Grey Owl's thoughts were

content. He dipped his paddle a few strokes; his hands were cold but no more than many a time before. A few strokes more, then he slowed, let the current help him along.

His thoughts turned to his son again—he couldn't stop them—to that moment when Allanaq must have realized he was lost. Had the open lead broadened, too wide to cross on foot? Is that what happened? Or had he set camp on thin young ice, foolishly out alone, his thoughts straying to the young women, perhaps, instead of where they belonged?

The boat rocked. Absently, Grey Owl dipped his paddle, pulled in to still the side-to-side motion.

He didn't want to keep seeing his son this way, thinking of his pain, his grief more than their earlier happiness. Sometimes, though, he couldn't stop the thoughts. He . . .

The boat heaved—more than gently this time. Had he hit a slab of driftwood? Seaweed dragging?

Grey Owl gripped the paddle. It was something else. An animal was down there. Dark-headed. Too large for a seal.

With a sudden, desperate stroke, he plunged the paddle into the water. One side. The other.

Something was fishing for his catch.

He leaned toward the bow for leverage. Forced a heavy stroke, another. He peered backward under his arm.

Not a whale. It wasn't large enough for that. But there was a shadowed line of white. A walrus! A walrus had followed. He'd never be able to outmaneuver it. Not in the water, not even with its poor eyesight. It was beneath him now. Coming for a taste of seal. He had heard of such things.

The kayak lurched. Grey Owl's head whipped back.

In a panic he reached for a harpoon. Thin sealing harpoons—that was all he'd brought. No man hunted walrus from a kayak. But something—anything . . .

The kayak was pulled backward, against the tide. The rear end dragged lower in the water, the bow rose sickeningly higher. Grey Owl twisted to his side, then behind. He raised his arm, tried aiming for the point where his line faded into the water.

And he threw it, the sealing lance, hauled it hard and quick and sure as anything he'd ever done in his life.

For one heart's breath, the kayak stilled. The point bit through the water, disappeared.

Grey Owl's blood pounded so loud, so deep inside his body, he never noticed the second shadow riding low behind him in the water. Never thought of anything but the grip of his hand on the next harpoon and where to aim, or whether this was the place where his son had drowned, and Allanaq was calling him. . . .

There was a single moment when he prayed his point had hit: the way the line spun out, uncoiling and stretching. Without taking his eyes from the water, Grey Owl reached behind for the end of the line where it was fastened to a flat square of wood—the floatboard with its male and female mouths—for luck, for the seal, for its soul, so it wouldn't fear death. . . .

He could just make out the oval of the walrus's back, the massive shadow swimming, diving in anger now.

But the line . . . The walrus was taking it out, and the line should have been fixed to the floatboard, and the board stored on his side on the deck just back of the hatch where he sat, except something was wrong and it caught. He turned, thinking to loosen it, but the walrus held the seal in its front flippers and it kept pulling and the line grabbed and twisted around his hand, cutting and tight and he couldn't free it.

His arm, his arm was caught in the line. . . .

"Cut the line!"

And the walrus was taking him . . . Taking him out . . . And he couldn't reach his knife because his parka had caught somehow around the hatch, and he couldn't get the line off his hand. And the boat was dipping.

"Cut the line!"

He was trying. He was tearing at it but it was slippery and too tight and a man's voice was shouting through the waves but no one had been there a moment ago and the walrus's tusks could easily puncture the boat and he was tearing at his skin and the pain . . .

The kayak lurched and a wave broke over the top, tipped the kayak to its side. His face dipped into icy water and there was an umiak come alongside. A man latched on, pulling hand over hand along the length of line, sliced it, and freed the kayak before it rolled, righting it in the water again. A man?

Grey Owl's hand was bleeding and his arm felt as if it had been torn from the socket, but the kayak slowed. Somehow, he was free.

Grey Owl coughed out the water he'd swallowed. His fingers were white and his face burned with the cold, but he was alive. The man in the umiak had saved his life, but for all Grey Owl could see, the stranger looked nearer to death than he. His eyes were darkly rimmed, his swollen lips cracked.

And now that he thought of it, this man who just saved his life—his voice sounded like a spirit's voice, choked and tight as if he was more used to speaking with the dead man he sat beside than with the living. "You're not of the Real People, are you?"

The man didn't answer.

Grey Owl studied the umiak. The walrus skins that framed it were loosening—a dangerous sign. From carelessness? Or what? There were no paddles, so how could he have reached this place? No baskets of food. No gear. Grey Owl readied his paddle. "How do I know you are a man and not a ghost?"

The man didn't answer.

Grey Owl sighed, lightened his grip. He didn't know why, but for some reason he wasn't afraid. He had almost died. And he was looking in the face of a man who would not speak, and there was a dead man sitting next to him.

Grey Owl followed the young man's gaze. He was staring at the foredeck of the kayak, not at the seal that was still lashed on, but on the bow, as if his eyes could bore beneath the skin.

He wants water, Grey Owl realized. Of course, look at him. He's alive and he wants water.

Grey Owl reached inside, between his legs, for a bladder of water, then passed it across. All the while his gaze kept flitting to the young man's face, watching as he drank, as he drenched his face in water.

Neither of the two men were Real People, there was no doubt about that. The man's cheeks were circled with tattoos—not his chin, as the women of the Long Coast wore, but more: circles within circles. And the clothing, the cut of his parka, his long hair below his shoulder, windblown and loose—everything about him was different. And yet not completely different. The line of the umiak, the wooden ribs inside—these things were much the same as his own. Different, yet the same. Different, yet familiar somehow.

His eyes are sad, Grey Owl decided, the eyes of a man who has been through an ordeal. Too human to belong to a spirit. And he's cold—his fingers are blood-cold, no color in his lips.

The man was watching the water behind Grey Owl's shoulder. Grey Owl hesitated, then turned also.

What he saw first was the line of his harpoon shaft coiled on the water's surface, a curve of sealskin line floating as if it were seaweed, a trail of blood and then the dark, upended shape of the walrus where he had never thought to see it coming near.

Dead now, floating the way a winter-kill, with its layer of blubber, would float instead of sink. He'd lost the second seal, but the walrus was his to bring home.

Grey Owl's thoughts raced. Never had he succeeded in hunting a walrus this way: alone, with only two strikes of a harpoon—and in the autumn season.

Carefully, in case the walrus wasn't dead, he paddled to meet the line, tested it, waited, then began to haul it in.

If he'd been with other men, they would do the butchering together, back there on Ayak Island, or on an ice floe if it were winter. They wouldn't haul it home until it was cut and stored in their umiak, or if they'd brought a sledge.

The walrus was immense—it would take three men just

to bring it up on land—and butchering took time—more than he had if he wanted to reach home before dark. And here was this stranger who had saved his life, as much in need of a fire's warmth as he was of food.

Food. The thought of fresh food and a new walrus hide brought Grey Owl's thoughts to his wife again. This walrus would make Nua happy. The hide would be a gift. He would shape some of the ivory into combs and needle containers, spoons, maybe earrings. Surely now, her heart would open. She would stretch as if she had been asleep, and she would give thanks to the walrus for sharing its life so they might live.

Grey Owl peered at the man and this time, his heart lurched. He swallowed hard. Cautiously, he said, "My son also died in these waters." He waited to see if the man showed some sign of recognition before he went on. But Grey Owl's thoughts lifted like a wave and he was suddenly too glad to be still.

"A year ago," he said, "my son died. And now you have appeared in the place he was lost. You have saved my life. You called this walrus and now we have meat and my house will be glad. You will come home with me and my wife will have a son again."

The words spilled from his mouth: "Perhaps you are a spirit, for you will not tell me where you came from, or what you are. If tomorrow you are gone, I will understand you were no man at all. But if you are here, I will know you are my son who has returned. I will give you his name and adopt you.

"This man with you, he must have come from the bottom of the sea, but I am not afraid. I don't know who he was but he has helped bring you home, and for that I thank him. I give thanks you are alive."

"I am alive," the man whispered. "My father is a ghost."

Grey Owl drew back. The man's voice was raspy and hoarse. And yet—understandable. The sounds were odd, but nearly the same as the words the Real People would have chosen. Different, yet the same. "You speak like a child," Grey Owl said, and then he laughed gently, as if it made more sense that way.

For the next while Grey Owl worked to tie a line to the walrus, passing it through a series of gashes he cut, much as he'd done with the seal, but more, and always checking that the knots were secure. To connect the lengths he used a series of ivory line fasteners carved to the shape of a seal and decorated with eyes to make it pleasing, so the animals would not be shamed.

He had made the right decision, he told himself, not to butcher the walrus here. He carried his tool kit and firestarter rocks, but the man was dangerously cold and Grey Owl had brought only a small amount of food. He didn't want to lose another son, so newly born.

"My father must be properly buried," the man said.

"Of course." Grey Owl glanced up. "We will do everything according to ritual. Nothing will be forgotten. There's no need to fear, so long as we do nothing wrong."

His new son nodded, but Grey Owl could see there was uncertainty hovering at the corners of his eyes. He was looking now at the harpoons Grey Owl had returned to the deck lashings.

"Why do you use that point?" he asked, "and not a better shaft and toggling head to twist beneath the blubber? Was this something a young man made?"

This time it was Grey Owl who didn't answer. *A young man?* Was this an insult? These points were among Grey Owl's best work, from the kind of pebbles any man would find along these beaches, flints that he'd smoothed and ground to an edge himself. Points he hunted with, that fed him.

Quietly Grey Owl considered the man, watching the way he turned next to take in the kayak's construction, the way he stared at the male and female charms set along the sides for luck. As if he had never seen such a thing as a face painted on wood before.

Grey Owl returned to work, securing the walrus to his kayak—not the umiak; his new son's boat had been exposed to the weather too long to trust. He passed a line around the rear flippers, pulling them in tightly. The head he secured so it faced upward, clear of the water, so it would tow more easily.

Grey Owl was determined to allow himself only joy. This man was his son, given back to him by the sea. If he needed to be taught the skills of a man all over again, then so be it. Olanna would help him. Others also . . .

With a jolt, Grey Owl realized that there might be some Long Coast People who would not feel the same as he. There might be jealousy, that he had a son. Or fear, because the son was unknown to them, because they didn't know who his people were. He would have to be careful. That dead body must be put away quickly, before its spirit made trouble. And everyone must know he has adopted the boy. That way it would assure him of relatives to hunt with, a house to belong in.

Grey Owl looked up. "My son's name was Allanaq," he said. "I give it to you."

The young man seemed not to understand. "I already have a name. Qajak."

Grey Owl recognized the name but he winced at the odd pronunciation. "It's a good name," he said. "Qajak. Here we would say Kayak. And you may keep it, of course. Names are good. A man can never have too many names. But my son's name was Allanaq and if you carry that name then his spirit will come and visit you, perhaps bring luck."

"Allanaq?"

The sound came out with a longer emphasis than Grey Owl would have given, but it was the name, and names held power, no matter how a mouth formed the sound. Grey Owl's expression opened into a smile. "Allanaq. It is our word for *A Stranger Who Becomes A Friend.* See how it must have been waiting for you, and I never knew . . . ?" Grey Owl started to laugh, then stopped when he realized the man's face remained just as distant.

Perhaps it was only that he was tired, Grey Owl hoped. Alone out here in a boat with a dead man—how many people would laugh?

Grey Owl searched for something to say. "Do you remember," he asked, "the way we cut our shares? That the man whose harpoon first strikes a walrus receives half the intestines and the better share of meat? The second man takes the hide?"

Qajak looked up. "Who takes the ivory?"

"The first hunter takes one tusk, the second is shared around."

"And after that?"

"The remaining meat is also shared." Grey Owl waited, pleased that his new son had shown interest. He said, "My wife has been ill. Perhaps, till she is stronger, we can find a woman to scrape the hide and sew for you—"

"No. Thank you, no." Qajak looked to the walrus. "Take my share of the hide as a gift, for your wife. What I want to know is . . . May I have the ivory?"

Grey Owl relaxed. "Those are kind words. It is right that a son thinks first of a mother, before anyone else. We shall work it so you have your ivory."

It was only when the range of distant hills and the grey strip of land in front of the Long Coast village cleared to a definite outline that Grey Owl slowed his paddling and brought the umiak alongside his smaller boat.

The sun sat over his left shoulder and the autumn dusk was near, as he had hoped. Even with the tide helping, towing a walrus had been no easy task. The kayak rode low, the drag of its weight slowing them, and he hadn't been certain whether they would have to camp and wait out the dark.

Grey Owl's arms ached, and even his thoughts were worn. All the while he'd paddled, he'd been planning their entry, racing for home, then slowing only when he was certain the shadows were long enough, that evening was near. He gave thanks it was no longer summer, that the sun would soon set. People would be curious but too polite, he hoped, for questions. The dark would call them inside. With morning there'd be the walrus hunt, most of the men would leave—which was exactly what he wanted.

It was not going to be a simple thing, bringing home a stranger and a dead man, a walrus and a seal. A dead man—that was worst of all.

Already, Grey Owl could make out the narrow shape of Old Ani, watching from his seat on the beach ridge. Old Ani would have recognized Grey Owl already—even for an old man, his eyes were sharp. He knew every boat that was out, and who had gone hunting and where. And that there was a second boat belonging to no one who was Real.

Grey Owl looked at his new son. He was sleeping. With a new parka he would not be so unpleasant to look at. And he would have him cut his hair short, so no one could joke that he looked too wild.

If only the boy wouldn't lean so close to the dead man—shoulder to shoulder. What a strange thing that was to do. Strange, and dangerous on two sides. Dangerous because the ghost might return to the body and who knows what trouble that could bring—illness or bad luck. Dangerous again because who could say what people would think of a man who hadn't the sense to stay back, to know when it was prudent to be afraid.

Grey Owl reached for the pouch beneath his parka, took out his lip pieces, the two ivory and jet labrets all men wore above their chins. More than a few people were walking toward the beach now and it mattered that he appear his best.

He slipped them in. With his tongue, he pushed the back plate comfortably in line below his teeth, against the gums. The outside with its fancy jet beads protruded like two tusks from a walrus's mouth. He sat tall. *Let them see a hunter coming home with his son and their catch. Let them see two proud men.*

The next time he turned, the young man was awake, staring at him as wide-eyed and surprised as if he were a child.

Grey Owl schooled himself. His new son might be large as a man, but who could say what he knew? Perhaps no one had ever taught him how ill-mannered it was to stare in another man's eyes? Grey Owl lowered his gaze, but not before glancing to see if his new son had labrets of his own. He didn't. Not labrets and not the holes where they ought to be worn. Grey Owl tried not to wince. "You saw something?" he asked, and he stiffened, waiting for the answer.

"Your labrets—excuse me. They're so large—Are you a shaman?"

"No. Only a man. You . . . You don't wear them?"

"I've seen them. On traders, and a man who came once, for a wife."

"They say—" Grey Owl searched for the best words. "They say the *inuas*—the spirits—see how much like the animals the labrets help us look. Like the walrus. They say it makes a hunter more pleasing, less fearful to them . . . Were those you saw very different?"

"Smaller. They were smaller."

Grey Owl let out the breath he'd been holding. Allanaq's answer was not so bad. At least he had seen labrets—size differences were not so important. And he obviously knew something about handling an umiak, and how to cut with a knife. Perhaps it wouldn't turn out difficult, bringing him home.

Always, there were stories of lost people, of strangers who wandered into villages after they had lost their way in a fog or been carried away when ice they'd judged safe turned out to be too young or rotten and broke loose, carrying them out to sea.

Sometimes it turned out that the person found relatives and all was well. Which is why he must be adopted. Other times the lost man was an enemy, in which case trouble often came.

"Perhaps," Grey Owl offered, "perhaps when we bring in the boats, it will be better if you let me talk, if you hold quiet for a while."

Qajak had a distant, tired look, but he didn't object. He turned, studied the shore as it grew larger.

Grey Owl watched with him. "There," he pointed. "The

Long Coast village. Our home. As far as that distant point where the land pushes out but it's not detached. There's good beluga hunting in the spring. And from there a long sandspit. And there are three small rivers draining into a sound. And the marshes are good. After the caribou hunt, when the rivers freeze over, I'll take you inland and show you the best hunting places, where the caribou drink and browse." He waited, but he was beginning to think his new son liked to talk less than other men.

Grey Owl forced himself to look at the dead man's face. Whatever resemblance there might have been between the older man and his son, death had erased it.

"Perhaps," he said, "until the Long Coast people know you, it would be better if you did not sit so close to someone dead."

Qajak gripped the skin-covered gunwale.

"Only so you don't frighten people," Grey Owl hurried to explain. "After all, is not the dead man's spirit already gone to the Land Above the Sky? Surely it won't matter to him where you sit?"

"Gone?" Qajak repeated. "How can his soul be gone when he isn't buried yet? Are you asking that I abandon my father's body before he is safe?"

"Abandon? No. I said nothing of abandoning . . . "

"Wasn't it enough that Red Fox allowed him no weapons, none of his amulets to help him find the way to the Dead?"

"Red Fox? Who is Red Fox?"

"Red Fox?" Qajak looked at the mask his father's face had become. "Red Fox is no one."

"Then perhaps you needn't fear . . . ?"

Grey Owl guided the kayak as the last of the breakers carried them in to shore. A few of the men had been waiting, not singing as they usually did, but watching, whispering among themselves. Behind him, the walrus lay beached in the shallows, chest pointing skyward, rear flippers hidden in the waves. Grey Owl winced as he caught sight of the men's questioning glances, the curiosity they didn't trouble to hide.

He looked for his wife, but didn't expect to see her. Most days she stayed inside—her hands busy, but her thoughts holding to the same few places she found safe.

"Walrus!" he called, wanting the men's attention on his catch. "There are walrus at Ayak Island."

Two of his younger relations, Weyowin and Lake, splashed into the water to meet him. Bear Hand, a man near Grey Owl's age, approached more slowly. He took hold of the kayak's bow—not the umiak—he was careful not to touch any part of the umiak, but he helped steady the smaller boat.

Grey Owl steadied himself as he climbed from the hatch. He made sure he was smiling, that nothing but joy showed on his face. Weyowin and Lake were young, the kind of men Grey Owl could persuade. Bear Hand was another matter. A respected hunter, an elder, he had a tongue that was too sharp, a way of reminding a man of every promise owed.

And there was one debt Grey Owl suddenly remembered—that Nua and Bear Hand's wife had spoken of a marriage between their son and his daughter Squirrel. Squirrel, who still lived in her parents' house, unmarried.

Grey Owl worked to keep his voice light. "Walrus," he called. "Enough to honor our village and teach our feet to dance." He squinted toward the beach. He didn't find Nua, but the other women were keeping to their line, none of them singing, children held by their hands, all of them with their eyes more on the umiak than on his catch.

Grey Owl moved quickly, untying lines, dragging the seal up out of the incoming tide's reach, turning it so the face was up, so it would remember this place when it was born again, so it would know where to come.

Each time he glanced over his shoulder he saw Bear Hand studying Allanaq and the father and the boat. Bear Hand would be more than curious, he would be counting the memory of his own dead—a brother killed by strangers when he was a boy, a cousin who'd been missing, found with an arrow lodged in his chest. He would be thinking of how Real People fought the Forest People, how the People of the River had always fought them both. The way everywhere in the world, Real People fought against strangers—for territory, for revenge, for the hope of stealing back a wife who'd been stolen as she went about her work.

Grey Owl pulled his hands inside his sleeves, hiding the way they shook. *Now. He must say the name now. Only by giving the stranger his family, could he hope to keep him safe.*

"This man found me," he called, "just as the walrus decided I might be a better meal than a clam on the bottom of a rock."

Bear Hand looked from the empty umiak to Grey Owl. "He brought weapons?" he asked.

"It was my harpoon, but it was Allanaq's song that called the walrus from the sea."

Bear Hand drew back. "What kind of song?" he started to ask, but before he could finish, one of the women raised her voice in disbelief. "Allanaq?" she called. "Who is it? Allanaq?"

Grey Owl and Bear Hand turned together. It was Squirrel. Grey Owl tried not to wince. He should have guessed, he should have planned. But there were so many people . . . Of course the girl would startle to hear Allanaq's name alive again. Promises had been made. Squirrel had brought her sewing, sat with Nua.

At least his new son was doing his part well. He hadn't yet spoken. He'd climbed from the umiak to the shore and was working now—with his back to the land—untying the lines Grey Owl had fastened to the walrus.

Grey Owl looked to the women. "Where is my wife?" he called. No one answered. Grey Owl tried again. "Someone might tell her I have a seal for her house. And where is Olanna? Our shaman will want to hear of his gift." Grey Owl made a show of searching for the old man's face.

One of the children, a boy so young he still wore a one-piece suit, broke free of his mother's hand and strolled nearer the water's edge.

Thankfully, Grey Owl knelt to speak. "Little one," he said to the boy, "Olanna would be happy to hear that a second hunter's share of walrus waits for him here. Tell him"—and now he made sure his voice carried over the noise of the waves—"tell him my new son and I hope he will be pleased with his share."

The boy stood there, two fingers stuck in his mouth, his eyes wide. "And ask my wife to bring water, fresh water, to honor the seal her new son called from the sea."

Grey Owl turned the boy's shoulders. He watched until he was sure the mother would let him go, then he stood back up and turned to Bear Hand. "This man," he announced, "this new Allanaq, who is my adopted son, offers you the third hunter's portion of his catch."

Bear Hand's posture remained tense, his arms at his side. "Third hunter's share? When I wasn't there? This is generous but—"

"But this new son heard me speak of you, of your daughter's loss, that she has no husband."

The women began murmuring among themselves. Two of the younger girls giggled and tried to push Squirrel out in front, but Bear Hand didn't want his daughter staring. He made a motion with his hand and obediently the girl stepped back, but not so far that she couldn't watch from behind the others.

"Where did you find him?" one of the women called.

"She has tattoos," a younger girl said. "Is she a woman?"

"Not a woman. A man who saved my life." Grey Owl stepped aside, wanting them to see the walrus, the seal, his boat—intact—the truth of what he claimed.

Qajak had freed the walrus and was fighting to position it near the shore. Finally, several of the men ran to help. They waded through the surf, pushing from behind, working with the tide until they managed to roll and drag the massive body out of the water and onto a level gravel shelf.

Bear Hand pulled a tangle of seaweed from the walrus's

flipper, then checked to see if there was breath inside its lungs. "You offer a gift," he said to Grey Owl, "but I don't know if your eyes see what my eyes are looking at. Are you asking that I eat from this walrus who may already have been eaten by the dead? Is this man a spirit to trick you into poisoning me? Poisoning all of us?"

Grey Owl felt as if he'd been struck. He looked from Bear Hand to Allanaq, to the umiak. "Wait here," he said. "I will go and speak with Olanna."

Qajak leaned, half-hidden behind the dark hill of the walrus's back. He felt weak yet keenly aware, as if he were a wounded animal, bleeding even as he ran, desperate for a place to hide.

Everything he saw was different than his home. Different beach, straighter, rather than a finger of land pointing toward the sea. Different smells. Different skies.

How long had it had been since he had seen stars or the moon? First the sun had stolen them away. And then the fog had stolen the land. Stolen his father. His home. Stolen everything but his thoughts, hovering endlessly around Red Fox.

The knot in his empty stomach and Red Fox.

The burning in his throat and his father and these beaches that looked like no beach he had ever seen and Red Fox.

And all that mattered anymore was to see his father buried and Red Fox dead. Forever dead. More than that, he didn't care.

It would be best if his father was buried at home, yet how could he do that? Winter would be here soon. The sea would be closed in ice. Finding his way back to the Seal People was no simple matter. Then again, if he buried his father here, in a place he never knew, how would his soul find its way to the Land of the Dead?

He would have to wait and plan. For now, he gave thanks that the man who had found him asked that he not speak. What would he say that wouldn't offend these people with their strange accents, their cut-off hair?

Tell them their village looked tiny? The tangle of bleached driftwood was so thick, it looked more like a graveyard of bone. The stone points he'd seen were of slate, probably soft, barely ground along the edge. How many houses? Two? Maybe three. He couldn't tell from here.

Women he'd seen, but they looked naked with hardly a tattoo on their faces. One girl had stared so openly, he wondered a grandmother didn't pull her back inside. And all of them standing and waiting around the walrus as carelessly as if it didn't have ears the same as they and couldn't hear them arguing over its meat.

He felt faint, his thoughts muddled. It would be better if he had something to do. If at least his hands were busy while he waited for Grey Owl.

Qajak reached inside his boot for his amulet knife. It was ridiculously small to cut up a walrus but what else did he have? He wasn't going to beg these people for something better. At least the ivory handle was beautiful. The walrus needn't feel shamed.

He whisked the sand from the walrus's skin so it would not dull the blade, then found a place to start, along the height of its chest. He felt with his hand, found the center between two bones, and pushed in. The skin was tough, his hands so weak they felt as if they belonged to someone else.

There was resistance but, thankfully, his blade was sharper than if it had been worn with daily use. He remembered a time, not so long ago, when Red Fox said he had a way with a graver, with a bit of ivory.

Vaguely, he was aware of the men standing behind him, watching from the side. He wouldn't allow himself to look up. They would be watching to see how well he cut, how fast and true, whether a man of the Seal People could be as aware of a walrus's needs as they were.

He kept his head down as he sawed through the more elastic layer of blubber, then turned the point in deeper, leaning in harder. Next, a series of cuts so that strips could be formed, the skin and blubber separated from the muscle, then peeled away. Last would be the center line, allowing the strips to fall. Later the heart and liver would be cut, the intestines laid aside. He only knew a little about how these people worked their shares but surely, Grey Owl would return before he got that far. Something would happen.

He thought of the harpoon head Grey Owl had used, without a hole to tie a line. How much easier it would have been with one of his flaked points rather than a barbed tip.

He had most of the outer strips marked now, from the height of the chest down toward the ribs, the first two laid out along the sand, with a slit in the end of each to form a handle. There. One of these fine-looking men could step forward if he chose, help haul the heavy meat away.

Or else they could kill him now, when he wasn't looking. He had no way of knowing how much status Grey Owl had, whether these people respected his family enough to hold back. Hadn't he seen men killed by his Seal People before? Forest People mostly—strangers.

He risked a glance. They were staring at his hand, all of them. No. Not at his hand. At his amulet knife. They were staring as intently, as if they had never seen Seal People's work before, never seen spirit faces carved into an ivory shaft.

He hung on to the thick slab of skin, steadying his hands, pretending he hadn't noticed. Then, just as he started to lay the second chest strip, the little boy to whom Grey Owl had spoken came running over the hump of the beach. He was hurrying a man by the hand—the Long Coast People's shaman, it had to be.

"It's Allanaq" the little boy sang. "See who it is. It's Allanaq come home."

Qajak stood up. The man coming behind the boy was old, older than his father had been, older than any man he knew. He searched his face quickly, before he approached, trying to decide whether to trust a shaman, when it was a shaman who had just killed his father.

And yet the man was smiling and so thin. Wouldn't a greedy man be fatter? A devious man less happy?

On his head he wore a smooth skin cap, fringed in fur and decorated with a small pair of caribou antlers, polished to a creamy white. He wore no labrets, but the slits beneath his lip said that he had labrets as large as Grey Owl's, large as a bull walrus's tusks.

Walking behind him, Grey Owl seemed less worried than when he had left. His steps were lighter, not so stiff.

The women moved in closer behind them. Bear Hand and the knot of men walked as a group toward Olanna. Qajak heard a few murmured comments, a hint of a raised voice, but they spoke quickly, and he wasn't yet used to the odd turn of their words.

The shaman lifted one arm. The other hung as if it had no strength—an accident, or a fight? Qajak glanced to see if these were warring people. How many other men with wounds showing? How many cripples? He couldn't tell.

Olanna began to speak and there was a richness to his voice, a rhythmic quality Qajak hadn't expected. He turned to listen.

"A dream. I saw a dream," Olanna called. "In it a bird was flying over the great sea, so high above the land that at first I, who was limited by human sight, could not see what manner of bird it was. In its talons it carried prey, food for its family, its people. The bird flew over our houses, circling our shore. When it passed directly above the cooking pots of our women, the owl—for now it had come close enough to be recognized—the owl dropped its catch, a hare, dropped it so it became a gift, so our people would not be hungry."

Olanna coughed, cleared his throat. He said, "The bird is this man whom Grey Owl has newly adopted, who saved his life. And so he must be welcomed. He is not so much a stranger—"

Qajak listened carefully, straining to understand each word the shaman said.

"—as the inland Forest People who do not even know the right words that name things when they speak."

Olanna lowered his head to show he was done. Grey

Owl made a quick motion for Qajak to come over. "You're a fortunate man to have been found by Grey Owl," Olanna said, "to be adopted into his family. To stay alive a man needs more than food. He needs relatives and hunting partners, women to call the animals to his harpoon."

Qajak listened, surprised to hear a shaman speak with such plain wisdom. His face was less stern than he had expected, his eyes no more, no less wrinkled than any man's. Qajak shifted his weight. He felt more at ease than he had earlier.

Olanna said, "You and that man who was your father have come to us because the world is not only that which we see. It has an end, but it is enormous. There is room for all the people living and for people who have died. Tell me, where is your village?"

The men jostled closer in to hear. Qajak let them. "I am of the Seal People," he said, "From the Place Where the Land Points Into the Sea."

The man called Bear Hand folded his arms over his chest. "There are many places where the land points to the sea."

Reluctantly, Olanna agreed. He said something. Qajak didn't understand. Olanna made a motion toward the ground. Drawing. A map.

Qajak knelt down. Without a pause he skillfully sketched out the outline of the coast surrounding his home, the point of land, the lagoons, rivers, and bays. Nothing was left out. No detail, no cliff or bend.

Bear Hand stood over him, following the line. "What are these?" he scoffed. "We don't know of such a place. Or these."

Qajak looked up in confusion, but before he could say anything Grey Owl stepped in. Starting where Qajak had finished he left an empty space then set down a pebble. One to mark the cape where the land turned. A few more to outline the distant mountains, the rivers coming down to the coast. More for the way home—every bend and inlet from Ajak Island to the Long Coast.

Behind him, a few voices murmured their recognition. Bear Hand wasn't satisfied. "We know where we are, but what is this?" He pushed at the unfinished section between the two maps. "What kind of man doesn't have sense enough to fear bringing the dead into our village?"

Grey Owl touched Qajak's shoulder in warning.

The shaman said, "His name was Qajak but he is Allanaq now. Grey Owl has adopted him out of thanks that he saved his life and because he has no son. It's a good name. Whatever dead are nearby, they will think he is already with them. They will not take the trouble to look here. We are safe."

"Safe?" Qajak's voice was flat and weary. "We may be safe, but my father must be buried."

Olanna nodded, assuming he understood, but Grey Owl grew more worried. He had heard enough in the kayak to fear Allanaq could say something, add to their trouble. "Weyowin, Lake," he called. "Will you help haul the boat out? We'll carry it to the graveyard."

Grey Owl leaned closer, whispered to Qajak, "It's good to ask my nephews for help. That way you'll owe them favors, and they'll have something to hope for."

Qajak was confused. "But why take him to the grave-yard so soon? Before he's properly clothed?"

"There are stones we can use there," Grey Owl said, "so you needn't fear scavenging animals, or dogs—"

"Dogs? You'd leave a shaman's body where dogs could reach it? I don't understand."

Grey Owl looked to Olanna for help.

"With death the part of the soul that travels during dreams, that enters and leaves the body, is gone. It becomes a ghost. Your father's breath soul will find its way to life again when a child is given his name."

His voice was kind, but Qajak had no patience left for kindness, for being spoken to as if he were a child. "How can a spirit return from the Land of the Dead," he asked, "if he was never given eyes of ivory to find his way there? If you bury him so quickly, where will he get weapons to hunt with while he waits? I have walrus ivory. At least wait until I can carve him spirit-weapons so he can hunt and eat."

Patiently, Olanna said, "Perhaps if his things were here . . . ? But isn't it more important that his ghost be released quickly, safely away from the village?"

Qajak felt as if he'd been kicked. The men around him nodded to Olanna. "At least," he said, "at least allow me to make a death mask while we wait, so that—as you fear— his ghost does not return through his nose or eyes."

"On the Long Coast," Bear Hand said, "it is only our shaman who knows which spirit masks to carve."

"If my father can be left in the boat, then I can stand guard until a proper burial . . . "

Olanna laid his hand gently on Qajak's arm. "You have done what you can," he said. "Already the four required days of mourning have passed."

Grey Owl nodded. "In your boat—you met these rules."

"You did not dance," Olanna said, "or sing or give joy . . . I have seen this, I tell you. In a vision. You have brought no evil."

Behind them, someone said, "His joints should be severed, so the ghost will not find a way back."

Qajak stared blankly. The strength was fading from his voice. "Cut my father's joints? My father is no enemy. He's a shaman."

A short, broad-shouldered man with heavy hands brought Qajak's amulet knife from the walrus. He turned it over to show the handle, the way the bearlike face was carved in the round, not on two sides only, the way a handle was usually made.

One of the younger men—was it Lake or Weyowin— took the amulet, handled it, then passed it to Olanna, but there were more who would not touch it, who looked and then stepped back. Finally, it came to the shaman. He studied the shape of the face, part bear but also human, beautiful yet grotesque, the kind of thing a man saw in a vision or when he'd been on the ice too long.

"What kind of a face is it?" one of the men asked.

"It's evil," Bear Hand said.

Unexpectedly, one of the men poked Qajak with a finger.

"I am not a ghost."

"This is yours?" Olanna asked.

"I made it, yes."

"So," Olanna held it out. "We have seen these before. All of you. What do you fear? We have traded these with the Big Lake People. This is no spirit catcher, it's the man's own amulet. Are we children that we haven't seen carved ivory before?"

Grey Owl rushed over. "Yes, he makes these. He has asked for more ivory from the walrus. He is a great carver, it's true. He makes these." Grey Owl raised the amulet, held it high.

"It brought luck," Olanna agreed. "It brought them together, saved both their lives."

"Yes," Grey Owl called. "Did I not tell you it was so?"

Qajak's strength fled. His knees began to buckle. He was alive, but he was only a man. How much could one man understand?

The two younger men Grey Owl had spoken to hefted the umiak, one carrying the stern, the other the bow. Slowly, they walked the boat up the slight incline of the beach. His father's body had slipped down, inside. Only a hand could be seen, the sleeve caught somehow against the gunwale and a crosspiece.

In front of them another man walked backward. He was urinating as he walked, disguising the scent of death, so no spirits would find a path to follow.

To one side, Bear Hand joked loudly. "It must have been bird shit that Olanna saw drop in that pot. Bird shit, not a hare."

Grey Owl caught Qajak under his arm, helped him lean against his shoulder. "Come," he whispered. "We will go and find your mother. It's better to go along with the shaman now. Stay alive. Later we can talk about your father's death. Later."

Inside the house the moss wick sputtered in the seal oil lamp, then brightened as Elik's hands danced past the flame.

Her grandmother stood at her side, the two of them with their arms shoulder high and out to one side, practicing again the motions that went with Elik's song.

Alu lowered her hands. "Wait," she called, grateful for the break. She lifted the wick from the shallow pool of oil and twisted it to hold more steady, then moved back to rest on the sleeping platform she shared with Naiya and Elik.

Elik waited, trying to be patient, but patience was difficult. The story was a sacred tale *quliraq,* from the First Times; it mattered that she remember correctly. When it looked as if her grandmother might go on to some other work, Elik touched her arm. "Grandmother," she asked, "please, show me again—the part that tells: *After the first two brothers had died and the third brother was out hunting caribou—*"

Alu chuckled and, with the privilege of age, studied her granddaughter's face. The girl was pretty, her chin a little strong but her eyes were sharp and very dark. It was true she didn't always take the trouble to tie her braids as fancy as her sister Naiya, but on Elik it didn't seem to matter. Her face had a way of shining sometimes, the way it did now, intent and curious. Not so shy as most girls were. More like a seal staring brightly from the water, black hair oiled and smooth.

She had to smile. This granddaughter had a way about her. Yes, it was true and the midwinter runner's feast would begin soon. She herself had made sure Elik would have a chance to recite the tale. And what girl wouldn't be nervous, dancing the story of How Eagle First Brought Feasting to the People? Dancing it alone, in front of so many guests?

Alu closed her eyes. Her vision blurred these days. One of her eyes had a cataract; the other was often teary. She felt the luxury of two fires against her skin—one of wood for heat, the other in the lamp for light.

Her son's household had known a good year. The winter storms had not been harsh, the animals had honored them with food. And though it was perhaps true that her son wasn't the best of hunters, still—his family did not go hungry. She never needed to send her daughter-in-law or her grandchildren begging for skins or meat the way she had when her two sons were young and she was newly widowed. More than once; some memories never faded.

And it wasn't as if Chevak was so poor a hunter he couldn't keep his mother fed. She knew he liked to go about bragging how his old mother chose to live with him, the generous son, while she could have stayed with Saami. But Saami had the two new wives, and she didn't always get along with them so well.

Besides, hadn't Chevak told her that a man with three children need never be afraid? A son to hunt. One daughter to sew, a second to trap ptarmigan and gather berries and wood. A wife to cook his food. He was a proud man, her son Chevak. A good father, the way he insisted his children learn their skills and work hard.

Naiya, the other daughter, sat leaning forward, a length of sinew looping its way in a complicated twist from her hands to her mother's. Gull held quiet, the way she usually did. And Naiya was a good girl, helpful, not lazy. If ever Chevak had too sharp a tongue, and he did sometimes—a mother could admit these things—it was because he feared his children would grow up lazy.

They were different, the two girls, though both were useful. Both were fast runners. Both had strong backs. And yet—if she was one of the young men coming from one of the guest villages for this feast, she'd look to Naiya first as a wife. Not that Elik wouldn't work hard. She did. But it was the things she chose to work at, like this song now instead of her sewing, when the girl already knew the verses better than Alu did herself.

"Grandmother?" Elik asked again.

Alu guarded her thoughts. She didn't want these girls growing jealous. Jealousy led to anger, not joking. It had happened between her sons. And anger in a small house, in a long winter, never could be good.

"Grandmother—is this right? *The third brother was hunting when he caught sight of a large, young eagle circling overhead.*"

"Yes," Alu said, and her flat, worn teeth showed with her smile. "The hands this way and you say: *The brother would have killed the eagle but that it landed on the ground nearby, pushed back its beak as if it were a hood, and became a man.*"

Elik pointed her raised hands higher.

She knew she was nervous, too worried about the song. But it mattered so much, knowing her grandmother trusted her, knowing she would be watched, that she must remember every detail.

The runner's feast would come. Today, perhaps tomorrow, and the guests would arrive. Already their fires had been seen, out on the flats beyond the bluff. The two runners who'd been sent earlier to their neighboring villages with invitations and requests for gifts had gone back out again yesterday. They'd brought word that the Long Coast People had arrived first, that there were three sledges plus more people walking, that the Fish River People were barely a half day behind.

But what if, with so many faces watching, she grew nervous? What if she forgot? People would say it was because she was young. They'd say it loudly, hoping her failure brought no bad luck. But people at a feast brought long memories. With a children's tale she might be given a second chance, not with a sacred tale.

Which only meant she must keep practicing. She would bring honor to her family, to her village.

She could not throw the weighted strands of a bola into a flock of birds as well as her brother, or spear a fish with a pronged leister, though her aim was fair. She could not sew a kayak's skin with the same precise double-lapped stitches her sister's bone needle took, though someday she might. Nor could she set a trap as silently as Sipsip, her uncle's wife. Or predict the weather as well as Kimik's father or most other elders.

But this she could do—recite tales, sing of the spirits. It was true she did not understand everything she sang, the way a shaman would, but she wasn't old enough to compose songs, only recite them. She would be content, if only she didn't forget.

With her arms extended, Elik matched her stance to her grandmother's. "*It is I who killed your two brothers, and I will kill you also if you do not promise to hold a Songfest when you return home.*"

"*Willingly I would do this,*" Alu sang, "*but I don't know what this means. What is song? What is feast?*"

"*Come to my house,*" Elik motioned, "*and my mother will teach you what you don't understand. Come to the tall mountains, where my mother's heart is beating.*"

"Go on," Alu said.

Elik stared into the glowing lamp, picturing the young eagle-man as he lifted his hood and his human-faced spirit showed from under the feathers. "*Human beings are lonely,*" she sang, "*because they lack the gift of feasting. Make ready as I told you, and when everything is prepared you must go out and look for people, and you will meet them two by two.*

"*The brother returned from the eagle's house and just as—*"

"There," Naiya interrupted. "It's done."

Gull knotted the caribou sinew she had been twisting

into thread, placed the short ends between her teeth, and tugged till it snapped. The snap echoed, louder than it could have been. Elik stopped, her hands poised, extended.

Naiya crossed to the pile of gifts they had been preparing for the feast. Out loud, she began naming each person and the gift they had requested through the runners. The clay pot for their aunt Nua because Long Coast clay dried more brittle than Bent Point clay. Cooking stones for Nua's niece Two Ravens because stones that wouldn't crack were worth handing down. The needle case, knife points, the skins. "What else isn't finished?" Naiya asked.

Elik hadn't moved.

Her grandmother had been watching. Protectively, Alu tapped the place beside her. "Elik," she said. "The song is good. It's enough."

"But if I forget—"

Naiya looked up. "I have a sister with the memory of a hundred elders. You won't forget."

Gull looked between her daughters, grinned, then hid the expression. "There is water there, to heat," she said. "And maybe someone remembers how to roll out furs for Grey Owl and Nua, before my brother has to sleep in a hearth."

Naiya laughed and Elik smiled a truce. They started together for the winter passage, where extra furs were stored, but then they stopped. Outside, one of the two dogs they kept tied near the house had barked. The sound was crisp, louder in the needled winter air than it would have sounded in the summer. The dog quieted. Its barking turned into the sound of Chevak and Iluperaq climbing through the entry tunnel.

Gull hurried to check the fire. She set her round-bottomed clay pot on its hook above the hearth. Inside was a stew of tomcod and preserved sourdock to make it pungent, a section of caribou leg bone for the marrow that would make it fat. A simple meal but the best had already been sent ahead to the *qasgi*.

Chevak first, then Iluperaq stepped up through the entry well connecting the lower winter passage to the house.

Elik started to greet them, but her smile faded before it began. Her father wore his fine pair of jade labrets but his mouth above them was drawn to a line. Her brother stood with his arms tight against his sides.

Gull took in the silence straining between them, then busied herself at the fire. She sliced a chunk of fish with her round, fist-sized *ulu*, pushed it to one side, then squatted back on the scrap of skin she kept beside the hearth. She sat with her chin pressed against her chest, her eyes lowered in that way she had when she wanted her daughters to know it was better if they, too, sat this way, without speaking. Naiya took up the ivory crimping tool she'd been using to shape the toe end of a boot sole. Elik slipped back against the wall.

Chevak noticed none of them. His gaze was all on Iluperaq as he crossed to the platform where the trade gifts were piled. Iluperaq pulled several of the caribou hides to one side, set two sealskins apart from the others.

Chevak spoke to Iluperaq's back. "Give me the gifts," he said. "I'll carry them myself to the *qasgi*."

Iluperaq didn't answer. He was counting out the number of skins. One brown, two calves with more white. Elik held her breath. She wished she had her mother's calm, her sister's careful disinterest. Iluperaq was a brother, not a sister; with every season passing, they spent less time together. And yet she could feel his heartbeat, the same pounding rhythm as hers.

It was Iluperaq's bridal gift for Kimik they were arguing about, the skins her brother had been saving. Elik remembered, too clearly, how proud Iluperaq had looked each time he brought their mother another caribou.

Gull would roll the hide out flat, showing Naiya and Elik which way to hold it. "You do it this way," she said, "scraping off the meat before you work the skin, because the animal has a soul same as you. Something could make you ill if you didn't pay attention." She showed the way to begin, scraping at the first membrane on the flesh side with her blunt stone blade, breaking the grain, careful not to tear the skins. On the floor and on her lap with sandstone first, before a sharper blade, working the skins till her fingers were red and the hides were white and supple as if they were alive again.

Those skins should not have been here. They should have been kept aside, waiting until Iluperaq had enough to carry all at once to Kimik's house as a gift, to show her family he was ready to be a husband.

"There were four I took at the willow's edge," Iluperaq said. "Where the bend comes around. It was almost spring."

Gull went through the motions of cooking.

Iluperaq glanced toward Elik. "My sister would remember. It was when she was a new woman."

"How could the girl remember what she did not see?"

Elik lowered her gaze. She might have a memory for stories, but her brother had a hunter's memory. He could easily name each animal he'd caught within the year, whether the wind had been blustery. Which arrow or lance he'd used and where it struck.

Except it was also true that a son should not raise his own opinion over a father's. A father should not give his son cause to argue.

Alu woke from a sudden nap. She wiped her nose, looked startled to find so many people in the house. "Are they here?" she asked. "Is it now?"

Chevak's expression changed. He smiled at his mother, came and sat beside her. He whispered something in her ear—no one else heard. But the wrinkles in the corners of her eyes woke. "Someone might bring a sack of *kivviaq* to eat," she said, and Naiya leaped quickly for the bulging skin stored in the entry.

She brought it back, an entire sealskin stitched at the flippers and neck, stuffed full of tiny birds. Alu plunged her arm inside, pulled out the first fermented bird she found that was solid enough to hold together. The small head fell limply to one side of her hand, legs to the other. The fat-slicked feathers slipped from the carcass to her lap. She smiled. "There'll be good feasting—more than enough to go around. Bring that," she said, and she held out a hand. "Help me up. I want to go visiting."

Gull motioned for Naiya to go with her grandmother. Alu climbed stoop-backed off the platform, into her boots, her parka. Naiya held her arm, and, in the tight silence, they left to go outside.

Chevak waited for his mother to leave before crossing the floor. Flustered, he looked at the pile of gifts, clicked his tongue. It was too large a pile for one man to carry alone. But if he asked for help, Iluperaq might be angry enough to refuse. Then both of them would be shamed.

Shouldering his way in front of his taller son, Chevak bent to the pile, dug his arms between the layers, and lifted what he could.

Iluperaq watched from the side.

Elik hoped they wouldn't ask her to speak. What would she say except that everyone in the house knew which skins were Iluperaq's and which her father had caught? That people whispered that the reason Chevak's brother, Saami, would not hunt with him was because Chevak slept too much in the *qasgi*? That a man who hunted with Chevak as partner caught less than if he hunted alone?

A wooden dipper slipped from Chevak's arm and he bent to catch it. With a sudden move Iluperaq scooped up the remaining skins, gathered them tightly into his arms.

Chevak looked pleased. "These people from the Long Coast," he said, "they'll be shamed when they find how much more we have to give than they do. Wait until next year. They'll try to come back with more. Skins and kayaks. They'll wonder how we grew so rich."

Without answering, Iluperaq shifted the load, then stepped down into the passage.

Behind him, Chevak looked toward his wife. Loudly, while Iluperaq could still hear, he said, "A boy's thoughts should learn to be sharp, like the point of a blade, with the animals, not with young girls."

Gull spoke with her head bowed. "He's not a boy, your son."

Chevak laughed. "He is a boy, with a boy's thoughts between his legs."

"Then he is a boy," she said quietly. "But let him be. . . . After the feast if there are extra skins, perhaps we could give him back a few?"

Chevak started to say something, then caught sight of Elik sitting with her eyes lowered, her hands working quickly as she could make them.

She didn't need to look up to feel her father's eye studying her. She was wearing only the short undertrousers all women wore inside the warm winter houses, no outside clothes. Her braids hung below her breasts, and her breasts—they were young but they were growing. "And keep my daughters near your side," he said to Gull. "Both of them. I'll have no one running off in the dark where I cannot see which way they go, or with whom."

Gull didn't answer. With a glance to Elik and then to the food no one had eaten she rose, slipped on her parka, boots, mittens, then turned to help her husband with the remaining pile. They left together, for the *qasgi* first, to add their gifts to the others, then out along the hardened paths beyond the houses, where the guests would be lining up their sledges.

Outside, on the snow-covered tundra, on the inland side below the houses, the first of the neighboring visitors had already formed themselves into a greeting-line. In front of them, seated on furs to block the cold, four men were drumming: two from the people of the Bent Point, two from the people of the Long Coast.

In front of the drummers, in a second line, a row of Bent Point dancers showed off the wolf masks and hides that had started the year with luck: a pack of wolves who'd followed the Fish River down from its course. An adult male, an adolescent, and three females. Silver, white, and brown, all of them.

One of the wolves, the long-legged adolescent, had walked right into the center of the village. Fearless, they'd thought, until after it was dead and they found the old, dry blood on the scruff of its neck. And the point that wasn't theirs, and the broken shaft protruding from the wolf's shoulder.

That was Nagi, Elik's mother's brother, looking out from the wolf's eyeholes. And Saami, her father's brother, inside the female with her tail hanging below his crotch. And the tall one, that was Singmiut, with his shoulder-high dance mittens clacking and rattling to greet the day.

Elik looked away.

Alone in the house, she had put on the parka her mother had sewn as a gift for her first woman's time. The seams were flawless, hidden and impervious to the wind. She smoothed her hands along the ground squirrel fur, admiring the work. This was no child's parka, straight-bottomed, unsexed. Her mother had used extra skins to shape a woman's hood, large as a womb to carry children. The hem turned up higher toward her hips, then curved down again, front and back forming two graceful panels so the spirits who saw her would know she was a woman of the Real People, not so different than the animals themselves, with tail and legs, spirit and strength to match.

There was an insert of the white underbelly of caribou sewn to the front, so that the fur which had covered the heart of the caribou now covered her heart. And a row of wolverine tassels stitched in with a line of red-painted seal gut. Five tassels for a woman's sacred number. Red for the blood the Sun spilt as she rose up in the sky.

And yet, for all the fancy clothes, for all the menstrual blood she now had to keep away from hunters, for all her father's warnings, she wasn't sure she was ready to be a wife.

Elik didn't know where the thought came from, only that it wasn't new. Perhaps it had to do with the way Naiya watched after every man. Or Iluperaq was so hungry for Kimik it made his words angry, made him stare at the walls at night.

But if she didn't marry . . . ? What if her father had one of his stubborn whims and gave her away? A father could do that to a daughter—give her to any man he asked, someone willing to take her. A girl could run if she tried, but a father could do that first.

She laughed suddenly, remembering the man who had stepped out of the Loon's skin, how handsome he had been, how straight his shoulders. She had gone back several times after the ice crusted over, searched but never found him. Now there—she smiled at her joke—there was a man she would marry.

She waited till no one was looking, then crouched, took a handful of snow, and filled her mouth. The snow melted. She spit it out, watched as it cut a line of holes into the snow. "For a drink," she whispered, "for you, husband Loon, so you will not be thirsty," and then she turned and made her way along the women's line, past her mother and grandmother, to where Naiya stood.

"You're here." Naiya glanced at her. "Come stand with me. Watching is better than dancing. This way, we can have a look at the men before they see us."

"If they see us." Elik laughed, and Naiya pulled her farther along the row. They found a place beside Sipsip, who stood with her younger child in her hood, the older one tucked in between her legs. Next to her was Salmonberry, whose ivory earrings were so long, the beads dangled in front of her ruff and chinked as she moved aside to let Elik and Naiya in.

"Who isn't married?" Naiya whispered.

"You," Elik said.

"No, silly." Naiya laughed. "The men."

Elik shrugged. This was her sister's game, one she played so often she had named the string figures she'd invented, a different knot for each unmarried man they knew. "There's Kahkik, with the Long Coast People."

"He's too short and he has huge ears."

"Huge ears make a good hunter," Elik poked her sister.

"He's married. He's too old. There's Singmiut."

"He's married too." Both sisters looked to see if Salmonberry had heard. With a hand over her mouth,

Naiya whispered, "Which only gives him more ideas, not fewer. But if father doesn't let us marry soon, we'll end up being carried off by a man too old to hunt. Both of us."

Elik turned to see the guests, trying to learn who had come from the designs stitched in their parkas, or where they stood. "There's our uncle Grey Owl." Elik smiled. "Where's Mother? She wanted to find him. Do you see Nua? Or Olanna?"

"You don't want to marry a shaman."

Elik didn't answer. Naiya's talk would only go on, longer than Elik cared to play. She looked to where Grey Owl was working the bindings free on the skins covering his sledge.

The sledge was well loaded down on its runners, the covering skins stretched tight, strapped with lengths of hide. The rear of the sledge, where a man could push, was made of caribou antlers and Grey Owl, with his back to her now, was working the ties free from the antler points.

Grey Owl was her mother's oldest brother and Elik's favorite uncle, a man as unlike their younger brother, Nagi, as her father was from his too-serious, always-quiet brother, Saami.

Both Nagi and Saami were the kind of men who paid attention only to the doings of other men, where they hunted, which women they liked best. Not Grey Owl. When she was little and Grey Owl visited, he would throw her in the air and make up songs and carve wooden dolls and give her bits and pieces of skin and sinew. And laugh. He always laughed.

He reminded her sometimes of Iluperaq, her brother, and the thought made her smile—Gull had her Grey Owl. Elik had Iluperaq.

Except this time, she remembered, it might be different, with Grey Owl's son, Allanaq, dead. Which might be why she didn't see Nua here.

With Allanaq gone, there'd been concern over Nua's health. Elik had not visited with them last summer, but

Iluperaq had. He'd gone during fishing season, knowing the nets they set in Grey Owl's smaller river would bring fewer fish, but knowing that, without Allanaq, the household needed not only help but the sounds of people laughing.

Elik tried to remember her cousin, but it had been more than a year since she'd seen him. They'd been children together, young children first, and then not so young. They had slept together once—not the whole night through, they had been too young for that. It had been long ago and she hadn't thought of it since the news had come of his death. They'd only done what most children did: running off together, teasing, their play fight turning to curiosity.

It had been before she'd become a woman and it hadn't mattered. Children play. They don't sit around a lamp like a house full of adults, figuring out to whom they're related, whom they'll marry.

Someone else walked up to Grey Owl. Not Olanna, the man was too straight-backed to be the Long Coast's elderly shaman. And now Elik remembered hearing her father say that Olanna would not come this year, that he was weary of keeping up the rivalry between him and their own shaman, Seal Talker.

"You see that man?" Naiya nodded toward the same man. He stood two steps apart from anyone else but nearest to Grey Owl.

"Who is he?"

"I don't know. I think he came with Grey Owl."

"Grey Owl? Why would a stranger come with our uncle? What would he want?"

"A woman," Naiya said. "But he won't get this one. Look how worn his clothing is. What hunter would want a woman to see him dressed that way?"

From the back, the cut of the man's parka seemed too long. And worn—beneath his arm ran a shadow where a seam had opened and not yet been repaired. Naiya was right, but it wasn't only that his clothing was old. It was odd also, without decorations, and in a style Elik had never seen before. A stranger's parka. Not Real People's.

The man turned. He was wearing no labrets—which was also strange for a man, and for a feast, when everyone wore their fanciest, newest clothes. Without labrets his face was like a child's, newly come to the world. Except he was taller than any child and there was a dark line of hair above his mouth and his face was tattooed—not like a woman's on the chin—the lines were too different for that—yet not like a man's either.

He took a step. Grey Owl blocked his face. Then someone else leaned to the side, cutting off the view, and finally Elik walked away. In a little while more there was shouting and a series of footraces began. Someone set a fox tail on a stand so that whoever was the fastest could grab the tail first, before the others.

It was during the second race that she saw the man again. He was taller than she'd realized and not so broad, with a long stride that would give him an advantage in a race like this, more than in a contest of strength.

Four men took off running and she found herself watching, curious. From the start the stranger pulled ahead, his legs moving in stride, until midway along the race when he turned, looked over his shoulder to see who followed. And then, deliberately, he seemed to change his pace. He was slowing. She was sure he was purposely slowing. He looked ahead again, still running, but he seemed to want to lose. Only when two other men passed him did he seem to put any effort back into the race.

And then it was over. It was the Bent Point man who had won. She took a step to one side to see her cousin Stillwater, Saami's oldest son, showing off the fox tail in his hand. People would say it was a good thing one of their own men had won. That, because Bent Point was giving the feast, it would put their men in a good mood, with less chance for anger.

Out of the corner of her eyes, Elik felt the stranger shift his attention and she turned, following the motion.

He was looking at her. Directly through the crowd.

Looking at her as clearly as a moment earlier she had looked at him.

She made a motion with her hand to ward off bad luck and quickly stepped back, blocking his line of sight behind Sipsip's shoulder. He must have seen her staring. What a strange man he was, not to look away.

The crowd was breaking up. Most of the men would be sleeping in the *qasgi*. The women and younger children would sleep in relatives' houses. Was the man still watching her? She held her head steady, refusing to turn around. Elik looked for someone to walk with and heard her mother's voice.

Both her parents were standing not more than a few lengths away, backed off from the group. Grandmother Alu was somewhere else and, without her constant warning, Chevak let his voice grow loud, "Grey Owl already told me he wants to stay with your brother."

Gull's disappointment showed. "Why with Nagi? He always stays with us."

"Why should I know?"

"Perhaps Nagi's house is less crowded?"

Elik walked away: her parents would work out the details of who slept where and who fed whom. She'd already heard her father's arguing; she didn't want to have to watch as other people raised their hoods, hid their ears.

The low winter sun had circled and was ducking down again. Back along the trampled snow, there was shouting, laughter rising. A few of the men were racing again, but most of the lines had broken. The drumming quit. Dark was coming and the first few stars were opening in the sky.

The trading feasts were always held in the midwinter season, after the Feast for the Dead and the Feast of the Seals. Always the days were short, the long nights a better time for eating and for songs. She'd lost sight of Naiya, but that was just as well. She felt edgy, as if she didn't know what to do with her hands, which way to turn her feet. Here and there, people were helping visitors haul in their loads, untie the harnesses on the pack-dogs.

Iluperaq was helping someone with his sledge—from the distance she guessed it was a cousin, Weyowin, with his wife, Two Ravens, a girl no older than Elik and already with a baby.

Their sledge was built, not with planked crosspieces and runners made of driftwood, but with makeshift runners, some dark material, perhaps bone covered in frozen sod and then iced over.

The thought of sledges and strangers and nighttime made her feel afraid suddenly. In all her life Elik had never seen a full-blown raid, nor lost a mother or a sister to violence. But others had, not here, but often enough so that it was easy to remember their stories, the fear.

If trouble came out of this feast, she would run. She'd heard of revenge raids where the enemies allowed one of the women or a boy to escape, to warn others what they'd done. She would help first, she told herself, help where she could, and then run. She didn't know where.

Elik climbed with her sister inside the house, rushing to have the lamp lit, to cook what little food had not been sent ahead to the *qasgi*.

The men came next through the winter entry, straightening their backs with a bustling, excited commotion. There was as much talking as as she ever heard inside the passage: Iluperaq and their father, Weyowin and his younger brother, Lake. Two Ravens was already inside, showing off her naked baby to Naiya while the boy whimpered to reach his mother's breast.

Grandmother Alu stroked his skinny, soft leg. "He has no amulets on his waist-string?" she asked.

"He did," Two Ravens said, "but he defecated on them so much, I sewed them inside a shirt."

Naiya lifted one of her fingers to the baby's wet lips, smiled as he tried to suck. Babies were a good thing, useless when they were new but for the joy they brought. Only later did a child have a mind to remember with. "Did you carry an amulet for yourself?" Naiya asked. "A swan's beak to make a boy?"

Alu laughed. "If she had any sense, she wanted a girl first, to help take care of all the boys who would come later."

Two Ravens smiled at the talk. She had taken off her outer parka, proudly showing how one of her breasts was fuller than the other with drops of bluish milk clinging to the nipple. She reached and took the boy from Naiya, put him to her breast.

Naiya smiled at the baby's sucking noise. "What else did you do?" she asked. "Did Olanna hold the afterbirth to a lamp, to see inside . . . ?" Elik squatted by the hearth, the few sticks of wood forgotten as she listened.

Gull clicked her tongue. "That isn't something to ask. What a shaman does to see an infant's soul is nothing to speak about."

Alu disagreed. "If something was meant to be, it can't be stopped. Did Olanna look?"

"Nothing." Two Ravens slipped her finger inside the baby's fist. "But he did search."

Purposefully, Gull dropped a bit of fat into the hearth, then pushed it against the coals to sizzle. "Go away," she murmured, "Don't see this house. Don't look here. Eat, and go away—"

The women quieted as the men entered, took off their parkas, and passed them to the women to dry. Weyowin looked to Gull. "It's so bright in here," he said politely.

"No, no—our lamp is small," Gull protested. Smiling again, she set aside the older stew for the women to eat the next day, then proudly, as owner of the house, she began cutting fat chunks of frozen salmon to share around.

Alu went back to tending the seal oil lamps, pulling the wicks longer, proudly showing their guests how there was so much oil to burn. Elik raised the fire, set the cooking stones nearer the coals to gather heat.

She sat with her back to the men, tending the fire but listening also. She had expected that, after the pleasantries, the men's talk would turn to the journey as it always did, the journey or the hunt. What they'd seen, whether the snow had been too gravelly for the sledges or too deep for the dogs, or whether the wives had pulled out front while they pushed from behind.

And they did talk of those things, but only a little. Quickly, the conversation wound back to the same one that had begun outside, their words all about the stranger.

Chevak looked to Iluperaq, as if expecting an argument before it began. He said, "A man without people isn't to be trusted."

Weyowin nodded. "His speech is like a sea gull's, screeching."

Lake agreed. He was Weyowin's younger brother, a smooth-faced boy Elik had met only a few times. He nodded his head in agreement, quickly and too sure, as if to make himself seem older and more wise.

"If he brings in meat and he works, what does it matter?" Iluperaq asked. "Nagi married Sipsip and her mother was a stranger, kidnapped for a bride. No one forgets that. But look now. Her children are Real People. She's a hard worker."

Naiya hung the men's mittens where the frost and moisture would not stiffen the skins. She made a face which only Elik could see, rolled her eyes toward Lake, then back. Lake was too young to suit Naiya's opinion. Too soft and overweight and young. Weyowin's skin was bad, not soft enough.

Elik filled the cooking pot partway with fresh meltwater, partly with water from the sea, for the taste of salt.

Weyowin said, "The man hardly knew what a net was. He was like a boy not knowing where to tie on sinkerrocks."

Iluperaq shook his head, trying to understand. "How can a man not know how to set a net? Does he learn?"

Naiya was seated on the women's side of the platform now, out of the way, while the men took their meal first. She leaned down to Elik, whispered. Both nodded. It was the stranger they were talking about, the tall man with the old clothes they had seen outside.

Using a pair of forked sticks, Elik lifted the first of the

fire-heated cooking stones and dropped it into the water. Steam rose and the water sizzled.

"When he came to us," Lake said, "he didn't know anything."

The baby had finished nursing and Weyowin took him from Two Ravens. He held the boy so his head was cushioned in the crook of his elbow, legs kicking on both sides of his arm. His tiny penis pointed in the air, ready to spray his urine.

Chevak pointed with an exaggerated expression. "And if he won't wear labrets like a man between his chin and his mouth, what does he wear between his legs?"

Weyowin and Lake laughed loudly. Gull placed her longest wooden platter on the floor in front of the men, filled it with choice strips of dry salmon. Lake picked up one of the strips, took an end in his mouth, then quickly cut off the remainder, his knife slicing the red meat just in front of his mouth. "It's good to eat," he said to Gull.

"It was my daughters who cooked the food." Gull smiled.

Chevak sent a look to Gull, hushing her comment about marriageable daughters. "If a man can't fish," he said, "what does he eat? And if he doesn't eat, how do we know he's a man?"

"He eats," Weyowin said. "I've seen him. And he hunts. Almost too well."

Grandmother Alu sucked on a strip of dry meat. "A man who hunts too well has to be careful not to be noticed, not to make others jealous. It's better if he gives away what he has."

"You haven't seen his carvings," Weyowin said. "No one wants to touch them. He gouges holes through the ivory so nothing is flat. And the faces, they're not human, not animal."

Elik winced, recalling how the man had looked at her.

"But when he hunts," Iluperaq asked, "the animals come to him?"

Lake leaned forward. "Maybe his carvings are spirits who trap the animals? Maybe they kill for him."

"Did he come here to trade?" Alu asked.

"Grey Owl adopted him."

"Grey Owl?" Elik couldn't hold her surprise. "That man is Grey Owl's son?"

"He gave him the same name as Allanaq," Weyowin said.

"But he looks nothing like our cousin."

Chevak laughed. "Who knows what Grey Owl was thinking?"

Elik hid behind her work. Naiya and she had joked about the stranger. And he had looked at her. Directly through the crowd, as if he'd picked her out. But these people, her cousins who lived with him—they weren't even certain he was a man.

But if he'd been given Allanaq's name, didn't it stand to reason the name had also given him some trait, some manner her cousin had? The name brought back the soul, but how much memory did it carry?

"He's like a child," Weyowin said. "Grey Owl did everything for him."

Iluperaq said, "But if he marries a girl and she knows the ways of the animals, they'll give themselves to her, and there'll be food enough for a house."

Elik lifted a cooking stone from the fire, but her hand was shaking and the stone slipped from the forks. The boiling water splashed up, burning her hand. She cried out in surprise.

Chevak's expression twisted to sudden disapproval.

Mischievously—he meant no trouble—Iluperaq said: "A girl who works as hard as my sister ought to have a husband. We could marry Elik to this new man."

"No!" Chevak stopped him. "My daughter is a child. Look at her, the way she spills her pot and cries. And what would this man feed her? Sand? Snow? When my daughters marry it will be to wealthy men, not boys who can't even tie a net."

Elik felt numb, burned and frozen at the same time. Her thoughts darted and whirled and then, for the second time that day, settled on the Loon who had shown itself as a man. He'd been handsome and richly dressed and he'd come to her—only to her.

Thinking nothing more than that she would stop their talk, Elik said, "I will never marry, no matter who the man who asks for me."

For one long, brittle moment no one spoke. But then Chevak snickered and then laughed. "And who would want you—a child who cannot even heat a pot?" And he laughed again.

The brief winter sun had long since turned the sky to night when Elik stepped down into the qasgi's passage, then up again through the hole in the center floor.

She had known it would be crowded but even so, the heated air took her by surprise; the people, the smells of fish and seal meat, the noise.

The ceremonial house was the largest in the village. It was the place where men worked their tools and ate and slept when they were not in their own houses. It was a place for guests to stay while they visited. And, with its walls of driftwood that had come, like fish floating up out of the sea, it was the place where shamans worked themselves into a trance and spoke with their spirit helpers, and traveled to the Moon. The place they drummed and sang and promised offerings until the spirits softened their hearts and sent their living relatives, the animals, to die so that people might live.

A light drumming covered the sounds of talking. The line of men nearest the entry hole were sprinkling water on the flat, round surface of their drums to deepen the sound and keep the gut from tearing. There was talking everywhere, and laughter.

Gull had given Elik a platter to carry over and she held it pressed against her chest—frozen blueberries mixed in a thick froth of caribou fat they had spent most of the afternoon chewing and then whipping through their hands. She started for the sidewall where other bowls had been set, then hesitated.

Everything seemed too close today. Too thin and brittle, as if all the world around her were tight as the men's drums, loud and straining. Fit to break.

She looked to the ceiling. Overhead, hanging from every rafter and crosspiece, were the giant wooden face masks that had been carved for the feast—elongated animal faces, twisted spirit faces, and all of them with eyes cut out like so many windows. Eyes that peered down at her from the sky, watching and following, listening to her thoughts.

She took a breath, tried quieting herself.

She had shamed herself with her comments today, spoken thoughtlessly and too loudly. She knew well enough she would marry someday—it was the way things were in the world. A man needed the skills of a wife. A wife needed a husband. How else could a family survive?

Overhead, atop the upright timber where she stood, an immense, carved eagle perched on a staff. Its wings were extended, its beak open so a true eagle's voice might speak through it.

She picked a bit of meat from her platter and placed it on the floor beneath the pole.

Iluperaq had done nothing but tease—she was the one who had answered in anger. And now, when she most needed to have her thoughts quiet for her song, everything frightened her, every noise, every shadow.

"Please," she whispered to the eagle, "help me not to be afraid. Help me, so I will not shame us both."

Elik rose and threaded her way behind the men to the wall where the mound of exchange gifts waited to be distributed. One side for the gifts the guests had brought; the other from them, the host village, to be given out. She found a spot for her mother's long platter on the floor, set it in between two other bowls, where it would not accidentally be kicked, then turned and looked for a seat among the women.

Naiya was there, on the women's bench along the opposite wall. She was crowded in with Alu and their mother on one side and Two Ravens with her baby on the other.

Elik had hoped to sit beside her grandmother, for confidence, before it was her turn to sing. But Naiya and Two Ravens were leaning in toward each other, whispering and laughing. She started toward them until Two Ravens caught sight of Elik and closed her mouth so tight, so quick, that the teasing could only have been about her.

Elik shrank back, pretending she hadn't seen. She glanced instead along the two other sides of the bench: there were her uncle Saami's two wives with their constant gossip. And a woman from Fish River she didn't know. And a girl, near her age, who looked familiar. And Sipsip, with her youngest pulling on her braid, talking to Salmonberry, with her boy in her lap.

She searched the floor where the men sat: there were no spaces. The circle nearest the hearth was reserved for elders. Finally, then, she saw one empty place beside Malluar, on the floor at the base of one of the qasgi's supporting house poles.

Malluar sat with her hood still raised, framing her face the way fur framed the face of an aged bear, silvery, distracted. At least if she sat with Malluar, she wouldn't be troubled with gossip of young men, of marriage.

Elik made her way over, then squatted down. "Grandmother?" She waited politely. "Grandmother? May I sit with you?"

Malluar glanced up to see who she was, but she seemed less interested in one girl than in watching the men as they darkened their faces with lines of soot, took down the dance masks, checked the mouths, the eyeholes, the ties that would hold them in place.

Elik pulled off her parka, rolled it carefully in on itself, and placed it against the house pole. She squeezed in beside Malluar, then turned to see if Naiya or Two Ravens had noticed where she sat. They hadn't—Naiya was engrossed with the baby, hushing him, balancing him on her knees. Two Ravens laughed with the girl in front of her.

It was better to sit here, she told herself. She would be safe from their gossip. And from the masks, also. Wasn't

Malluar a shaman with spirit helpers of her own to call on? Nothing would come for her, not here.

The air had changed. Elik took a small breath, tasting it. Someone had pulled the gut window back over the smoke hole overhead, closing them inside. Food came around, salmon roe and more fat with berries. Malluar squeezed the red eggs between her fingers, pushed a clump into her mouth, but Elik's stomach felt too tight to eat. She passed the wooden dish on.

Overhead one of Seal Talker's carvings began to move. It was a human figure, a man with wooden labrets above his chin. Its arms and legs were rotating. How did it do that? There was a drum in its hand, a gut drum, and its mouth opened and shut as she watched.

Seal Talker's voice came as if from far away. The shaman ordered one of the lamps put out: only the one where the dancers stood would burn.

The *qasgi* went quiet. The singing would begin now— not the Bent Point People first, theirs would come later. These early dances belonged to the guests.

Malluar leaned against her shoulder. She gestured for Elik to look at Seal Talker. He was wearing short, plain leggings to his waist, an amulet of eagle's down on a string around his chest. His ribs showed beneath his skin, thin, like those of a hungry caribou, yellow in the lamplight.

"He's afraid, that cousin of mine."

Elik wasn't certain she heard correctly. She turned. Malluar's face was so close every line in her skin seemed deeper, older. The lines of her chin tattoos looked wider, more blue than black.

"You see that man they've brought?"

Elik followed Malluar's gesture toward the stranger. He was seated next to Grey Owl.

"My cousin doesn't know what kind of luck that man brings with him. And so he is twice frightened. Once because of that man. Twice because the sight of his own fear frightens him. See how many gifts they've brought?"

Elik's gaze shifted toward the wall where she'd set her food. She hadn't noticed before but it was true: the exchange gifts that had come with the visitors were heaped higher and took up more space along the floor than the Bent Point People's pile. And if the Long Coast People and the Fish River People had been so blessed by the spirits that they had more wealth to give away, then as hosts, the Bent Point People would be shamed. Seal Talker most of all.

"My cousin is jealous," Malluar chuckled. "But the joke is that five years ago he would never have admitted such a thing. To his wife Ema, maybe, but never to me. If he felt it, he would hide it." She shook her head, whispered, "No. Never let fear show."

Elik lowered her gaze. She had never heard anyone speak against Seal Talker, as if she were throwing away secrets. Certainly not Malluar, and certainly not to her—a girl of a hunter's lineage, not shaman.

Behind them a tiny voice began to wail. Two Ravens' baby: Elik was vaguely aware of her cousin trying to hush the child, then finally leaving the *qasgi* to go somewhere and put it to sleep.

Seal Talker was singing now, a Wolf's Song to begin the feast. He jumped out, growling, stalking the crowd. His entire face was hidden beneath the skin of a wolf, its nose covering his, his eyes looking out from within. He danced forward, stomping his feet so close he could have reached down and touched her, stepped on her foot.

Her heart beat so loudly, she wondered whether the Wolf Spirit borrowing Seal Talker's skin could hear her. Whether it was hungry enough to come and smell the meat that was her body. She pulled her foot in, tucked it against Malluar. She didn't want him touching her. Not even by accident, not even in the dark.

And then, just as suddenly as he'd leaped out, Seal Talker was done. A few more lamps were lit. The empty floor of the *qasgi* surrounding the entry hole brightened again.

Elik was surprised to see Grey Owl's stranger standing at the edge of the men's line. The only one standing. What was he going to do? A man who didn't even know how to fish, how to eat?

Grey Owl squeezed the man's hand—she could see it—the way he touched his arm. Elik winced. She hadn't had a chance to greet her uncle. He hadn't come to talk to her. She wondered whether this new man could have secretly done something to him, fed him food that was taboo? Something that could take the thoughts of a good man like Grey Owl and twist them, change them, so he no longer knew what was right?

The stranger—she couldn't bring herself to think of him as Allanaq—was naked. His shoulders and body, arms and legs, everything but his face and penis, were painted red with spots that were white, almost like a crab with barnacles on its shell, like something that had walked along the bottom of the sea.

Even if her mother was disappointed, she was glad Grey Owl had chosen Nagi's house to bring him, not theirs. Maybe he was the reason her aunt Nua hadn't come? What had Weyowin said? That it was possible he wasn't human?

And yet there was something about him that was almost shy, the way he glanced back to Grey Owl and Grey Owl nodded. He was nervous, just as she was nervous about her song, frightened in front of so many people who to him would all be strangers.

He bent down, took paint that had already been mixed out of a rawhide-hinged box on the floor, rubbed one part of his face with black—only half of it, the other half he left human.

He seemed to change then, the shyness falling away, as if the colors masked his fears, gave him strength. The beat of the drums picked up. He glanced once to Grey Owl, then, with a deliberate rhythm, began to sway. He was using his hands in the same motions any of her people would have, acting out the story with his hands.

There was a boat he showed, but he wasn't fishing or hunting. He'd been cast out, he and another man—his father. They'd been forced out of their village by a shaman and their hands were bound and then suddenly there was no father. He was dead. Not this man, but the father.

The stranger's moves grew more and more insistent. His knees bent lower, his back swayed. Elik leaned forward, her hands on her ankles, pulled into the beat.

The man's arms were long and well muscled, tight with veins that twisted like a river to his wrists. He was showing his umiak, the way the water cupped it, without paddles, in a fog that took him beyond sight.

He looked into the distance, as if he could see the boat, see his father, his home, so far away, and the shaman who had wronged him. The drum quickened. Elik held her breath. She could see him. She was there. In the dark chop of the water. Inside the boat. She felt the pitch and roll and the loss not only of his father but of his people also, all his people.

It was the story of how he came to Grey Owl, to her uncle, how they saved each other from the sea. How they would have drowned and died and wandered with hate inside their dead hearts were it not that the fog spit him out and Grey Owl came.

And then silence, sudden and demanding. The drummers quit. The man's arms hung motionless until a few moments went by and his chest moved heavily. He caught his breath, and then he left the floor. That was all. Elik felt drained, empty and alone.

Maybe it was true what her cousins said about him, that he could do nothing, not hunt or fish. But surely he was a man? There was his chest heaving and the sweat running between his shoulder blades, gathering to the small of his back.

Malluar leaned close. "You see," she whispered. "Seal Talker grows old and suspicious. He doesn't know whom to trust. Who will turn on him."

Elik didn't see. She turned—Seal Talker was standing near the drummers again, talking to the men. One of the other guests had also risen, a man near her uncle's age, also from the Long Coast. From the look on his face, he definitely thought he was going to dance, that it was his turn.

•

But Seal Talker was shaking his head no. He was shaman, and it would be his turn again. First.

Malluar chuckled without caring who heard.

Elik watched as Seal Talker moved toward one of masks that hung on the wall. Someone put out the lamps again. Seal Talker was going to dance, or else go into a trance—she didn't know which.

There was a cry and a shuffling and then a clacking sound Elik knew from other times in the *qasgi*. It was the bones on Seal Talker's shaman's belt, the call that would summon his spirit helpers. They would gather inside, around her, in the dark.

In another moment the *qasgi* would become the door through which Seal Talker would travel to the Land Below the Sea. In another moment it would be forbidden for anyone to leave, to risk breaking the membrane through which he would journey.

Except she couldn't breathe. The walls felt as if they were closing in around her. As if with one accidental touch Seal Talker could drag her down with him if she remained, down inside his trance, beneath the waves. She'd be down there with that man's dead father and with Seal Talker.

Malluar's cold hand brushed against hers and she jumped. She grabbed her parka and pushed herself up, then lurched forward. With a hand raised to feel her way she stumbled for the opening in the floor before it was closed. Before the air drowned her, before Seal Talker's spirit helpers came and took her . . .

Outside . . . She had to breathe . . . Had to get out.

The snap of cold surprised her. The absolute dark of the sky and, overhead, so far, so high, a thousand tiny holes. People could be peering down. Watching her from above. She didn't want anyone watching her. Didn't want the light of the moon to touch her.

Almost at once her eyelashes frosted together. Where she'd been sweating she felt a line tickling her skin, and then the burn of cold air. She fought with her parka to get it on, and then stood there, swallowing air so cold it stung her lungs.

Dizzy, she felt dizzy, but she would be all right. It was only that she needed quiet for a moment, she told herself, that was all. She had to get somewhere, calm herself before she went back and faced her own dance.

Sipsip's house was just there, closest beside the *qasgi*. Elik remembered hearing Two Ravens' baby cry earlier, before the stranger had danced. Sipsip's house was closer than her own and it made sense that Two Ravens had gone there first. She would be inside, lying down, nursing her baby.

Directly overhead, a band of red-and-green lights danced across the sky. Elik covered her head with an arm. The lights were made by people, by boys playing at a game of ball with walrus skulls. She didn't want them to see her. Not now. Not ever.

She hurried to Sipsip's house, through the thick darkness of the tunnel entry. She felt dizzy still, and there was a high-pitched keening in her ears, almost like a song, but she couldn't make out the words. She pushed aside the inner hide curtain, straightened through the floor entry. With a shudder of relief, she felt the warmth from the banked fire and the familiar odors of a lamp and food and fish.

She turned, expecting to see Two Ravens with her baby.

Instead, a man stood facing her, there beside the hearth. It was the dancer, Grey Owl's stranger. *Allanaq.* Quickly, she looked away. She didn't dare allow him to see her eyes. It wasn't safe. If Weyowin was right, and he was a demon, he could jump inside her body through her eyes.

The man was wearing the parka she'd first seen him in outside. The parka was worn, it was true, but now she wondered if it might be the same one he'd been wearing that day he was forced from his home, in his story. There were parts of the fur she couldn't recognize. Was it dog— the balding legs of a polar bear?

Everything he did seemed contrary to what she knew, the right idea, the wrong way. His parka might once have been beautiful but it was old now. Did he think his father's spirit would be content to see him that way, without pride?

The man leaned over and picked up a clay pot that had been sitting on the hearth.

"How do you make this?" he asked.

"The pot?" The question surprised her.

"I'd been wondering what it is—" His voice was deep and he spoke too fast. She could follow, though some of the words were different, others strung together in the wrong ways.

"It's made out of clay," she answered. "Earth. The ground."

"That's all?"

Elik stole a glance to the man's face. Maybe the man wasn't as strange as Weyowin said, but more like a child. He reminded her of something her grandmother said: that the most painful thing in the world was for a person to live as an orphan, helpless, without family. "The clay," she said, more slowly this time, "is mixed with down from a ptarmigan's thigh. We add seal oil, to bind it."

"We don't make these in my home."

Elik didn't understand. "Nua has no cook-pots?"

"I meant at my own house." The man stared for so long at the far wall Elik wondered again if maybe Weyowin wasn't right. Maybe he wasn't a man. Too many things he did were wrong.

Finally he sighed, looked around the single large room of the house as if seeing it for the first time. "There's so much driftwood wasted. And your doors—they should face the sea, but they don't."

Elik watched the man's gaze flitting around the house, like a bee, like a mosquito. Is that what he was?

He said, "You're a shaman, aren't you?"

Her eyes flew from his face. "No. Of course not. I . . . I was sitting with Malluar. Is that what you saw?"

"I thought I heard you call a loon's sound?"

"No—I wouldn't . . . " She shook her head, protesting. How could a stranger dare speak so directly? Even if he was a child? Didn't he know that words held power? What loon?

"In my home," he said, "there was a man. He spoke often of how he wrestled with a powerful Loon-spirit, and how he won. That whatever he asked, the Loon would do for him because he was a great shaman. Even drown a man in his kayak if he asked."

Elik's thoughts flew to the one time she'd been with the younger Allanaq. It had been during a winter visit to the Long Coast, not here. They had gone to play inside the older, ruined qasgi, where no one ever went. She and Kimik, Iluperaq and Allanaq—they had all crawled inside the qasgi's collapsed tunnel. They had been laughing, exploring, the way they often did when they were young. Except that this time, inside, Kimik and her brother thought nothing of finding a corner together, of rolling in the dark. When all around them on the floors, in the walls, there were bits of yellowed ivory sticking out from gaps between the floorboards. Splintered wood with eyes and faces and shards of painted bone watching them. Watching her. She had backed away—she remembered now—she had run and Allanaq had followed. He caught her in another cousin's house. He was laughing and so was she, relieved to be free of that place. Safe. No one else had been home. By then, she was glad to have someone to hold. . . .

He wouldn't remember. Or else, if he did—he would only remember about her and Allanaq. Not about the Loon she had seen. He couldn't. But even if he did, she needn't worry. The guests would leave again, soon after the feast. She would never see him again. He would go away, him and his strange talk and his boat.

But then, with a sudden curiosity, she asked, "Was it true—your dance? The way my uncle found you?"

"Grey Owl thought it might go better for me if I told the story, so people here knew, from the first. My people are Seal People."

"I don't know any Seal People. Who was your father?"

He looked away. "My father is a ghost," he said, and then, looking back suddenly, he met her eyes. "There are so many things to remember, so much to think about—a man's heart could snap with the weight of it all."

Elik shook her head. She had never heard a man speak this way. Not her father. Not Iluperaq. Not to her. "I should go . . . "

She took a step, but he called her. "Wait," he said. He had taken something from inside his parka. He was holding it out, something small and white in his hand.

It was an ivory carving of a loon. *A Loon!* Lying sideways in his hand.

The smooth, tiny figure pulled her in. "You made this?" she asked. She started to reach for it, then stopped. She had never seen a carving so beautiful, so smooth, so true. There were lines etched and blackened like a necklace of feathers around its throat. And there was another mark for its heartline and another for the *inua* inside of it. And other markings around the eyes she had never seen before except to know that if a carving ever held power, this one would.

"Take it," he said. "I don't want it. My father spoke with the *inua,* but Red Fox's spirit helper was stronger. Maybe this amulet will be more useful to someone else."

She tugged her hands up inside her sleeves, not to touch it. She didn't dare. Was he trying to say it was a gift? Or only showing it? Was it something good? Or bad?

*No.* She held her breath, stepped through the entry, hoping he didn't hear the thundering inside her heart.

Elik woke earlier than the others, then lay with her eyes closed, the heavy caribou furs drawn to her neck.

She had dreamed that she was a harbor seal basking on a thick pan of floating offshore ice. Even now, awake and with the sounds of her sister and her grandmother, Two Ravens and her baby's thick breathing in her ears, she could feel the warmth of the spring sun move from the curve of her seal-back down along her ribs, the way droplets of water tickled her belly, then evaporated.

In the dream, her human fingers had been tucked inside mittens and the mittens were her flippers, elastic and strong. Her skin was nothing like a woman's, but more a layer of nostrils and ears, smelling and listening into the air, everywhere.

A sound had come, thick and frightening, a human sound, and she had pushed her way off the ice. Not quickly—though she wanted desperately to be quick—but with awkward, laborious movements that tasted like fear inside her mouth.

Until, finally, she reached the water's edge and dived back inside the sea, where the water was safe and comforting. She swam, but not deep, then looked back at the path she had opened. Two shadows had appeared on the surface. They were long and slender, seallike, but they weren't seals. They were humans inside skins that had once belonged to seals. But that wasn't bad, because the people inside—they were good.

And that was the strange part, how even while the dream was happening, she knew she had become a seal so that she might learn what it was like to live beneath the sea, an animal inside a coat of fur and flesh. Not so different from a human, except that a seal could sense the smell of the human in a way that a human never could. Not just its presence, but its heart. Not just its scent, but the kind of person it was. Whether it came in respect or with greed, whether it was thankful or too loud.

Then she woke and lay there, savoring the dream, watching the light of the shallow house lamp her mother kept burning through the night.

She thought that, maybe, the seal in the dream was the same one Grey Owl had caught in his kayak. It made sense because she had not been able to stop thinking about the new Allanaq's story, the way two men who would have been dead were alive because a seal had died so they could find each other.

Elik would have told her uncle about the dream if she could. He would have liked to hear how his kayak looked from below, that the seal she had become believed he was a good man. Except that he and his strange son and most of the other guests had already packed their sledges and carry-sacks and left.

Elik rolled over and stared at the greyed roof poles overhead. The feast was over and, though nothing had gone wrong, nothing had gone well either.

She'd danced the Eagle's Dance and, in spite of the way her hands had started off shaking, she hadn't forgotten a word, not a move. Afterward, her grandmother had put her arm around her shoulder and praised her. Her mother had smiled in that slow, quiet way she had, then just as quietly gone back to the sewing in her lap. But that was all. Not another word. She was done and nothing had changed.

The guests were gone. Inside the houses, ice-pits, and raised caches, their food stores were mostly emptied. Outside there were tracks beaten through the crusted snow and the feeling that something had been going to happen, and then it hadn't.

Elik sighed, quietly pushed aside the stitched-together fur she shared with her grandmother, and rose. There were urine pots to move and ice to melt for water and, if her mother wanted to feed Two Ravens before she and her family started the journey back to the Long Coast, there was meat to cut in shares. Elik slipped her boots and parka on over the waist-apron she slept in, then left quickly, before her mother woke or her father came in hungry from the *qasgi*.

Though it was time to wake, the sky outside was a dome of night with only a smudge of grey showing from the east. The snow along the path to the nearest freshwater pond was well packed, shadowed and wide enough in the dim light to find her way without stumbling.

Near the center of the frozen pond, she traded her empty waterskins for the long-handled ice-chipper that was kept there. Methodically, she placed her feet on both sides of the hole, then began chipping. The hole was well used, the new layer of ice clear and thin, and she needed only to punch it a few times before water swelled from the hole and sloshed up toward her boots.

She stepped back, chipped a little at the edges to widen the hole, and used a scoop to pick out the small chunks of floating ice. With a practiced motion, she looped the handle on the skins across the end of the stick, circled it down so it filled with water, then drew it up and set it on the side to fill the next skin.

When she finished, she bent to catch the handles. Then straightened, turned; Iluperaq stood watching her. She jumped, before she realized who he was. How long had he been there? She hadn't heard him walking—not a sound.

The hair on her brother's forehead was a sharp black against the lighter color of his raised hood and his eyes seemed darker than usual, not angry but intent. He was wearing his double-layered winter clothes, the white fur hunters wore when they were stalking seals beyond the pressure ridges, hoping they wouldn't be seen.

"Where are you going?"

"Hunting." He listened toward the houses, then bent to help her with the skins.

Elik looked to see what gear he carried: coiled lines, two harpoons, one with an ice-testing point on the handle end. He'd looped a carry-sack over his shoulder for gear.

"For ringed seal?" she asked.

He nodded. "There's a lead open; I saw it yesterday, the reflection of a water sky in the clouds. Out a distance to the point, if the wind hasn't changed." He carried the skins as far as the looser snow at the pond's edge, then set them down again. "There's moonlight still. It'll guide me till the sun comes up."

Elik looked back along the path. "You're going alone?"

He nodded, started to say something, then stopped. Elik waited. She hadn't followed her only to say he would hunt. Men hunted. They hunted alone. They hunted together. If it was breathing-hole sealing he meant to do, then it wasn't a strange thing going out early in the moonlight.

Iluperaq straighted his shoulders, lowered his voice against the winter air that carried sounds so far. "Tell Kimik . . . Tell Kimik a man hunts for his food."

"So." Elik nodded, understanding. Husband. Man. Hunter. The words were nearly the same. "You've packed food? For one day? Or for two?"

Iluperaq looked toward the houses. "For however many days it takes to satisfy our father."

"Did you tell him?"

Iluperaq shook his head. "Father keeps us too much at home," he said. They were nearly the same words she'd heard Naiya use, though from her sister Elik hadn't taken them seriously. Naiya used them to speak about men, of wanting to be married. Iluperaq spoke less often.

She said, "It's only that he wants us around still, that he doesn't want the house to grow empty or too quiet."

"He could have grandchildren. That isn't it."

"He needs your help."

"Who doesn't need help? Where do you hear a man say

he doesn't want a son at his side? A second pair of ears, or hands?"

Elik thought of Grey Owl and his new son. Was that why her uncle had adopted him? Because he was growing old and had no daughter to bring a husband into the house? Her eyes lit with a conspiratorial glint. "I'll come with you," she offered. "A wife for you means a sister for me. I know how. I've gone before . . . Not a lot. But some . . . ?"

Iluperaq smiled back. "Next time. This work belongs to me."

Elik nodded. If the need had been for food only, he would have taken her along. Women fished and trapped ptarmigan and fox. If there was need, they'd hunt for more. But this was more than just food. She turned—there was a whining sound, something moving in the snow. "You brought a dog?" she asked.

"To sniff out holes."

"It would be good if you found a bearded seal."

"It's too early in the year."

"Do you remember—the last time we went together?"

"With father, yes." Iluperaq's voice sounded flat again.

"We found three breathing holes that day." She waited, thinking he would smile with the memory. He didn't. His thoughts were as firm as his anger and anger, they both knew, was better kept inside. "He means well," she said softly.

"Will you tell Kimik for me?"

"I will. And I'll hold my stitchwork till you're home, so the seals will come."

The carved bones rolled toward the *qasgi* wall with a rattling sound. The first two hit at the same time: *Neqaraq,* the Salmon; *Kegluneq,* the Wolf. The slower ones followed with a sound like pebbles scattering on rocks. *Issuriq* the Spotted Seal; *Nayiq* the Ringed Seal.

Anxiously, Seal Talker leaned past the other men to see if the bones fell out any better than the first time.

It was possible he should have used a different set, thrown some newer bones and saved the power inside of these, his oldest. But the runner's feast was over and the

Bent Point People looked to him as shaman to find game. Tomorrow or the day after that; it had to be soon.

Too often in one life, Seal Talker had learned what hunger did to people. The way it turned men's hearts to stone, women's mouths first to fury and then to fear. It brought weakness and made people's thoughts too muddled and foolish for them to hunt well. To steal, to murder sometimes, that they could do. But to hunt wisely? No.

Two more of his animal carvings rolled unevenly to a stop. Sea Gull, then Wolverine. Another from behind leaned with its short neck across the first.

The knot of men behind Seal Talker pressed closer. He didn't look but he could hear one of them sighing, someone else coughed. "Which way? What is it?"

He didn't answer. Sea Gull covered Salmon. Caribou, his own helping spirit, hid beneath Wolverine's body. A sign of females alone. Which was not a bad thing in itself, but it wasn't complete. No more than males alone would have been complete.

He'd have to roll again. And again after that if need be, till they answered with a sign of where to hunt. Or else refused to speak and he had to search some other way.

The shaman crawled forward, scooped up the bones, and then, shutting out the men with their nervous glances, squatted on his haunches and studied the carvings.

Caribou first, the surefooted *Tuttu;* he blew on it, warming it with his breath. Then the Spotted Seal, then the Cod. He blew on them all, then licked them, so they would see what he saw, want what he wanted.

It was his uncle, Kashek, who had first taught him to read the bones, as Kashek had taught him all things. He could still remember the old man's face, his downturned mouth—like a crescent moon carved upside down on a mask. The way he used to stare at a thing with eyes that were darker than any man's had a right to be.

Kashek taught him it wasn't the way the bones were carved that gave them power—whether the neck on one was sufficiently long or the shoulder on another as angled as it might have been. It was that they spoke to him—that was what mattered. That the carvings pleased the spirits enough so they came and spoke when he called.

Except sometimes, sometimes it was true and an amulet or a song did lose its power after it was used. He'd known it to happen with masks and certain magical words. But his bone set? What if he'd been wrong all these years and it did matter how well they were carved? How truthfully?

Then again, what if it was his own age that brought weakness, and not the bones at all?

Like the dream he'd had of his uncle—how many nights ago had it been? Two? Or was it three? Seal Talker didn't like the way he forgot things anymore: a day, a season, a small gossip his wife shared in bed one night, then had to remind him again the next.

Still, wasn't it a good sign, to have his uncle speak? A sign of strength that even though one of them was dead and the other alive, they still understood each other's words?

In the dream, Kashek had been teaching him—just as he had when Seal Talker was a boy—where to set joint markings in a carving to show where a soul could enter or leave, and how to scratch ownership marks with a burin, so people would know whose hand had done the work.

Strange, how some days had passed so long ago and yet seemed more clear than all the others since.

Malluar had already been grown when he'd gone to live with Kashek, already married and round-bellied with her son, the one who'd lived almost a year. Kashek had already taught her to be a shaman when Seal Talker's turn had come, though she seldom had the chance to work her skills, what with the babies, either hers that never lived, or the ones she wet-nursed, always crying at her breast.

Seal Talker started to smile, then just as quickly stopped. Their uncle had trained Malluar first; pregnant or not. And because of that, because she had known Kashek when he was strong, had him for herself—Seal Talker could never be sure there weren't things she knew that he had never been taught.

Young men die but old men forget—wasn't he proof there was truth in that? And if that was true, then wasn't it also possible there were secrets Kashek had taught Malluar and then forgotten when his turn had come?

And yet, even as he thought these things, he felt foolish. To be jealous, even to this day, for a slight that might never have happened?

Quickly, Seal Talker rubbed the carvings, then tossed them toward the wall.

The men leaned forward from behind, watching.

Nothing of this feast had gone the way he had planned. And now, with the last of the guests leaving, Seal Talker could barely hide his anger, his disappointment.

First, he had looked for his only son to come, and he had not. And here it was, a second winter that Arveq sat in Fish River, refusing to come home. He'd even sent word with the runners announcing the feast: *Seal Talker was not young, but his son was. Seal Talker was shaman and had more than enough for food for his son to find a wife and bring her here.*

Arveq should have been with him. He should have been home and he, Arveq, should have been the one throwing the bones, learning to read their tracks, to be shaman after his father and Malluar, his aunt.

And what had his son sent back? Nothing but gossip. That his wife was fat and well fed and he was the father of a new daughter and a relative of men in Fish River. That he honored his father but he was a hunter, not the kind of man who fought with spirits and rolled on the floor clutching his knees to his chest with the pain of listening to them, fighting them, pleasing them so the people could be strong while he grew weak.

That was Seal Talker's greatest shame.

The second shame was lying on the floor along the wall at his back, and it stabbed at him each time he walked by the mountain of gifts the Long Coast people had left behind.

Women's *ulus* with fine, sharp edges. Skins and fish-hooks. Needle cases and more antler than he had seen carved in a full year. Even a sledge was there, even a kayak! And what did it mean but that the spirits had been more pleased with the Long Coast People than with his own?

With more anger than he meant to show, Seal Talker scooped up the bones, scattered them against the wall. Sea Gull again. Wolverine and Salmon . . . Blind, all blind today!

So be it. There were other ways he could search for game. And there were other ways he could get a child of his blood to follow where Arveq wouldn't dare.

If his only son was not called to be shaman, that did not mean that Kashek's line—the blood that flowed inside his veins and Malluar's—need die without a future. None of Malluar's children had lived, and she was too old now to try again. But he wasn't. Who knows but perhaps he'd get another? A child who wasn't afraid to wrestle spirits.

If he had not wasted so much time waiting for his son to come back home, who knows but he would have thought of it sooner.

Seal Talker looked about the qasgi. A few of the younger boys were sleeping. On the bench, Blue-Shadow's oldest son sat wrapping sinew for a cable on a bow. The men nearest him held quiet, their murmurings swallowed inside their mouths.

He'd frightened them: he could see it in the way they'd taken out their tools, pretending to work. The way Chevak concentrated over a splice he was trying to make in a line of bearded seal skin, when everyone knew the man's fingers always fumbled, hating small work, that he traded what he needed for the skillful baskets his wife made.

"Have the sleds left?" he asked. "All of them?"

Nagi had been outside most recently. "There were still two sledges," he said, "waiting for daylight maybe. Someone was working on the cross slats. Maybe the lashing came loose?"

The shaman nodded. "Then we aren't too late. Chevak, Saami, all of you, go home and see what food you have. Nagi, tell whoever's still here from the Long Coast to wait.

Their Bent Point relatives would be shamed if our guests left with nothing to eat while we have plenty."

Chevak stood in front of his daughter, his expression skewed in surprise. "Iluperaq didn't say he meant to go hunting."

Elik kept her gaze carefully to her work, her hands moving in a downward, twisting motion, taking up more of the caribou-back sinew she had already split, lengthening the line.

*Tell Kimik a man hunts for his food.* Those were her brother's words, but had he also meant she should keep the hunting a secret?

She lifted her head enough to see the black bottoms of her father's crimped boot soles as he paced the short distance from the entry to Iluperaq's side of the sleeping platform. He squatted, pulled one of Iluperaq's storage baskets out from underneath, then sat with it in his lap.

With a grunt of displeasure Chevak fished through the contents. "Did he take one of my blades? The grey chert is here. Why would he leave that one and take another?" Chevak shot a glance toward Elik. "You said he left before light?"

*Yes,* Elik nodded, but she didn't offer the next answer, that there was more than enough moonlight on the snow to see by. That with the wind calm as it was today, a man could easily follow Iluperaq's tracks.

There was a scuffling sound from the passage—Gull searching for the food Chevak said the shaman had requested.

Elik looked to her grandmother. Alu had drawn a fur over her shoulders and seemed sunken, exhausted now that the visiting and eating were done. Naiya also sat quietly, not for Alu's reasons, but more the same as Elik's, because quiet was safest when Chevak worried about meat.

He reached deeper under the platform, pulled out another basket. His mouth hung open as he counted out the blades. "I saw no tracks," he said, "nothing to say which way he'd gone."

Elik added a few strands of sinew to the others, lengthening the thread. *How could he have searched for tracks when he said he didn't know Iluperaq had left?*

Why did her father lie? Because he didn't want to admit he slept late in the *qasgi* while Iluperaq went hunting? That he was a father who didn't know which way his son had gone?

But then, if she did tell him that Iluperaq said he'd follow the clouds' reflection on open water, would it not shame her father more, being told what he should have seen himself?

Gull climbed in from the entrance passage.

Chevak froze with his hands poised over the open basket—until he saw it was Gull—then he pulled it to his lap again, fingered his way among Iluperaq's things.

"I found salmon in the outside cache, enough to make a meal," Gull said. She looked toward Alu as she spoke, rather than watch her husband's hands. "It must have fallen behind the rolled-up tent skins. Do you think Seal Talker will need more?"

Chevak shifted his anger from his son to the shaman. "For them he gives anything. For us he grows too old to find caribou."

Quickly, before Naiya had a chance to say it first, Elik rose. "I'll take the food," she offered, and she crossed to her mother's side.

Alu came suddenly alert. She pushed back her blankets, made a motion shooing Elik from the house. "Take it," she called. "Do you want someone to think we feast on meat instead of sharing?" And she made her voice loud, as if to be certain Seal Talker knew it was no fault of hers there was food left in the house.

Outside, the cold air sharpened Elik's thoughts. The sky was unusually clear. The hills in the distance caught the sunlight, turned the snow-covered passes to orange, blue, and gold.

She looked toward where the Long Coast lay, a three-day journey along the winter trail if the weather was good.

And in the other direction, inland where the river cut a pass between two hills—the place where Fish River People lived. She watched a moment. Inland seemed more dangerous than the coast. As long as people followed the shore, it seemed they could never get lost. But inland— what if a fog came in? How could people find their way?

When she was young, Naiya used to brag to the other girls how Elik was the bravest, climbing on rocks and roughhousing, hiding in washed-out gullies. It wasn't true. Iluperaq was braver. She wouldn't want to go out to the lonely places by herself, the way a man had to. Crossing the tundra for caribou, climbing the hills for dall sheep, listening as wolves closed in their circle in the dark.

There was a spirit who lived inside that nearest hill, people said. A *yua* that had no human form, no animal. It was named *Yuilriq,* the spirit who owned the mountain. He could walk on air and find a hunter trespassing. He could spoil a man's aim. Maybe kill him.

Naiya said that stories about spirits had frightened her more as a child, less as she grew older. For Elik, it was the opposite. She'd felt braver when she was young, when her thoughts were not yet awake. She wouldn't want to hunt the way Iluperaq did now, alone, with the night sky watching from above.

Closer in about the houses the snow was trampled, marked with scuffling dogprints, with the flat, skimming lines the sledges cut in the snow. She turned to see the last few visitors leaving now, fitting packs to the sides of impatient dogs. The bulky figure of a man straightened, turned to watch the *qasgi.* Seal Talker must have asked him to wait.

Grey Owl had been among the first to leave, taking the trail that veered past the small canyon, then led to the sea. He and his new son had disappeared so quickly Elik never had the chance to sit with her uncle, or tell him about her dream of the seal he had caught.

And yet, if he had stayed longer, he would have visited in her house. He would have heard her father's complaints, the embarrassment of his anger. And not just Grey Owl, but his new son also. She would have been expected to cook food for him. . . .

Didn't the new Allanaq know how improper it was for an unmarried man to offer gifts? Was it possible that someone could speak their language, yet know nothing of their ways?

*Iluperaq and this new Allanaq. Her father and his anger. The feast and all her dreams.* Where did they come from, she wondered—all her thoughts, her questions, strong as an undercurrent, secretive as water below ice. What could a person do with so many thoughts?

Elik made her way inside the *qasgi*, then waited. After so many days of feasting, the supply of seal oil had dwindled. Already, with the guests gone, fewer lamps were lit. It was a moment longer before her eyes adjusted to the light, till she saw that the only people left inside were Bent Point People. Her mother's younger brother, Nagi, stood beside Seal Talker. Her father's brother, Saami, near the long wall, where the gifts that had not yet been shared out were spread along the floor.

She looked sideways at Nagi, then at Saami's longish face. It was true Nagi had a stronger resemblance to Grey Owl than either did to their sister, Gull, though all three shared a little of the same wide cheekbones, a similar curve to their eyes.

She and Iluperaq looked less alike than Nagi and their mother. And some people said she and Naiya had the same mouth, though Naiya was adopted. And Saami and her father looked nothing alike, and had even less in common. Saami was older, and had a quieter face. He was serious, while Chevak was often angry. He hunted, while Chevak settled for smaller shares.

So perhaps it wouldn't matter that Grey Owl had taken a son who looked nothing like he did. After all, it wasn't the shape of a chin that made someone into a relative, or the way he stood so tall.

Elik set down the salmon she'd brought, then crossed behind the men toward where Ema, the shaman's wife, sat huddled in the corner on the bench, asleep. Elik took a seat nearby, then looked up to see her father enter the *qasgi*. Quietly, she moved behind one of the beams that held the roof.

Ema woke at her jostling and straightened herself. She said, "My husband looks for caribou—did you hear?"

"No, Grandmother, I hadn't."

"Often it's like this—late in the winter we feast, then go without."

"Yes, Grandmother."

"Do you remember the last time we were hungry, truly hungry, all of us on the Long Coast?"

"Yes, Grandmother, it was—"

"No," Ema stopped her. "You children know only the little hunger. The short hunger that fades with the first catch of fish. You don't remember what we do, your elders." And then she stopped and gave a laugh. She poked Elik in the ribs, smiled her nearly toothless smile.

"If you're afraid, you needn't be. My husband—he's still a man. He wakes up at night, and his legs are stiff. All three of them. He could get you with child, if he wanted. If he sees caribou, he'll call them. They'll come the way the girls came, the way I came, when I was young. You'll eat. You'll see."

Ema went quiet after that. She reached for the skins that had slipped to her waist, fixed them around her shoulders again, then took her sewing: a child's ball she was sewing from alternating strips of white and dark caribou.

Elik edged her way out from behind the shadows of the post. The men were standing in small groups now, separating gifts into piles, laying them out for the women and the houses they'd belong to.

Her father held his arms out and Nagi handed him a thick, long roll of hides. He brought it around to where Seal Talker sat beside a lamp, set it down, then pulled back a length from the roll. One of the men let out his breath. Seal Talker's eyes narrowed to a slit.

The hide was brown, larger than a caribou, the fur too

long for a sea mammal. "What is it?" someone asked. "It's not caribou."

"It's coarser than caribou," her father said.

"But what is it?" The men leaned in to check, to touch.

"They haven't dall sheep near the Long Coast."

"It's not heavy enough for brown bear."

"I've seen it," Nagi said. "Though I didn't notice before—it was the same as the sleeping skin Grey Owl brought for himself."

Seal Talker rose from his seat. The other men backed off, gave him room. There was something in the way he walked, an anger in his posture. Elik tried not to think of Ema's words, that he was a man still. That he could get a woman with child. He squatted down, took an edge of the hide in his hands, smelled it, rubbed it together. "It's moose," he said and his voice was low and tight.

"What?"

"*Tuntuvak,*" he said, then again, in another tongue: "*Moose.* But it's none of theirs. Nor anything the Real People know. They traded it from the Forest People. Though how many blades and what they offered . . ." Seal Talker shrugged but his anger was back, like a layer of smoke spreading in the air.

He made a slight motion and her father snapped the end of the hide, unrolling the full length so they could see the size of it, the shadings.

On the bench behind the men, Elik sat taller, trying to see.

She heard a sound, but she couldn't see well enough. A light tumbling. Something had fallen. Scattering. There and again. Here. Over there.

Pebbles tucked inside the hide? Blades? Is that what they were? Elik was only partly aware of the men scrambling to catch the pieces, Seal Talker calling them to bring it in, all the pieces, back to him.

Something grey spun across the floor toward the bench. A moment later and her father was on it, pecking like a sea gull after a fish.

Elik started to say something, to show her father where another had come to rest. It tumbled toward her, not in a straight path; it was no smooth circle to roll in a line. White. It was white and oblong. Odd-shaped. Not round.

Elik moved smoothly and quickly, with an eye to her father to make sure he didn't see. She slid from the platform. With one hand she picked up the toy ball that had kindly fallen from Ema's lap. With her foot, she slid the ivory carving closer in, away from her father.

No one had seen. She bent and picked it up. It was the loon. The carving Allanaq had tried to give her. The realization brought a shiver: the loon amulet had come of its own will. *It had come to her.*

Her hand was shaking as she returned the ball, then slipped back to her seat. Ema had closed her large, slanting eyes, but she woke, smiled her thanks.

In the dark of Elik's fist, the loon amulet felt sharp and smooth. Familiar somehow, as if she had always known how it would feel. The way the tip of one wing dug in against her palm here, the way the other wing wedged itself against the base of her thumb.

"Show me," Seal Talker asked, and Elik slid her hand beneath her leg. Not her. He wasn't looking at her. The shaman stood with his hand open and waiting in front of her father. She could see the disappointment on Chevak's mouth, the reluctance as he handed over his catch.

The men were all talking, passing the blades, the open-worked carvings and worked antler tools they'd found. "Look at this one. Look at the flint work, how it's angled. Look at the way this one is done."

Seal Talker examined the keen, double-sided edge of the blade Chevak had handed him. "Grey Owl made these?" he asked.

Nagi compared the bifaced blade he'd picked off the floor to the one the shaman held. From her seat, Elik made out the flash of a black stone so smooth it caught the fire's light. "Obsidian," Nagi said.

"But even if Grey Owl traded for an obsidian core," Seal Talker asked, "how did he learn to make these?"

"Perhaps he didn't make them. Perhaps he traded them already finished. From the same place as the hide?"

"No," Chevak disagreed. "Grey Owl carves no differently than any of us. It was his son who made these."

"His son?" Seal Talker winced. "Will someone tell me why Grey Owl should be given a new son when his son is dead and my son, who should have been here feasting, is so far away, I can't even say if he lives?"

The men went silent.

Seal Talker moistened his lips. He was hungry and tired, and he wasn't enjoying any of this. He said: "I hear the Long Coast People keep the bones of that man's dead father near their house."

No one moved.

"Who knows what harm a stranger's ghost might bring? It could lie to them, trick them in ways I cannot even guess. Not even I, with my spirit helpers, could begin to guess.

"It's possible," he went on, "that the dead father's ghost followed his son here. And if he did, then the reason the bones told me nothing has everything to do with that man, and nothing to do with me." He waited, thinking through this newest idea.

"Listen," he said. "Go, and call everyone. Tell them I will hunt for caribou. I will go into a trance and I will search with eyes that see inside the darkest places. And if I find caribou, we will know which way to hunt, and all will be well. If I find nothing, we will burn these things and try again. We will know what chased the animals away."

The men let the blades and carvings drop back to the hide.

Elik forced herself to stay calm. She wanted the loon, whether the men kept theirs or not. She glanced to the shaman's wife, then quickly felt beneath her parka for her amulet bag, and dropped the loon inside. The weight changed, pulled heavier against her neck.

Elik pushed herself from the bench, took the first step

toward the passage. "Here, where are you going?" Ema called her back.

Elik turned. The old woman pushed a sliver of fish toward Elik. The fish was dry and hard; there was no odor. "Go on, take it." Ema spoke as if she was talking to a child. "Throw it in the ashes, for the spirits. It will go up in the air, to the other side. It will grow and be enough. We'll all be hungry together. Go on."

Elik did as she was told. The ashes in the empty hearth puffed. The fish disappeared inside. Elik stepped for the passage again.

"Can you carry something?"

The loon swayed beneath Elik's parka as if it were fluttering its wings. "Yes?"

"Can you carry these for Malluar?"

Elik followed where Ema had pointed, to one of the small piles of exchange gifts that had been separated from the others.

"Malluar could use the help, not to have to walk so far herself."

"I can bring them." Elik hid her relief.

In the background, the men were still talking: ". . . We don't know who he was," Seal Talker insisted. "What kind of man has hands so small to carve this way? Don't touch them, until we know."

Night had come on, hovering and watchful. With it came a stronger wind out of the hills and snow—swirling around barely visible houses, smoothing them, blending them into the land.

Elik shifted the load Ema had asked her to carry—it was awkward more than heavy. She pushed in against her parka, feeling for the loon. Was it the same one, she wondered? She would have traded every gift in the *qasgi* for a way to know whether it was the same Loon she had dreamed about, thought about, called to, ever since she'd seen it on the late-fall beach.

And what of the man? Had he meant for her to find it?

Could a stranger have that kind of power? Or was that part of the Loon's power, traveling through a man's hand into hers?

And how could one person hold so many questions! As if there were a wind inside her mind, turning everything white and difficult to see.

But then a smile came to her face. Whatever else was true, the Loon had come to her. Not only had it protected itself, but here it was bringing her to Malluar's house. And who more than an elder shaman would understand? Not only about the Loon, but also why Allanaq had asked if *she* was a shaman.

Elik pushed aside the frost-hardened hide that hung across Malluar's winter entry, then stepped down to a long passage tunnel.

Baskets were heaped along the floor, one atop the other. Stuffed, round seal pokes sat like old men along the length of a narrow bench. And overhead there were bundles of dried beach grass and skeins of tomcod tied and hanging from a planked ceiling. And the ceiling itself was supported by two whalebones—the long, log-sized jaws of the bowhead that was so rare on their shallow beaches.

Her father spoke so often of other people's wealth, Elik seldom listened. And yet what else was here: oil and fish, food enough to last a winter, a year. Shares and goods traded for a shaman's service. Enough to take care of the one woman in the village who lived without a husband, without a son or brother to hunt for her.

There was talking inside—more than one voice. Elik listened, then called, loudly, so they would know someone had come. She waited till someone answered, then climbed up into the house.

The first thing she saw was Malluar bent over a woman lying belly up on a grass mat on the floor, clothed in a woman's inside trousers, nothing more. It was Water-sky, the younger of the two sisters Saami had married, the sister with no children.

Beyond Water-sky's brown shoulder, Sipsip sat cross-legged, tapping a slow beat with one of Malluar's drums. Her hair was braided on two sides, wrapped with a thong in that odd style she'd worn since she was a child. Sipsip nodded once, then turned back to her drumming.

There was a sleeping bench along only one wall, leaving the floor more open than in her own house. Elik set the skins down, found a place to sit on the floor with her back against the bench. Beyond her, outlining the walls, a circle of wolverine skulls faced inward toward the hearth. White-faced and with their sharp teeth intact, their empty eye sockets watched the way she sat.

Carefully, she pulled her legs in. The one thing she didn't want was for Malluar to say she was too young to be there, that she was troublesome or distracting.

She wondered why it was Sipsip who came with Water-sky instead of Marmot, the older sister, but then she remembered Alu complaining about the two wives Saami had brought home. How married sisters spent their days bickering. Water-sky, Alu said, was jealous of the older sister, jealous because Marmot had two of Saami's babies at her breast, while Water-sky had only the one son who had been left on the tundra, dead before he had a name.

But here was Water-sky now, with a stomach that looked as if someone inside might be growing again. Which might be why she thought it better, safer for this new child, if Sipsip came with her to the shaman, rather than a sister jealous enough to bring who knows what kind of trouble.

With her hands hidden inside her long shaman's mittens, Malluar began walking a slow, narrow circle around Water-sky. She took small shuffling steps, changed direction, shook the mittens, chanted.

Elik made out only a few words—something about eyes beneath the sea. And another word, *tuqu*, for death. But most of the words were secret, magical things. Not something a shaman lightly shared.

The dancing ended and Malluar bent over and pushed Water-sky's trousers lower till the dark triangle of pubic hair showed out below her stomach. Farther up, a line of paint had been rubbed along Water-sky's breastbone, but she was sweating, and the paint had spread, trickling to her armpit.

Malluar moved lower, fixed a band around Water-sky's ankle, knotted it tightly just above the bone. "Lie so your legs are flat," she said, then added a length of rawhide to the ankle-band and straightened it beyond Water-sky's feet. A good-sized rock had already been set beyond the grass mat and Malluar took her time knotting it carefully to the end of the rope. "Can you move the rock?" she asked.

Water-sky tried to slide her foot in, to lift her knee, but the rock was too heavy. It slid once, barely rolling, but that was all.

Malluar checked the line again. She had Sipsip put out all but one seal oil lamp. This she placed on the floor between the rock and Water-sky's foot, so that the only thing in the house that could be seen was the rock and the circle of light outlining the hollows beneath Malluar's eyes.

"When I ask a question," Malluar said, "don't speak. You must try to lift your knee and move the rock, and I will see which way it answers."

Sipsip backed away a safer distance and Elik moved to see. This was *qilaniq*, divination by the stone. If a taboo had been broken or forbidden food eaten or a spirit dishonored—even if Water-sky didn't know it—the rock would know. Elik had often watched Seal Talker try this, but only in the *qasgi*, drumming and cajoling his spirit helpers to answer. Never had she been allowed to sit so close.

A sheen of sweat covered Water-sky's forehead. She lifted her head, tried to see what Malluar was doing.

With both hands, Malluar pressed down on Water-sky's soft stomach, palpating it. First with her palms, then with her fingertips, as if searching for something. Water-sky groaned—short, guttural sounds she was too frightened to hold back.

Malluar hushed her, pressed again. "You have eaten

something forbidden? Perhaps out of season? Did you fail to give a seal its drink of fresh water? Don't answer with words—move the rock."

Water-sky raised her knee and the rock hesitated, still too heavy. Malluar asked again, badgering, demanding. "Have you sewn on a caribou skin with your needle while your husband hunted?" Water-sky twisted her head from side to side, working to keep silent, not to cry. And then, suddenly, her knee moved. The rock broke free, rolled with her foot.

"It moved!" she cried, and she raised her head to see the shaman's reaction.

"A good sign," Malluar said. She rolled the rock back the full length of rope. "Tell me again," she said, and in the dim light, her face seemed to hang like a moon, suspended in the sky.

Elik shrank back. If she were the one lying there, she would never cry, she told herself. Never make so many noises.

In a thin, high-pitched voice, Malluar said, "There is a small-sized person inside of you. A person who wants to stay warm and safe."

"She will be born?" Sipsip smiled broadly. "Is it a boy?"

"It is a person. I cannot see between its legs."

Water-sky turned to Sipsip. "I knew it. I knew it was so."

"Be careful," Malluar warned. "Twice someone has tried to come out, and twice they waited for a better time. Now someone will come. Someone who wants to be born."

Malluar moved to Water-sky's other side. Behind her, the lamp flickered, folding shadows down from the ceiling, directly between the eyeholes of a wolverine. The next time Elik looked up, Malluar was watching. "You—" she said. Elik glanced to Sipsip.

"Not her," Malluar said. "You. Come here."

Elik hesitated, but only long enough to compose herself. Then, before Malluar changed her mind, she hurried closer. The older woman gestured for her to squat, exactly at Water-sky's side. Malluar took her hand, set it atop

Water-sky's rounded stomach. "Push here," Malluar said, as if this was something Elik did every day. "Push hard."

Water-sky jumped at her cold touch, but Elik did as she was told, pressing the soft skin only a little, then with interest, pushing and watching as Water-sky relaxed, as her skin pressed back around Elik's hand.

"Now here," Malluar said. "And here."

There was a dark line, less than half the thickness of a finger, drawn from out of Water-sky's pubic hair to her navel, dark against the yellow-brown of her stomach. Elik had never touched a line like that before, or felt anything like Water-sky's stomach—the way it was tight, not softly falling the way her breasts were, to her sides, more like a full-size seal poke, dried and hard and inflated, as if someone had breathed inside. "What should I feel?"

"If you feel anything, tell me."

Elik closed her eyes. She pressed with a harder touch, then lighter, moving her hand. Her fingertips felt hot, as if there were a fire inside the woman's stomach. Or a breath, as life was a breath, giving heat.

Inside, beneath her hand, something moved. Elik startled, pulled back her hand. "Something's in there—"

Sipsip laughed and turned to Malluar, "It's a good sign. Perhaps you have an amulet Water-sky could carry?"

Water-sky pushed away from Elik's hand. She was smiling and nodding, obviously pleased. Malluar brought out a hinged box with smaller wrappings inside. "I have bees," she offered, "for a strong head. And here"—she held out the open box to see: an ermine pelt with the skull attached—"for strength," she said, "agility."

While Malluar spoke with Water-sky, Elik rocked back on her haunches. She felt awed and a little frightened, proud that she hadn't shown fear. She reached for the drum Sipsip had laid aside, felt the willow root stitches tying the rim in a circle, the taut gut stretched across the top. She ran a finger along the edge of the grass mat on which Malluar had laid Water-sky and tried repeating to herself each word Malluar had spoken, the way the shaman's voice had sounded.

Elik hadn't expected a house could make her feel this way, strong and weak at the same time, curious and frightened. She only knew she wanted to stay, not go home and listen to her father belittling the size of Iluperaq's catch, or to the *qasgi*, where Seal Talker might find her loon.

The next time she looked up, the two women were gone. She hadn't noticed when. Malluar squatted on the floor beside her hearth. A tripod stood braced inside the rocks. She poked the ashes underneath with a stick, turned them over to search for coals. It wasn't until the trail of smoke tapered to an obedient line that she turned and looked at her guest.

Elik stared at her hands, hoping Malluar wouldn't yawn now, ask her to leave. She said, "Seal Talker's wife asked me to bring these."

Malluar glanced at the new hides. There was a long quiet. Elik searched for something to say, but the most that came out were small things—how fine the feast had gone, how delicious the food.

Malluar crossed to the platform, unrolled the hide, and looked inside.

Elik fought back the urge to hold her new amulet. *What if, like Seal Talker, Malluar found the loon evil. What if she thought a stranger's work could bring harm?*

Maybe it was better not to mention the loon, not till she knew which way Malluar's thoughts would turn. But there were other questions she could ask, circling the real ones. She wet her lips. "There was that man," she started, "the stranger Grey Owl brought?"

Malluar lifted a hollowed-out wooden bowl she'd found tucked inside the skin.

"He will be my aunt Nua's son in Bent Point?"

Malluar turned the bowl over to see the bottom. "It's a difficult thing to be an orphan," she said.

Elik nodded. Alu had said the same. "But if Grey Owl has adopted him, then he isn't an orphan anymore, is he?

Does that mean he is also related to my mother—her nephew?"

"If he has Allanaq's name, then he has Allanaq's aunt. And Allanaq's cousins. If I were Grey Owl, I would have done the same. I would take him to every relation, every neighboring village. I would bring gifts and feast him. Tell his name, his story."

"But what if someone says those ties are not real blood? What if . . . " she hesitated, started again. "What if some people say a stranger's hand brings trouble?"

Malluar seemed thoughtful, enough so that Elik hoped she might talk more. She leaned closer, waiting. But Malluar noticed the change in her posture. Her mouth softened. "So?" she asked. "Has anyone said that of your Naiya?"

"No. But Naiya is a cousin."

"Of Sipsip?"

"No, but Sipsip was born here. Were people afraid of her mother?"

There'd been a day—Elik remembered it suddenly—when they were very young, and Naiya, who teased Sipsip often about the braids, had finally teased too loudly. Sipsip jumped on Naiya, straddling her chest. She tweaked her chin and pulled Naiya's braids, and wouldn't let go until Naiya promised that Dzan, Sipsip's Forest mother, was more beautiful than any woman. And even then she refused to let go until Naiya's sat and allowed Sipsip to pick out her lice and braid Naiya hair the same as her own, the same as her tall, long-nosed mother always wore hers.

Malluar set the box aside. "They were afraid when her mother first came, that there would be a revenge raid. That we would be attacked because of her. We were lucky that time," she said, and then she hesitated.

"All my life I've heard tales of blood feuds and raids—so many it seems they run with the seasons. In the end, a person who lives with adopted family only, no hunting partners, no wife or husband, could never feel safe. If a mother hasn't milk enough for her own child, how much will she have for another?"

"But this man is no child."

"Then perhaps we should ask different questions?"

Elik flushed, but she didn't stop. "Why does Seal Talker fear him?"

"Ah—" Malluar laughed. "Now I understand. You're afraid because Seal Talker found no caribou, and if we're to find game, he needs to learn who chased them away. But come—your uncle is a wise man and by now he and his stranger-son are far away. You needn't be frightened. Would you like water? You could fill the pot. I would not complain of younger hands to help."

Elik's face fell. Malluar had misunderstood. She was not frightened of hunger. Not asking for potential husbands. She looked away, hiding her disappointment.

While Malluar took down a waterskin from its peg, Elik watched the hump of the old woman's shoulders, her rounded back.

Perhaps, she tried convincing herself, perhaps things were better unsaid. The new amulet was safe against her skin. Wasn't that enough?

A frozen salmon Water-sky had left on the floor was thawing; the slime on the outside opaque, a thinner pool of water forming beneath. Elik found a ptarmigan's wing near the hearth, pushed it closer to mop the spread.

Malluar turned about. "The skin feels empty." It was the way a parent talked to a child, suggesting, never pushing.

Elik stood up. "I'll gather snow to melt," she said, and took the bucket from Malluar and left quickly, before her thoughts tricked her into saying more.

The wind was calmer outside than it had been earlier, the stars not so distant as they sometimes appeared but close, watchful. Elik didn't want to go as far as the freshwater pond, but even so—with all the guests there'd been trampling and peeing in the snow—she had to trudge a distance over a drift, behind the raised food caches. She found a place; she scooped the bucket full, packed the snow down hard, then filled it again.

It wasn't until she reached the path below Malluar's

house again that she caught the odor of smoke. She stopped, listened to the sounds of dogs whining, then followed the drifting air, closer toward the other houses.

The smell was woodsmoke, sharp and burning. But it was more than a fire from a smoke hole, not enough for a house-fire. The snow ahead of her was painted with an orange glow, outlining the curve of their low-lying houses. She was near enough now to hear voices, people talking. She slowed, leaned out beyond the snow-covered frame of an upturned umiak—And then she saw it: the flames, the fire.

Seal Talker stood closest to the blaze, his face glowing red with the heat. He was heaving the wooden masks that had been made for this year's runner's feast into the fire: Eagle and Raven, Caribou and Wolf, burning them until next year, when new eyes would be opened and new spirits returned to the feast.

Sipsip was there, this time with her baby peering out from her hood. Water-sky stood with her arms easy on her stomach. Most of the men were helping Seal Talker with the fire, throwing in driftwood to add to the flames. She watched her father drag a long, narrow pole from the back of the crowd, then heave it with a shout—almost too loud. Her mother hung back, her arm linked with Naiya's. And she saw Kimik, but not Iluperaq. She would have been surprised to find him back so soon. Her brother was too proud to return without something to show.

Elik heard a step. She took up the bucket, then turned to see Malluar walking with a careful side step over the slick snow, so as not to slip.

"There was smoke blowing into the house," Malluar said.

"It's the masks; Seal Talker is burning them."

Malluar nodded, but neither of them moved to stand closer. Elik came and stood beside her, a little taller, leaner across the shoulders. The fire snapped, and though they were too far to feel its heat, they could see the sparks shoot upward, like spirits rushing toward the sky. Abruptly, she asked, "How does he call them, that they speak to him?"

"Who?"

"Seal Talker's spirit helpers. Do they hear his drumming first, then come? Or only if he calls? Or with the caribou—does he see the herd in his trance, or do his spirit helpers guide him?"

Malluar chuckled. "So many questions from one girl's mouth. But listen—spirits find joy watching people dance and celebrate. The Eagle would not tolerate food that wasn't shared, or was wasted after a feast. And yet it's also true that by feasting now, we may go hungry later. We know this. Seal Talker knows this. And so he does the things our elders taught, hoping that if someone among us forgets what's proper, the spirits will not hide the game from our eyes. A shaman works to keep evil from looking our way."

Elik's voice came out a whisper. "Don't make me go. I don't want to be down there."

"Why?" Malluar no longer laughed. She was surprised by the words, that a ritual meant to close the eyes of the masks should frighten Elik so deeply. It was almost backward. "What do you fear?" she asked. "Have you broken some taboo?"

"No. Nothing. Only that—I don't want to watch . . . "

"You're an odd child, frightened and curious in your own way. Stay with me for the night, then, if you prefer. There's no reason to join them." She looked at the gathering about the fire. One of the men had picked up a drum. The women began a farewell song to the masks. Malluar smiled, nodded to herself. "Perhaps you're in your bleeding time?"

"Not yet . . . No." The question surprised her.

"My cousin prefers an audience for his tricks," Malluar said. "When he succeeds, it's important the people know. But it makes no matter if one person is with me instead of with him in the *qasgi*."

Elik didn't understand "But it isn't my time—what if someone asks where I am? Wouldn't that be a lie?"

"A lie? Sometimes a shaman sees truth where others

never look. No one will be hurt. There is no taboo broken."

Elik felt torn, wanting to go, not understanding a lie. "There are spirits, in the air, in the sky—They would see . . . "

"A woman's power is strong when she makes blood. But if nothing's there. . . ?" Malluar left her words unfinished, till she saw Elik still hesitate. "It would only matter," she added, "if you were bleeding and said you were not. But if you were not, who will know? Would your mother tell Seal Talker: my daughter had no blood on her thighs? Who will say a spirit could be offended, when there is nothing to offend with?"

Malluar looked away, but then she laughed, as if at a joke she'd just remembered. She pointed toward the drifted snow that held the *qasgi*. "You cannot see the *qasgi* walls and yet they are there, hidden beneath the snow, just as smaller things also hide inside. I'll tell you something, though. This will not be the first secret I've kept from my cousin." She pointed toward the bucket. "Maybe you can carry the snow? I'll send word you'll be with me." She turned and started away.

Behind them, the fire had grown smaller. There were no masks left to burn. One by one, the men were disappearing inside the *qasgi*, the women back to their houses.

Elik stood there, trying to recall the lessons her grandmother and mother had taught during her first woman's time. That a woman must be careful when she bled and always tell lest an animal's spirit sense the human, hide from the hunter who unwittingly mixed an animal's death with a woman's blood . . .

But if there was no blood, there was no lie. And if there was no lie, then wasn't it good and right for a younger woman to help an elder?

And when would her mother, her shy, compromising mother, ever ask to see the moss toweling that should have been burned after it was used?

Elik set her shoulders, then picked up the bucket and hurried after Malluar.

~

The blood and fat had thickened the stew and it was done now. With a scrap of old skin, Elik lifted the clay pot from its hook above the fire and carefully, because the pots were brittle and she didn't want Malluar to regret her invitation, set it on the floor between them.

"It's good." Malluar smiled her approval. With her long-handled knife, she stirred the broth till she found something to spear. She took a bite, chewed once, then spit it in the fire so it would rise and feed the spirits.

With her fingers, Elik did the same. They ate the fish first, then passed the broth back and forth until it emptied. Politely, Elik bided her time, waited till they sat back and belched and wiped their bowls with their fingers. Then, in a rush of questions, she asked: "Why didn't you dance in the qasgi, the way Seal Talker does?"

Malluar laughed as if she had been wondering how long the girl could sit with her questions. "I did dance," she said, "though you're too young to remember when my legs were stronger. What I do now—making songs, curing people—these are skills that strengthen with age."

"Are they secret things?"

"Some, yes."

"Secret from Seal Talker? Or do you both know the same things?"

"I'll tell you something," Malluar said. "Though I don't know why I'm talking so much, except that you asked, and it's been a long while since anyone was so little afraid. But listen—my cousin's greatest fear is that I know things he never learned."

Elik leaned forward.

"Because we are cousins, we both inherited our shaman's strength from the same uncle. That man was a very great shaman, thought he never married, never fathered children. But his sisters did. Both his sisters. One of them became my mother, the other was Seal Talker's. When the time came and each of them had children, their brother helped bury the placentas, so the babies' souls could not be hurt.

"My soul is hidden," Malluar said, "and remains secret, though in time, my mother told me where the afterbirth was buried. But—here is the part that matters—because I was a child, it happened that my uncle never noticed how I was playing nearby after his youngest sister gave birth to a son, and he left her hut with the soul in his hands, and hid it. I know the place and the words that were spoken that day. And Seal Talker knows that I know."

"Why doesn't he kill you?"

Malluar laughed. "Seal Talker may be able to harm lesser people, who have no helping spirits to fight back, but he cannot harm me. Not without fear of what I could do first." Malluar's eyelids slowly closed. There was a long silence.

Elik waited, staring at the fire. Suddenly, before she knew what she was saying, she asked, "Could you teach me?"

"What?"

"Could you teach"—Elik's voice cracked—"teach me to be a shaman?"

Malluar's eyes shot open. "Who has been putting thoughts in your head?"

"No one."

"But child—" Malluar's gesture echoed her surprise. "Neither of your parents are shamans. Neither have been called by spirits. It is not in your blood."

"But, I thought—" Elik searched for the words. "I wondered—since you let me come, and told me things . . . You would perhaps—"

"Perhaps what? How? To be a shaman a person must first have the blood of a shaman's lineage inside of her. Where were your ears when I explained how Seal Talker and I are cousins?"

Elik's voice grew smaller. "Some people learn?"

"Oh yes, to be weather forecasters, or how to chase away the little pains, the ones not caused by soul loss. How to poke with a blood-letting awl and set broken bones. You could learn divination, which anyone can do. You could be one whom we call *angatkungaruk*, a lesser shaman. You might even try a few of the shamans' words I use. But they would grow weak and you'd have no way to find others. And it is possible a spirit would help you, but it wouldn't come into you." Malluar waited a moment. "Surely, you didn't expect more?"

Elik lowered her head, hid her disappointment. "No. Of course not. Excuse me. Please. Could you tell another story? About your uncle?"

"Ah, my uncle." Malluar sounded relieved. She had known the girl had strange ideas, but this—this breaking of custom—she hadn't been prepared. Her voice fell into a storyteller's rhythm: "Now here was a shaman such as never is anymore. He had dreams that came when he called, and dreams that brought fits when he didn't. And the people—they were so afraid, seeing the frenzy that came over him, the way he fell writhing on the floor. But listen"—she threw Elik a glance—"I'll tell you something. The power that came to my uncle's family was so strong that only by marrying hunters with no shaman's blood could his sisters, my mother and Seal Talker's, ever hope to bear live children. And even so, Seal Talker's two brothers died. And I myself never had a brother or a sister. Seal Talker and Ema had two daughters, and they also died at birth."

"And you?"

Malluar made a face. "My children didn't like to live. And now Seal Talker forgets how glad he was when Ema, who has no shaman's blood, gave him the one son who did live, Arveq."

"Arveq who went to Fish River?"

"Arveq who married in Fish River rather than argue with a father who hoped to make a shaman out of him, never caring whether Arveq had visions or not."

"And that was everyone, in your line?"

"Almost, except for Olanna in the Long Coast. Seal

Talker remembers hearing that our uncle's mother had a sister who was also a shaman and who also gave birth to one live son. Olanna denies it."

"What do his relatives say?"

"He has only a sister, Little Pot. She says she remembers little of their parents."

"Then how does Olanna say he became a shaman, if not through the blood he shares with you?"

"He tells of the time he was eaten alive by a wolf, but the wolf farted and the wind he passed—because it contained part of the wolf's soul—also contained Olanna. When Olanna woke, he was alive and naked, alone in a cave and half-frozen to death. But ever after, he says, he has been a shaman.

"Now, enough stories. I grow tired and you with your ears so hungry for talk, should practice an old woman's trick and sleep more often."

Elik didn't answer. She felt young, and very foolish. Malluar was right, of course. Nor should she feel disappointed. It was no small thing forecasting weather, learning the ways of the lesser *angatkuq,* the shaman without spirit helpers. It could be good work, vast as a lifetime. She didn't know why she had spoken so rudely.

She took the cup Malluar had passed, turned it upside down, so nothing evil could enter.

Grandmother Alu had once drawn up a creature in her fishnet, a sea creature with the face of a dog and the hair of a man. Horrified, she had freed its hair, asking only that in return the creature send a bearded seal in its place, and it had. More than once afterward she had called on the sea-spirit and it had helped. Willingly, which was no small thing. Perhaps someday a spirit would also willingly fill her pot. It was possible. Elik should be grateful; Malluar had given many gifts.

"Surely, you haven't more questions?"

"No. Thank you. No."

"Then come, and we'll roll out our beds. Tomorrow, if you like, you may go home."

It was on the spring ice, not yet the Moon When Geese Return, no longer the time of the long dark.

The grounded ice that hung against the shore was quiet and still today. No sounds of cracking. No upward heaves. Anchored enough to be trusted, not yet eroded by the hidden currents. In the sky overhead, the sun circled longer, higher, warmer each day.

Allanaq stood with his feet apart to spread his weight. He held the straight section of the netting in his teeth, the tangle in his hands, working the loop through the nearest open mesh as Grey Owl had shown, around and in on itself, then again.

*It isn't right trapping seals this way,* he muttered, then quickly glanced to where Grey Owl held the opposite end of the net.

He should never have said that out loud; he hoped Grey Owl hadn't heard. Words couldn't be trusted. They had a way of changing, of twisting themselves. Like the words Red Fox had spoken to his father: *Come,* he had said. *Come and we will be shamans together. . . .*

There was one truth Allanaq had learned over the long winter: life went easier if he guarded his words. Besides, what use was there hurting the one man who cared whether he ate or starved, lived or died?

"This way." Grey Owl circled his arms in a large motion. Allanaq copied. *Over and through . . .* His hands moved uncertainly, like a boy's, needing twice the time that Grey Owl used.

And what would a hunter know about nets? Except what any man knows—that a seal in the winter must come to its breathing hole, or drown. That the same seal would go to a different man, rather than someone fool enough to call as if it were a fish . . .

The last tangle fell away. The heavy net unfolded neatly from his arms. Grey Owl chuckled, then walked backward on the flat offshore ice, the net wide between his hands so Allanaq would see which way to hold it and where the sinkers needed to go.

They had come out on the ice yesterday, a time when, Grey Owl said, the seals would be swimming with the currents, following the path of the headlands. At night. The nets had to be set by dark, so the seals would not see the shadows of their feet. They had set three nets below the ice, marked the sites with tall poles, in case new snow blew in to hide their work. Then checked their knots and gone home.

All winter before that, they had worked on the nets: Grey Owl in the *qasgi* with his older nets, some of caribou sinew, some of willow, piled around his lap. Tying new lengths. Mending tears, while he and the other men talked about the prospects for the coming season. Which way the caribou might come, down through the pass or in from the hills. Whether their ribs would show hunger when they came. And how many young they would have.

Inside their house, Nua cut length after length of dehaired seal thong, starting from the outside, circling toward the center. With a marline spike and a shuttle and an antler gauge that was fastened to a handle—large mesh for *ugruk,* the bearded seal, heavy as three men; smaller-sized mesh for smaller fish.

Early this morning, Nua had roused them, so early the sun had not yet woken. With a cup of thick, boiling seal's blood for strength—the only meal they would take until a catch was made—they gathered their tools, took turns hauling the sledge by a line around their shoulder.

His father used to wake him just as early. *"The sunrise,"* Anguta would say, *"Whispers a story to those who listen: Where the seals have hauled out on the ice and which way the caribou have gone to browse."*

Their first net came up empty, with a huge circle of a tear where something had chewed or broken through.

It had taken most of the day chipping at the ice with their pointed antler picks, laying out four holes, to push their net down through the spring ice, first at this site, then at two more.

Grey Owl had chosen the place, knowing where the land jutted out beneath the tumbled ice and where the hidden currents would be strongest. They'd brought chippers and mesh ice scoops and fastened the net to lashed-together willow poles long enough to guide the nets down through one hole, up again through the next.

He showed Allanaq the way to tie grooved sinker rocks along the length of the net and how to spread Nua's lines so that, although their eyes could not see, their hands could feel the pull and weight of the net as it passed down through the first hole, then back up through the next, until it was spread between the farthest holes, anchored so the corners were strong against the weight of a thrashing seal.

Allanaq had spent his youth learning to find the depression that marked the widening hole of a seal's breathing hole in the ice. But he hadn't known this way of surrounding the hole with a net that hung horizontally into the water.

He knew how to listen for a seal as it scratched its way below the surface of the ice. And he knew as well as any man how to stand absolutely motionless with a harpoon until a seal came for its second breath, because its first was too quick for a strike.

But he didn't know anything about this fishing for seals with a net that dragged below the ice. Not too close, Grey Owl said, or the seal would find another place to surface.

Not in daylight, and not too deep, or it would easily avoid the mesh and swim away.

Underice netting, Grey Owl called it. Or skylight sealing, to describe the thin window of ice that formed overnight in this season.

But no matter what the names, Allanaq still didn't understand how a net could be left alone to trap a seal at night, while a man went home to his own bed, ate and slept.

At the second hole, as soon as he felt the net drag, Grey Owl knew they had something.

What they hauled up was a ringed seal, stiffly curled in a half circle, its flippers trapped in one end of the mesh, nose jammed and caught through another. Dead for lack of air. Drowned.

They peeled back the net and Allanaq grabbed for his harpoon, expecting a fight. When the seal didn't move, he lowered his arm. "It's already dead," he said.

Grey Owl caught the dismay in Allanaq's voice. "It's a good size," he said, as if he'd heard nothing. He quickly knelt on the jagged ice, rolled the seal over so its face was up. With his knife he cut a slit in the seal's upper lip, threaded a slender bone probe through the hole he'd just made, then looped it back to a notch.

Together, they straightened the net and set it back below the ice before it froze too stiff in the air. They hauled the seal to their sledge, rolled it on, and covered it with a hide.

Allanaq hurried to grab the dragline ahead of Grey Owl. He leaned his shoulder into the weight, trudged toward the next marker—ahead of his father, hoping Grey Owl didn't notice the way he didn't admire the seal, or thank it, or offer a song.

At the third net the ringed seal they brought up lay stiff and straight. Again its flippers were knotted in the mesh, its two eyes open, round and blind.

Grey Owl reached to free the net from the seal's face. He pulled back: the net caught. He tugged and lifted harder. The mesh slipped and suddenly, the seal moved. With a sound like a cry it sucked in a breath, then thrashed itself, heaved up on its flippers, panicked, and rolled back into the tangle.

Grey Owl jumped clear. "Club it." He motioned, but Allanaq didn't move.

"Club it," he yelled, but by then he'd jumped for the heavy braining-stone himself, grabbed it by the corded loop. With a circling motion he swung it once, then down onto the seal's head, striking the round of its skull, the side of its face.

The seal slumped, then lay heavy and quiet. A line of blood trickled from behind its ear to the snow. With the toe of his boot, Grey Owl nudged the seal. Waves of fat rippled beneath its fur. The seal rolled on its slippery blood and then rolled back again.

Grey Owl caught his breath. "We'll call Nua when we bring it home," he said. "We'll listen to her laugh how two men never let a woman rest."

While Grey Owl squatted to peel back the net, Allanaq studied the seal's dead face, its black nose, the thin line of its mouth. Quietly, he said, "There's no honor here. No honor in drowning a seal this way."

Grey Owl stiffened. "No honor?" he repeated, but he kept his hands moving. He had been waiting for this, or something like it. One winter with this son—there were signs. He was beginning to learn. Gently, he said, "If the seal comes to our net, how can it be wrong? How can it be wrong to eat?"

"Not to eat. To hunt this way—tricking it. So it never knew the man who took its life, never saw the beauty in the blade. It's dead," he added. "No different than eating carrion."

"And yet . . . " Grey Owl tried to sound reasonable. "If a wolf killed a caribou and your people took it after they chased the wolf away—not by hunting, or stalking or corralling it, but taking—would that be wrong? If it made the difference whether your children ate or starved?"

"That isn't the same. We eat where we have to. But while we are people, we don't hunt caribou as if they were fish. Fish we spear. Or catch with a hook, jigging. But we don't depend on fish: most times when they come, we've left for caribou. Seal we hunt with a harpoon and a lance. We give it fresh water, for the thirst of its soul."

"We do that too—Nua will, when we bring the seal home."

"This seal. But what about the next one? Will it come to you? Knowing it will be killed without honor?"

Grey Owl sighed. He tried to remember if his first son had been the same way, too young to know how little he knew. He said, "I'm not always wise, but I've lived long enough to know how to catch a seal with a harpoon at its breathing hole. And in the open water, from a kayak, which is most difficult. And stalking it on ice. Calling it with a seal-scratcher. With an arrow. With a club. And also . . . " he said, "with a net. That seal did not hide from our net."

Allanaq looked away.

Grey Owl fixed the band on his snow goggles more comfortably behind his ears. The glare of the spring sun was sharp; everywhere there were signs of ice melting into water, softening, puddling. He heard something—a flock? He turned, looked up. As if they were a gift, he saw the armspread V of a flock of geese. A string. A necklace. The first of the year.

"Look there." He pointed and then he waited. Then carefully, so his voice sounded the way any man's would sound, when he spoke of his tools or hunting or the land, he said, "Tell me—what do your Seal People try for, when the geese return?"

Allanaq peered toward the sky. He could hear them before he saw them, the honking sound, deep and inviting, gentle and strong at the same time. It seemed early for birds to come, but then—maybe it wasn't. Maybe the ice had stayed late this year, or this was an early flock. He'd been taught to hunt by the wind: blowing from the north, the ice could break free. Southside hunting—inshore—that was dependable.

In his own home, the women would be lining up on the beach, singing a greeting to the first birds of the new year.

A heavy-winged song for the geese. Louder for the long-necked cranes, the quarrelsome gulls, fat-bellied auklets, the kittiwakes, the black-skinned cormorants.

He smiled in spite of himself. "When the first snowbirds call," he said, "and the days grow long, and our kayaks are all repaired, we paddle out in the widening leads. The ice is all around us, floating, almost dancing. We hunt beluga."

"The white whale? From a kayak?" Grey Owl hoped his voice showed admiration. "How do you catch them?"

Allanaq laughed and for the first time that day, his motions grew animated. He hefted his ice-testing stick, bent his knees, and pointed in the distance, as if he'd sighted a village of long, sleek white belugas. "We herd them down the leads between the ice shelves. Kayak after kayak, pressing them together. The whales are afraid, but the spears are carved with amulets and we sing. The men but need to raise their points and the belugas come."

"So many?" Grey Owl's eyes danced as he pictured the scene. "You should tell that story in the *qasgi*. During the night—while the women are listening—" He stopped suddenly, gave a quick, loud laugh. "Ha! There's the reason why you worry."

Allanaq lowered his arm, not at all certain he wanted to hear.

"Winter in an empty bed." Grey Owl shook his head. "It only makes the nights seem colder. Now here's spring and, surely, a young woman has been thinking the same thoughts, combing her hair, wondering what the men are saying." He slowed his talk a moment, then, more quietly, asked, "You never told me—did you have a woman already, where you lived? Were you married?"

"No, no one." Allanaq shied away from the memories. "I carved for my father—most of the time. Inside our *qasgi*."

"But now you can. You should have come to me. You should have said something—Here I was glad that you weren't the kind of man with his thoughts only on women. Never thinking you were shy." Grey Owl stood back, considering Allanaq's face. "Labrets," he said, and he was nodding now, smiling and planning. "No wonder none of the women have spoken of marriage. When they see labrets, they'll start looking for the meat behind you in the cache. We'll find out who's available, if any of the girls have strong hands. And wide hips—there's a good sign. Nua will know. She'll talk to her sister, the other women."

Allanaq felt less sure. "What wife," he asked, "wants a man who argues with a net, and then gets lost every time he looks for shore?"

"It isn't so," Grey Owl protested. "Maybe when you first came. But you learn quickly—I've watched. You're lonely, that's why you talk this way. You're hard on yourself. Tell me, with words, what do you think we'll pick up in the next net. What kind of seal?"

"Ringed seal," he said without hesitating.

"You see—you do know. Why ringed seal? Why not another?"

Allanaq shrugged. He scanned the ice. From where they stood, the hills of pressure ice rose in a jagged range of boulders—greys and shadowed blacks, whites and blues. Nearer the land, the grounded ice appeared deceptively smooth, marked by scattered knee-high ridges where the wind had opened cracks, then sealed them again.

He had passed more than a few of his days here studying the ice, realizing that without his Seal People's point of land to break the winter ice into a north side, and a south, there was less he was certain of—only the stretching Long Coast shore-line, the wind. A few more stable markers. And the seals.

And for all he could figure, their behavior remained the same. They had shared secrets with him. Shown him that what he had known before, he still knew. He said, "Bearded seals don't keep their breathing holes open, not so close to the grounded shore ice. On the ice edge more likely, not here."

Grey Owl hid his smile. "How would you hunt a beard-ed seal?"

"On the late season ice? They like to feel the sun. A man would do well to stalk them, wearing white." Allanaq kept talking, but there was another part of his thoughts that had shifted—down the winter trail, around the point of land that led to the Bent Point village and a face he remembered well. The girl from after his dance.

There'd been a loneliness in her face that seemed to match his own, though he wasn't sure why. He'd asked, though not directly. Grey Owl said she was a cousin, one of many. Allanaq remembered her eyes, the way they were bolder than the eyes of other women here. Almost too bold—more like a shaman's than a young girl's. And shamans, he had reminded himself, he would never trust again.

"There's not so much you have to learn," Grey Owl was saying. "Only the shape of the headlands in the summer—I've seen you making maps. Your eye is good. Your memory better."

Allanaq allowed himself a smile. "Perhaps. But a man who has nothing should not boast."

"Put the labrets in your chin and you won't have to boast. I will, and your mother will do it for you."

Allanaq couldn't see the men from where he stood, but he could hear their muffled voices, hidden behind the umiak. Someone had taken the boat down from the rack, turned it on its side for a windbreak. He recognized Bear Hand's deep voice and Weyowin's lighter one. The hacking cough would belong to Bear Hand's middle brother, Kahkik. Someone else answered and someone else laughed—the way men do when they work together, trading stories, planning where to hunt.

With spring approaching the qasgi had grown too damp to work inside. The seats, the walls, even the fire pit dripped the smell of mildew and rotting fish, moisture and too much dark when outside all was light with the high, spring sun.

None of the voices belonged to Grey Owl; he was with Nua, dragging their tent skins from the tall storage cache. After that, he'd said, he'd come for Allanaq. The ice would be out soon and traders would boat past the Long Coast. It was time to sort their baskets. Now, while they could plan what else to make. With the knife handles and harpoon heads and foreshafts Allanaq carved full of his animal and human faces, they could make a good trade. Flints, jasper, jade and slates for his fancy bifaced side blades. Wolverine and martin, beaver and eagle feathers for Nua to sew.

The wet ground absorbed the sound of Allanaq's footsteps. The men couldn't have known he was coming till he was well around the point of the umiak's bow and he could see them, first.

Bear Hand sat with a section of caribou antler by his feet, the beginnings of a barbed tip in his hand. He was laughing, pointing to his face, his crotch. Till the moment Allanaq's shadow lengthened on the ground and he stopped talking, they all did. As suddenly as if a shaman had tied a string around the men, from his hands to their jaws, pulled it, and they stopped. The laughter changed, too quickly. Round-bellied Kahkik coughed. Weyowin leaned forward, stiff with embarrassment. Bear Hand smiled and went back to his story.

"So the Dog Man went on hiding his long tail inside his pants"—he jabbed his finger toward his rump—"Where it couldn't be seen. But these pants were the ones his Dog Wife had made, and she always waited till dark to sew because she didn't want the Real People to see how she couldn't hold a needle properly with human hands. Only at night, when her hands turned into paws could she sew, except then her stitches were always too loose. And those last few stitches she made just before sunrise were the same stitches that needed to be torn out first, the next day."

Allanaq found a place in the circle. He sat down. His hands were shaking, but he forced himself to open his tool bag. He laid out his antler-handled knife with the flint end blade, his flaking tool made from the walrus penis bone Grey Owl had given him, his engraving tool with its sharpened ground squirrel incisor for a bit.

Bear Hand's gaze followed. He stared a moment at the carved knife handle—a bear's face with three lines, the same as the tattoo marks near Allanaq's eyes.

"And so"—Bear Hand turned, not wanting to seem curious—"the people discovered her husband's tail, the way it wagged, the reason why he ate only when he was alone—because he didn't want anyone human watching him put his face down in his food, his tail between his legs . . ."

Allanaq leaned forward, past Weyowin and Kahkik and Lake, to where Bear Hand sat. His voice would shake when he spoke—he knew it—but it was better to answer an insult rather than let it hang, like fish on a windless day, letting dung flies gather. "Is that a new story?" he asked.

"No, no," Bear Hand objected. "That's the story we were telling because our hands always feel clumsy at the end of winter."

"Yes, I heard that one," Allanaq said, and he glanced to Weyowin, nearest his shoulder, then to round-faced Lake, who answered by lifting his hood, hiding his face. It would be best if he knew which of these so-called cousins he could count on if an argument arose, if it came to a song-match, or wrestling.

"That story was told in the *qasgi*," he said. "But I heard it differently. I heard that one day the Dog Man was visiting in a house where the husband wasn't home and so the Dog Man and the Real Man's wife made their beds together because the fire had gone out, and both were cold. But the wife grew fond of the way the Dog Man warmed her cold hands at night, and how whenever he lay on top of her, she had no need to find a second blanket. So she asked if he would stay with her because there was more heat in his fur than in all her husband's hard bones."

Bear Hand's smile fell away. No one answered Allanaq's story. Loudly, his brother Kahkik rummaged in a basketful of shuttles wound with sinew. Lake split a feather quill with his teeth. Weyowin wedged four clawed hooks into an ivory shaft.

Allanaq wasn't certain what had happened. Maybe he had merely walked in on a story being told. Maybe it wasn't an insult, only a coincidence.

Weyowin and Lake were brothers, his younger cousins

through Nua, who was sister to their mother, Little Pot. And Little Pot, perhaps for Nua's sake, had from the start spoken kindly toward him. Still, he wasn't certain of Lake, most likely because Lake was promised to Kahkik's younger daughter. Whenever there was talk of Lake's choosing a hunting partner, he made it clear he intended to look among Kahkik's relations. Not his own.

A wind rose from off the tundra, grew sharper. In unison, the men watched it lift a leg on a caribou hide someone had left hanging on a rack. They opened their circle, then moved closer inside the umiak's shelter. Bear Hand and Kahkik shifted their seats nearer the stern; Allanaq sat near the bow. They sat on old skins to keep the water-soaked ground from seeping into their clothes, and scraps of sealskin lay in their laps to cushion their work.

It was the same thing Grey Owl kept warning: that Allanaq didn't need enemies. That—since Grey Owl had been born in the Bent Point village and only come here to marry Nua—that theirs was a family with few relations. Allanaq needed to mind his tongue better.

He opened his tool bag and brought out the stone he'd brought for the day: a greenish, almost translucent jasper, more like the flints they found on the beaches at home than the porous, hard-to-flake stones that were so plentiful here.

He turned over the fist-sized rock, examined each facet in the rough outer cortex. On the outside the surface was pitted and dull. But inside—inside it would be like a dream, like a spirit offering up treasures.

For the first blow, he set the flint down on another stone, a hard, dense rock with a flattened, well-balanced bottom that he kept for just this purpose.

He set his eye toward a point near the center, brought the hammer down freehand style, with a solid blow. There was a crack and a smaller sound. He opened his hand: the flint lay in sections now, no longer a whole.

He held them apart. The blow had struck true; the rounded upper piece pulled away to reveal a flat working surface for his next blow. There was no waste and only the smallest circle to mark the impact. Grey Owl had traded for this stone from a Fish River man at the Bent Point feast.

The trading had gone well. Both Grey Owl and the Fish River man had walked away believing he'd struck the better deal: this rock with all its flakes buried inside for two ivory handles Allanaq carved into spirit faces—one to please a walrus, and one to please a bear. He remembered the black eyes he'd inlaied in the bear's figure, the row of holes he'd pecked out, then plugged with his own hair that he'd set with a glue of boiled fish oil. To him, it was only two carvings, nothing near so precious as a good stone. Nor had they taken him long, though the man acted like a child when Grey Owl brought them out, running to show his wife and son. If he had been that man, he would have been more careful not to show emotion, not to show he cared.

More carefully now, because the next blow would decide the shape of the entire piece, he set aside Grey Owl's hammerstone; that one was best for heavy work. He took up a narrower one, more pointed, easier to aim. Cupping the flint at a steep angle, he rubbed the hammerstone against the corner to strengthen the edge, aimed for the steep side, then struck. A long, tapered flake came away in his hand; the corner now had a new ridge up on its back. The edges of the flake were sharp enough to slice the heaviest hides.

He marked the next angle, struck again. He worked so intently, he didn't think to watch the men, to follow their eyes following his hands.

From the scattering of flakes around his feet, he chose a wide oblong, started working the edge, preparing it on one side then the other.

It was a guess, because he hadn't asked directly, but he didn't think this flint had come from Fish River. He'd asked and Grey Owl said there was no more of it on the Fish River banks than here. More likely the man had traded it from someone else. There was a place Grey Owl mentioned, south along the coast, a Place of Many Rivers, where people said these better stones were found.

In the end it didn't matter where it came from; only that

he struck it well, that none of the stone was wasted. There were many fine blades hidden inside the rock, and inside those—more to retouch when the edge grew dull.

He planned the way he wanted each blow to fall, following the faults and angles on each stone, using his first blow to make a striking platform, then deciding whether to work the core further or start a flaked point. His Seal People shaped their flints on both sides. Strong, thin blades worked best, with edges shaped out of diagonal ripples running upward from the center, covering the entire face. He was a fine craftsman, though he was too young to consider himself an elder, for all the blades his hands had made.

His best work, not these blades but the ivory swivel-chains he was saving to bury with his father's body, were hidden in the house. He didn't even trust himself thinking about them when people were around. Sometimes thoughts crept out, turned into words. Words into trouble.

Even so, he liked to take the memory out sometimes, picture the way people used to come and stand behind him when he was a boy. They used to watch and pat his shoulder, handle his carvings when he'd finished. Walrus. Bear and Wolf. Otter and Bird. They would hold them toward the firelight, the better to see, to take back home and copy for themselves.

For all the things Red Fox had taken from him, he'd never been able to steal the knowledge inside his hands. It wasn't arrogance, or pride. It was the way sometimes he felt as if there were eyes inside his fingers, eyes that saw the way to make a striking platform and how to shear off exactly the flakes he wanted.

No. Red Fox hadn't stolen his sight and neither would these people, with their white quartz flakes and soft slate, their clay pots. And the way they scraped their points, rather than flake the edges. The way they kept using barbed dart heads rather than toggling points. No. Some things could not be taken from a man.

By the time Allanaq stretched his back and thought

about looking up, he'd finished two large side blades, as perfectly similar on one side as the other.

Bear Hand, Weyowin, Lake, and Kahkik were watching.

Allanaq quickly picked up a harpoon foreshaft and head. He pulled out a large end blade, one already finished. Hiding his discomfort, he checked its fit into the groove, stole a glance at Lake: the hook with its leader made from a gull's quill was long since finished. Lake might have been younger than Allanaq, but he had already started a series of net floats: rough seal-headed shapes with holes to take a line. Smooth and simply done, but done. The pile of Weyowin's sinker rocks rose higher than his ankles. Bear Hand had set aside his antler and was helping Kahkik with a net.

They were working on fishing gear, all of them. Hooks and nets, sinkers and weights. Allanaq brushed off the shards of flakes that sprayed his lap. For a second time he checked the chipped end of the blade to make sure it wedged securely into the head. Had he done something wrong? Again? What?

He looked up. In an open area between the houses, a few boys had tied a rock behind a puppy's harness and they were chasing it, laughing as the confused dog frisked and yipped at the unfamiliar weight. The boys ran past and a young woman approached. It was Bear Hand's daughter, Squirrel, a wooden bowl under her arm. With careful, self-conscious steps, she walked to her father's side, set the bowl full of steaming food down on the ground, whispered something in her father's ear.

Where the boys had played, there were two other girls now, younger than Squirrel. One of them had a loop of sinew in her hand, the other held a grass basket slung across her shoulder. *They must be going to set traps,* Allanaq thought. Waiting for Squirrel rather than go alone.

While her father plucked a biteful of meat, Squirrel glanced at Allanaq's work, then up to his face and away, quickly. But not so quickly her glance didn't touch on his.

Bear Hand looked beyond her to the other girls, then said

something to his daughter Allanaq couldn't hear. Her expression fell, but she said nothing. Obediently, she turned to her mother's summer tent instead of toward the girls.

Allanaq watched after her, but carefully—an unmarried man didn't look too long at a woman he wasn't interested in. Not that he hadn't noticed her before—the Long Coast village was too small for that. And the girl was pretty, round-faced, slight of shoulder, with a walk that turned gracefully from side to side. And obedient. If he ever took a wife here, it would be best if the girl were obedient.

Squirrel's long hair was worn in two braids, wrapped with tassels of orange-black puffin beaks. Her chin had been beautifully marked with tattoo lines, though only a few. But then—she was young still, and his own face held more tattoos than most of the women here. And no labrets.

Maybe Grey Owl was right. Maybe he would frighten people less if he was more like other men here. He was being stubborn about the labrets. He knew it. And being stubborn was one way to die more quickly.

Allanaq picked up the large blades he'd been holding, lifted it toward Bear Hand.

Bear Hand glanced once, then went back to fixing a splice in his net.

"This is not the best blade," Allanaq started. "I chipped the sides too quickly, but a man might be willing to trade?"

"Trade?" Bear Hand looked sideways to his brother. "Trade what?"

"Your fish hook for this blade."

Bear Hand held still, but Kahkik leaned forward. "Here, let me see," he said. Allanaq passed the blade to Lake, who looked at it, passed it to Weyowin, who also took a moment to turn it over in his hand.

Allanaq tried not to pay too much attention. It would be a good sign if Bear Hand's brother wanted the blade. He was younger, which allowed him some foolishness, but he was also considered a decent hunter, which granted him respect. But he would not cross his brother, no more than Bear Hand's daughter would. And Bear Hand didn't trust

Allanaq. He never had. If he allowed his brother to trade, it would be almost as good as if Bear Hand took it himself, only simpler.

Bear Hand said, "You struck off flakes from both sides." It was not a question.

"It's sharpest that way."

"It's sharp because you work it longer. But because you work longer, you make fewer blades. In the end, your blade will catch the same animal."

Allanaq hadn't expected that. He said, "The blade that meets an animal is the blade that pleases it, is that not so?"

Bear Hand didn't answer.

"Perhaps," Allanaq reasoned, "if it's true that my hand takes longer, perhaps the walrus will know I mean only honor."

"Walrus?" Kahkik said. "Is that why you made the blade so large and spent so much effort chipping instead of grinding?"

"Yes." Allanaq leaned forward to show them. "You see, the line ties into the round hole here. When it finds a walrus and the weight of the long shaft bites in, the blade catches inside the muscle. The harpoon releases. No different than any other—"

"What are these?"

"The socket takes the foreshaft."

"Yes, but why do you carve so many circles and eye-dots?"

"So the point will see which way to fly."

"And this?" Bear Hand pointed to the ground, to the slender harpoon head that would hold the point. The blade had been flaked from flint, but the head was made of ivory, decorated with a series of lines, four from the point to the hole, others in opposing directions.

"It holds the point on one end, the foreshaft on the other."

"I can see that, but why? Why do you assume this will be pleasing when it may just as easily anger the animal's spirit and chase it away. Does it work?"

"This one is new, but I've used the type before."

"What are these?"

"The closed socket takes the foreshaft."

Bear Hand reached across, hefted the piece the harpoon head would fit on. "Why so heavy?"

Allanaq didn't understand why he asked. "For walrus, of course."

"Walrus?" Bear Hand almost smirked. He made a show of shielding his eyes from the sun, looking to the sea. "Where do you see walrus? It's herring we catch, and early salmon. If we aren't ready, we'll miss the largest run we can depend on."

"But," Allanaq started, "but there will also be walrus, out of the ice floes, migrating north with the spring."

"But first there'll be fish. Why waste time on a blade so large, it would cut a fish in two?" Bear Hand rose, letting the blade fall to Allanaq's lap.

The other men stood, all at once. Kahkik with a touch on his brother's hand and Lake quickly folding his tool kit. Weyowin hesitated behind them, then—with an awkward, murmured farewell, he walked off alone.

Allanaq sat a long moment without moving. Breathing deeply. Thinking as little as he could. Then slowly, he too began putting away his tools, the harpoon head, the ground cloths.

He kept breathing. Steadily. Fighting for calm. Even in this place, even with these people, a man must never let his anger show.

The elbow-shaped tent that Olanna and his widowed sister, Little Pot, set up for a summerhouse was only a short walk from where Grey Owl and Nua weighted their own stitched skins over a framework of upright poles.

For days Allanaq kept his eye on the flap of their door, watching the shaman and his sister enter and leave and go about their business until, finally, he made himself approach.

It was a windy day, glaring and bright. Offshore, only a few remaining ice pans floated on the waves.

The door flap was open, pinned back with a rock on the ground and a line tied to an upper corner of the skins.

Outside the tent, Little Pot plaited strands of willow into a narrow, tapering fish trap, tended her fire, and—whenever there was anything to tell—called to her brother inside about which of the men had gone where and with whom, and whether she thought the wind might change.

Allanaq started forward, stopped, then started again. *This has nothing to do with cowardice,* he told himself. *He was no boy, to fear a knife.* What kept his feet walking in circles were two questions. First, how Grey Owl and Nua, Olanna and Little Pot, could all be so certain that, along with everything else a man must do to please the spirits, he must also cut holes below his lips. The second question was how he could go home again, scarred and with a face that looked so much like a mask, people might wonder if he were still a human being.

His Seal People wore no labrets, though he had seen them a few times during trading feasts. And the animals came there, as well as here.

But then again, his father was dead and he was here. And here, while a girl who wanted to look beautiful threaded a coal-blackened needle beneath her skin, below her mouth, the boys cut holes beneath their lips, then decorated them with their finest stones.

A man must look the same as other men. Not like an enemy. Or a boy. But like a hunter. Just as a walrus wore tusks, so a hunter, to please the walrus, must wear labrets. He started forward.

Little Pot looked up from her work and smiled. Her hands kept moving, twisting the willow in and around, growing the oval fish trap longer.

"Olanna? He's here?" Allanaq asked. He knew well enough the old man was inside. That he had just finished the meal he had not felt up to eating the night before. That the weather made his joints ache, his left ankle swell. He knew that Olanna had heard the story of the trade he'd offered Bear Hand and been refused. And he knew that Olanna was waiting for him to come.

Little Pot pushed one of her braids behind her shoulder. She was a smiling-faced woman, with a few strands of hair speckled grey near her face, darkest black behind. Everything he knew about her came from Nua's stories; a few from her son, Weyowin. Though the shaman was her older brother, she herself had no inclinations toward shamanizing, no particular gift for healing or divining or listening to the voices of spirits.

Her husband, who had been Nua's brother, had disappeared two springs ago, kayaking on a day when the south wind chased away the north and opened a lead too wide in the ice for the man to find his way home.

Which was the reason Nua often added their food to the food Weyowin and Lake brought home—because she was married into their family. It was also the reason Olanna had sided with Grey Owl, the day Allanaq first came, because of the food they shared.

Little Pot set down her work. "Olanna is inside," she said, then she rose, stepped aside, and followed in behind him, not to miss any talk.

"It's better inside," Olanna called—he was leaning against a sidewall, a place where, while hidden himself, he could easily see the younger man's strained expression. "In the dark, the mosquitoes won't find you so quickly."

"There is almost nothing here of use," Little Pot said politely, "though maybe I can find something old to eat."

"If you have water?" Allanaq said, but Little Pot was already standing over a clay pot that hung from straps over a low-banked bed of coals. In spite of her words, the tent was filled with the sweet, flavorful smells of a cooked summer meal.

She held out a bowl full of large gull eggs, two hands' count and more. Allanaq took one, sat down next to Olanna. The shaman was wearing a suit of fishskin clothes, the way they did here. Fishskins that were cured like hides with urine to remove the fat, welted with a strip of caribou for strength, stitched with a waterproof seam. He tried not to show dismay. Among the Seal People, no one but the poorest orphan would have worn clothes that remembered where scales had sat. Not willingly. And certainly, never a shaman.

While Olanna also chose an egg, Allanaq used a knife to

peck a hole in the pointed end. He sucked down the thick white, the warm yolk. He smiled his thanks.

Little Pot pointed inland. "We picked them from their grass nests; there was ice crusted on the grass, and runoff water flooding everywhere."

Little Pot held out another egg but this time, Olanna raised his hand. "Perhaps we should talk first, before we decide if we should eat."

Allanaq glanced at Olanna. He was old, little more than a frame of bones inside his parka's skin. Certainly he had a frail look, except that Allanaq knew about shamans: that their eyes had a way of deceiving. That strength could be hidden inside, below the veins, beneath the brittle, dry skin.

Allanaq lowered his gaze. Olanna had been watching him, but the odd thing was, he didn't frighten him. Not the way Red Fox had. Not the way, he knew, his own father sometimes frightened people.

In all the time he'd lived here, Olanna had never threatened him, never blamed him for some trespass. He sat near Grey Owl in the *qasgi* and visited their house and, each time he came, they spoke of only the usual things. Which way the wind had turned and whether this man or that had gone seal hunting, and where and carrying what.

Allanaq swallowed his questions. "Grey Owl says that a boy who is ready to be a man should wear labrets."

Little Pot squatted with a fistful of moss beside the coals. Her hand was lifted, her ears waiting. She said, "It's a good thing. A caribou, when it's grown, wears a rack of antlers."

Olanna nodded. "And the walrus fights with his tusks."

Allanaq remembered his first tattoo: the way he had climbed from his bed one morning and his father had looked at him once, thrown back his head, and laughed. Before the day was over he had brought him to Little-Creek's house. Only Little-Creek, with her bone needles and her hands that were said to sew the smallest, tightest stitches, of all the Seal People would be allowed to draw his son's first tattoo. He'd been little more than a boy, digging his fingernails into his skinny, long-legged thighs, drawing his own blood but refusing to move or cry.

Olanna glanced about the tent, trying to remember which tools he'd brought out from his winterhouse, from the *qasgi*, where water and dampness had a way of seeping into everything. "We can do this now," he said, "or we can wait."

"Now," Allanaq said.

"It won't hurt," Little Pot encouraged him. "The boys never scream."

"What should I do?"

"Stay there," Olanna said, and he rose, then crossed to a storage basket that hung from the lacings on the wall of the tent.

A moment later Nua leaned in the open door. She was smiling, broadly enough that Allanaq wondered how long she'd been waiting.

"Where is your son?" she called to Little Pot. "Grey Owl asked me to tell him it would be a good day for fishing." Her excuses made, she came in, sat next to Little Pot, and gave up any pretense of coming for another reason.

Olanna pushed something at Allanaq. "Here, wear this over your head."

"What is it?"

"For an amulet. To guard your soul."

Allanaq looked to Nua. Her face was beaming, filled with pride. He tried remembering when he'd stop thinking of the three tattoo lines on her chin as plain and too weak.

He took the small package, unfolded it to find a raven's head with the dark feathers shining above the beak, then scraped away to form a band to wear around his brow. Opposite the head the raven's feet were also left intact, sharp and scratchy. He opened the band, slipped it on so that the feet dangled over one ear, the head on the other.

Allanaq remembered back, only a few days earlier; he and Grey Owl had gone out hunting eider ducks along the shore. The afternoon had been brisk and cold, the last of the winter ice bobbing and melting with the tide. The low-flying birds had returned, filling the sky, the orange of their beaks bright against the black of their heads, the white V of their necks.

Together, they had swung their bolas overhead. Allanaq remembered his thoughts clearly: that here, finally, with the small stones of the bola tied so they circled as they flew, was a weapon no different than that which his own father had taught him to use. He had been content, for that one moment, he and Grey Owl, swinging the line that joined the stones, aiming toward the front of the flock, spinning the line then whipping it till the rocks spread out the full length of their cords, circling and gyrating.

They had brought the birds home to Nua, Grey Owl wearing three and he four ducks hanging over his shoulders, thumping his chest as he walked.

Nua felt the bulk of meat beneath the chest feathers, spread the wing out in a fan. She took Grey Owl's catch from his shoulder, carried them inside their tent. And then she stood there, with feathers, feet and head all intact, making no move to skin them or cook. She said, "These birds are not mine."

Grey Owl looked confused. "The ducks are not good enough?"

"The ducks are good," she said. "But they aren't mine." And she turned to Allanaq. Very clearly, she said, "People have been saying that a man's catch belongs to his wife."

Allanaq's stomach tightened. "And who would marry me?" he asked. "Is your word that means *orphan* not the same as the word that means *poor?*"

"You aren't an orphan," Grey Owl insisted. "We talked about this; I thought you agreed?"

In a gentler tone, Nua asked, "Perhaps you have a wife already?"

"No," Allanaq said, but the word came out angrier than he meant. "I had no sisters. No wife. No mother except the one who died when I was young."

"Then a wife will be good," Grey Owl said.

Allanaq had sighed. His memory opened: there had

been women, no matter how he tried not to think about them. There had been mothers who came and sat with his father, and his aunts, who talked about their daughters, named their relatives. There had been Small Spider, a cousin through his aunt's husband's blood, who some had said he might marry someday, when she was older. And Nanogak, who oiled her hair with the smell of dry flowers and who, for two nights in a row, had come and pulled his blankets over them and muffled her laughter as she rolled him underneath, as she took his hand and pulled it down, there in the dark, shown him where she wanted him to be, and where to touch, and why.

But if he did marry here, he wanted to ask, was that not one more way of saying yes, he was dead to his own Seal People, and they to him? If he married here, how would he find the will to leave a family? Or the time away from hunting? How would he keep his anger burning enough to lead him back to Red Fox?

And yet, there was truth in Grey Owl's words also: *If you are dead,* he had said, *who then will avenge your father?*

"Look around," Grey Owl had said. "Think of the people you see. No one here is lean, no one hungry. The year has been good. But even so, some people are fatter than others—do you see this? Some people are better fed. And one man may be a better hunter than another. But if this had been a hard year—and hard years will come—then we would starve together. All of us, sharing until there's only death left to share.

"If you have no woman, except Nua, who depends on you, if you are not married to someone's daughter, then why should a father or a brother or a mother care whether you live or die? People would ask—why should their relatives starve, so that you, who mattered to no one, could eat?"

Allanaq's hands felt empty, his fingers ached for something to hold, to do.

Nua pulled over one of the eider ducks. With one elbow on the bird's long neck, she stretched it out so the breast was pointing up, the legs and feet pulled tight.

With her curved woman's knife she made a quick, deep cut into the breastbone and up along the line of the body cavity. She pried the bones back, a few of the ribs snapping until the chest lay open. She reached in, jerked out the stomach contents, the liver, set them to one side.

"When a husband kills an animal," she said, "that animal's *inua* flies back to its nesting ground and is born again." She looked up to make sure he was listening. "But once the hunter brings the dead animal home, it becomes food, and the food belongs to the wife."

Nua found the socket where the wing attached. She dug in, made a cut, and removed one wing, and then the other. "It is the wife who shares out the food. The wife who knows—

"If it were winter and these were the hunting shares of a bearded seal, the first share would be *kuju,* the loin." She cut a section of the back, just above the legs. "This goes to the *kuju's* wife. Because that man you call by the same name as his share. Then *talia,* the flippers, for the second share. This goes to his wife." She made another cut. "And *tulimai,* the ribs, for a third share. What is left," she said, "is sometimes for a shaman, sometimes for an old woman, so she doesn't go hungry." She severed the neck, whole, with the bill, "*Niakrok,* we call this section. Do you understand?

"Life is dangerous. The man you hunt with is the man who shares his food with you. He is your partner or he is your relative. It is his sister, or daughter, or niece who ties you so. You need a wife."

Olanna returned with a fishskin basket, sat, and unpacked it beside Allanaq. An antler chisel, two blocks of wood—one in a small size, another larger. He reached up, felt Allanaq's chin. "Show me the size you brought."

"Size?" Allanaq didn't understand.

"The labrets you made. Did you bring them?"

"I did." Nua called, and she pulled a pouch off her neck, opened it into her hand. Something clunked—a flash of ivory, a green bead.

Allanaq felt foolish. He should have known; he should have asked.

"First Ones," Nua said, and her voice was proud. "They were my other son's." She turned to Little Pot. "See the green stone—that's hard to get."

"Jade, yes. It's beautiful," Little Pot agreed.

"The girls will want to find out what else he has."

"Let them look—his walrus teeth won't be the only thing that's hard."

Allanaq's face grew heated.

"Put your hands over your ears," Olanna said. "Can you hear me?"

"Yes."

"Give him a stick to hold," Nua suggested, "So he won't scream."

"I won't scream," Allanaq said. His voice sounded oddly distant.

"Move around so your back is in front of my knees, and lean down. Keep your hands covering your ears; I'll hold you between my knees. Can you still hear me?"

No reaction.

There was a pressure inside Allanaq's ears, as if he were underwater and the sounds of the earth were far away. He felt the shaman move, then lift something: the blocks of wood he'd taken from the bag.

A dark wood, a lighter piece, a small one: Olanna chose the larger block. He squeezed to feel the thickness of Allanaq's lower lip, pressed the gum where the teeth joined the bone. He pulled the lip down and slipped the first block inside, held it out as he reached for a knife.

Allanaq's eyes followed but his line of sight was cut off. He saw the stone knife coming up. Felt someone tug his head back, pull his hair. Tightly, he shut his eyes, not to shame himself. He pressed his knees together, felt his groin tighten.

There were sounds, outside and around him. The old man's fingers making his dry mouth gag. He tried to swallow, couldn't. And then another sound, a churning. Saliva inside his mouth.

He thought he heard Nua's voice. "Straighter," she was saying. And then Little Pot's laugh, but he wasn't sure.

Fingers probed his mouth, his teeth. His tongue. He fought the urge to choke.

He shifted his legs. There was nothing to hear except the pressure of air, like a wind, like surf. And then another sound: a tearing deep inside of him. The taste of blood, thick and warm, then cold. *Was this how it felt for a seal mammal? Bursting from water into air, cold reaching where it never had before.*

Someone was stuffing a rag inside his mouth, wiping at his chin, his neck. He didn't want to look.

*What else would they cut to call him one of them? His hair, because it was long? His hands, because they didn't like what they made?*

Olanna's knees eased off his head. "Spit," he heard him say. "Spit." Allanaq sat up, but he was dizzy, and too hot. Olanna pressed a horn-dipper into his hand—urine. "Drink it and spit it out. Spit through the cut." Allanaq did as he was told, felt the new place with his tongue, the open gash, burning.

Behind him, Nua and Little Pot kept talking, "Foxskin and Drummer have a little girl: Runs-around," Little Pot said.

Nua shook her head. "Too young. Even if he were willing to wait."

"She's promised anyway—to a cousin in the Fish River village. And Lake is promised to Kahkik's daughter, as soon as he has enough skins to cover a boat."

"Lake might trade?" Nua wondered.

Allanaq tugged Olanna's sleeve and signaled, *No.* He tried to speak but the pain flared. Olanna nodded, turned to his sister. "No," he repeated, "Allanaq would have a knife in his back if he tried taking her, if not from Lake, from the girl herself."

Little Pot said, "There is Bear Hand's daughter, Squirrel."

Nua shook her head. "Bear Hand is difficult . . ."

"Perhaps, but sometimes, where wealth is concerned—"

Allanaq closed his eyes. He felt nothing. No excitement. No hunger. No room inside his heart. And yet, there was one question. He tugged Olanna's sleeve. The shaman leaned closer. Allanaq pointed. Olanna thought a moment, then said, "The boy asks his mother if a wife must come from the Long Coast? Or perhaps another place?"

"No." Nua's firmness surprised him. "A wife you need from here. Hunting partners, trading partners—those people you find in other villages, so you'll have help if you're hungry, or if there's trouble. But a wife—" She tapped the ground: *Here!* "What if you brought your wife to me, and she cried that she missed her family? What if she was the kind of woman who wanted to visit all the time? Or live near her sisters? For another man, perhaps. But for you— No. You would be a stranger again."

Allanaq motioned: *It was only a question.* He pointed again, this time toward Bear Hand's tent.

Nua smiled. "Squirrel is young—this is the first year she became a woman. It would not be a bad thing if you married there. . . ."

The talk went on; Nua and Little Pot naming their relatives, the stories of who had married whom and where and when. Olanna took hold of Allanaq's shoulders, pulled back so his face pointed toward the dark ceiling. He pressed the two halves of the labrets into Allanaq's mouth, one outside, one inside, snapping together.

Allanaq raised his hand, but slowly—the touch would jar the plugs. He felt around the edge of one of the circles. Ivory. His tongue knew that taste. He wondered if there was blood on it—not his blood but older, dried blood from that other Allanaq, the one they were trying to turn him into.

"You have to wash it with urine," Olanna was saying, "till the skin closes. And run a piercing tool through the cut, like this." The shaman made a circular motion in the air. "You have to be careful, or else something could find a way inside. Bad things."

"We'll do it," Nua answered for him. He couldn't speak.

He wouldn't cry, but he wouldn't speak either. He was thinking of his father, wondering if he would recognize him now, a man with two holes in his chin, dressed in ivory the way a walrus dressed.

In the season after Rivers Start To Run and Birds Lay Eggs there is nothing but light inside the sky. No moon glistening on snow. No stars. No dark to hide behind.

Allanaq knew he had been seen, walking toward the graves, even so early as this, with Nua and Grey Owl still asleep, but what was he to do?

Not for all the breath inside his body could he pretend his father's bones weren't here. That he had drowned in that umiak. Or been properly buried in a well-lined log grave instead of here on the open tundra, where these people insisted he leave it.

"But I did come, Father," he whispered. "I made a song about the revenge we will one day have: *Red Fox's death; for yours; I will travel through the earth to find him. He made a mistake, that man, Thinking he could kill you. Thinking he was strong. Red Fox's life. I will trade it back for yours.*

Allanaq glanced along the mounded pile of rocks. He made a sound, part in grief, part disgust; it came from low down, in the back of his throat. Not even enough rocks, not even solid enough a covering to be certain some loose dog or prowling wolf couldn't paw its way down to the wrappings.

*And then they warn me not to come here. That it isn't safe standing near the bones of someone dead. I'll tell them what isn't safe—it's leaving a ghost without the means to find his way free of the body. Without eyes to find the Land Above the Sky, without charms to protect himself with, or burial weapons to hunt with. Without respect.*

Allanaq had been squatting with his arms wrapped around his legs, chin on his knees. He stood now, walked the two remaining steps to the mound, then walked a circle, properly, the way they would have done at home. He walked four times, following in the direction of the sun. In his Seal People's home it was said that the soul of the dead could often be seen at this time, peering from the mouth of the corpse, drawn by the smell of life.

He didn't think he would see anything now; his father was too-long dead, but there was a thick feeling in his throat, in his stomach, just the same.

He'd brought his father gifts to replace the amulets Red Fox had stolen. Quickly, he brought them out. They were only a few things but he hoped they would start his father back on his journey. What the dead needed was only a little bit, the same as the living.

A wooden spoon to eat with. A fishing spear, a small one, for if there were any rivers where he went. Arrowheads, five. Six. Seven. Daggers, more highly decorated than a man would need in life. And last of all, the loon-headed chain carved from a single piece of walrus ivory. Noisy, powerful because of its noise. Because the sound of its chain rattling was like a shaman's song: even in death it had the power to chase away evil, to keep the spirits away from an empty body, this corpse, this village.

With death, one part of a man's soul, the breath soul, is free. One part becomes a ghost. The ghost travels to the Land Above the Sky and makes its home there, hunting, fishing, and visiting. Unless, Allanaq knew, any death taboos had been violated. As they had been here. Leaving his father's ghost bound to these rocks, this place he did not know. What was left for the dead but that they seek vengeance? Repay their insult with sickness and death. More death.

Allanaq looked to the other graves: low mounds of stones scattered without pattern, nothing like the ordered burials at home, on the spit of land. He glanced over his shoulder back toward the village. The graveyard wasn't so far from the houses that someone couldn't have followed if they wanted to.

And yet—what else could he have done? He had stayed up nights, thinking. Waiting until the frost went out enough to move the stones. Till the snow first, and then the mud, would show no tracks.

Quickly, he shifted the first rock. It was large, but not too heavy. He lifted it, rolled it, set it down on the ground. He swatted at the mosquitoes buzzing around his face, then pushed the next stone aside, moving it only as much as necessary to make an opening large enough to press in the arrowheads and the ivory chain, until he felt resistance. Not so hard as a rock. But no longer soft. Not flesh. He pushed again, felt something move. He winced.

Something warm slid across his face. Not rain. But what? He glanced to the ground. His mouth cuts—they were dripping again: splotches of dark on the grey-green rocks. He wiped at his chin with his parka sleeve, then sucked in air when his hand accidentally touched the labret.

He cursed and looked down again. Another spot of blood had run between the rocks he'd opened, down inside the cracks.

He felt young, and frighteningly ignorant. If only his father had survived. He would have shown him what was right, what was good. Allanaq had spent so much of his life learning to pay attention to the ice, to the wind when it changed. He knew well enough how to right a kayak if it rolled, and how to carve. For the rest, he'd trusted that others would be there to teach him the rules of living.

He stepped away. Even he had sense enough to know this wasn't good. A man with blood spilling from inside— he shouldn't be here. He stood, turned, and glanced. He didn't want to see any shadows. Didn't want to know—

They were here, even if he couldn't see them. Spirits. They could find his soul and try to steal it. They could bring illness. Or death.

He backed away, glancing behind, to the side.

No one was watching. Nothing human he could see.

He tossed the harpoon down, nudged it closer against the rocks.

He took another step, tried convincing himself the buzzing of the mosquitoes, the call inside the wind—that it was only that: the wind, and nothing more—then he turned and started walking. Not running. Running would anger the dead. But he could walk . . . Faster. Back for the houses, someplace safe.

They sat inside the tent, with the door open to control the fire, the wind outside blowing loudly. Squirrel's mother Meqo scooped a second dipper full of the stew she'd cooked of grayling and young shoots of fireweed dipped in oil. She ladled it into the shallow tray on the floor in front of the men.

Allanaq waited until Bear Hand and Grey Owl had each picked out his share before taking his own turn.

He was wearing the new labrets: not First Ones, but a larger pair Grey Owl had made to help the cuts increase slowly, without pain. There had been a scab around the two holes in his chin, and he winced when he put the new pair in, but not badly. It was a good sign, the pink skin under the darker scab. A sign of healing. A sign he was a man.

And the new parka he wore: Nua had stitched it during the sewing months of winter—that was a good sign also. It was too fine a parka to wear out hunting—something in which to be seen, by which to be recognized.

He tried to remember each lesson Nua had whispered to him: not to eat too little or else Meqo, as owner of Bear Hand's house, would think it an insult. Not to eat too much, or she would call him greedy. That he should lean back with his hands on his stomach when he was finished, and not to look at the girl if he could help it. And most of all to let Grey Owl speak for him, so they would think of his gifts first, and not the odd way he had of shaping his words.

When the men were done with the food, Meqo pulled the bowl away, then squatted next to Bear Hand. She was a quiet woman, Allanaq saw, quieter than Nua. And the daughter was quiet, also. More like her mother than her father.

He stole a glance to where she sat with her round woman's bowl in her lap, safely guarded against the shadowed tent wall, behind her mother. She was pretty enough. And he had remembered her smile, but not her voice. Perhaps that was what he needed, a quiet wife. Someone mild enough not to question his different ways, not to speak out.

". . . A good sign for fish camp," Grey Owl was saying. "The way the clouds are moving quickly."

"The river's open. We'll take our umiak up the mouth to the near fork," Bear Hand said, "my brothers and I, and our wives."

As if none of this had been planned, Grey Owl pulled the sealskin full of gifts from his side, out into the open. He nudged it away from the center, so the girl could see without having to move. "You'll want food for the journey?" he suggested.

Out of the corner of his eye, Allanaq tried to watch. Squirrel, that was her name. He tried pronouncing it beneath his breath, not the way his people would say it, *Siksrik* but *Cikik. Cikik,* for its sound, Squirrel.

She leaned forward to see what was there.

Allanaq found himself wishing it were winter. In winter, in the warmth of their burrowed house, she would have sat without the parka she wore now. He would have been able to see her better, the smoothness of her legs, her thighs uncovered but for the tiny flap of an apron. And that itself would have been so small, hiding almost nothing.

He caught a motion, turned. It was the younger sister who came forward and unrolled the sealskin. With her small, plump hands she took out the eider ducks, left the gift of side blades open to the air. The flints were flaked with sets of smooth, parallel ridges on both sides—the best he'd done in a long time and better than anything he'd seen.

The girl was young, hardly old enough to lift a cousin into her hood, let alone grow a baby inside herself. Too young for Allanaq to notice.

*But why was the older sister acting so lazy, with food in her lap when she should have been working, showing off her stitch-work, her cooking, anything to show what a hard worker she was. But not this eating, this laziness.*

Still, Allanaq wanted the gifts to be accepted. He wanted

this over with, but he wanted a wife also. *Could she really be so lazy? Or was she merely young?* Maybe Bear Hand hadn't found the gifts pleasing. But Grey Owl had been so careful with the selections. *Not that one,* he kept saying, *That one will only remind Bear Hand what you are not, more than what you have become.*

Allanaq's ears were ringing. He'd caught only part of Bear Hand's words ". . . And how would a man catch enough fish to keep a wife, when he doesn't know where the best creeks run?"

"Are those not eider ducks?" Grey Owl answered with a laugh. "With a layer of yellow fat, sweet as a clam in oil?"

"Of course, of course. But you yourself went with the boy, so he knew which way to hunt."

*The boy?* Silently, Allanaq repeated the taunt. *The boy.*

Grey Owl said, "But is it not the wife the animals give themselves to, through the husband? A man's wife shares her food, and it is her generosity that pleases the animals, that makes them willing to come to the husband's harpoon."

Bear Hand nodded. "It's true. But it isn't the wife who listens for where the caribou will cross. Who knows where the wolverine hides."

"But a boy becomes a man. And a man learns, all his life. Knowledge is shared, the way food is shared. And even you can see how my son's carvings will make a rich woman out of his wife."

Bear Hand rose and crossed to the open door of the tent. Outside the winds had risen, blowing off the water with strength enough to lift a kayak from its scaffolding and send it tumbling over the land. The tent skins fought against the wind, flapping, pulling against the rocks that weighted them down.

Allanaq waited. If Bear Hand agreed and Meqo accepted his gifts, if the girl smiled, these would be the last few days Allanaq was called a stranger.

Bear Hand came and sat back beside the smoking fire. Very quietly, he said, "There are people who say they saw your son sitting in the graveyard."

No one spoke. The wind beat against the tent, made it talk, made it sing.

"Who said this?" Grey Owl asked. His voice was very tight.

"Everyone saw." Bear Hand shrugged as he looked at Allanaq. "He didn't have the sense to hide."

Meqo motioned at the tent wall, billowing and flapping round them. "Such things bring bad luck," she said.

"But it hasn't." Grey Owl pinched Allanaq's arm, warning him not to speak. "A full winter he's been here. There's been no bad luck."

Bear Hand opened his hands, placating, condescending.

". . . And there is the question of family," his wife added.

Grey Owl rose. "He is my son." He motioned Allanaq to follow. "And he is Nua's son. Wherever among the Real People he travels, he will have family."

Bear Hand touched his daughter's shoulder. "Then perhaps we should let the girl decide for herself?"

Allanaq glanced at Squirrel. Quickly, he tried reading her lowered face, the way she lifted her shoulders, tightly, against her father's touch. The way she kept her legs demurely together—exactly as her father would have instructed her to sit.

*The girl will say only what her father tells her to do. No more,* Allanaq told himself. *No less.*

Elik pushed herself up from the tundra and brushed away the bits of moss and tiny leaves that clung to her hands and summer caribou leggings.

She'd done well with her picking. This last place especially, by the pond with the line of cattails—there'd been more greens than other places she'd gathered.

The wooden basket Iluperaq had made her was full now, as was the larger fishskin carry-pack she had learned to make herself, before the busy summer season began. Her mother had taught her how to plan the bag: from the moment the fish came to the hook below the winter ice, until the first welted stitch was sewn.

It was the way a woman needed to think, Gull said. Not like a man, who hunts each day, then rests to hunt again. But forward into the seasons: a woman waits for spring to pick green willows, then splits them, stores them, turns them into a net. In the summer, when the river runs, she sets that net and catches her fish. And dries them. And stores them. Like the willow. Like the net. A circle for each next season coming.

It was a humbling thing, trying to hold so many thoughts inside of her. Not only what her mother and grandmother taught, but those thoughts that came on their own: how a living thing could change into a carrying thing. How the skin that had contained the fish, now contained the roots that she'd been picking.

To make a fishskin bag, the skin must be carefully peeled in an upward direction, following the backbone. And the meat, of course, must first be eaten, never wasted.

She had borrowed her grandmother's seashell to scrape the inner membrane—only with her grandmother's well-worn shells did she make fewer mistakes, ruined fewer skins. After the scraping the skins were soaked in urine, and this too must be done correctly. She had used little Taku's urine—Kimik's nephew's—because, as Alu said, a nursing baby's urine was soft with a mother's milk. Overnight, that was best, then the skin could be rolled away or stretched flat and stored until the time to sew.

Elik rummaged through the basket, pushed aside the skinny *ekutuk*, the root she'd picked to eat along the way, and the mat of wintercress—it was young with no buds yet, the way her mother liked it for a soup. And there were a few tops of the dark green *ayuq* her grandmother made into sickbed tea.

And there—tucked inside the larger, folded leaf was a new plant, one she hadn't known. Fair-sized, compared to most of the low-lying flowers that grew here, with a running stem, yellow petals. Not marsh marigold. Not yellow saxifrage. Something else. She didn't know what.

She would have asked Grandmother Alu whether it was edible, or if it had a name. But this was the second year her grandmother had had to stay behind when the rest of the family left for fish camp. Her legs were too tired, she said, even for the umiak, even if it wasn't necessary for her to walk the bank with Gull and help to drag the boat.

Elik hefted the larger pack she'd already filled with stalks of sourdock, fixed the wide band around her shoulders, but then she stopped and set it down again.

But for the wind and the calling birds, no one was here. Kimik would stay close to camp to be near Iluperaq. And Naiya seldom went anywhere alone. There wasn't reason for her father or mother to come.

Quickly, while no one was about, she tugged free the cord that held her amulet pouch around her neck.

From inside the pouch, she pulled out the smooth loon

figurine, set it down on a nest of bunchgrass. She picked a few tiny blades, set them near its mouth, so it could eat. Then she stretched out on the ground to watch. She felt hopeful, as if she were a seal and the Loon was floating nearby. As if this way, maybe, finally, it would recognize her, trust her. Perhaps, she hoped, it would speak to her.

"I've heard you singing, Loon," she said. "I know your voice, the different ways you call. I know the way your wings sound when you lift off the water. But I don't know how to speak to you, or if you hear my voice?"

And then she waited. She waited until her wrists hurt from holding her head and a sharp blade of dry grass dug in at her elbow. She moved, tried sitting with her legs folded under her, then with her legs out, then lying down again.

Behind her in the sky, two white-fronted geese with their short necks glided past, the tips of their wings so close, they seemed to touch. Elik picked the loon up in her hand, lifted it to see: "Is that what you want?" she asked. "Are you lonely for something else to live with inside my bag? If I found you a mate, would you talk?"

She rose and hunted in a circle till she found the hump of a ground squirrel's burrow, the dark hole where it entered the ground and stored its food. "Ground squirrels are good," she said. "A scrap of fur from its body? Or else the seeds it's hoarded? The squirrel's strength might come into the seeds?"

The Loon didn't answer.

No, she decided. An amulet for the Loon must be closer to its own kind, something of its own choosing. Perhaps, then, the Loon would help her understand the voices she heard, sometimes in the wind, always when she was alone. Like a drumming inside, deep and ringing in her ears.

It wasn't a difficult thing for Elik to find her way back: her family set up fish camp in the same place near the river's mouth every year at this time. One day along the coast by umiak from the Bent Point village to their fish camp, sometimes two days, depending on their load. No one else would have fished there. Nor would they, so long as the salmon returned, need look for a different place to fish.

Nagi and Sipsip set their nets at the next mouth of the same river. The Place of the Small Stream, they called it, though they always brought in more salmon, more sheefish and grayling, than Elik's family.

And her father's brother, Saami, and his wives fished at the Place With a Shallow Crossing just down from Nagi. If the season went well they hauled the dried fish back to the winter caches, then returned for a second load. Or dug a pit and stored what fish they'd caught till summer's end.

She could have drawn a map if someone asked. A picture of how Real People moved out of their settled villages each summer, families traveling to the rivers, to the places where the fish showed them they liked to come.

Elik hurried when she could, but she didn't run. The pack bumped low against her hip and the walking was riddled with burrows and hummocks. Finally, she caught the drifting smell of woodsmoke, pushed through the line of willow brush that followed the river, then scrambled down the waist-high drop to the bank, and around one bend.

She saw her father first. Chevak was standing beside their tent, the old tent they covered again each year—not the new one Iluperaq and Kimik had recently set for themselves. That one stood a few paces upriver in a slower current, closer in against the silty water's edge.

*Too close, in case there's flooding,* Chevak had warned when they first arrived. But he said it after Iluperaq had already gone to the trouble of cutting and dragging down willow poles and bending them to a frame. And Kimik had already covered the new frame with skins. Iluperaq had stared hard at the ground while Chevak spoke, then let the tent stand just the same.

Three other people sat around the gravel-edged fire: Naiya and her mother, so close they looked as if they shared one skin. Iluperaq sat opposite, cross-legged, hands busy with his work.

*Quiet. There was too much quiet.*

Even from a distance she could see it: the way her father leaned against his pronged fish spear, arms angrily crossed as if his heart was beating so loud, it was all he could do to hold it inside his chest.

Iluperaq glanced behind: Kimik was walking from their tent toward the fire. She moved slowly, one of her hands near her throat as if to hold the food back down. She smiled when she saw Iluperaq, then lifted her arm and waved at Elik.

Elik pulled free of the shoulder strap and let her pack fall to the ground. It was still new for her, having Kimik here at fish camp, different but good—hearing her laugh that was lighter than Naiya's, quicker than her own.

So many times their father cautioned Iluperaq to wait. *Another season longer* he kept saying. *A family of four women needs two men—not another woman—to find them game.*

Was that what they were arguing about? she wondered. Kimik eating too much? But the fishing season was good; there was more than enough for all. Or perhaps it was because Kimik was ill with her pregnancy, and Chevak thought she didn't work enough?

In the end, it had been because of the baby that Iluperaq had his way. The baby, and because Saami had opened his mouth in front of the other men, reminding Chevak how it felt to be young. How anyone could see from the size of Kimik's belly that Iluperaq was no boy to sleep alone at night.

Gull waved Elik toward the fire. "We cooked some fish." She pointed to the small trout speared through the mouth and leaning on a stone. "Everyone's eaten."

Elik looked to the sky first, then the fire. It was spring; the light was full, the sun high. It was easy in this season to forget dangers, to stay out longer than she realized. There was only the remainder of the few bones no one had eaten, the scudded trail where one of their dogs had dragged off its catch.

Elik took the place next to Naiya. She thought about the plant she'd found, but she didn't bring it out. There was too much anger in the air, words hanging that couldn't be taken back. She didn't understand why her father grew so easily annoyed, why he allowed his jealousies to show.

Her mother had spoken of it only once that she remembered, ever. It had been for Kimik's sake, recently. They had set up camp and were waiting for the salmon run to start, and Iluperaq and Chevak had gone to hunt, and the women sat together, skinning ptarmigan.

Into the circle of feathers and sticky fingers, Kimik had said: "Chevak thinks I'm lazy, but I'm not. I'm ill with this baby. . . ."

She had spoken suddenly and so softly Elik almost didn't hear, but Gull had. "No," she answered quickly, almost as if she'd had the answer ready. "It isn't so. Chevak is a father. He knows. I was the same with Iluperaq, and with Elik."

"He doesn't remember." Naiya laughed. "That was too long ago."

"Is he angry with Iluperaq?" Kimik asked. "Or with me? He teases my cooking. My sewing. He says I have no strength. . . ."

"No, daughter. Hush. It's just his way."

Kimik chewed her lip, then said, "My mother says it's strange, the way you go to fish camp in such a small group."

Naiya's eyes widened. Elik looked to Kimik, to her mother.

Kimik said, "When we go to fish camp, most all the women in our family fish together. My brother's wife, Salmonberry, and sometimes her cousin. And my mother, and sometimes her older sister, Ema. But you come alone, and Chevak stays with you."

No one answered.

Kimik said, "I worry for this person inside me. That his new ears will hear the loud voices and learn to be angry before he learns to talk."

"Hush," Gull said. "It's better not to speak of such

things. Chevak . . . Chevak doesn't always know how to be happy. It's his age—He grows old and he doesn't like it. Sometimes it makes him feel clogged up inside. He sees Iluperaq, how strong he is. He sees the way his brother Saami hunts well enough for two wives. Alu says Chevak was too small when he was young. That's why he speaks so loudly. He doesn't mean to."

Elik tested the fish with her fingers, waited for it to cool. The skin was brittle as paper birch, part charred, part golden. She brought it to her mouth, found a place where she could bite.

"Here's our wandering squirrel," Chevak called, and he came and stood behind her. "What did you bring? More sourdock?"

Elik lowered the fish. Was he saying he had seen the sourdock? Or complaining that it was sourdock and not something better? With him, there was always one word, two meanings.

"It's a good daughter who brings her mother food," he said, and he moved to stand in front of her.

"There was one plant—" Elik started to explain, but when she looked, his gaze was on Iluperaq, not her. He wasn't listening to her at all.

Iluperaq and Kimik sat with their long gill net stretched between them, a tear in the midsection flattened to repair.

Elik glanced to the river, to the first line of floats that marked Chevak and Gull's net, then beyond that to her brother's small boat, upside down on the gravel at the next eddy, where the gill net should have stretched. His and Kimik's—the net she had worked on all spring, while Iluperaq worked for the gift of sealskins.

Kimik rotated the heap of ruined net in her lap. She took up her tapered, wooden netting needle and started on a tear. Iluperaq worked with a marline spike. On the ground, a pile of notched sinker rocks was neatly arranged to one side, wooden floats to the other.

"It's only the one load you lost," Chevak said.

"One load now. Another in the morning," Iluperaq said. "This will take all night to fix."

"Not all night," Kimik reminded him. "You have four hands to do the work, not two."

"The salmon run is still strong," Gull made her voice hopeful. "Tomorrow you'll do better."

Gently, not to make trouble, Elik asked what happened.

"A log floated down," her mother said. "It jammed the net. The branches tore the mesh."

"The log could have been caught," Iluperaq's voice was tight. "A boat had time . . ."

Elik looked to her sister, but Naiya had carefully turned away.

Chevak said, "No one can catch every log that jams and breaks. Or if your kayak stroke is so quick, you catch the next one. Besides"—he shrugged, swatted a mosquito—"your net should have been placed better. Everyone learns this. And now you have a wife, so if it's broken, she only needs to—"

Iluperaq raised his voice, "Only needs to—" he stopped.

Kimik had risen to her feet. Her face was pale. One hand covered her stomach, the other her mouth. Quickly, before anyone else had moved, Gull was at her side. She took Kimik by the shoulders, helped guide her away from the fire, somewhere she could be sick alone if she had to.

Iluperaq watched after them. Without saying more, he rose, went inside his tent, and closed the door flap.

Elik lowered her eyes, hoping her father wouldn't speak. Naiya found a song to hum. Chevak buried the bits of food that clung around the ashes, then buried the ashes.

It seemed like the longest time till Kimik returned and followed Iluperaq inside their tent. Gull followed after, into theirs.

Chevak took a few steps, then stopped. From Iluperaq's tent came the definite sound of laughter, a woman's first, high and bright, and then a man's. Chevak stood listening, a little too close, a little too long before, finally, he turned and followed after Gull.

～

It was the sound of birds arguing over their morning catch that woke Elik first, ahead of Naiya. Ahead of her mother and father, who had gone to their bed across from hers in a silence that turned into the rustling sounds of bedding, her mother's soft encouragements, a mingling of their noises, and then later, sometime in the night, to sleep.

Elik slipped outside the tent and stretched the tightness from her shoulders. Overhead an eagle bent back the tip of its wings and veered away to hunt. A long-beaked king-fisher swooped to the water, dipped its head so quickly, the movement almost couldn't be seen, till it flew off with something narrow in its mouth.

Elik turned to follow the bird; with surprise she saw that Kimik and Iluperaq were already down at the river, already working.

Near Kimik's feet, a thick line held one end of their gill net fast to a stake. Iluperaq sat in his narrow boat, partway out across the river, where a large painted bird float marked the end of the net.

The net was full. All along the line, smaller bird floats bobbed and marked the weight of trapped salmon fighting, dragging against the net.

Elik stared a moment, surprised at how late they must have worked repairing the net, then setting it back again to catch the run. She called a greeting. Kimik smiled, pointed out their load.

Behind her in the tent, her mother was waking now. She heard Gull's soft voice, then Naiya answering. And then her father coughing, asking for water.

For a moment, Elik feared it would start again, his anger. That he would be shamed to see his son at work before him. But no—behind her came the sound of her father's rushing footsteps, and Gull behind him, then Naiya. Chevak smiled toward the river, toward the heavy work awaiting them. He ran to help Iluperaq bring in his boat, turning the bow to shore while Iluperaq anchored the boat with his paddle.

Then, so quickly there was no time for a meal, they were down in the water, all of them, soaking their boots and splashing and hauling in the nets. The work turned to a blustering rush, freeing the tangled fish from the mesh, heaving them up on shore.

Once the fish were safely out of water, cleaning them became the women's job. Chevak and Iluperaq stayed until the first hectic rush slowed to a steady pace. Then, together, they took their birding spears and bolas, and left the women to their work while they walked inland to see what they could hunt.

With practiced hands, Elik, Gull, Naiya, and Kimik ran from fish to thrashing fish, laughing as they slipped on the fat pinks and silvers, as the strong, cold tails slapped their legs, struck their feet.

If a fish still struggled, Naiya stepped on its back, or the tail, holding it in place while Elik clubbed and Gull sang and Kimik laughed whenever she missed and clubbed again. Until all the fish were safely thrown from the shore to a shallow, willow-lined pit that was already dug and waiting midway between the river and their drying racks.

And then the cutting began. Elik took her first fish, and then her fifth, and then her tenth. The slime was wiped from their scales, the scales flicked away. With curved stone knives and quick, sure strokes, the first cut was opened along the length of the belly, from the head to the tail, then split around the fin.

Into one wooden tub they threw the organs, the intestines. Out on the rocks they set clusters of round, red eggs to dry, then pack later in the hard frozen ground. Nothing was wasted, nothing lost. What people did not eat, their dogs would. The fins, the organs. The heads they buried in grass-lined pits, left them to ferment and dig up later when the taste would come to the tongue, sharp and ready. The air bladder was saved to stuff with the eggs, to dry and eat the same as seal intestines.

They turned the fish over and split down the length of the backbone, separating the meat from the ribs, then scoring through the thickest part, so the wind and air and smudge fire could dry them quicker. When enough were done, the work was divided: Gull and Naiya cleaning and cutting while Elik and Kimik hung the salmon over the drying racks, one by one in neat rows, careful so the red meat faced out to the wind and flat, so the smoke from their slow green fire helped dry the undersides.

All through the day they worked, hanging the fish, talking lightly, sharing the eyes for a treat, a bit of raw fish when they were hungry.

It was only once in a while, when the work slowed, that Elik glanced sideways at Kimik, wondering at the way her new sister wore her clothes: no different than she or Naiya. Or the three straight tattoo lines marking her chin—also the same.

Except for Kimik's eyes, which had an upward slant, lovely and narrow, more the way Malluar's eyes must have been shaped when she was young. Less like Elik's and Naiya's.

Malluar's mother and Seal Talker's mother were sisters. And Seal Talker had one son, Arveq, who no longer lived in the Bent Point village. And no daughters. And Malluar also—no daughters, no children, just as Malluar had said.

Except that Seal Talker's wife Ema was the sister of Kimik's mother, which left Kimik as Malluar's closest young female relation.

And if that was true, Elik wondered, than wasn't it possible that Kimik knew things Elik had never been taught? Things Malluar might have told because Kimik was more closely related to the shaman's line than Elik could ever be?

Elik stopped her work. With all the anger bristling in the air, last night had been the wrong time to ask about the plant. She could now; with the men gone Kimik would feel freer to talk, less worried about Iluperaq.

She hung the split fish, stopped at the river to rinse her hands in the numbing water, then came back with the basket she'd filled last night. "What is it?" Naiya asked first.

"I want to show you what I found." Elik spread the leaves on the ground. Carefully, she unfolded the outer leaf first, then the one she hadn't known.

"They're wilted," Naiya said.

Gull glanced once, then shrugged.

"Wild celery?" Kimik glanced down to see.

Gull leaned over, touched the leaf with the clean part of her hand. "Not celery. I don't know what."

"Let's finish the fish," Naiya said.

But Kimik was still looking. "If it has a root that goes like this"—she showed with her hands—"then it isn't wild celery. It's rare, though."

"Here—" Elik brought it closer.

Kimik wiped the fish blood from her hands. "It's marsh marigold," she said. "I couldn't see it before. The leaves are poisonous if they're not cooked."

"You mean if I had eaten them—?"

"Yes. See how this red follows up the vein." Kimik turned the leaf over, pointing. "I don't know what would happen. But cooked, they're safe."

"You knew that? So quickly?"

Kimik shrugged, her attention back on the fish.

"It's because she's a wife now," Naiya joked. "She has to know more."

"But we've always gathered plants together."

Kimik lifted the next split fish by the tail. "I know only what plants we eat, what not to touch."

"Someone told her," Naiya said. "That's all. Why with you must everything alway mean something?"

Kimik laughed, then leaned to Naiya. "She asks so many questions. Before I was your sister—was she always the same?"

Naiya laughed and nodded. Elik returned the plants to the basket. The teasing didn't matter, she told herself. This was no different than she always heard from Naiya, except that now there were two voices instead of one.

She lifted a fish by the tail, held it on the flattened drift-wood table, and made the first cut into the belly. The next toward the backbone, halving the fish without cutting through. Whenever she could, whenever Kimik wasn't watching, she glanced to her face.

The long night's work showed beneath Kimik's eyes. The early months of pregnancy, the lack of sleep, all made her new sister look pale and tired.

What if it was true they had grown up together, practiced their first stitches by the light of the same lamp? If they learned to fish by dangling the same shared cod-hook beneath the ice?

Wasn't it still possible for Kimik to cut a salmon's flesh in a way Elik didn't know? Or set traps differently? Or learn songs, shaman songs?

Elik's blade stopped moving. "Maybe Malluar taught you something?" she asked. "Maybe there are things you know that Naiya and I weren't taught?"

Bewildered, Kimik stopped her work. "Malluar talks sometimes, when she visits. But only about the same things as my mother."

"But what if . . . " Elik was insistent. "What if Malluar taught you things, but you didn't know they were secrets, because no one told you? So how could you know?"

Kimik looked to Gull for help. "Malluar keeps secrets," she said, "the same as she always has. No one knows everything. Not even Malluar. Not even Seal Talker."

There was a sound behind them, brush cracking, men's voices. Kimik set her blade down, relieved to have the strange talk end. She wiped her splattered face with the back of her pushed-up sleeve and stepped forward to greet Iluperaq. Gull nodded at Elik, telling her to hush.

Chevak and Iluperaq came walking from the upper river trail. The women smiled; Kimik stepped forward. Gull waited at her shoulder.

They had only reached the farthest drying rack, the empty one beyond Iluperaq and Kimik's tent, but already the women felt it, the tension, the anger. There was no game that anyone could see. Empty hands. Empty packs. Only an anger smoldering between them. Again.

They started talking, as soon as they saw the women. Words they must have carried all the way back. Gull started a song, a high-pitched humming she hoped would cover their anger. Naiya joined her.

Chevak raised his voice louder, wanting them to hear. "The caribou was there," he complained. "That close. I could have touched him."

"He was alone and acting strange. And he wasn't close—no arrow could fly that far."

"A man could try, if someone hadn't been too lazy to carry a spear. . . ."

"It wasn't laziness. We were going for birds. This was one caribou. A human shouldn't eat meat from an animal acting that way."

Chevak's shoulders stiffened. He held his hands tight against his side. "There is a tale," he said, warning, "of a man whose father told him to find some food."

"And there is a another tale," Iluperaq started, but Chevak had walked away, behind the fish-drying racks, where the women stood—Gull with her blade in her hand, Kimik with a fish, Naiya and Elik openly watching.

Chevak studied the ground, the crotch of the upright pole. He smelled the air, tasted his fingers. He said, "There is a tale of a man whose new wife ate so much food, nothing was left for the others. . . ."

Kimik set down the fish without even caring that she'd put it on the sandy ground. She held her hands to her stomach, the same motion Elik had seen her make before.

Iluperaq held so still, he seemed to have forgotten how to move.

Chevak crossed to his tent, stepped in, rustled about loudly. A moment later he stepped out again, this time with his sinew-backed bow and fishskin quiver flung over his shoulders. His steps, as he walked away along the riverbed, were louder than any hunter's ought to be.

Iluperaq hadn't spoken. In long, hard strides he passed beyond them, down to the river, where he'd left a pile of sinker rocks he was working. He grabbed the first one his hands touched, started retying the line ends that had come loose from the groove. They were wet and slippery with bits of salmon and river debris. The knots wouldn't hold. He picked up a second rock, raised it to gouge the notch-end deeper.

He brought it down once. Hit. Raised it again. The second time the sound of a rock smashing turned to a shout—angry and loud. Iluperaq clenched his hand to a fist.

Briskly, he sped to the river, plunged in his hand and let the icy water cool the finger he'd smashed. Blood was running out the open gash he'd struck, too angry, too wide of the mark.

On the way to his tent he threw a look to the women. "I cut it," he said. "That's all. I cut it and it's bleeding." And he closed the flap of the door behind him.

Kimik hurried after.

Elik stared at the shuttered door flap. Gull watched her daughter, as if worried Elik might do something, go in there and say something that would make it worse. She put her hand on Elik's arm.

Elik looked questioningly to her mother, then to Naiya, seated now at their outside hearth. Naiya had picked up some sewing, buried herself in the work. Her hands moved so quickly that Elik wondered if her sister didn't have a power in her needle that taught her to stay calm, to keep her thoughts whole while Elik never had learned how.

"I'm going walking," she said.

"Not far," Gull asked. "Please. Not now."

Elik chose the quickest path away from camp, scrambling up the cut bank, ducking through the waist-high brush, shrub birch and willow. She started toward a place she knew, where a sandy washout gave way to rock and then rose higher to a hill. It would have been good to rest, to sit and watch the view toward where the brown water of the river met the bluer sea, but . . . No.

It wasn't her father she wanted to see, or their camp, or anyone except the land. The way it opened in a circle, no matter how far she walked. The way it gave her different things to think about: not her father's anger, not the spattering of too-proud blood dripping from her brother's hand.

She walked awhile more, found a clump of salmonberries: too hard and bitter to eat yet. A little farther and she tried a few stalks of wild spinach, sour, but pleasant in their own way.

She continued through an open flat of lichens and tiny flowers hidden in patches of moss: yellows, greens, and early reds. Past that awhile longer to a place where the land was drier, more level beneath her steps, with a hedge of taller grass, then cattails. Through them she could see the catch of light sparkling on water, a pond.

Elik stopped, then listened. She'd heard something. Not the wind, but what? There was a cawing sound, overhead and toward her right. Ravens. Yes—there: with their wings black and strong against the clouded sky. She started forward, stepping quietly, not wanting them to scatter.

But then she stopped. There was another call. Not a raven this time. Something else. A man? But who would shout out in the open like that?

With a jolt, she dropped to the ground. Instantly, her heart raced, so loud she thought it would give her away. *What was she doing, to follow a raven, when anyone knew that Raven followed people . . .*

The noise grew louder, a pounding, echoing in the ground. People running. No; only one pair of feet. Louder, coming toward her, then softer again, moving away. Faint. She waited a few moments, then risked lifting her head.

She pushed aside the tall grass. With a shock, she saw her father's dark hair, the whitish color of the gut parka he'd worn when he went stamping with his anger from their camp.

He was talking to himself, making noises and talking loudly. Was he hurt? A man hunting should be quiet, not to frighten or anger the animal he stalked. He dropped down near the pond where the ravens had landed. Elik edged along the tall border grass till she found a better view.

He was kneeling over a fallen caribou; a male, huge and beautiful, its antlers still growing toward the rutting season. Was this the one he and Iluperaq had seen? It was possible, though she couldn't be sure. His arrow could easily have found that one, or another, then stalked it here, following until the bull grew weak enough to drop.

The caribou was partially hidden by her father's back, but even so she could see the dark hooves lifting from the ground, the way the flanks heaved, hungry for a breath, the line of blood running where the arrow stuck—not a heart shot but in the shoulder, piercing, deep and strong. The caribou kicked. Its chest heaved and then it went quiet, beautiful and still.

Respectfully, Elik lowered her head before looking up again. Its ghost would be watching now, listening for her thoughts.

A few paces beyond the caribou, the first of the ravens landed on the ground. It opened its black, laughing mouth, then hopped to one side, waiting. Ravens always knew about food. First, before any creature. In a moment her father would give it its share.

She almost stood up, called out to share the work. The caribou would be a heavy load to haul: the antlers, the head and skin. Winter hunting was often easier, with a sledge to glide on snow. But now, in this season, she ought to help.

Her father stood over the caribou, knife in his hand. He would pull out his arrow and cut the head first, the proper way, so the caribou would not be offended, would not have to see itself suffer.

*Except why was he waiting?*

He turned, surveyed the land as if looking for someone. Did he think Iluperaq might have followed?

Elik shifted the grass aside. Her father was lifting the caribou's rear leg. *What was he looking for? A penis? Why?* Her father had never been a brave man, to anger the dead. . . .

He let the leg fall, just like that. As if the caribou would not know what he did. And then he came back around, squatted in front of its face, and started singing.

Elik relaxed. This was better. He would sing his hunting song now, a song of joy. Hearing it, the caribou's spirit would be free. There'd be no reason for it to linger, causing illness, warning other animals to stay away.

Except—there was nothing of respect in her father's song, only anger. Anger in his face—she could see it—clutching and hard; in his words, the same anger he had thrown like a net about their camp.

"If you were my son," he sang, and then he laughed. "If you were my son, then my son would be lying here now. You who thought you could run as fast as I. You are gone. You who thought you were man enough to bed a wife. Who said to me, I can hunt. I can run. But all you do is feed your wife. See where you are now? You think you know the ways to fight, because you carry antlers, the way a boy carries a knife. You who think you can run, because your legs are long instead of old. You see this blade?"

And then he held his knife to its face, as if the eyes that were watching him were alive again and not above them, around them, listening now.

Elik pressed her hands to her mouth, not to call, not to shout at him to stop, to be careful.

He took his blade but instead of severing the head and releasing the soul, he moved to the stomach and sliced down, one long line and then another crossing that. He tore back the skin. Tore it, without care, down into the meat. He cut around the upper legs, the joints that were easiest. There was blood on his face, on his hands—carelessly he wiped them on his trousers.

He was angry at Iluperaq and because of it, he was throwing his anger on the caribou, letting it rise, like smoke in the air. And like smoke, it would be seen. He was worse than a fool. A fool hurt no one so much as himself. But what he did here, this anger, it would turn on him, on his family. He would bring hunger. Maybe illness. Maybe death.

The caribou were travelers, always and forever the great

herds came and went as they wished. This one must have strayed, driven wild by mosquitoes. And wild it would remain, without chance for a new birth. With one name in its thoughts: her father's. His family.

Chevak took hold of the antlers, yanked back so the neck came up, exposing the throat. He cut in, then around. A rope of dark blood followed his knife. He pressed the antlers back, hard toward the ground. Bearing down with his weight till, with a snap of bones, the head came free. The eyes, white and black, turned from the sky toward the pond.

"You are like sky without wind," she heard him say. "Like nothing I can feel. You think you can make me work for you, when you should work for me?" He gave the head a kick, then turned his back as it rocked to the side.

He was done. The organs and intestines that should have been cached till he could take proper care, he left piled on the ground. What parts he could easily carry, he lifted to his shoulder. The legs for Gull's sinew, meat from the chest, the white-striped flanks for new clothes.

And then, so quickly that she wondered if her eyes had watched a demon instead of a man, he was gone. She crouched in the grass for what seemed a great while, listening to the rain that had begun to fall. She wiped it from her eyes and cheeks, then slowly she rose and walked to the caribou.

There was a smell of wasted blood soaking into the moss. Tufts of coarse white and brown hair where his knife had cut. Clots of blood. Black eyes staring at the world.

What did it see now, she wondered. Her? Or her father? Was it watching to see which direction his trail led, where his camp lay?

She would have to make amends somehow. Apologize, confess her father's wrong. Perhaps, if she was not too late, she could undo the harm he caused. But how?

She felt flushed, hot and cold at the same time. She yanked off her parka to keep it clean. The cool rain tickled her breasts and she shivered. She wasn't thinking clearly and she knew it. She was tired, terribly tired. How many days had it been since she had slept a full night through?

Since the fish started running? Since they left their winter camp? How long since she had slept at all?

And what could she do? Not burn the head; the smoke would be seen. Not bury it; there weren't enough rocks and the ground was frozen too shallow beneath the moss. The pond? Perhaps she could drag it to the pond?

It took all her strength, straining and pushing, to drag the huge head by the antlers, to the cattails, then farther, into the open stretch of water. She waded into the pond, pushing the head in front of her, until it was deep enough, till not a single point of its antlers showed above the surface. And then she left it. She backed away from the water's edge.

There was sickness on her hands; if not on hers, then surely on her father's. She didn't want to go back to their camp yet. Tomorrow maybe, but not today. Today she was too frightened, confused.

The sky was light as morning, but there was a white circle of a moon, so thin she thought she could see the sky behind it. There were clouds and the smell of wet earth. There were the ravens watching her now, the way they had watched her father. She noticed her arms; she was shivering. She crossed them over her breasts, hid her stomach. She felt empty inside and out. She pulled her parka back on.

Near her feet, the point of a raven's feather marked the bloodstained ground. She picked it up. The feather was black as coal. Blacker. She tossed it up, threw it toward the sky. "Go away," she told it. "Go back to your home. Don't look here. Don't remember this place."

Elik swatted her cheek where a mosquito had bitten. She scratched her neck, the knuckles on her hands. With a start, she sat up. Not in her bed—she was on the tundra, asleep on the moss. Below the watching sky. There was the trampled grass where her father had knelt. And there the pond. She turned away. She didn't want to remember.

The rain had stopped, but foolishly, like a child, she'd let her clothes get soaked. The furs of her parka felt heavy on her skin, wet, maybe ruined, unless she dried them and rubbed them soft again.

Nearer to the tall grass she lowered her trousers and squatted down to pee. Instantly the mosquitoes found her, buzzed around her face, her naked legs. She slapped her knee, the back of her thigh where she couldn't see. She tried to get done quickly. What if something got up inside her while she squatted that way? If not the mosquitoes, then something smaller. Invisible.

She jumped and tugged up her pants, then just as quickly grew annoyed. What was the matter with her, thinking that way? Scaring herself? Sometimes, she had heard, people went crazy after a long winter. They ate dog shit. They slashed their own skin with knives.

She couldn't figure how long she'd been asleep. Where the sun had been, if it was night. If she was sick with cold, or if she was crazy. She scoured the line of hills, took her bearings, and started walking. She didn't want to be crazy. She wanted to be home. She wanted someone to tell her that everything was the way it had always been. Before the caribou. Before her father's anger.

It wasn't.

Even before she saw the tent, she heard their sounds: people talking, eating, feasting on a catch of meat. She smelled their fire, its smoke at the back of her throat. It made her feel cold, even the thought of it, sweating, then shivering all over again.

Elik jumped down the cutbank. She walked slowly, taking in the way the smoke rose, not disappearing toward the clouds but lingering, low to the ground. And the way parts of a caribou were roasting: legs, a strip of ribs, no more than that. She wondered what her father told them, whether he'd explained about the rest of the caribou. He must have lied or they wouldn't be eating it. Would they?

Gull rose when she saw her coming. Naiya and Kimik stopped and watched her approach. There was something in their faces. Worry, yes. But not for the caribou. What then? For her?

With a troubled thought, Elik searched the camp. There were tents and boats. Fish racks and piled stones. Kimik but no Iluperaq. Her father but no Iluperaq.

She waited till she was close enough not to shout. "Where is my brother?"

"Inside." Naiya nodded toward his tent. She spoke softly, the worry in her voice barely hidden.

Her mother's arms hung at her sides. "Where were you?" she asked. "Did something happen?"

Elik looked at the ground. "No. Nothing."

Chevak made a sound, a snickering. "Your brother is sleeping." He laughed. "Not hunting. Not sharing work. Sleeping."

The words hung for a moment, bitter and small. Kimik set down the roasted caribou she had been eating. "I fed him blood soup," she explained, "but his fever grows. If you touch his hand, you can feel there's swelling. Below the finger, moving through his wrist. Maybe, something is inside . . ."

Elik looked from face to face. Their mouths and chins were moist with grease, shining with the fat of the dead caribou. As if they were dwarf-people, to eat from their kill without burial. Not Real People. Not humans at all.

*But no*—she told herself. *None of them knew what meat they ate. Only Chevak . . . The others hadn't seen.*

"We talked about setting snares," Chevak said. "Up by the higher boulders—for mountain sheep. Now who will help me?"

The hood of Elik's parka rubbed against her neck, irritating. She reached to pull it looser but her fingers grazed something sharp stuck in against the softer ruff. She picked it free, then stared in confusion at the feather in her hand. It was black: the tapered, pure black raven's feather she had tossed up to the sky. The one she tried to send away.

Elik stepped back, off-balance. She searched in the empty air for where the upright poles of the fish rack should have been. For something, anything, to grab on to . . .

It was her mother's arms she felt, catching her as she fell. As she closed her hand tighter around the feather, hiding it. Her mother's strong arms, lowering her to the ground. And her mother's voice, as if from far away: ". . . Not sick . . . She's falling again. I hoped we were done with this. . . ."

And behind her, above the fire, inside the wavering air—What was it she saw? A caribou? With its head thrown back like a hood and its inner face peering from the chest. Did it know she was the one who tried to help?

The next time Elik opened her eyes she was lying in a bed of caribou skins, inside, on the floor of their summer tent. The soles of her father's black crimped sealskin boots stood near her face, her mother's bare feet just beyond. Elik made slits of her eyes, pretending to sleep.

"It isn't safe—" That from her father's voice. "A shaman visiting this camp. Spirits trailing after him."

"But if we leave Iluperaq lying that way? With illness—"

"Then who should go? With so many women, one man needs to stay."

"I will."

Elik dared a look. Naiya had spoken. Her sister sat with her head lowered and respectful, wary of her father's changing moods.

Chevak's pacing stopped. "You? How can you handle the boat? You're too young."

"I won't take a boat. I can run. Who else is there?"

"Let her bring the shaman, please." There was fear in Kimik's voice. "His soul—who knows where it's gone?"

"Naiya? Are you sure?"

"Elik can't, and Kimik shouldn't leave. I can run, Mother. I *want* to."

Gull's voice was very small. "How long?"

"One day there. Maybe two coming back with Seal Talker?"

"One day to visit, she means. But what about this one?" Chevak stopped in front of Elik. "Shouldn't she be with her brother, in the sick-tent?"

No one answered. Then Chevak's voice again, flat with

annoyance. "We should have married her already. It might be harder than I thought, finding a man for a wife who faints, who wanders and talks about voices."

Elik closed her eyes. She was shivering again, so cold. She lay with her knees pulled up to her chin, the weight of so many furs piled on top. She didn't want to hear any more. Kimik had slept with them, rather than Iluperaq. Which meant her brother's illness was bad enough her parents would not risk the spirits that found him finding her and their unborn child as well. And Naiya was leaving. But that didn't matter. Elik wanted nothing more than to sleep. To sleep and dream of other places. Other voices.

She could almost hear them, if she kept her eyes shut tight and listened. Not the human voices. They were too loud, like thunder. But those behind, she could hear them now: the voice of the Raven, whose feather was safe in her pouch. The voice of the Loon. They were calling her. She had only to listen and she could hear them:

*In the sky. Look for us. In the fields. On the ground. Look for us. In the sea. In the air. Look for us. Look for us . . .*

They were done with their meal. The shaman pushed away the wooden guest bowl, then belched loudly to show his appreciation.

With a cautioning glance from Gull, Elik rose and walked quietly toward Seal Talker.

Their mother had cooked a fine meal of boiled eggs and salmon, but Naiya should have been the one to serve him. As older daughter it was not only her duty, it was her privilege. Except that Naiya had grown suddenly busy elsewhere, stripping willow bark, mending netting, anything she could find, so long as she was able to avoid the shaman.

Naiya had been whispering pieces of the story to Elik ever since she had returned. There was something about Seal Talker's delicate stomach: flatulence, Naiya had laughed. But then she'd leaned closer, whispering that there was a new man, a nephew, she started to say. But each time she began the story, someone called and there'd been no chance to finish.

With small, gentle steps, Elik lifted Seal Talker's bowl, held it carefully, so as not to trip or stumble. It was important to do this right, these small things. She had promised not to faint again. And certainly Seal Talker had more important concerns than whether one girl followed or watched too closely the things he said and did.

"We are so poor. A family of women," her father complained. "Two girls, unmarried. A son too sick to hunt."

Elik filled the shaman's bowl full of caribou fat they'd mashed, then stirred to a white foam. She took a seat beside her mother, watched as Seal Talker shifted his legs. Without realizing it Elik set her hands in the same position, open on her knees. Seal Talker moved a hand toward the belt around his waist and her hand went to hers.

"What are you doing?" Naiya nudged her.

Elik startled. "Doing what?" she asked.

"Put your hands inside your belt, little sister. You might as well open your thighs. He'll think you mean the same thing."

Elik rearranged her legs. "I wasn't thinking," she said, and she reached for a duck's wing to wipe out a bowl, then noticed her sister's hands: empty. Naiya had put aside the willow she'd been splitting earlier. Her lap was filled with her own bowl, her own food.

"You have to look lazy," Naiya whispered. "While they discuss payment for working on Iluperaq. Otherwise, he'll ask for you."

Elik studied her sister. "How do you know so much?" she whispered.

"How do you know so little?"

Elik drew her eyebrows together. Had she missed something while she'd been ill? It wasn't sleeping for two days that troubled her; it was this feeling as if she'd become a child again with no sense, no thoughts inside her mind. It would have helped if she knew more of men. What little experience she had—it had been so long ago, in the toppled-down *qasgi* with her cousin, the first Allanaq, and with other boys. She knew what had happened, but with all the rolling about, the hands and fingers, a boy's quick poking . . . Sometimes she still wasn't certain what she had felt, what they had been doing down there in the too-quick scramble of body parts. "What does Seal Talker want?" she asked.

"Whatever he can get. But hush—you don't want him watching."

The shaman swatted a mosquito, then slid toward the smoky side of the fire, where the insects would be less bothersome. "Your racks are full," he complimented their father. "The fish come to your nets."

"Torn nets," Chevak protested. "Torn nets and nothing to eat. A man's catch is poor this year."

"A man needs his son. It's true, I may be of some small help . . . "

"Though already," Chevak backtracked, "Iluperaq has woken from this fever. The swelling's gone down. Though we worried for him. Naiya, the older girl . . . "

Seal Talker looked to the women. His glance swept over Gull, over her breasts that still were round, for all that she'd been twice a mother. On Kimik, though, being the wife of a man so ill, he was less interested there. But then again, her stomach was rounded and full—what man wouldn't prefer a woman who'd already proved she could bear children?

He looked to the women's fish racks. The salmon glistened and hung full. Storage baskets clustered near the tents. His gaze lingered on Chevak's boat—there was something of value.

Chevak sighed, carefully. "Ah, my daughters, yes. What would a man do without daughters? The skins on our umiak are so thin and poor this year. The older daughter offered to run for you, while the younger one tore her fingers restitching the boatskins. They were so old . . . "

"The younger one?" Seal Talker pulled himself taller.

"Yes—and she cooked the fish. It's tasty, isn't it?"

Seal Talker made no attempt to hide his interest. "Which one is younger?" he asked.

"That one. But the other helped as well. Both helped. Either one. Which one do you like?"

Seal Talker filled his mouth with pink salmon meat, chewed, then swallowed. "A man needs daughters, as well as a son," he said. "They show the animals how lovely they are. The caribou come to admire their work. And you, with so many girls. The younger one—her name is Elik?"

A light rain fell from the piling, grey clouds, heavy enough for them to raise their hoods, but not to chase them inside. Naiya took Elik's hand and pulled her to the nearest place they could talk, behind the fish racks, where no one would hear.

Close against the outside wall of the tent, Gull sat with Kimik, both of them kneading bits of feathers and down into the clay they had dug a few days earlier. Seal Talker and Chevak sat beside the fire, talking. Iluperaq remained inside: Elik had been warned not to go near his swollen illness till her own fainting was fully gone.

Naiya's brown eyes shone with excitement. She tugged Elik's arm, started talking. "His name is Whale Fin. Don't let him see me here."

"Who?"

"Seal Talker. Who else? I don't want him to find me alone. Here, take this. If he sees me working, he'll think I'm trying to show how fine a wife I'd be—" She took the grass boot liners she'd been plaiting, pushed them into Elik's hands.

"Who is Whale Fin?"

"I told you. Didn't you hear? He's Seal Talker's nephew from Fish River. We talked together, while I waited for Seal Talker to get ready. He walked with me . . . And then a little bit more." Naiya smiled. There was something different in her voice, less childish, more serious. "He has a son," she added, "a little boy, but he left the boy in Fish River with his mother's relatives—she died." Naiya touched Elik's shoulder. "You shouldn't stare so much."

"I wasn't . . ."

"Sister, you haven't stopped watching him yet."

"He's an old man. His wife is older than our mother."

"He's young enough. I can tell you what he did."

Elik's gaze shot up. "Did Seal Talker say something?"

"He didn't *say* anything. He showed me."

"Showed you what?"

"That a shaman is no different than another man. Even an old shaman . . . " She made a gesture. Elik's eyes widened. "We found a place to make camp, to rest. It was already more than half a day's walk out of the Bent Point shore. I made a bed for him of willow boughs. I cooked his food. I helped him carry. I did everything a woman should. He said he couldn't sleep. . . ."

"He said that? Is that all?"

"No."

Elik looked away. "Did he . . . Did he hurt you?"

"No. But he would have if I had tried to stop him. You need to know that. Even Whale Fin refused to speak against his uncle."

"That was all?"

"One time was enough. Another time wouldn't be so good."

"What do you mean?"

"I mean if Father lets Seal Talker pick one of us to sleep with, in payment for coming here, for working on Iluperaq, I don't want it to be me." Naiya peered around the fish rack to see if anyone could hear. "Whale Fin said he told the aunts who kept his little son that he would stay only long enough to help with the salmon run. But Seal Talker has already asked him to stay longer. He'll be there, at the end of the season. I don't want to go home as his uncle's wife."

Iluperaq stretched flat on the grass mat in the center floor of the tent, as Seal Talker instructed. He had woken from his earlier fever, slowly, unevenly crossed the path between the tents. He spoke to Kimik, which was good, though he wasn't smiling and his voice was weak. His sleeve had been cut away and he held his hand at a careful angle, the finger swollen, the color wrong.

Crowded inside the tent, Chevak sat stiff-backed behind Seal Talker. The women sat opposite: Gull, Naiya, and Elik. Kimik kept a separate distance, nearer to the battened door flap than to people, trying not to see. She hadn't slept; she hardly ate. As soon as the shaman arrived, she had begged for amulets, for Iluperaq to be healed, for herself so her unborn child would grow strong. She sat there now, pulling on the hem of her parka, too troubled to move closer, to do anything but what she was told.

Seal Talker set his tools on the white polar bear skin he'd brought: his lamp, his puffin-beaked mittens, a drum. He filled his lamp with oil from a skin—his own, a shaman's lamp, not something borrowed from Chevak. When the wick caught, he signaled, and Chevak secured the door flap, tightly so the light was shut out, the room transformed. Seal Talker folded his legs and sat to Iluperaq's side, leaving the small light to outline Iluperaq's chin, his parched lips and open mouth, the hollows beneath his eyes.

Gull coughed and Elik looked away from the shaman to see her mother watching her, a warning in the corners of her mouth.

She lowered her eyes. She had overheard her father asking Gull to take Elik aside, warn her not to call attention to herself. "If there's talking to be done," he had said, "tell her, people wiser than she will do it. Tell her to be respectful. That man—he knows how to make a woman barren. He could steal her brother's soul."

Elik glanced to Seal Talker's shadowed face. She saw a man who was old, but not frail. A man she had known all her life and all her life been taught to fear, to respect, to avoid. His face was lined in shadows. His narrow eye scanned the dark rim of the tent; his wider eye crossed hers. She looked away.

Why did they think she would anger him, when all she wanted was to watch? Her heart raced, then slowed, raced and faltered. Was that so different from what her mother wanted? Or Kimik? If Seal Talker summoned his spirit helpers to this house, they would tell him of the caribou. If her father confessed, no harm would come.

The tent filled with silence; the shaman let it hold. He waited till the lamp shrank the light to a crack across Iluperaq's shoulder, till Naiya edged uncomfortably toward Gull and Kimik's worrisome noises hushed, then disappeared. He pushed a scrap of skin under what was left of Iluperaq's finger. Beside the skin he laid out a wide, wood-handled knife.

Only then did he take out his shaman's drum and raise a beat: *aaya aaya aaya aaya,* as if the sound he called on was the heartbeat, as if the heartbeat belonged to his spirit helpers coming near. . . .

Iluperaq moaned. *Does he see my brother's soul?* Elik wondered. *Does he see inside?*

Seal Talker threw back his head. The veins on his neck were like cords, dry and brown. His hair was like wild grass and his breathing, not like a man's, and yet not animal. Like nothing she could name.

"You must close your eyes now, all of you," Seal Talker said. "You must not watch, or you might be hurt."

Elik lifted her hands, covered her face. Her brother lay still. The quiet thickened. She heard her mother's breathing on one side, felt Naiya's shoulder graze hers on the other.

She heard the rustling of the shaman moving to Iluperaq's side, the side where the knife had been set. She heard the sound of Iluperaq's arm being lifted from the floor. Then her brother's breathing changed. It knotted, stopped, turned into short, tight gasps. She heard the sounds a knife makes at the caribou butchering place: stone seeking out the joint. Cracking through to the ground below. She heard the shaman trying to hold her brother still. And his little breaths coming like huhn, huh, huhn now.

That was all.

And then a different sound grew. This time it was like the wind but not the wind. It was like a person—Seal Talker's spirit helpers . . . He had brought them inside the house. She heard them sliding through the opening at the top of the tent. There was a scratching sound. Sharp claws on a rocky beach. Fox first. Elik knew that sound. Then Caribou's heavier step. And then something new, a trembling from inside Seal Talker's body. His arms and legs were shaking—she could feel it through the ground. His face would be twisted in pain, his eyes turned inward.

She didn't know what was happening, except that he was with his spirit helpers. Talking to them. Listening. They would lead him to the evil that the caribou had become. His spirit helpers would wrestle it. Seal Talker would appease it. Knowing that all the evil that came to people came because of the souls they themselves killed, animal's souls they killed in order to eat.

A voice came, high as a whistle, shrill and loud. It filled the tent, the air all around them. Not Seal Talker's voice, but from somewhere above him. He would learn of her father's actions. Now. He would see the caribou's death. The voice said, "You who are the forces of wind, of the air, take pity on our fears, on the small humans who cannot see you.

"Who here has neglected the proper rules of conduct? Who brings illness through a failure to obey? We ask you to release us. Fling away evil."

No one answered.

With the slightest motion, Elik opened two of her fingers. Only a slit, only a little. The tent was dark, the air close. She moved another finger.

*We beseech you. You whom we cannot see. Whether you are dead and are watching. Whether you are angry, or ignored.*

A slit of lamplight bent across Iluperaq's chest.

His shoulders shook. A moan escaped his lips. Gull gave a start. Kimik made small, whimpering sounds. From her father she heard nothing, nothing at all.

Her brother's eyes flicked open. If his soul was lost, what would happen to his body? Would he die? Would he curse them? Elik leaned forward. Everything seemed to move in strange, jerking steps.

She turned to Seal Talker; she couldn't help herself. She wanted to see: the way he stared into a distance; the way he no longer looked old, but strong as any man.

Seal Talker held his hand over Iluperaq's. Nothing had been there, until he took his hand away. There on the floor in front of them—something had been taken out. What was it? Something brown? Like mud, shapeless.

What had Seal Talker done? What had he called?

Elik slid back, terrified suddenly. Whatever it was, it was sickness. It was disease. Seal Talker had taken it out from Iluperaq's hand. The shaman's power—it was greater than she had thought. Ever.

He started to speak, and she jumped. "I see blood spots on the gravel, in the ashes where someone spit." Seal Talker's voice chilled the tent. "Who has eaten of the heart? The kidneys or the intestines of a caribou?"

Elik's heart beat wildly. *He had found the caribou. It would speak. Now! It would tell the shaman and Iluperaq would grow strong again.*

She lowered her hands. Naiya also had opened her eyes, and her mother. Except that, instead, from Kimik's mouth, a cry erupted. And then Kimik's voice, small and very frightened. "Aii!" she said. "The caribou . . . Mother, I forgot . . ."

Every face in the shadowed tent turned on Kimik.

Kimik? Kimik had broken taboo? A woman with a child inside?

With a shout, almost too glad Chevak turned on her. "What did you do? Confess."

"I ate the liver of a caribou when I was hungry. It was so little, I thought . . . I thought it wouldn't matter."

Seal Talker rose on his knees, his chest glistening. "What else? You must tell, for your husband's sake." He loomed over her.

"That's all." Desperately, Kimik shook her head. "I swear there was no more."

"And I see no more," Seal Talker shouted, "Only those. All will be well." Kimik buried her face in her hands.

"Listen—" Seal Talker said. "Do not go out unless your hands are covered. Never eat an animal shot through the heart. Drink ice water, not hot, and only through a bone tube. Do not be careless, for your child's sake and for others."

And then Seal Talker was done, exhausted, but done. Gull came and helped Iluperaq to sit, to hold the scrap of skin tightly over the stump of his finger.

*Was that all then? And the power she had watched had removed the disease?*

Her father leaned back satisfied, his arms hugging his chest. Kimik wiped the runny mucus from her nose. Elik looked to her brother; already he seemed less pale. Was Seal Talker done? And the mistake had been Kimik's? Not her father's?

She looked to Seal Talker. To her father. Certainly Chevak had no power to fool a shaman's sight. Seal Talker's curved back glistened in sweat. His skin hung away from his ribs. He started putting his amulets away, neatly, carefully. She didn't understand. Seal Talker was powerful, his magic strong. But Chevak hadn't been seen. How?

Elik searched her memory. There was one thought, only one she could piece together. It was this: the caribou spirit had not spoken because it was not here to speak. Not in this world, not in the air nearby. It was she herself, burying the caribou's head in the pond, who had satisfied its anger. She herself who had erased the wrong. The caribou's spirit had gone to its proper place. There was nothing here to find.

Very quietly, Elik reached beneath her parka. Between her breasts, her amulet pouch hung on its string. Inside, the ivory loon and the raven's feather nestled side by side. Speaking with each other. Sharing what they knew.

Elik leaned out over the river. She hooked her fingers through the salmon's gills, fingers toward its mouth, careful of its small, sharp teeth. With her free hand she dug the clots of blood from the stomach cavity. Then with her scraper, flicked away the last bits of intestine, set the fish on the driftwood board. She looked toward the tents to see if she was watched, then upriver, where her father and Seal Talker stood beside their umiak.

Her father was talking. He seemed to be pointing out the shape of the river, how far to the mouth in one direction. Which way it meandered to Sipsip's fish camp in the other. Seal Talker ran his hand along the sides of the beached umiak. What was he looking at, she wondered? Whether her mother greased the overlapped stitches? Whether the ownership marks along the prow were her father's and not some other man's?

The fish slipped under her hand; she jabbed the tail with her knife, catching, then holding it, then forgetting it again as she watched the two men. If she had been braver, she would have opened her mouth and asked him questions: why did he set his shaman's lamp toward the east? How did it feel when his body shook inside the trance and did it hurt?

But she hadn't asked. She hadn't been brave at all. Ever since that night she'd fallen asleep on the tundra, and then even more so after Seal Talker arrived, her mother watched her more closely than ever. There was no chance to be alone with him. And if there had been, even if there had, she wasn't certain what she'd have said.

Chevak laughed and thumped Seal Talker on his back, then started walking up the gravel bed and toward their camp, smiling as he went. Elik flipped the fish over, dug her blade in, then down, behind the gills.

The sky above was a cool grey. The river rushed along, pushed by the northern wind, carrying its floating sticks and foam. Now and then a salmon jumped, silver against the brown water.

She glanced up to see Seal Talker still standing beside the boat. He seemed to be watching the river, the way she had been, watching the waves bring down the silt, fast on the far bank, slower at the bend where the salmon came. He watched the bobbing floats on Gull's net and the way one sea gull led three others on a chase.

The next time she looked, he had started walking. Toward her. She was certain—he was walking toward her. Her heart skipped. Quickly, she grabbed the next fish. Was he looking at her? She cut off the fish's head. Sliced through the belly. What had her father said? She slipped in her blade, searching for the layer of bone. . . .

His shadow fell over her. He had never approached her before, not alone, not without her father or mother present. She clasped the antler handle of her knife so her hands wouldn't shake. When she looked up he was smiling, crookedly. One long wrinkle dug in from his narrow eye to the corner of his mouth. He wasn't a large man. He didn't need to be.

On the higher ground above them, her father stood speaking with her mother. Gull must have felt her glance. She turned, so she wouldn't see Elik, walked on to some other work. They knew the shaman was there. Both of them knew.

Seal Talker picked up a rock, tossed it in the water.

Some reflex told her to hold quiet, to hide her thoughts the way her mother warned. She thought of the brown soul-thing Seal Talker had taken from Iluperaq's stomach, the way it came out of him and moved. If Seal Talker could do that to Iluperaq, then surely, he could do anything, anything he wanted to at all.

Seal Talker squatted down beside her. He tossed another rock.

She rolled the fish she had just finished gutting into the waiting basket, picked up the clump of roe that had separated from its sac, ate it, then wiped her mouth. She was lucky he hadn't seen her peeking inside that tent. She wouldn't want to feel his anger.

"Good-size salmon," he said.

Elik didn't answer.

Awkwardly, he picked at the side of his face, placed his hands on his knees, on the sand. "I was thinking of leaving soon," he said. "Before the weather changes."

Elik lifted the new fish by the tail; it slipped and her

knife fell. She laughed, started to pick it up, then stopped. Her sister's warning came back: don't stare at him, don't look—unless you want to share his bed. But she had looked. More than once. And now, it seemed, her sister was right. Naiya was out searching for the berries it was too early to find. She was here.

This was about payment, she told herself. That was all. He hadn't seen her peeking during his trance. No one had told him how she fainted. This was about payment: just as Naiya said. A short while with her in exchange for helping Iluperaq. Her father must be pleased with himself, making so easy a bargain.

Perhaps, though she knew he was strong, and she was more than a little afraid of him, perhaps it wouldn't be so bad.

Maybe it would turn out he was kind. Maybe she could ask him things. Little things. That would be all. She started making circles with her finger in the sand, lazy circles. Childish circles. She glanced once; he was older than her father, yet not so old as Malluar. His narrow eye was watery, not clear, but in the end—no different than another man.

He would only take a little time. And Naiya said he hadn't hurt . . . And then . . . While their legs were entwined, and his thoughts were gentle? Who knew but he would find her harmless, her questions amusing?

Finally, Seal Talker laughed at their shy playing. "The salmon sees a beautiful girl," he said. "And it thinks to itself—here is a good place to come again next year."

Elik allowed a smile.

"I like a quiet girl," he said.

She looked to the river, to the dance of water lit up by the sun.

But then, instead of leaning out and touching her, as she expected, he kept on talking. "A man's house should be filled with beauty," he said. "Not only on the outside, for all to see, but inside his house—with children's voices. . . ."

Something told her not to move. These weren't the

words Naiya told. Naiya said he had climbed one night inside her blankets, and that was all . . .

"A shaman calls and he has anyone," Seal Talker said. His voice was almost sad. "I don't want anyone. I want a wife. I want a son who is my son. Not some other man's. What I want is to be certain . . . "

Elik heard her sister's warning: *Work, and he'll think you're ready to be a wife.* She lowered her knife. *For sewing, and for children, he would want me for that, but not to teach me what he knows.*

"A man says these things," she whispered, "but a man's wife has different words. A man's wife says . . . "

Seal Talker's laughter cut her protest. "My old Ema would only be glad for a pair of younger hands to share her work."

Elik told herself to breathe, to swallow. Her father watched from higher on the riverbank. Chevak was right about this, if nothing else: there was no way she could refuse. Try, and a shaman such as he would take where he wanted, send his magic where he chose.

With her gaze lowered, Elik reached slowly across. She touched his hand. She felt his breathing change. She started to lean back, making it easier, wanting him to hurry. To take her, then go away. *Maybe he won't like me,* she prayed. *Maybe he'll finish and then go away.*

She thought of her father's anger that day she'd boasted she would never marry. And Naiya's fear that Chevak could make it true. She remembered Ema in the *qasgi* last winter, laughing that her husband was still a man beneath the covers.

She lay back on the wet gravel, squeezed her eyes against the watchful sky. His hands moved up, inside her parka, scratchy on her skin. She tightened against the cold. He squeezed her breasts together, his thumbs pressed her nipples. She felt her amulet bag slide to her armpit and nearly panicked: her loon, she didn't want him to find the loon. She held her breath, frozen. She thought of the face of the stranger who had carved it. Eyes like crescent moons. His long chin, kind and sad at the same time. She pushed the thought away, hiding it.

Seal Talker hands moved from her breasts to her bulky trousers. She opened her eyes. He lowered himself closer, pressed his face against her cheek. All she could see was the black and grey of his hair; all she could smell was the fish smell on his skin, his sweat. He tugged her trousers off, pushed them aside. He straddled her, then moved his legs together, hers apart. He slipped his hands beneath her buttocks. Shifted her to a better position, then up toward him.

He was stronger than she would have guessed, and his wife was right—he knew what he was about. She bit her lip, pressed her hands to the gravel, not on him. She didn't want to touch him, didn't want to feel him anywhere she didn't have to. He moved inside her. Harder. She turned away. Squeezed shut her eyes. The rocks cut into her back, her heels, her head. Her skin prickled with cold. She didn't dare move for fear he would think he had pleased her.

In the end, it was over quickly. Breathing heavily, he pulled himself away. She opened her eyes to see the drops of sweat that had formed themselves on his forehead, the bits of sand clinging to his face.

She sat up; she could tell he expected her to say something, but what? In a house she might have cleaned herself. Here, she only pulled her trousers back, gravel, sticks, and all. She wanted him to go away. Please.

Kindly, as if he were a suitor, not wanting to frighten her, he said, "This parka, did you make it? It's very beautiful." He ran his fingers along the stitches.

An idea sprang to her mouth, sudden and sure. "My mother made it." She smiled, shook her head as if it was all so obvious. "I'm too young to do such work."

"Too young?" Seal Talker drew back, amused, but then annoyed. "How can you be too young to sew? You bled. More than once already."

But Elik had found her chance. She said, "Just this year. The first year." She added: "I can make mittens. I can make boots—"

"So can a man. But you're no man. Are you playing with me?"

"No . . . I . . . No—"

"What? Say it. You with your eyes so hungry—Say it."

"It's just that, I'm young. If you wait another year, only one more, perhaps we could consider a trial marriage. If we agree, and if there's a child . . . We would know . . . "

The shaman sat back on his haunches; for a moment he seemed to be figuring the days, the length of time till each moon passed, and then, just as suddenly as he'd grown angry, a smile settled onto his mouth. "Yes, I see." He nodded, satisfied. He brushed the sand from his hands, then rose and stood over her. "So," he said. "We will do it that way. I will start a shaman's healthy son growing inside of you. And you will learn to sew. Both at the same time." He pushed himself heavily up from the gravel. Without looking back he climbed the beach to where Chevak stood, still watching from their tents.

Bear Hand's daughter Squirrel walked ahead of Allanaq, leading him out along the flats of windblown soil and green tussocks, away from the village and toward a place where, she said, the sun warmed the ground earlier than along the beach.

Allanaq watched the way she walked: small steps, carefully taken. Then every little while, a leap and a run, childlike, as if she had forgotten she was here to be a bride.

He hadn't. Not for a moment.

He glanced ahead, wondering which place she'd pick for them to lie down together. He hoped it would be quiet and soft. A place where he could catch his hands inside her braids. He would unknot them and he would bury his face in her hair. And his hands, he would lower them to her hips. And she would move the way she moved now, legs rubbing, her buttocks climbing.

The girl was quieter than he would have liked, though Weyowin kept telling him that was a good trait in women. In her father's house she'd hardly raised her eyes, and never spoken—which wasn't because of her name.

Squirrel had been given the same name as her grandfather, a man who, Allanaq heard often enough, had owned many hunting songs. She was small, as the grandfather had been small, with straight, narrow shoulders. With hair that was pulled into tight braids that hung to cover her small, pointy breasts.

Bear Hand had given him the seat of honor when he visited, farthest from the cold. He had sat sheltered from insects and been well fed with a meal of caribou liver cut in strips and stitched inside the sac of its stomach, left to sour for a hand's count of days. Squirrel, he remembered, had sat idle as a child, while a younger sister passed a dipper full of water. Bear Hand had taken it first, emptied it, then given it to his wife to fill while Allanaq waited.

All these signs: hospitality mixed with disrespect. Allanaq wasn't sure he understood. He'd been given a guest's seat but no fur to sit on. Offered water but Bear Hand drank first. They spoke of a wolverine Bear Hand had trapped with a ball of fat pierced with antler slivers thin as needles to open in its gut. But that was all the story he shared: the wolverine's size, the beauty of its skin. Nothing of where he'd caught it, or how the trap was placed. Nothing useful a son would need to know.

Last of all, Allanaq had reached beneath his parka for the pouch he carried, the gift Nua had chosen for Meqo— the mother, not the girl. The girl's wishes would only matter later. At the beginning, others would do the talking.

It wasn't until after they'd eaten that Grey Owl motioned for Allanaq to bring out the sewing kit—a packet of soft leather with an antler closure that doubled as an awl. And inside—he watched as Squirrel's mother opened it—five of the most delicate bird bone needles he had ever made, with smooth tiny eyes and shafts as strong as any woman could hope.

Except that Meqo was careful, untying the roll, opening it. She showed nothing of her thoughts, covered the silence with her humming. She glanced to her husband and Bear Hand made a sign, so small Allanaq almost didn't catch it. But the mother nodded, and Squirrel rose, walked behind him and out of the tent, and there was nothing to do but follow.

It wasn't until they reached a level place on a knoll, part rock, part moss and curling lichen, that Squirrel turned and offered him a smile.

*She was pretty, with her half-open mouth and the three tat-
too marks on her chin.*

Not like the tattoos the Seal People's women wore not
on their chin but with heavier lines circling round their
cheeks, beside their eyes. And yet, he realized, plainness
could be pretty. Perhaps, with time—even beautiful.

"Quiet," Squirrel whispered, and she pointed to the tundra. "Eggs—and the nest is empty. Gulls. They aren't being
watched." She glanced to his face, then away. She pointed
to the higher knoll. "More eggs there. But this is enough."
She reached for his sleeve, hurried him along.

"Here, there's three, so we'll take two"—she stopped
suddenly, looked at her feet—"I forgot to ask—you do eat
eggs?"

Allanaq nodded Yes, but the question surprised him.
Did she think he was as different as that? Not to eat an
egg? And here she was, not even wearing her better
clothes, on the day she went to meet a husband? No ornaments. No pieced stitchwork. And yet, she was pretty. And
he wanted to touch her—it was true. He wanted to feel her
skin beneath his hands.

She passed him one of the large buff-colored eggs, took
the other for herself. "Come," she said, "before the gulls
return." And she started ahead.

They spoke little, but he liked the way that felt. The
way her head reached no higher than his shoulders. Maybe
Grey Owl and Nua were right, and this was the way he
should live. Mated, like wolves, like sandhill cranes with
both the mother and the father sitting on a nest. He wondered if he had a scent about his skin just then, if she
could smell the musk of his thoughts.

To live, Grey Owl kept reminding him, a man needs the
skill of a woman's hands. To travel without fear he needs
her relatives. Brothers and uncles to share what they knew
of the land.

She looked back once, laughed to see he hadn't broken
the egg. Then she led him on again until they reached a
place where an outcropping of rock blocked the wind.

Squirrel waited for him, then sat, then motioned for him to join her.

From the small pack she'd carried she pulled out an ivory comb. For a moment, he thought she would loosen her hair. He closed his eyes. He sat so close he could smell her, the scent of her skin, her hair. He breathed deeply, then felt her touch his hand. He opened his eyes but all she did was to take his egg, then, with the sharpened comb, pecked a hole in the narrow end, handed it back. She peeled the cracked part of her shell away, let the pieces fall. "Drink it," she said. "Go on." And he watched as she set her lips to the narrow end, lifted her chin, sucked, and swallowed. He watched the way her throat moved, her neck tightening and loosening. He didn't know how much longer he could wait.

"Go on," she prodded. "You eat." And he did. He reached a finger inside the shell, broke the yolk, then drank.

He wasn't sure exactly what order to do this in: he had never been with someone who could be a wife. Should he be the one to start? Or wait till she offered?

No. Something in the way she sat there, watching the spring runoff drip from a patch of shaded snow—she wasn't someone to start first.

Purposefully, he moved around in front of her. Her knees had been raised but she lowered them, letting him near. She was small, a tiny thing. She would be even smaller without her clothes on. He brought one leg over, straddled her legs. He smiled, put his hands on her shoulders, but she was looking at something. What? Something on his chest. He stopped. She giggled. "What is it?" he asked.

"Your necklace." She tugged the strip of rawhide that had caught itself, half-exposed, on the neck of his hood. She wrinkled her nose. "What is it?"

"It's a bear. But it's more than a bear, also."

"You talk so funny. You're never plain." She pulled it out to see. "It doesn't look like a bear. It looks like a whale. Why is it angry?" She started to make a face at the carving, then caught herself. Quickly, she let go, winced as it fell to his parka. "Did you carve it?"

Allanaq grew annoyed. She knew very well that the work was his. He wished she didn't seem so young, like a child with a toy. But she wasn't a child. Nua had assured him she had bled, more than three times now. More than enough.

Her expression changed again. She took in everything about him: the shape of his eyes, the straight bridge of his nose. Her glance stole unashamedly over him, till finally, she asked, "Who gave birth to you?"

"What?"

She said it again, "Who was your father? Who gave birth to you?"

Allanaq shook his head, almost sadly. "Quiet," he said. He put his hand over her mouth. "You speak too much."

Then he rose and moved toward her. This time he didn't wait. He leaned her to the ground. It was soft, he noticed, shaded from the watchful sky. The kind of place young people came, to do their rutting above the sea.

He moved his hands up under her parka, higher, till he felt her breasts, one beneath each hand. Like hills. Like two rocky promontories on a moss-covered hill.

He felt her stiffen, then draw a breath.

He shifted his legs. The girl made no sign of resistance, but neither did she help. He slid his hands beneath her buttocks; she let him, but that was all. She turned her face to the side. Closed her eyes. She lifted a foot. He pulled off her boots. He pulled off her trousers.

She wore no short women's apron but a light, narrow belt with curing amulets and something for fertility.

He started to lift her parka but she stopped him. "It's cold," she said. He buried his face in the fur of her ruff and stroked the soft skin of her thighs, then higher, drawn to the warmth between her legs.

He raised himself partway. She lay still beneath him, eyes closed, face turned away. Impassive, with no sign he could read, none of interest, not rebellion.

What did he know of women? he asked himself. Their

glances? Their little sounds? Not a good deal, but then—it didn't matter. He was ready. He took off his leggings, his clothes, all of them. He wanted to feel the wind touching his back. He didn't care now what she'd said about the cold. He worked her parka higher till her breasts were showing, then he lowered himself till he could feel her nipples against his chest. Someday there would be milk inside her. And someday, if the milk she gave went into the mouths of children who were his, then he would drink that milk also. It was something he had always wanted to do, drink the same milk that fed a child who was his. He would drink from her, every place that was warm and wet. And she would open for him. Not the way she was doing now.

He glanced to her face again. Still nothing. No matter where he went with his hand. Nothing. Except this time, somehow, he knew it was what her father had told her to do. Nothing. He had known it all along.

Abruptly he pulled away. He grabbed her shoulder, then her hips. She opened her mouth in surprise, but he was the one this time with nothing to say. Without a laugh or a sigh one way or another, she let him roll her over to her hands and knees, lifted her hips backward toward him. Her shoulders and face she kept toward the ground.

He pushed up against her, laid his chest on her back, his hands on the ground beyond her shoulders. He leaned closer. Harder. Again. But all he could think as he rocked himself back and forth and listened for the sounds she never made was that he didn't want it to be her he had to marry. *Please—* He squeezed his eyes closed. *This girl—let it not be her.*

Grey Owl stood on the graveled beach below the houses while Allanaq watched to see which way the skies were moving and how fast.

"Maybe there'll be a storm," Grey Owl said, and he squinted to the horizon above the blue-green water, searched for a line of changing clouds against the haze to prove how the weather could change at any moment, in any way. "Fish River is closer than the Bent Point shore." He gestured inland to show exactly where. "If there's heavy water, you can find it by the willows, and there's a bluff that comes down where people corral rabbits, then pick them up—it's easy hunting."

Allanaq didn't turn to see. It had only been two days since Bear Hand's daughter trailed behind him down the hill, but two days had been more than enough to decide.

"There is that other Allanaq in Fish River—" Grey Owl spoke quickly, hopefully. "Both of you named for the same relative. You'd be welcome there. It wouldn't be so far to come back."

Allanaq turned to watch Nua making her way toward them, slowing her pace to match Olanna's. Behind them, Bear Hand and several other men gathered next to a row of upturned kayaks. They craned their necks, trying to hear above the sea breeze, pretending work.

"Trade with whom?" Nua asked, and she set down a large grass basket she had brought.

Grey Owl quieted, looked fondly, almost sadly, to his wife. "Who can tell me what food a woman eats to make her ears so sharp?"

"The same food you eat." Nua poked Grey Owl's stomach. "The same water. But a woman learns to listen through the walls. While you, my husband, listen only to yourself. . . ."

Allanaq relaxed his shoulders. It was good, the way Grey Owl and Nua lived together. Agreeably. With joking in the morning and a muffled laughter rising from their bed at night. He had no wish to bring them grief. He only meant to learn the shape of the land from here on the Long Coast as far as the Bent Point village.

It was true he had made the trip before, but that had been overland, along the winter trail, and not yet alone—Grey Owl hadn't thought it was safe for him to go alone.

It wasn't safe for him not to go, he had replied. Did a man not need to know—for himself, not from stories only—where fresh water could be found? Where there were places that driftwood collected, places where the caribou liked to cross?

But Allanaq had not named his other thought, the one about the girl named Elik. Grey Owl's sister's daughter. The one who danced.

He hadn't named her. And the reason was the same as the reason that he'd noticed her in the first place. The way she danced with a look in her eyes as if she was watching into two worlds at once, the invisible behind the visible. As if she were a shaman. The thought had repelled him, then attracted him. Followed him, even to his dreams.

He glanced to Olanna, then away, remembering how his own shaman-father had been able to hear other men's thoughts. He took a step farther.

If the girl was a shaman, he would go away quickly, without speaking to her. If she was an ordinary girl, he would speak. But he had to know first, without risking trouble.

"If someone in Fish River already shares my name," he said to Grey Owl, "then I already have a hunting partner there. So isn't it better to visit in the Bent Point village, and find someone new? You named a cousin—Iluperaq?"

"My sister's son. He's a good hunter. He would be *iluraq,* your cross-cousin."

Nua squatted beside her basket. "You'll want these," she said, countering Grey Owl's warnings. "The comb you carved for me."

"After you taught me how—but that was yours."

"And you'll make another. But if you mean to visit, then you cannot go empty-handed. And perhaps"—she waited, made sure Grey Owl listened—"perhaps it will turn out that people want to trade. Whether they know you or not. The more you have, the more people want to see. The safer you'll be. Take this: this box, this necklace. These needles."

"You packed more?" Olanna asked. Allanaq nodded. "Show me."

Allanaq hesitated. He would have preferred to refuse, but the truth was, he hadn't enough reason. Though he avoided the shaman, Olanna had never spoken harshly to him, never given him cause to fear. He had thought about this, trying to understand. The one reason he had figured was that Olanna and Grey Owl were related through Nua. There was no other reason Olanna should offer kindness.

Allanaq crossed to where his small umiak waited at the water's edge, tilting with the incoming tide. He sorted through his gear, brought out the grass basket he'd used to pack most of his tools and carvings.

"Have you traded before?" Olanna asked.

"Not alone," he said. Nua spilled the contents of Allanaq's bag out beside her own, sorting them. End blades, side blades, drag handles, scrapers of different sizes. Some like the inset side blades, in his Seal People style. Some polished, the way he had learned here.

"There are things you need to know," she said. "A container full of seal oil is worth maybe five caribou skins, depending on whether it's spring or fall when they're taken, or the skin of one wolf. Or two pokes for the pelt of a wolverine. And these blades"—she pushed a few of the better worked blades to one side—"may be traded for skins, or for straight-grained wood, or ivory."

"Be careful who you trade with," Grey Owl said. "Try to learn first who a man's relatives are."

Allanaq looked behind him. Bear Hand, Kahkik, and now their youngest brother, Drummer, were carrying one of their kayaks toward the beach.

Olanna reached out, touched the sleeve of Allanaq's gut parka. Thankfully, Allanaq turned back around. Olanna moved his hand lightly to Allanaq's chin, to the lip plugs he wore now, as often as any man. "You are a man here," he said. "Where anyone can see."

Olanna lowered his hand, moved it to between Allanaq's legs. "And here also." He pushed in the layers hiding the crotch below Allanaq's parka.

Allanaq started to protest, then just as quickly held still, listened.

"Bear Hand sent his daughter to look here, where he himself would not. He wanted her to tell him if there was a man down there. She did. And there is. But what he still hasn't decided is whether you are a man here." He tapped Allanaq's chest. "Till then, make sure you give him no chance to doubt."

Olanna lifted his face to the salt air. "This is a good time for your son to journey," he said to Grey Owl. "Now, while all is well. While we have food, and no one argues or questions why he goes.

"I have something for you." He turned back to Allanaq. "Before you forget." And he pulled out two flat wooden plagues he had carried, charms that brought luck and doubled as harpoon guides. "Your boat must have eyes," Olanna said, "Male and Female. This one smiles"—he held up the male—"this one frowns. Both are needed for a path, to bring you home."

The ribbed floor of the umiak was covered over with harpoon heads, foreshafts and extra shafts, lengths of seal hide line wound around mounting guards. Loaded in the stern were slabs of seal meat stitched into bundles of their own fat and skin, bladders of fresh water to drink along the way, and his baskets, repacked, and stored along the sides.

Grey Owl steadied the boat as Allanaq climbed in. "If you do trade," he said, "remember to keep your face like a mask, like a carving, with one thought hiding inside another."

Allanaq anchored his paddle against the bottom, relieved to hear Grey Owl's encouragement. "This Seal Talker," Allanaq asked. "What kind of man is he?"

"That depends," Olanna answered, "on which kind of man he decides you are."

"When you reach the Bent Point place," Grey Owl called, "look first for my younger brother, Nagi. When his son is grown, you'll be *ataata*, male children of two brothers. For now, Gull's son, Iluperaq, is closest to your own age."

Allanaq leaned his weight against the paddle, pushing off. The keeled bottom scraped, then lifted with the incoming wave, scraped again then pulled free. The umiak rose into the waves. While there was still time, he cupped his hands, called out, "There was a daughter, also?"

"Two. Naiya and Elik."

Nua lifted her hands to her mouth. "Look for Naiya—her work is as good as her mother's."

Allanaq had the bow turned to the open sea now. He looked back over his shoulder. "Not the other one?" he called.

"Also good, but with a younger girl's hand—"

"Both in the same house?" Allanaq veered east and Nua started walking, following as the boat turned east, following the shore. "Unless they've married," she called. If she said more, he didn't hear. The wind stole her voice. Allanaq steered into the line of incoming swells.

Allanaq dipped the paddle into the water on one side, lifted and circled tightly, then again on the other.

He'd started out later in the day than he wanted, but it didn't matter now. It felt good to be free of the land. Moving. To be someplace where he didn't need to guard each word that fell from his mouth, or worry whether someone took offense, or thought him boastful because of his carving, or foolish, too handy with a harpoon, too clumsy with a net.

He was here, in an umiak of his own making and he felt as near to being content as he had in all the time since Grey Owl had found him.

Content? He wasn't sure the word fit. But at least he was doing something. And he would still meet Grey Owl and Nua at fish camp, later; they would manage fine till then. What he couldn't bear was another day watching the younger girls stare as he passed—even with labrets in his chin and his hair cut short. The way the young boys followed behind him, watching when he pissed.

Differences. They kept coming back, comparisons. Like the ice. He was sure that the ice at home would have been in still, perhaps puddling, but certainly not ice-free the way it was here. At least, he didn't think so.

Or the boat he had built over the winter. Here they built kayaks with the bows bent upward, split and turned like a single eye to peer above the waves. The prows on his Seal People's kayaks were single, straighter, as was the umiak, the entire boat longer and more narrow.

Yet both floated. Both held a man. Both were built by bending the steamed wood to a curve. Hammering pegs against a form, to hold the shape, lashing the framework with rawhide cords. In both places they gathered driftwood for the boat. Though here, gathering driftwood had seemed a little easier, a little quicker.

In both places they hung amulets and charms. In both places the seals still came. Yet upturned prow or not, if any man but Grey Owl had found him, he would be dead now. He knew that. He'd been more than lucky; he'd been guided by a spirit. And not just him, but Grey Owl also, because both their lives had been saved.

The swells had died down and the tide long since turned.

Allanaq drew his paddle in and tucked it alongside the ribs. Grey Owl had given him one last gift: a flat, greyed length of driftwood. Allanaq had almost forgotten: he pulled it from under his baskets, looked it over while the boat moved with the current.

"A man might carve a map," Grey Owl had said, and he'd pointed along the beach, showing where the land tucked in and there was a promontory and then a smaller bay. "You carve the wood to remember the shape. This way"—he had showed with his hand—"and this."

The soft, water-aged log was as long as from his elbow to the end of his hand, but wider and warped as Allanaq sighted down the length. He flipped it over, placed a knot so it matched the point where the Long Coast turned.

He set the board down, took up his paddle again. He turned his attention closer to the land as it floated by, familiar near the Long Shore coast, less so as the day wore on. He stayed close in toward shore, noting where the distant foothills rose to a haze of snow-crusted mountains.

Which beaches were gravel, which were sand. Where there were rocks. Lagoons or bays. Strips of driftwood floated in from foreign lands. Grassy marshes and shrub birch.

There was no night, and so he paddled as long as he could, and then more. With every stroke, rivulets of water ran from the blade to his hands, from his elbow to a puddle in the lap of his sealgut parka.

He paddled till he found a landing with fresh water trickling from between cracked rocks. The tide was in and he only needed to drag the boat a short haul up the beach. He gathered rocks to set it off the ground, turned it over to dry, to check the seams. He ate while he worked, tearing off strands of dry meat while he combed the beach for tinder, then leveled a shelter, using the boat to break the wind.

When he'd hung his leggings to dry and tucked his feet into his sleeping furs, he took the driftwood out again. He left a straight part for the Long Coast, then used his finger to mark off so much wood for so much distance. He began to carve.

He peered over the top of his boat to see the horizon: a black line of ice-free water. How far from his Seal People's place had he really come? He didn't know, except that he remembered the endless length of sandy beach, lagoons, and the few stands of higher ground he'd passed before the fog closed in. He knew by now that he was farther from his Seal People than he had first dared to think. Yet not so far that he wouldn't return someday. Return, and kill Red Fox for what he had done.

Allanaq opened his eyes. He had fallen asleep with a picture of Red Fox in his thoughts. When he woke, the face in front of him was a girl's. Elik. He said her name out loud. In his dream, they were lying together in his father's house in his Seal People's village. There had been the dry smoke of a hearthfire and the smell of her hair in his nostrils. The way she lifted as he put his mouth to her breast, softly, like the sea.

What would he say when he reached her village? Would

he ask if she were a shaman? Would he talk about Red Fox? Or his father? And what about Olanna? He was a shaman. Unless maybe, the Real People's shamans were not so jealous or angry as the shamans among his people. But then what about Seal Talker? No one named that man with any kindness. Troubled, Allanaq closed his eyes.

A man couldn't know these things alone. It wasn't possible to know, and it wasn't possible to decide. He closed his eyes, rolled over, and, with his hand, finished what the dream had begun.

All through the second morning there was a steady wind, cool and singing. The rain held back till midday, then lightly fell, a pattering of fresh water falling to salt.

The paddling and the water's mirrored glare, the ringing wind in his ears—they lulled him into a droning calm. Earlier, he had turned the boat farther out to sea, at first to get a wider view for the map but then he'd kept paddling, farther, on a whim. Without land, the wind became his primary navigation aid. And for all he could tell, there was little sign of a weather change. Still, he began to wish he hadn't turned so far from the coast. The green-brown swells he stared into were like music—constant, drumming.

His eyes were closing, the boat nearly rocking him to sleep until, out of nowhere, a larger swell followed on another. It rose, lifted him, brought him awake. The umiak came down, not with a slap but with a flexing that moved through every rib in its frame, through the length of his legs.

It wasn't the wind—a calm followed just as suddenly as the waves had risen. His hands tightened on the paddle. His boat waited between swells. He heard something. What? A sound. Not birds and not waves breaking. Not wind. He rested his paddle on the prow, listened.

Allanaq was not the kind of man to seek out visions, but he also knew there were times when visions came—peering through a fog, from behind the giant ridges of pressure ice, or sometimes when a man sat too long in a boat, watching the endless sea.

What he saw was not a vision.

There!

A spume of spray, water shooting, upward and then . . . It blew again.

A bowhead whale! Agviq to his Seal People, Arveq in the Real People's tongue—except words didn't matter. Names couldn't hold the power of who this was. A bowhead! Alive and huge, so huge he wondered how it was possible for people and whale to share the same air, to live in the world together.

Foolish or not, he climbed to the prow, leaned out to watch the spray erupting from its blowhole, the dark curve of its back, the flip of its tail as it dived, down then up again, so clear he could nearly predict it.

He had seen the long white belugas near the point beyond the Long Coast shore. And the smaller shining black killer whales, one then another, side by side or in a line. He and Grey Owl had steadied their kayaks, watching as they dipped past. Beautiful and serene. But they were not Agviq.

Grey Owl spoke about how the whales allowed Real People to find them sometimes, how it was most often in the open seas, when the ice went out. They seldom came so close toward the Long Coast shores.

Here, then, was one thing they shared: neither Seal People nor Real People hunted the bowhead, not in the way they hunted walrus, or a sea lion, a seal.

Not that they wouldn't harvest the whale's meat if they came upon one beached, or already dead. They would. They did. They used everything: the bones for house poles, the oil, the rows of malleable baleen for baskets, bowls, the baleen's fringe for fishing gear and ties. And the meat, the sweet, thick *muktuk* of its skin and fat. But to hunt them— with amulets and magic songs and proper actions, the way they hunted other sea mammals—by chance yes, but not often.

Even if they could harpoon them from their boats, even if his walrus points were large enough, bit deep enough, even if they twisted beneath the layer of blubber and held.

Even then a whale so large would merely suck the boat in to drown. It would upend them, smash them with a flipper, drag them and their lines and their lives down into the sea. A single flip of its tail and boat and men were dead.

And even if the boat didn't flip and the hunters didn't drown—what use if their points aimed true and held? No man he knew had ever succeeded in tracking a wounded whale out in the open sea. Or dragged it in to shore on a rawhide, sealskin line. Once, twice in a lifetime, a man heard such a story. But that was all.

Here then was his question: how could a man, a hunter, shape a weapon beautiful enough, strong and respectful enough, to entice the whale to give itself to him willingly? Not a bloated carcass chanced upon a shore; not a single beached whale, out of water. That wasn't what he meant. But to have a magic so powerful that the whale would come.

The whale surfaced, nearer this time. Startling, how close. The waves rose, rocked the boat. Allanaq grabbed for the gunwale. He took up his paddle, braced against the wave to hold his boat. Agviq—it was beautiful: white on the chin, dark, dark black on the height of its sleek, long back. It submerged. This time it didn't rise.

Finally, he slipped back to his seat, started to backpaddle, away to safety. He angled his paddle out from the stern, drew in toward the hull, then rolled it to change direction.

It could not have been a new thought, the possibility of taking a whale so large. But it was new for Allanaq. The idea that a man could shape a weapon beautiful enough to entice the whale to come to the harpoon and die.

Or—if not the weapon alone, then the weapon and a song. A magical hunting song so strong that the whale could hear the thoughts inside a man's heart—and not just the man but his wife, calling from the shore at home— thoughts of reverence, a song of beauty.

Allanaq moved to a better position in the stern for steering. He rotated the paddle underwater, pulled out, circled, and dipped in again.

The next time he thought to look, he was closer to shore than he had realized. He must have drifted. Certainly he'd lost track of the day. The sun was at his back now. One more night, depending on the wind, and he would reach the Bent Point place.

With a thought, he freed the driftwood map from where he'd stored it, set it near his legs. With a small side blade leveraged against his thumb, he notched a place where he'd seen rocks that came down to shore. Another point with three old houses that looked dead, abandoned. And a mound beside the mouth of a creek. And a sandspit, then another place with many willows. Another creek.

He was paying more attention to the map than he was to the shoreline or the white lick of smoke rising on the pebbled beach, the four people hastily standing, moving, peering at his boat.

With a sour feeling in his stomach, Allanaq scanned the camp: three men, one woman. One of the men was already walking to meet his boat—something neither his Seal People or the Real People would have done. Still, the woman was a good sign; perhaps they didn't mean to fight. No tent. A simple lean-to. A single, narrow, open boat.

Allanaq hid his fear behind a smile, signed to show he held no spear. *How fast till they could right their boat? Three men paddling after one? A harpoon wound was not always the fastest way to die. . . .* He climbed out of his boat.

*K'ozokkaak'at.* The man pointed toward a small creek coming in from upland, behind them.

Allanaq didn't understand. Westward he pointed. *"The Long Coast."* He touched his chest. *"Real People,"* he said.

"Tooth People," the man said, this time using a proper word as he pointed to Allanaq's labrets, then to his chest.

Allanaq relaxed. At least an attempt had been made to speak. He followed the few steps to their fire. The man who had met him was older than the others; he saw that at once. Grey Owl's age, a little younger. He motioned Allanaq to sit at the log where they'd made camp. The man spoke quickly, with low, rolling sounds that came from the back of his throat. He waved his arms and made so many motions, Allanaq wondered how he expected anyone to understand.

He stole a better look at the woman as she offered an empty bowl. She was older than he had thought at first, shrunken, with most of her teeth gone. A single straight tattoo divided her face from the forehead to her chin, with four more lines to each cheek, like a river. And no labrets, and on the men also—tattoos and no labrets.

The tunic she wore over leggings was made partly of caribou and partly of another skin, something with no hair—he didn't know what. The hem was shaped to a point in the front with a red-painted line up the center as if Raven had walked there. The seam line above her heart hung with fringes, and above the fringes the remains of a few cracked porcupine quills still showed—winter clothing, too heavy and no use in summer rains.

He scanned the camp for weapons: there were shafts of some kind—spears or harpoons—leaning against the boat. Three in a row. And if he saw three, then somewhere there could be more.

The woman returned with food, a stew of meat with something green and a few thin bird bones floating on the surface. She ladled out a portion, glancing all the while at the way his gutskin parka was put together, the welting in between the whitish horizontal strips.

He didn't know what the meat was, but he couldn't turn it down without insulting them. He found the smallest chunk, picked it out with his fingers and chewed. *Good meat,* he signaled, trying to be polite. *Good.*

The older man nodded his approval.

*What did they want? Not food—they didn't look hungry.* He saw no fishing nets, but a long meshlike basket that could have been a fish trap. *Perhaps they wanted to trade?* He hoped that was all. Certainly it was likeliest. Warring parties left their women at home. They came in the night. They killed, then quickly left.

They could be Forest People—he'd heard of small bands coming with their beaver, marten, and wolverine furs asking to trade for seal, oil, the kinds of skins they could only get near the coast. Grey Owl had told him of places inland where trees grew taller than a man. Not one, but many. Places where the driftwood that lined the Real People's shores were still alive.

These people were more different from Grey Owl's people than he had been, even from the start.

The woman spooned out food into the men's bowls. Definitely, she was the mother; the two boys were sons. Younger than he was: a hot-blooded age. An age when boys counted themselves men if they killed first, thought later.

The one on his left eyed Allanaq's meat knife. Carefully, he opened his hand so the antler handle showed; he held it out. He wanted no fighting. Not these three alone against one.

The boy glanced to the father for permission, then took it. The second boy, the younger one, leaned closer. They would have been tall for Long Coast People. And their hands, the fingers on the one who'd taken his knife—they were longer and thinner than those of most men he knew. He didn't like the way the boy's hands felt as they touched, too much like claws. Wolf's or a bear's.

The father said something to the woman. Allanaq didn't understand. He watched; the father added a hand sign. The woman rose, then came back a moment later with a birchbark basket, larger than the kind he was used to seeing. She set it down on a trampled thatch of beach grass.

The father pointed with his chin. *Look through it. Go on.*

Inside the brown bark of the basket, there were stone blanks: cherts and chalcedony—blades of every color and size. Pyrites for starting fires. One fist-sized egg of obsidian, unused. Grey on the outside, it would be black within. He let out a breath, realized how tense he'd been. *They wanted to trade. That was all.*

Allanaq made a sign. From his umiak, he pulled out one

of his baskets. It wouldn't be a bad thing for him to practice trading before he reached the Bent Point village. Who knows but he'd find something rare, something an unmarried girl would like?

The woman stepped behind the man's shoulder as he laid out more: seal-faced hat ornaments, boot creasers, lice crushers, wing-shaped balances for harpoon ends, most decorated with circles within circles, lines within lines.

The next time Allanaq looked, one of the boys was standing over his umiak. Fingering his harpoon foreshaft, the embedded point.

Allanaq stiffened, but the boy set it down. He picked up the driftwood map next, looked at it curiously one moment, then as if he suddenly realized what it was, flipped it over the right way. He brought it back, said something to the father. The man turned with it till his shoulder matched the line of coast, east to west.

And now the younger boy started talking, quickly and too loudly. The father hushed him, set the driftwood down, then beckoned Allanaq beside him. *Trade,* he said, this time using the Real People's word. He said it slowly, precisely, so Allanaq would understand. Allanaq shook his head, *No. Not that.*

The man pulled over his basket. One by one he lined up the stone blanks. Allanaq tried to hide his surprise—the man was a better trader than he'd realized—he had followed Allanaq's eye, marked the ones he wanted most. The blue chert, the grey flint, the obsidian.

"It isn't finished, the map."

Either the man didn't understand, or he didn't care. He pulled over the driftwood. He barked an order and one of the boys sidled against Allanaq's shoulder, close enough there was no mistaking the threat of his blades: one showing in his boot top, another at his belt.

The woman brought a second basket. There was a chinking sound of ivory against stone. The father took it, dumped the full contents to the ground. With a sweep of his hand, he fanned them out for Allanaq to see.

Arrowheads. Light darts for small seals and repeating heads for lances. Blades for inset handles and knives. Stone scrapers and awls. Spiked bone hooks for tomcod, and ground stone hooks with gull tendons for sculpin. Barbed and toggling harpoon heads made for ice-thick waters. And there, peering out from beneath a scatter of other blades, was a wooden plaque with a whale carved on it.

The plaque was no bigger than his open hand, but the painting on it—the painting filled the wood—a bowhead, as beautiful and real as the one he had just seen. A charm so powerful, surely it might entice a whale to give itself to the man who held it?

Allanaq wanted it. He nudged one of his larger points toward the man. "For walrus?" he held his fingers like tusks to his chin. "You hunt walrus?"

The man stared blankly a moment, then gave a single, loud laugh. *Me?* he pointed, then to the sea, a diving motion with his hands. *No,* he shook his head.

"For whale?"

"Yes! For whale. Bowhead whale."

"Where did you get this?"

The father nudged the older boy. He squatted down and, with Allanaq's knife, scratched a few lines in the dirt. Allanaq winced as the blade struck a stone—it would chip, or dull, but he held quiet and leaned closer to follow. The younger boy excitedly pointed up the valley, to the creek, a fork, a watershed where two rivers joined.

"Here?" Allanaq tapped the ground. "You traded this here."

The boy drew more: a series of drainages, lakes, a pass between two hills. The father interpreted: "*Homin Zagheelton Dinh,*" he said, "The Place With Many Lakes. *K'its'a Hughnotohoonee'onh Dinh,* The Place Where the River Changes Course. *Dotson' Da'oyh Dinh,* the Place Where Raven Puts Up a Nest."

"Someone else made this, and traded with you?"

"Trade, yes."

Allanaq asked again, "You made, or traded?"

"Trade." The man pointed to the map, pushed the whale plaque forward.

Allanaq nodded. It didn't matter where the whale came from. It came from somewhere. Somewhere it had been traded. Somewhere else, carved. Somewhere, a man honored the whales so much, he had made these, for the great whale to see.

For this, Allanaq signaled, he would trade. The map didn't matter. He had memorized it, not only the shape of the land but the stories attached to it. He could make another if he needed. If someone else wanted. For this he would trade.

Allanaq had planned on bringing the umiak in slowly, drying then greasing its water-soaked hides while he waited to be seen, recognized, and welcomed to the Bent Point village.

He had hoped it would be Grey Owl's younger brother, Nagi, who saw him from the shore; they'd met before. He was an easygoing man; he would be welcome. Or his sister Gull. Her daughter he would see later, outside their summerhouse, bending over her work or gathering driftwood. That was the way he pictured her.

He had paddled, and he had thought about the way he would greet her brother. He remembered him as a calm man, near his own age, keen-eyed. The kind of man you could depend on while hunting. Iluperaq, that was his name. Iluperaq would admire his work—not like Bear Hand and his relatives, who found shadows inside every carving they hadn't worked with their own hands.

He and Iluperaq would trade stories and eat together. And sometime, while they sat, Elik would come with food. He'd take the bowl and maybe his hand would linger, and maybe hers would brush against his. She'd leave and then, afterward, as if he wasn't interested, he would ask about her. He would ask the brother first, before the father. Grey Owl seldom mentioned the father.

It didn't happen that way—any of it.

He had judged the season wrongly and come too late. On the Long Coast, the people were only now beginning their seasonal move to fish camp. Here, where the rivers dreamed of water the color of a salmon's back, the village was already deserted. An old man's camp, an old woman's fire, no more than a few people remained. The shaman Seal Talker and Ema, his old wife. And a nephew, a large, quiet man whose wife had just died near Fish River. And Malluar, whom he'd heard about during the runner's feast, but never spoken with. And a young boy who had been lent to Ema to help fetch water. And that was all.

It was Ema, the shaman's wife, who saw him first. The fire she'd built outside her tent was smoking, waterlogged from the sea, and she'd gone to search for drier wood above the tide. With her arms full of sun-bleached wood she'd started back, then caught the straight line of his boat approaching from the west.

But then, instead of going for the men as he had thought, she waved him in and called, and stood there waiting. A brave woman, not what he would have expected from someone who couldn't possibly run fast, in case he'd been an enemy. Perhaps because she was the shaman's wife? Or were all the Bent Point women so forward?

It was only a little while later, under a sky that had turned to constant rain. Allanaq waited by his boat until the boy was sent to bring him. For himself, he was glad it was the boy. It gave him time to put away his disappointment, to pack his trade goods in the open, without worrying who saw. The whale plaque he'd just traded for was already lashed to the bow plate of the boat. That was his. He took only one basket. After all—how much could two men and one woman need? The rest he left behind.

The boy was young enough to take his hand without fear. He seemed glad to have a guest, someone to chatter at. The village was too quiet, he said. And he was tired of helping Whale Fin with his heavy nets, carrying water for the shaman. Yes, he knew Iluperaq. Iluperaq was married to his sister. Her name was Kimik. They were in fish camp together. Iluperaq had caught five times a hundred seals and caribou and given all the skins to his sister. Perhaps next year he would be big enough and Iluperaq would take him hunting, too.

Ema unrolled a caribou skin on the floor of the summer tent, motioned for Allanaq to sit. Seal Talker already sat to one side, Whale Fin, the nephew, on the other.

Opposite his seat, the tent flap was tied open, enough to keep out rain but not the light. Seal Talker's summerhouse and all his belongings were there to see. And what Allanaq saw were riches, more than Grey Owl possessed, more than Olanna. And if behind what he saw here there was also a *qasgi* and a winterhouse and caches, then perhaps this Seal Talker kept even more than his own father had acquired.

Ema ladled out food with a spoon made of musk-ox horn that couldn't have been easy to find, or trade for. There was a separate wooden bowl for each of them. He dragged out a chunk of meat, glanced up. Seal Talker looked like any older man: his teeth were worn flat, the skin bagged heavily under his eyes. His face drooped lower on one side than the other. But he smiled and nodded, so often that Allanaq couldn't guess what his real thoughts were, behind the bantering words.

Allanaq hoped they didn't see the disappointment that sat like a stone on his shoulders.

It was dangerous for a shaman to be richer than other men. Hadn't Red Fox taught him that lesson? Stingy men had less because they were lazy. The young because they were not yet wise. And the best hunters—they had less because they shared.

Seal Talker began their trading with small talk. "So. Olanna has gone to fish camp this year?"

"Not yet, though they were watching for the weather to change."

"You left us in a hurry the last time you were here also, after the runner's feast?"

Was that a complaint? Or a question—Allanaq couldn't decide. His thoughts narrowed to the loon carving he'd left behind. Who had found it, he wondered? Seal Talker?

Allanaq hadn't been gone even half a day when he realized that had been the wrong thing to do, leaving the loon behind. He had felt foolish and too shy. At least he'd carved no ownership marks on the surface.

Allanaq spread his carvings on the clean skin. There was a knot in his stomach in place of the calm he had hoped to feel. The nephew, Whale Fin, looked at the blades without touching.

He seemed fair and honest, not the kind of man who was too full of himself. Allanaq turned over one of his boxes, so the painting he'd done on the lid with a powder of ground hematite would show.

He felt Seal Talker's eyes on him whenever he looked away. How much did the shaman know about him, he wondered. Would he trust him, for Grey Owl's sake? Allanaq wished he remembered which of the Long Coast People Seal Talker was related to.

The sounds of geese calling filled the tent. Ema peered outside. With his wide, strong hands, Whale Fin picked up a blade. It was a long blade for a lance, one of the finest Allanaq had made from Grey Owl's striated quartz. He'd worked it in the Seal People's style, with both edges flaked into rows like waves covering the face. Allanaq tried not to look as if he cared. Whale Fin passed it to Seal Talker. The shaman gave it hardly a glance, passed it back.

"This stays sharp?" Whale Fin asked.

Allanaq nodded. The man had wide cheeks and a flat nose. Heavily muscled shoulders. Nothing like the longer, narrower lines of Seal Talker's face. Ema had said he was a nephew, but if the blood was close, it didn't show. What did show was his interest in the blade.

If he were more certain of himself as a trader, he would know whether it was proper to say more. He would have told Whale Fin to take the blade, that he wouldn't be disappointed.

But he didn't say that. Instead, almost in anger, he opened the lid on the small box he had just turned over. No one had touched it, so he would. He was tired suddenly, sick to his stomach and tired of hiding who he was.

Out from the wooden box tumbled an ivory charm, a walrus spirit made of ivory, and very fine. He could see it caught the shaman's eye, no matter how he tried to hide it. The rear flippers leaned forward to the body, the foreflippers that he had worked so long to polish also pointed forward, as if to hold a fish. There were eye sockets inlaid with black stones, and all over the surface were the lines that showed its skeleton, with spine and ribs and joints where the soul passed in and out.

There was a long silence. The shaman stared at the walrus but he refused to touch it. If anything, Seal Talker pulled his hand back, locked it on his thigh.

Allanaq remembered—again, the lesson Grey Owl and Olanna had tried to teach—that what was beautiful and right to Allanaq could be strange and dangerous to another man. He didn't care anymore. He was tired of worrying.

Seal Talker leaned heavily back. He yawned, acted tired. He complained a little of his age. He waited till Ema stepped outside, then said, "I regret I have no woman to offer you—my wife is old, too used to having her own way. She'd cook me bitter food if I spoke of offering her in hospitality—"

Allanaq felt his anger begin to fade. He had thought Seal Talker would say something worse. The shaman looked to Whale Fin, then gave a laugh, as if they shared some private joke.

"We could have made you comfortable, but you see," he spread his arms, showing the deserted summer village, "most of us have already gone for the season. I myself just returned from a visit to one of the fish camps. The river where Chevak's family set their nets. You know him, of course?"

Allanaq's throat tightened. "His wife is the sister of my father."

Seal Talker laughed, then poked Whale Fin in the chest. "This one has been dreaming about the daughter."

Allanaq could not have spoken if he tried.

"There are two. You remember?" Seal Talker asked. "They would be your cousins."

Allanaq shrugged, picked up a blade, set it down. His hand was shaking.

"Whale Fin took a liking to one; I tried her for him. She was lively and eager." Seal Talker's eyes danced with his joking and Whale Fin showed no offense.

"Did I tell you Whale Fin is a nephew? I had a son, you see—but he wanted a wife—" Seal Talker opened his hand, closed it. He looked as if he were going to say something, but forgot, or decided against it. "She had sharp teeth," he said instead. "And she made so many sounds in my ears, I told this nephew he could have her."

Whale Fin smiled.

"And I would take the other."

"The other?" Allanaq's voice sounded like wind in an empty shell.

"The other sister," Seal Talker said, and he made a different motion with his hands, as if pulling her rump to his lap. A motion no one could mistake. "She was like salt, that girl, like the sea."

"You are a shaman," Allanaq murmured.

Seal Talker didn't hear. "What?" he asked.

"The father," Allanaq said, covering his words with a cough. "Of course, he offered you one of his daughters. In payment for something you did?"

Seal Talker nodded. "We talked, yes. The brother had taken ill. The father sent a message that I was wanted, to work over the boy. The sister Whale Fin wants was sent to bring me—it was no small journey. And the father . . ." Seal Talker lifted his hands as if to apologize for all his wealth. "Chevak isn't the best hunter. It's no secret. What else could a poor father offer that I would want?"

Allanaq gritted his teeth. He didn't answer.

He stayed but one night through. He made his bed in the lee of his umiak, out of the wind, tucked in away from the endless light. He listened to the sound of the water, birds, the insects, the hundred sounds along the shore. He didn't sleep.

In the morning, he relieved himself in the ocean, then climbed back in his furs to stare. It wasn't until the laughing noise of the young boy playing with a stick woke him that he realized he had been asleep.

He sat up. The tide was in; the wind coming from the north, turning east, devious as a shaman's tongue. He had no use for this place. An empty village with empty racks. Too filled with shadows of people who weren't there.

He looked to the sky. The moon that had lit the snow when last he'd been here was buried in the summer light. There was no reason for him to stay here. None at all.

He looked back toward the black tent where the boy had said Elik's grandmother lived for the summer, alone. She had not come out, nor had he been invited in to visit.

He flipped the boy the hinged box with the walrus carving inside, for a present, and then, not only the box but the whole basket. Everything in it. He didn't care. The boy's eyes widened and he wrinkled his nose in thanks. Allanaq let him help slide the umiak down to the waiting tide, into the sea.

The shape of the year was like a circle: the way the dark of the year, the ceremonial season, gave birth to the returning sun. The way the spring caribou drive in the Time of New Antlers grew into the Berry Picking Time of summer. The way the fishing season passed, and *Real People* everywhere returned to their winter villages.

Inside their houses again, the women took their seal, walrus, and otter skins and set those to one side, land animals to the other, so that out of respect, the two would not be mixed. And Seal Talker and Malluar announced that the summer rules against the making of new clothes was ended and the season of *Kakivik*, the Sewing Time, had once again returned.

Except that this year, along with the growing dark, the first snows came on earlier than the elders thought to look for them. First during the light of one day, then into the dark of another.

The winds blew angrily, so strong they threw tomcod up on the shore and the women gathered them and strung them, hoarding the fish in case of hunger.

Old men sat atop their houses, waiting to see when the slush ice grew strong enough that they could send their sons out, safely hunting.

Chevak had brought his family home early from fish camp, even before the last run of salmon had a chance to think about his nets.

"Why stay?" he muttered. And he scolded Gull and watched after Iluperaq, who, like an old man, coddled and worried over his lost finger. Chevak complained about his luck, his women, even about the way they found his mother on their return.

Alu had lost weight over the summer; the surprise of her sallow skin only added to Chevak's poor humor. First Iluperaq's illness caused them to lose part of their catch. And now his mother's wheezing stole his sleep, changed the singing that used to fill his house to noise and too-loud fits of coughing.

Alu stayed inside, sleeping often, but sometimes sitting up and asking where, in the early storm, the caribou had gone. When she heard that Seal Talker had decided that they dared not host a runner's feast this year, she grew fretful and kept asking if the women had set their snares. She repeated instructions for things the girls already knew: how to knot twisted sinew into mesh for a ptarmigan net, how to hoop a willow snare into baited circles: low down for ground squirrels, larger ones for fox.

When the wind finally lightened, Gull and Kimik, Naiya and Elik slung their grass carry-sacks over their backs, took their pronged birding spears, and tramped through the new snow to check their snares.

Kimik, with her stomach high and pointing to show there was a boy growing inside, went one way with Gull behind the houses. Elik and Naiya went the other.

Earlier, the two sisters had stretched a sinew net in the willow brush where ptarmigan liked to browse. They circled back quietly, peering ahead until they saw two round-chested ptarmigan—males, caught by their necks and already frozen: dead since before the storm.

"They followed the berries," Naiya said, and Elik pulled the birds free, taking care not to lose too many of the brown-and-white-spotted feathers. "Here's two the fox won't get," she said.

"They'll make a good dinner," Naiya said, and then she smiled wider. "But I'm thinking of who I'll cook it for."

Elik glanced at her sister. "You should ask first," she said, reluctant to talk about Whale Fin. "Mother said that with so few caribou this year, we're already eating more salmon than she planned."

Naiya went back to resetting the net's head and footline into a V shape. Elik smoothed the wings flat and slipped the birds in her carry-sack. "Should we leave the decoy?" she asked, but Naiya still wanted to joke. "Maybe the next male will want a wife instead of a brother to sleep with?" She laughed. "Like us. Maybe we'll both have husbands before the winter's through."

Elik stiffened, then turned to hide it. She lifted her hand against the sun's glare, searched for their mother and Kimik. "I hope they find plenty of burrows," she said. "We still need more ground squirrels for our parkas."

"Whale Fin has wide shoulders," Naiya said. She had reset one of the sticks that held the mesh fence in place and was strengthening the other. "Grandmother said that for so large a man, I would need five more skins than the forty we plan for Iluperaq."

Elik tried thinking of something to say, anything that would end Naiya's joking about husbands and men. "Mother tied four bundles of grey skins, and two of brown—" she started, and then she heard something, stopped.

Naiya also heard: there was a call from near the houses. They listened a moment, but it was Naiya who smiled first. "It's the men." She tugged Elik's sleeve. "Do you hear?"

"Caribou?" Elik said, then, seeing a chance for quiet, she busied herself with the traps. "Whale Fin will be there." Naiya's face brightened. "You go ahead," Elik urged, "I'll finish these."

Elik watched the shape of Naiya's hooded parka grow smaller. She finished what little work remained, then started back. She wasn't sure if Naiya knew about the bargain she had made with Seal Talker; certainly Elik hadn't spoken of it. But her father might have, or Seal Talker; Whale Fin, perhaps. She hoped not.

The season at fish camp had been different this year than when she was younger, difficult. Perhaps it was that Kimik had been there, pregnant and not yet used to Chevak and Iluperaq's arguing. Or else only that her father was right and she was a secretive, sullen girl. More afraid of Seal Talker than she had realized.

Elik chose a different path to the frozen beach than the one her sister had taken, farther out of sight from where the men were now standing in a line. Naiya, she saw, had joined the women at the end of their row, nearest to Whale Fin.

He seemed a good man—she'd said as much to Naiya as soon as they'd returned from fish camp and he had started visiting, obviously interested.

He spoke kindly and listened to their father for as long as Chevak wanted to speak. And he was large, built wide rather than long, but not enough to slow him or make a poorer hunter out of him than another man.

The only problem was that he was also Seal Talker's nephew, and Elik would have preferred that he was not. Once married, he would draw her sister closer to Seal Talker's house. And Naiya would pull Elik to come also, to make a home together, or at least nearby. Two sisters sharing company and work. Naiya would point to Saami with his two sister-wives, to Kimik's mother near Ema, her closest cousin. Surely, she had said, Elik could see the wisdom.

How could she explain what she didn't understand herself? That she didn't want to marry though her suitor was the most respected, the richest man—not only in their Bent Point village, but perhaps among all the houses of the Real People?

Elik turned at a sound: the women were singing to greet the men. A song she recognized, but had hoped not to hear: No caribou had been found. Again.

The men had returned empty-handed. Still, there was gladness in their safety. Tomorrow they would try again. In the meanwhile, there was plenty of fish to eat.

Elik turned, walked awhile, not on the rocks, they were

slippery even if she tried being careful of the few new patches of snow.

The tide had come in under the crusting ice. The sun glimmered off the sea, but for one dark place—there: something small floated in the water, not far. A line of dark rising in the triangular pattern of waves. Small. A flicker, then gone.

A moment later and she saw it: an otter. Its pointed nose lifted skyward, legs and chest extended, floating on the waves. The otter rolled over. With its dark eyes watching her, it did something she had never heard of before.

Without diving, it started to swim. Not away and not following the shore, but toward her, with its sleek, wet ears pulled back and its eyes watching as it skimmed the surface.

She stood still. Water dripped from its fur as it climbed to the beach—in front of her, like a gift. No more than a few lengths away. She watched it walk: less graceful out of water, its webbed feet dragging behind, short toes scratching along frosted ground.

Then, as if she weren't a human woman, as if these were the oldest times, when people didn't need to take the lives of animals for food, as if it had no fear, the otter sat. It looked at her, and then it left, that quick. It slipped back into the sea.

She was shivering, suddenly cold. Had it been real? She thought so. There was the wet line of its trail. And there— something white where the otter had sat. A pebble? No. She glanced toward the houses. No one was near. She crossed the few steps, scooped it up. It wasn't a rock. A shell, maybe? She brushed off the sand.

For a moment it looked like the empty husk of a clamshell, cracked open and already dead. But no—it was a whale's bone. Part of a vertebra from a young, small whale: spiked and porous, brown on the underside, the surface facing the sun, white and old.

She thought of a story her grandmother used to tell, how an orphan walked along the shore and the amulets came to him. As if the spirits who lived inside the rocks and the ground had noticed him and sent them. And what strength the amulets had in life, so the orphan also gained. A walrus's whisker brought him safely through the waves. An eagle's claw helped bring food.

The best amulets, no matter what they were, the strongest, were those that came when a person was alone, walking in silence. Listening.

Quickly, before someone saw and decided the bone would make a good dipper or a line fastener, she slipped it inside her amulet pouch, listened to the chink of bone landing against ivory, nestling against a feather.

And then she smiled, remembering—It had been a year ago, hadn't it? Just this season, she had stood near this shore and heard the Loon.

She remembered the feeling that had come to her, as if with that single call, she understood she was not alone. As if, for the first time, the soul that gave her breath could see, finally, the souls of others who also had breath. Not people only, but Wolf and Wolverine, Rock and Bay. All had souls, as she had a soul. She was not alone. She never had been.

And the question that had grown inside her, bursting to be heard was this: how it was that a girl who could not be a shaman should hear these things—the way she did.

A shiver ran through her. She had never before felt so certain she could learn, would learn, when the time came, how to be a shaman. How to hear and how to see. How to understand the voices of the *inuas*.

She would speak to Malluar. In all the time since she'd asked Malluar to teach her, she had not once been alone with her again. She would go back. This time, she wouldn't be afraid to explain. She did hear voices. She did see the soul-spirits inside the animals. Couldn't Malluar have been wrong? Why would so many voices call her, if she wasn't supposed to hear?

It was the day after the men came home without caribou that Seal Talker sent his wife to visit. There was anger bristling in the house when Ema arrived. Elik, with her legs drawn tightly out of her father's and Iluperaq's way felt it and wondered if Ema would also. Or if the food they offered and the lighter comments they tried to make could push the echoes out the skyhole, canceling their sting.

Grandmother Alu lay beneath her furs, a sharp-boned figure who coughed but seldom moved. Gull had set fish broth in a bowl beside the lamp. It waited for Alu with a sheen of fat skimming the surface, clouded underneath.

The seal Iluperaq had dragged inside lay in the middle of the floor. Kimik knelt to one side, her curved stone blade in her hand, considering which way to start. If the seal was to become a poke, a full-size container for storing oil and food, the skin would not be cut, but pulled off instead, like a parka over a child's head.

If it was to be used for line, the skin would be kept whole, then sliced into a single full-length strip, starting at the outside and circling toward the center. This was not the large *ugruk,* the bearded seal, and so the skin would not be saved for a boat cover. But it could be used for a parka top, or boot soles, in which case a circular cut would be made around the head and then the flippers, a length-wise cut slicing through the chest.

"Where is the other seal you caught?" Chevak asked.

Iluperaq looked at the floor when he answered, "Outside. I'll bring that one too."

Chevak studied the seal with annoyance. "The wind must have changed," he said. "This morning when I checked, it seemed too rough to go out."

Iluperaq crossed to a tub of meltwater, lifted the dipper, drank.

"My bow was broken," Chevak went on. "I told you about that. How I had to fix the tightening strands. They snapped. Maybe—" Chevak stepped to the other side of the seal. "Maybe it would make a good cover for my bow when I fix it."

Iluperaq glared sideways to Kimik. She had lowered her sewing, set her hands on the sides of her rounded stomach.

He touched her shoulder. She seemed uncomfortable

inside herself, her breasts swelling with the weight of milk, the weight of all the rules she must follow: not to drink unmelted snow for water, or the child would be cold. Not to sleep late or the child would be lazy. Not to hear the weight of talk inside this house, or the child would be cruel.

Gull too must have caught the tension. "Elik—perhaps you would like to make a poke?" she asked, and immediately Kimik brightened. "I could take the one outside to my mother's house, and work there," she suggested. "Elik, this seal could be for you."

The house quieted at the overhead sound of snow crunching near the skyhole. "It's Ema," Chevak said, and a moment later, the shaman's wife called a greeting.

Elik opened her mouth, closed it without speaking. How had her father known it was Ema? He turned, offered Elik a smile. Her stomach tightened. A moment later Seal Talker's short, square-shouldered wife peered through the floor entry, then climbed, a little unevenly, into the house.

"The winds are heavy." Ema shook the wet flakes of snow from her parka. "Did you feel it? From the north?" Her eyelashes were moist with the snow, but she smiled broadly, ducked her head in greeting.

"A man has to be careful where he hunts," Chevak said, as if he, not Iluperaq was responsible for the seal lying on their floor.

Iluperaq offered a farewell, then quickly disappeared to haul the other seal to Kimik's mother's house. Kimik stayed only long enough to pull on her parka, then crawled out backward, behind her husband.

"So." Ema made herself comfortable. "My husband says the wind from the north is rising again."

"It's good that way," Chevak said, but then he stopped. His expression was awkward, as if he wasn't certain whether he should be there or not. He said, "With the ice crusting, we can hope to hunt for seals."

"The small pond where I get water has been frozen for days."

"Thick enough to walk on?" Gull asked.

Ema waited for Chevak to answer. When he didn't, she

turned to Elik. "My husband went walking last night, but the wind was sharp and too fast—Were you out?" She peered at Elik, lifting her eyebrows to see how the girl answered.

Elik shook her head no.

Ema went on. "When he came home he said that the wind was chewing on the ice and any man wanting to hunt should wait till it was done. Two days—he said his spirit helpers told him—two days."

Chevak shuffled his feet. He looked to Gull, looked away. He nudged the seal, looked again at Gull, and then, suddenly, slipped on his parka, mumbled a farewell, and was gone.

In the sudden quiet, Elik found a stick, used it to push the lamp wick back into the melted blubber.

She should have left with Kimik, she saw that now. She had done her best, trying to keep out of Seal Talker's way. Walking only with other women, avoiding places he might have walked. And while it was true she'd felt him watching her, she had hoped he'd forgotten. Why then was Ema here? She seldom brought her sewing anywhere but to Sila's house, or Salmonberry's.

A circle of light rose from the wick. Behind her, Grandmother Alu's breathing changed from a rasp to a cough. Elik turned just as she woke, lifted her too-thin hands, and pulled her sleeping furs higher. "Who's there?" Alu asked.

"It's Ema, Mother. She's brought her sewing." Gull said the words brightly, as if the shaman's wife was a sister or an aunt, come to talk and visit the same as any day. "Elik is going to make a seal poke," she added.

"Seal poke?" Elik repeated, but she no longer wanted to make a seal poke. Or sew, or do work of any kind.

From her place on the bench, Ema studied Elik's furs, the quality of work that had gone into scraping the hides, stretching and softening them.

Elik stared at the seal: its eyes weren't looking at her and she was glad. Glad it was dead. Glad it couldn't hear her thoughts.

Gull grew nervous. She tried to cover her daughter's

neglectful manners. She moved to the floor, knelt over the ringed seal's small, oblong body, took hold of a flipper, and shifted it to a better position on the floor. "My daughters were just talking about how badly we need a new seal poke to store oil—We have so much oil this year. . . ."

"She's a good girl," Ema agreed. "A hard worker." She set the sewing she'd brought on her lap. But that was all she did—set it there. She didn't pull any sinew from her kit, or even look at it. She merely folded her legs, drank the broth Gull offered, and watched.

Elik had no choice but to take the curved blade her mother pressed in her hand.

"Here, start it here. . . ." Her mother tapped her arm: closer. Using her smaller blade, Gull showed where to press for the first cut—around the seal's head—with a sawing motion, very slowly, not to slip or make a hole.

Elik took her own knife, worked the blade in a slow curve around the base of the neck, above the shoulder, knowing exactly why Ema was here. Knowing that she had brought this on herself, following a man as if it meant nothing. And now her parents—both her parents—wanted the same thing: Seal Talker's wealth in their daughter's house. Her father would be more than content. Gull would hardly disagree.

Her mother pulled with her till the skin began to peel, backward, leaving the hair on the inside to flavor the food, leaving the claws with the skin. Later the holes would be stitched tight so no oil leaked out. The neck would be gathered, tied with a seal thong.

Any other time she would have welcomed the lesson, pressed her mother to let her try. It was no child's task removing the skin without tearing holes and ruining it for a container. She wondered if her mother had secretly asked Kimik to take the other seal, leave this one for her.

"These hands," Ema chatted as she watched. "These hands of mine are bent, the bones so old and useless now. My poor husband—you understand—being a shaman, he must have a helper. A shaman's wife is called to no ordinary work. For years, he asks me, *Do this, Do that.* He needs me to fetch things, to hand him his drum—Did you know I do that, even during his trance, I hand him things." She nodded, impressed with the truth, proud.

For the first time, Elik looked up, interested. "Help him? As a shaman? How?"

Ema smiled. "A shaman's wife, even more than another, must look good to the spirits. If we would have the seals and caribou give themselves to us, we must perform all the rituals they require. Everything. This is important work. A work of trust."

Elik was surprised. "He teaches you things?"

"In the *qasgi* sometimes. I am the one who must know when to darken the lamp. I hand my husband his things, sacred things, the bone tube he uses for sucking out illness, the spirit masks he wears. When he speaks to his spirit helpers, I am the one who helps him recover, after the trance has racked and hurt his body."

Confused, Elik stared at the seal, at the moist blubber, the thick layer of meat. *Hand him his drum? Is that what Ema meant? Lift him from his trance? But what of the times I have fallen? What of the spirit-voices inside my ears?*

Ema drank from the water dipper, then started talking again, this time in a different direction. "Any child Seal Talker gets must be from a wife of a different family line, a wife who is young and strong and appreciates the demands of a shaman's life. Because of my blood, weak as it is, a baby could be born. But our son is grown and gone while my husband still waits." Ema paused, stole a look to see whether Elik smiled or showed fear.

"Of course," Ema said, "it is one thing for a man to want a girl beneath his blankets, another thing to want her for a wife."

While Gull nodded Ema tried to get Elik's attention, to see which way her thoughts had turned. She couldn't tell. She said, "A child of my husband's could have great power. Seal Talker's shaman-sight, but without the trouble of his blood—such a child would surely live."

With a satisfied look, as if finally, she had spoken

plainly and clearly, Ema unrolled the sewing she had brought. Gull kept smiling, nodding her head, and—while her daughter seemed to have forgotten her work—finished pulling the skin from the seal's body.

The next time Elik looked, Ema was twisting two lengths of sinew into one. She held the lengths together in her hand, made a looped knot and then a twist.

*It's not Ema's fault,* Elik tried convincing herself. *She means no harm. . . .*

Ema reached for a third length of caribou sinew to work in with the others. What Elik had thought was Ema's rolled up pair of boot leggings, she realized now, was merely a sewing kit; a simple roll of leather. One place inside for needles. A flap to hold the sinew. It was different than her mother's kit or her own. There was no sign of a needle case—hers was a hollow bone tube made from the humerus of a swan, with a strip of leather pulled through to hold the needles. No needle was safe without one.

But it wasn't the roll itself that stole Elik's attention, or the way the needles were wrapped in soft leather, not bone to keep them safe. It was the carved ivory closure that pinned the entire thing shut. A closure that was also an awl, and also the figure of an animal, with a head engraved on each side. Legs cut through. Ears protruding. "Where did you get that?" she asked.

"This? I wanted a knife more first, but he didn't have the kind I liked."

"He?" Elik's voice cracked, too high. She hoped Ema didn't notice, or her mother. She recognized the work, at least she thought she did.

"He had needles, bird bone, tiny, and with perfect eyes. But needle cases, no. He said the women among his people wrapped their needles in squares of skin, like this, then folded them away. Seal Talker traded this one for me." She lifted it, assuming it was her wealth that impressed the girl. "For a present," she added.

Elik reached to the awl, then hesitated. The ivory was white with a golden patina, perfectly smoothed. Not a mark showed, not a rough edge. The same as the loon she carried against her breast. "Who was the trader? Someone you knew?"

"No. Well, yes." She looked to Gull. "The one your brother adopted. You remember? He was here for the runner's feast—"

"Last winter? You mean last winter at the feast?"

"No, this summer. You like it? It's too bad you weren't here, you could have made a trade. He'd brought full baskets, in his umiak. But the man didn't even know the worth of his goods; he gave this to a boy, to Kimik's brother, Olah. Other things also."

Elik stood. She made herself cross to her grandmother's sleeping place. It was him, Allanaq. Her cousin. But why would he come during fish camp, instead of helping Grey Owl and Nua? And why give away carvings, to a child, instead of in trade?

She brought the dipper to her grandmother. Alu was still asleep, her body a tiny hump beneath the furs, dry fingers showing near her loose braids.

Sometime after Seal Talker had left their fish camp, he had come here and worked over Alu. Alu had told Elik about it herself, only recently, when they returned. The way he had whooped and danced around her, scaring away the evil that had stolen her soul, sucking it out with his tube. It hadn't hurt, Alu had said, but it had frightened her.

*Had Ema sat in this house and helped Seal Talker?* She wondered. Later, perhaps, when Alu was stronger, she would ask her grandmother.

Elik followed Alu's hand. The cup Gull had brought still lay untouched. And now that she thought about it, Alu did seem to have grown weaker since yesterday, when the men returned without caribou. Her breathing was labored, uneven and noisy. She hoped her grandmother would feel better later—after Ema was gone. She longed for the quiet reassurance of her stories, her humming.

Ema had rolled her sewing kit together and risen to

leave. She and Gull shared a few kind remarks; Elik answered with a respectful farewell.

Gull waited until Ema was out of hearing. Then she stood looking at her daughter. Awkwardly, as though she were not the mother but the child, she crossed to Alu's bed, gently touched her shoulder. Alu was asleep.

"You will be a wife," Gull said. She was looking at Alu, but her words were for Elik. "Someday, you will bring life into the village, and food into your house."

Gull turned halfway round. Her slanted eyes had a troubled look. "It isn't right for a woman not to marry," she said. "It isn't right. Elik—you have to pay attention. Think—if Iluperaq should leave the house—" She stopped, lowered her voice. "Not that he will, but if he should. Your father—he isn't the strongest hunter . . . Alone . . ." She stopped again. Alu was awake; with darkly rimmed eyes she watched Gull fill the dipper.

Alu took the drink, then lowered herself back down. Gull waited till she was settled and quiet again before moving closer to Elik. "It's the same for a man," she whispered. "He brings a seal home from the sea, but without the pot a woman has made, he cannot cook it. Without the grass she has gathered, there is no basket he can carry it in. Without a woman, a man cannot remember with whom to share his catch, where his sons may marry, who is lazy or who is honorable.

"And you, my little daughter, should likewise remember. Without a man to hunt you could not eat. You should not be so dissatisfied. Who are we to know the ways of the world, of the spirits? We spill blood. We make blood. There are no answers how or why."

Elik was already awake when she heard her mother slip away from her father's side. There was the sound of bare feet pressing on grass mats, and then the hushed and solemn words her mother spoke each day to greet the morning light. The familiar crack of tinder struck, followed by Gull's huffing as she blew the spark to life.

And now her father coughed to show Gull he was awake, waiting till she brought his drink. And Alu, waking with her shallow breaths, pushing up from sleep, for air.

And there, behind it, a panting sound. Elik listened. It wasn't her grandmother's breathing. This was coming from her brother's side of the platform. Kimik? Elik lifted her shoulders. She caught her mother's eye. Iluperaq's gear had been lifted off the wall pegs. Her brother was out somewhere, waiting ahead of the dawn.

"Kimik?" Gull crossed to her daughter-in-law's place. Naiya crept in beside Elik. "Sit up," Gull whispered, and then, "How long?"

"The belt, it's tight." Kimik's voice was low and strained.

"Get her into older clothes, quickly. Whatever she's wearing, it will have to be burned." Alu had sat up, her weight on her elbow, her voice the surest it had sounded in days. "Wake my son. Has he built a birthing hut?"

Gull glanced to Chevak. "The hut is done," he said. He sat up, scratched his head for lice.

"Iluperaq?" Kimik called, and the fear in her voice was plain.

"Tell the girl to hush," Grandmother said. "Not to be loud, else she'll scare the child and it will hide inside her womb."

Chevak dropped his blankets and walked naked to the hearth. "First Iluperaq asks me to hunt with him. Then he leaves without telling me when."

Chevak glanced to his mother. "How long?" he asked.

Kimik caught hold of Gull's arm. "How long? I don't know . . ."

Alu called toward Gull, "Pull down her blankets."

Gull nodded, tried to help with the leggings, but Kimik's weight was rooted, immobile. "It's all right." Gull tried to soothe her. "A first time, women always worry too much."

Gull smiled for Kimik, but Elik saw the worry tighten around her mother's shoulders. While Naiya crawled from Elik's side to her grandmother's, Elik moved along the platform, then helped until Kimik was sitting, her back leaning heavily into Elik's chest.

Gull made a sign and Elik slipped her hands beneath Kimik's armpits, lifted, while Gull tugged down the furs. Gently, Gull opened Kimik's knees: a dark circle matted the furs beneath her, wetness shining on both her thighs. Elik peered over the hump of Kimik's tight, high stomach. It was like water, she noticed. And a strange smell, not urine, not like a man's semen, but strong.

"I suppose I'll have to find Seal Talker," Chevak said.

"No!" Alu grabbed a sudden hold on Naiya's arm, lifted herself. "Bring Malluar or no one. Seal Talker would bring his spirit helpers fighting the spirit that fights with me. In this house. I won't have them. They listen to his name. Don't let him in." She glared at her son as she seldom had—shaming him into obeying.

Gull's face showed fear. She looked toward Chevak. "You could do that? Please? Bring a woman to help a woman . . ."

With a sudden move, Elik freed her hands. "I'll go," she called, and she held her breath, praying they wouldn't think to stop her. That, finally, she could have her moment to speak to Malluar, beg her again to teach her.

She helped Kimik lean against the wall, then jumped from the platform to pull on her boots, her trousers. Her hands slipped through her parka sleeves at the same time as she felt the touch of wind against her cheeks.

At Malluar's house, she climbed quickly inside. The shaman was already awake and fully dressed. Elik opened her mouth, thinking she would ask finally. That all the words inside her heart would pour out, sudden and clear as water.

They didn't. She stopped, looked about. Malluar sat hunched near an oil lamp, her round face reflecting the lamplight. A pottery vessel hung from a line above the sky-hole, but no food was cooking. She lifted her eyebrows, waited for Elik to speak.

Except—she couldn't. Elik heard something, a sound like Raven, cawing overhead. She stilled her breath. It was nothing. Only the house. She had forgotten how anxious this house made her feel. There was the circle of empty-eyed wolverines, watching. Malluar's spirit masks, looking at her from the walls, the ceiling.

*What was I thinking?* Elik wondered. *Talk to me now, while my brother's wife waits to give birth? While her woman's blood spills on a man's hunting things?*

Elik stood quietly while Malluar questioned her. How loud, she asked, had Kimik cried? And was the water clear or was there blood? Elik answered carefully, but she had the distinct feeling each time Malluar asked her to reach for a basket, or lift a dipper from a peg on the wall, that the shaman was watching her. Not just to help her find her things, but watching. Peering beneath her skin. Looking for something.

Elik helped her gather the last few things, not Malluar's amulet belt, which was sacred, but those things an ordinary girl was permitted to touch. A special water pail, which afterward would be destroyed, a birdskin to wipe the child if it lived, a sealskin if it died.

Outside the sky had lightened. The line where the sea ended was barely distinguishable from where the sky began. Elik shivered, lowered her head into the wind. She looked once to Malluar, walking quietly at her side. She had been right not to ask yet. The time wasn't right. And Malluar was so difficult for her to understand, different from her mother, her grandmother, from any other woman she knew.

Ahead of them, she saw Gull and Kimik already outside, angling away toward where the tiny birthing hut had been built, far enough away that any spirits drawn to the blood wouldn't also see the houses.

Elik raced to meet them, then helped take Kimik under her arm. "There's time," Kimik said. Then, managing a smile, "Maybe." They slowed and waited for Malluar to reach them. Gull stepped aside, relieved to have someone else take over.

"Is there moss for the floor?" Malluar asked. There was.

"And a strap to grab on to?" Yes, Elik had watched her mother tie it near the peak. "You may leave," Malluar said to Gull. "Go home and untie every knot you can find. Remind this girl's husband to do no work while she labors—"

"Iluperaq?" Kimik asked again.

"He's out hunting—could that make trouble?"

"Perhaps not. When he and Chevak come home . . . "

Kimik stopped. "Chevak isn't with him."

"Never mind." Malluar shooed away the girl's worry. "It doesn't matter—if everything else has been done to protect the child. Tonight"—she turned to Gull—"if you haven't heard from us, you may come. And you"—Malluar squinted to see Elik—"it would be a good idea if you piled dog turds, shovel them up the sides from the ground, along the skirting. Enough to circle the tent. It has to be disguised, covered in dog's scent, so there's no hint of Real People. So the place is hidden, and safe."

They had reached the birthing hut: a small, conical tent, with a layer of drifted snow rising up from the ground and down from the peak where the support poles gathered. It was scarcely large enough inside for Malluar and Kimik. Gull returned home and Elik ran to fetch the wide walrus scapula they used for shoveling, and a container. She picked out an older, uncomplaining bitch who had just whelped a litter, tossed the scraggly mother a scrap of fish, then smacked the frozen turds loose from the frost-hardened ground. The work took two trips, back and forth, filling the cracks between the ground and the tent skins, masking the scent of birth with life, working to keep out death.

It was late morning when they started, afternoon when she sat down outside the hut, head to her knees, hood drawn close to block the wind.

More than once she crawled forward to hear the sound of Kimik's clutching breaths, Malluar's encouragements. And then her shaman drum, like a prayer. Elik lifted the hide door, let in a crack of light to peek. Centered under the patch of roof light she saw Malluar's hand like willow

branches reaching from behind Kimik, twisting under her
sweat-soaked breasts.

Elik squatted back on her haunches. Evening came,
passed into night. There was too much time to think, too
many thoughts and too many worries. For Kimik first and
the way, all her life, she had heard about women dying in
childbirth. For Iluperaq's impatience with their father that
had risen past all caution. For Grandmother Alu's eye that
had turned blue with its cataract, a crescent moon at the
beginning of the summer, an eclipse now, at its end. And
for the way Malluar had watched her just now in her
house, not with the same disinterest she had shown a year
ago, but something different. Elik didn't know what.

Daylight was a thread drawn across the lower sky when,
finally, Elik heard a baby's cry. She raised an ear, listened:
Yes! A healthy cry, strong and brave. She straightened from
her vigil, waited till she caught a word: Kimik's voice, weak
now, but a word—*He.* The child was a boy. They were
both alive!

Elik's heart sang. Families longed for children: a girl to
help with other children, with her hands and the joy of her
song. A boy to hunt, to build umiaks and help to feed his
grandparents, to laugh and grow strong and tall.

She waited till she was certain she heard no calls for
help, then raced for home. Much remained for Malluar to
finish. She would cut the cord and the placenta would be
delivered, wrapped in a shield of moss, then hidden away.
Only a shaman or an elder knew the proper words for the
burial, the way the part of the soul that lived inside must
be taken in secret, the way the health and life of the child
was tucked in with its keeping.

Snatches of her own early memories leaped out at her:
peering from her mother's hood while a man's nose bled
from a wrestling match; being told to repeat, over and over,
the story of who her relatives were: Great Grandmother and
Great Grandfather, Mother's sister, Father's brother. She
remembered an early winter, pushing aside the frozen hide

door, peering outside while her brother stood naked in the strong male North Wind with the other boys, so that they, too, would grow hardy and strong.

This new boy would do that someday. Kimik would nurse him and she would help carry him. He would be held and passed around and admired till someday he would be strong and wise with reason.

It wasn't yet daylight when she reached the houses. The stars were hidden and the wind was empty; snow no longer fell. She had been running so she hadn't heard it at first: the commotion. The heightened drumbeat. It grew louder, centered near her house.

Someone had lit a fire outside, a small one, only large enough to see by. Except that was odd—people didn't do that for a birth. No one could know about the boy. She'd come straight here.

A hollow feeling stole her joy. People were standing about. Seal Talker first, a huge wooden spirit mask covering his face. Her father. His brother Nagi. Sipsip. Gull and Naiya standing near Whale Fin.

It was Naiya who took hold of Elik's sleeve, as if to hold her back. "What is it?" Elik asked.

"Dead," Naiya replied.

Elik thought she meant the new boy. "He's alive. A boy, Naiya—no one's dead."

"What are you saying?" Naiya snapped. "All day you're gone, and Grandmother is dead."

"Grandmother?" Elik wrinkled her nose, not understanding. She had been with Grandmother that morning, though morning seemed so far away. It was Grandmother who sent for Malluar. Asked them not to bring Seal Talker because his spirits would fight against hers.

Elik stared blankly at the fire. Alu had known, hadn't she? Her soul had wandered, gone out of her body, and she had known.... And here was Naiya, wearing someone else's older clothes. Her new ones—the parka she'd finished with Whale Fin in her thoughts—those were somewhere in the house. It would have to be burned now.

Death lingered inside, and clothing that touched death must never come near life.

At the sound of a man's voice they turned: Iluperaq had appeared. His eyes were all on the house. "Kimik?" he asked. The fear in his voice was plain.

"No." Niaya shook her head. "Grandmother."

Elik winced, turned away. The sledge Iluperaq had towed back from his hunting was empty, as was the carrysack thrown on top, and the bag on his shoulder: all empty. No seals had come. No land animals. It wasn't good. The kind of sign that came with death, with a soul unhappy with its treatment. She reached up, touched her brother's sleeve. "There is a child. A son. All is well," she said, praying it was still true. "And Kimik—also well."

Iluperaq dropped the towline, swallowed hard. The three of them stood watching as the men sealed the house, preventing the soul who had been Alu from coming back, throwing anger out on them. Nagi and Whale Fin and Kimik's father, Blue-Shadow, pissed streams of yellow water around the house: tracks to disguise the scent, so the ghost wouldn't find them.

Seal Talker set aside his drum. With his red-and-black shaman mask in hand, he approached Chevak and Saami. Their hoods pressed close as they spoke, made plans for the burial. It must be quickly done, the body removed through the skyhole, not an ordinary door. Alu's personal possessions must also be buried with her: her lamp, her woman's knife. Other things would be shared around. Gull joined them and they spoke a little longer, than started toward where Elik, Iluperaq, and Naiya stood in a quiet row.

Gull carried a fishskin basket over her arm. She reached inside—there was a clanking sound.

"What is it?" Naiya asked.

"Your grandmother's hearth rocks." Her voice shook. "All her life she saved these. She told me—more than once—they were hers from an aunt. They never cracked. They knew how to heat. She said . . . " Gull stopped, collected herself. "She said they should be passed to you, for the houses you make when you are wives . . . Last night . . . She had me take them . . . "

Naiya touched her mother's arm. "You did right," she said.

"She only said I should give them to the wives . . . " Gull stopped suddenly, noticing Elik. "Kimik?" she asked. "There's word?"

Elik tried to smile. "She's well—you have a grandson."

Gull bit her lip. By then Saami had walked away from Chevak. With his arms tightly at his sides he left to stand with his own family, his wives and grown son. Chevak and Seal Talker walked slowly to stand with them. In quiet tones, Kimik's news was repeated.

Seal Talker shifted the spirit mask he carried. Then, as if there were no one else beneath the sky but him and Elik, he stepped up to her. His face glistened with the sweat his mask had made, but the sterner look of the shaman was gone. He wore an old man's face and an old man's hungry smile.

Elik lowered her eyes, stepped back. Seal Talker laughed and stepped after her. "I like a woman who's shy," he said, not even troubling himself to whisper. "With most women, when they're shy, it's a game. . . . " With a quick move, he looped his fingers through the caribou belt on her waist.

Elik hadn't been prepared for the gesture, the lewdness of it, with death all around them, with the powerful blood of birth. . . . "Don't," she protested, and she pulled away, freed herself from his hand.

Ema was wrong—those things she had said, about allowing Elik to be a helper—Seal Talker cared nothing about that. He cared only about his own shaman's blood— exactly as Malluar said. He would never see her as someone with the strength to be a shaman—never.

Seal Talker's eyes narrowed. "What is this? Some teasing girl's game? I am your husband—"

"The girl is an aunt, not a wife!" Seal Talker spun about.

Malluar approached from out of the fire's shadow. Smaller though she was, she planted herself firmly in front of her cousin, looked up with eyes as daring as his own.

The moment stretched. With a sudden thought, Elik remembered how Malluar taught her to lie. She lowered her head and said—softly—"I am *kongak*—close to the spirits."

Seal Talker sneered. "What? With blood?" He ran his gaze down the length of her body, as if his spirit helpers were too strong to fear a few mere drops of blood on a woman's thighs.

Elik glanced nervously to Malluar. "From my sister-in-law's birthing hut—" She stopped, searched for what to say next, but this time Seal Talker hesitated at her words. His nostrils flared, and she caught it, the way he leaned back, uncertain.

More bravely now, she said, "Kimik has a son. My hands—there's blood on my hands—" She held them out, praying the light wasn't sufficient to show the difference between dirt and her lie. Praying even more that Malluar wouldn't side with her cousin.

The cold air was crisp with threat. Elik swallowed, dared a glance to Malluar. Her thin mouth was drawn in, holding back a smile. Her eyes danced with Seal Talker's discomfort.

It was Gull who broke the tension, innocently, burdened with the family's concerns. "Iluperaq," she said. "You have a son, a child who needs a name." She turned. "One of you girls should go to Kimik—"

"I'll go," Elik interrupted, but Malluar held her back.

"Not you," she said. "You must clean yourself of any birth matter. Who knows which spirit might see the blood on your hands." She took a step, placed herself defiantly between Elik and Seal Talker, who stood, his hands in fists, barely holding in his anger.

Loudly now, before he found a way to stop her, Malluar said, "Naiya, it should be you. Tell Kimik the name for her son is Alu. Tell us if the child cries or if his new soul recognizes the name. Spit water in his mouth when you say it, so the name enters his body. And tell Kimik also that the boy will be *qongoaktuktuk*—someone whose amulets grow strongest near things of the dead. Now, for the—"

"The body," Seal Talker fought for control. "The body should be wrapped in burial skins in the morning, when there's light to see by."

Malluar glared. "And removed through the skyhole," she said.

"—Tonight and for five days," Seal Talker called, louder than she had. "While we wait for the ghost to leave . . . "

". . . None of you may sleep in that house."

"Do not enter it. Do not remove your things." Seal Talker folded his arms defiantly.

Malluar did the same. She turned to Elik. "You," she said, "will stay with me. Iluperaq, while your wife is in her seclusion, stay in her mother's house. Sila won't complain of a son-in-law's help."

She turned to the rest of the family, but Naiya had taken an obvious step toward Whale Fin. Malluar nodded. "Chevak and Gull," she said next, "Perhaps you'll stay in Saami's house? Or Chevak—you in the *qasgi* and Gull with Sipsip. Either would be allowed."

Then, quickly, before Seal Talker could stop her, she pulled off the sack she'd been carrying over her shoulder, passed it to Elik. "Fill it with snow," she said. "We'll need water . . . " And then quickly, before Seal Talker found a way to stop her, she turned, pulling Elik away.

It was the fifth day of Kimik's confinement, the fifth day following her grandmother's death, but still, Elik had not found a proper time to ask Malluar her question.

With the five days gone, she would be leaving Malluar's house; there was no longer any need to fear Alu's death. And word had already come, more than once, that Seal Talker meant to hold a caribou séance, that all the people must gather.

With the winds holding so harsh, wives were cooking

their winter stores. Few hunters had been able to go out in search of seal. There was worry and talk and fear that even inside a trance, Seal Talker might not learn which direction to search for meat.

Elik glanced around the house. So often while she'd been at fish camp she had taken out the memory of this room, as if it were something she could hold and touch and turn over in her hands. The eight square hearth stones, the circle of skulls, drums, the carved and feathered spirit masks hanging from the roof poles and the pegs.

She glanced to where Malluar leaned against the wall of her sleeping place, her legs stretched out, eyes closed. Was she sleeping? No. She was humming: the sounds so light, so constant, it was hard to notice. Like the wind outside, ceaseless, touching all.

Elik looked at her hands; they felt tight, glovelike, as if the skin had grown too small. She had been allowed to cook, but not to sew. She could sing, but only certain songs. She wished she knew how to sit so quietly as Malluar. What was it her grandmother used to say? That Naiya's thoughts flitted like a bird, but Elik's stretched too tight, like the skin of a drum.

She lifted her hand to her mouth, coughed lightly.

Malluar opened her eyes. "So," she said, as if they had been speaking all along, "it seems my male cousin is in the rutting season and wants you in his bed."

Elik stared at the lamp.

"But I am wondering—" Malluar went on. "If you have noticed how demanding Seal Talker becomes? Loud and hungry. More so the older he grows. He becomes a nuisance, do you think?"

Elik didn't answer. If there was one lesson she had learned, it was that nothing Malluar said was certain or clear or plain.

"I have been thinking maybe—" Malluar pulled on her lower lip. "Maybe I will keep you for myself."

Elik held her breath. *Don't speak*, she warned herself. *Wait*.

"I have been thinking how good it would be to have your younger feet to warm my bed." Malluar chuckled.

"You would like water boiled?" Elik jumped without waiting for an answer. She lifted a water bladder, set her fingers to the ivory nozzle. She tried to quiet the shaking in her hands. "Who told you about Seal Talker? Ema?"

Malluar laughed. "Of course. From Ema—she tells me more than people think. She's brave, that woman. She knows when to come between us—two old fools who don't remember how to agree."

The next time Malluar spoke, her voice was lower, more serious. "But I've already shaped my life around what Seal Talker wants. What I don't know is why you're afraid to do the same?"

Elik set the water bladder back down. She didn't want to talk about Seal Talker. She had something more important to ask. Now. Before the chance was lost. Hadn't she earned the right?

Spirit-voices spoke to her. They brought her amulets. Filled her with visions. She fell and hurt herself and cried and frightened her family. And in spite of what Malluar said about shaman's blood and weaker blood, these were true things that happened to her.

"You . . . you lived near him, but not as his wife. You aren't married." Elik circled closer near the question.

"Not now. And not to him, but I was. Twice."

"How . . . How are you able to live alone now?"

Malluar shrugged, gave the obvious answer. "Because I am a shaman. When I help people they share their meat, food, their skins—anything I ask for. I have relatives to stop the leaks in my roof, and bring oil. Sila sews my clothing when my fingers don't want to work. And I am given a hunter's share of each catch. But there were also years when a husband's back warmed my nights, and I preferred it that way."

Elik looked up. "Were you always a shaman, even when you were young?"

"Of course. I was shaman through my uncle Kashek, even before I had the sense to understand."

"You said once you were a wife, but never a mother?" The last square of blubber hanging on a string above the lamp slid in. The wick dimmed, then brightened.

"You've asked these questions before," Malluar said, "and I've answered. But it's also true that the duty of elders is to instruct the young—because they weren't born, they can't remember. So I'll tell you: I have no children because the spirit helpers my uncle gave me are too jealous and too strong to allow anyone else to grow inside.

"I had two husbands. Both good men, and both of different lines. Even so, both died in hunting accidents. Neither was strong enough to start children inside me who could live. If Seal Talker had been a woman, it would have been the same. With Ema he was lucky to have one son.

"For a while, I despaired. I grew frail, I refused to eat. I waited to die. I missed my husbands. That was the only time Seal Talker suggested we marry—did anyone ever tell you that? I refused of course. It was a game—he wanted only to spy on me. What he didn't realize, was how his attentions taught me my value. It was his fear that gave me back the will to live."

"Did you practice as a shaman when you were a wife?" Elik asked, "Or only after you were old?"

"Both," Malluar said, "though all shamans practice more as they grow older. We become more sure of ourselves. But it isn't only that—shamans can no more deny the voices that call inside of them than a hunter could deny the hunger inside his stomach, or a child hold her breath. . . .

"I'll tell you another secret," Malluar said. "Seal Talker suspects that because I am a woman, there are things I know that he does not. And it's no comfort to him that being a man, he may know something I do not.

"He knows that the shaman who is a woman is potentially more powerful than a man, for there are things she can do that no man would dare. Though he traveled to the moon and back, though he fought below the ice, he would not dare. And yet for a woman, it is no great deed. We who give birth to life, we know best how to touch these things, if ever any human can."

"What things?"

Malluar lifted an eyebrow, then waited. After what seemed a very long while she asked, "Is that what you came for—answers to your questions? But what are you afraid of, child? Seal Talker? His penis stands up, then it falls down. No different than another man."

"No," Elik stopped her. "It's not that. Not him. I fear so much—" She looked at Malluar. "The Wind. The Air. The spirits I hear but cannot see . . ."

Malluar shook her head. "You are too young to have so many fears."

"Young? I didn't think it was youth that mattered. Perhaps fear is not what I mean. Perhaps it is that I feel a presence . . ."

"A presence? Perhaps you do. But only shamans feel their bodies invaded, as if they are not theirs alone. As if your thoughts, that you believed you knew, turned stranger on you, deceived you. And all you can do is to go where it takes you, see what it shows you, speak if it lets you."

"Yes—" Elik whispered. "It is so."

"What is so?" Malluar's voice turned hard.

Carefully, as if words were as perilous as hunting on the cracked ice, Elik started, "If . . . If I have seen the places that the *inuas* see, if I have met them, spoken with them, journeyed with them—what does this mean?"

"It means you ask a great many questions. And here is my answer." With difficulty, Malluar made her way off the platform to the floor. The house was warm and, like Elik, she wore only her short women's trousers. Her breasts hung low and heavy. The tattoos that reached up her wrists and along her calves, from her ankle toward her knee, made her look almost like a carving, a length of old ivory, black and brown, yellow and red. She stood opposite the hearth from Elik and she said, "If I teach you my magic, if I share with you the words that even Seal Talker doesn't know, what gift would you give me?"

"Gift . . . ?"

"A gift, yes. This is what I'm saying. I will give you what you ask, but only after I have judged you by your gift."

Elik's eyes went wide. "My woman's parka?" she said—it was the finest thing she owned.

Malluar smiled the way an aunt might at a child. "If I needed a parka, I have but to ask any woman, and it's mine."

"A knife? I have a knife my brother made . . . "

"I too have knives. Anyone, my little Elik, anyone can say they want to be an *angatkuq*, a shaman. Anyone can sometimes cure, sometimes see the world of spirits. This is not rare. But does that mean I must teach anyone who asks? No. Why then should I teach you who do not even share my blood? Why you and not some other?"

"I have a lamp that is my own."

Malluar sighed, stepped away.

"Ptarmigan I snared myself?"

"No. It's not enough. You should go now."

"Go? But I thought perhaps—"

"Perhaps?" Malluar reeled on her. "There is no perhaps. There is only your blood that tells the name of your grandfather and his wife, and which of the men in his line were skilled hunters and which of the women gave birth so that your life would someday begin. How can you be different from those who come before you?"

Elik's hands shook as she stood. "I will go," she said, and she crossed to where her bed was made. With her back to Malluar and her disappointment too huge to put away, she rolled her sleeping things in on themselves.

"Where are you going?"

"Kimik's house, with my brother."

"Don't return"—Malluar's words dimmed through the entry—". . . without bringing a better gift. . . ."

It wasn't until Elik felt the slap of wind against her cheek that she stopped. She turned, looked back at Malluar's house, from the outside this time, a rounded hut of sod and dirty snow.

Malluar's meaning grew suddenly clear. It was a challenge, not a refusal. A chance. Not an ending. She had almost misunderstood.

Elik caught her breath, turned into the wind. The day had brought her possibilities, a second chance, like a guest that came to live inside her house.

Malluar stared at the empty floor where Elik had just climbed down, at the hearth where the girl had sat. For five days the girl had filled the house with talk. So many questions. Malluar walked a small circle, began humming a song. Any song. It didn't matter which. She'd felt alert while the girl had sat there, excited almost.

What had she done with herself before Elik came? Sat near her lamp, or the hearth or on her bed, singing? Certainly not troubling herself with questions, so many questions.

Malluar smiled. She leaned across to fix more fat above the lamp, tying it on so it would drip through the day. It wasn't the first time the girl had come to her this way. And— she was certain now, where before she had only wondered— it would not be the last. This one would not go away. This one was different. Persistent, curious, strong-willed.

Malluar sighed. Her bones felt weary. She was old. She had been alone for a long time.

If it was only persistence that had brought the girl, Malluar would never have invited her to stay. There'd have been no talk. No request for a gift. Nothing.

It had a little to do with Seal Talker; his interest in the girl had sparked her enjoyment for the game. But more honestly, it had to do with the light she'd seen showing out from the girl's own eyes.

Young though she was, the girl would make a shaman. The animals, the indwelling spirits—they watched her walking by. They knew she was there. If Malluar tried any longer to deny it, the peril would be hers.

Still, there was much to consider here: too much to think about alone. She needed help.

She would go into a trance, and ask her spirit helpers what to do.

She looked about her house—at the small things one woman owned. The house seemed empty. No sounds of children. No husband telling of his hunt. Hers had been a different life than most women knew. She had no regrets. Would she have chosen it if she knew? That was a different question. She wasn't sure. Would this girl?

Perhaps she and Seal Talker had been wrong and there were some people who opened themselves to the spirits, even without the blood of another shaman showing them the way.

Perhaps it was not something this girl had chosen, any more than she had chosen it. This giving up of one way of life to receive another. The way one must close one's eyes to the outer world, in order to see the next. World of Spirit. World of Wind.

The next time the girl came—and she would, she would come with her questions and her gifts—Malluar would give her a different answer.

There was a sound, outside and on her rooftop, as if something were scratching the snow away. She held still, listening. Not a person. No. This was something with claws. Malluar took a small step. Another, to stand where she could see. This time, through the translucent gut window, she found it: the four legs of its shadow first. The slender, dark-nosed snout smelling at her roof.

A smile of recognition lit Malluar's face. Wolf lifted his muzzle, pulled his ears purposefully back—listening. How much of the girl's talk had he heard? "Wolf," she called, and she nodded a greeting. "You have not visited my house in so long. . . ."

The *qasgi* had been readied for the ceremony. At a signal from Seal Talker Ema had gone to all but one lamp, silencing their lights. Three men had been chosen to drum: Saami, Blue-Shadow, and Chevak. But for Seal Talker, they were the eldest in the village. And this would be a ceremony, more than many another, when age and wisdom and discretion were advised.

The caribou had not come. The seal had not come. The north wind that blew fiercest across the frozen sea—that wind had come. And it was because of it, because of the wind, that Seal Talker must trance.

He would ask his spirit helpers to show which way the caribou had gone. And whatever requests they made of him, whatever it took to find game, it must be done. If the people wanted to live, it must be done.

Elik found a seat along the rear platform. She took off her parka as the other women had, folded and set it neatly behind her. Naiya leaned against her shoulder on one side, Sipsip on her other. Beyond Naiya sat Gull, then Sila, the two older women whispering but not laughing, nodding but carefully, without raising their eyes. Kimik, with her new son on her breast, had stayed at her mother's house, her first day following confinement.

The *qasgi* was warmer than usual. Earlier the men had lit the fire for a sweat bath, preparing themselves for Seal Talker's trance. The heat they used to set the paints on their faces, arms, and chests still lingered, along with the smells of their sweat, the urine they washed through their hair. Even their fears were like a scent in the air—like the musk of a bull caribou facing the harpoon's blade, the smell of human hunger, prickly and thin.

Ema appeared in front of Elik. She carried a small wooden bowl painted with male and female figures: copulating caribou, seal, and people. Ema smiled, lifted it closer. "Eat," she said. "The men have finished. This is extra. A woman needs strength as much as a man."

Elik glanced to her mother but Gull refused to look her way. Naiya pressed Elik in the ribs. She took the bowl, but when she lifted it, her eyes found Seal Talker watching from behind the men, not even troubling to hide the way he looked at her. Quickly, she lowered the bowl, passed it back.

For his first dance, Seal Talker brought out a whip made of seaweed. Elik leaned closer, wanting to know: had

Ema made it? And if she had, was it weaker because, as Ema said, her old hands were losing their strength? Would a weakness in the braiding make it more difficult for Seal Talker to locate caribou?

Seal Talker snapped the whip. A few of the women had been talking; they quieted now. The double beat on the drums quickened.

"Enough!" Seal Talker shouted. The knife amulets on his belt clacked and scraped, trying to cut the hard weather. "It is enough! The empty seas! Our harpoons that cannot see!" He set down the whip, took up two harpoons complete with foreshafts, heads, but no retrieval lines.

Elik watched the way Naiya leaned forward, eyes all on the shaman's harpoon, watching as he struck to the left. Gull and Sila watched also. No one troubled with Ema, the way Elik did now, watching as she hid herself down in the entry tunnel, sliding the whip away from her husband's step. Setting a coil of rope on the floor just as his hand reached out. The way the whip in his hand became the rope that would bind his hands and feet during his trance-journey.

The silence spread. Two men, their faces painted so thickly she didn't recognize who—approached the shaman. As if afraid they'd scorch their hands, they bound his wrists with Ema's rope. Behind his back, then up again and through his ankles, his knees, knots no human teeth could ever cut or slice.

The final light was smothered. The drumming heightened. The beat rose faster than hands or ear could follow.

Seal Talker would ask his spirit helpers to guide him to the Moon because it was there that Alignuk dwelt, Alignuk who would convince the animals that the people were good. Alignuk whose heart could be moved by Seal Talker's plea.

The story of the Alignuk was the story of the Moon, of the brother who had lain with his sister, Suqunuq, in her house where she lived alone near the center of their village. It had been in the autumn of the year, long ago in the First

Times, when the world was thin and things were not the same as they are now.

At night, in the dark, a man had come and slept with Suqunuq, loving her though she did not recognize him, lying beside her.

He came again the next night, and the next. By then Suqunuq had grown curious. What if it was a spirit lying with her? Not someone human at all? And so she touched her lover's face with soot, under the left eye. She marked him.

It was the next evening when Suqunuq peeked down through the skyhole of the *qasgi* toward the men. She searched for the soot mark and found it, there on the face of Alignuk—her brother.

Out of shame she cut off her breast. Out of anger she let her blood drip into the same tub that she urinated in and defecated in. Out of anger she threw it at him. "Eat this," she cried. "If you love me so, eat this."

Alignuk threw down the bowl and ran after her. Round and round they ran, circling the *qasgi*, circling the village. Round and round until they were lifted into the sky. Into the sky they rose.

The sister became the Sun, and her blood the light of dawn. The brother followed her into the Moon where it is cold. Where he lived in his house, casting the lesser light. The moon. And it is here, in the moon, that the souls of all the animals live, the sea mammals in a pool on one side and the land animals on the other.

Naiya leaned against Elik's shoulder. Her hair smelled sweet with the oil she had combed through her braids—if Seal Talker found no caribou, it would be the last time this year she used oil for anything but food.

The shaman's frenzy was on him; they could hear it though they couldn't see: his body racked, contorted with the journey. His back bunched and rose, knees lifted; his head slammed the floor.

There were cries from outside that matched his own: from the smoke hole, from the tunneled winter entry: walrus and cormorants, the pained cry of a lynx, a bear alone on the ice.

It was impossible to know how much time had gone by. Half a day, or more? Elik breathed heavily. Someone else coughed. There was a sobbing sound—Seal Talker? Crying? Nobody moved. Nobody dared.

Finally, a lamp was lit. Seal Talker lay in the center of the qasgi floor. His eyes looked wild. There was blood on his hands and a gash on his forehead. The rope that had bound him lay in two pieces now, one near his feet, the other where the drummers sat.

"I have gone to the Moon," he said. His voice was hoarse and thick. "I have asked for the game to return."

"All will be well now," Naiya whispered. "You'll see . . . "

Elik did see. But what she saw, she didn't like. Seal Talker had chosen the tale of the Moon and the Sun for a reason. This caribou séance, he had chosen this too for a reason: the same as the reason why Ema had put the caribou bowl in her hands—made her drink. That bowl, and not another. Her, and not someone else.

"Do the spirits not enjoy the same things people enjoy?" Seal Talker asked. There was a murmured assent. Elik could have guessed the words, even before he spoke them.

"And if we are paired, so the animals will pair themselves, and their offspring will return, like blades of grass unending. There was a place I saw, With Many Willows. You all know it. Many caribou were passing—"

"East of the tall rock," one of the men called. And another answered. And by then, the pitch of excitement had risen. The tension broke, the women pulled in closer, the men relaxed. And now there were glances being cast from the women to the men, the men to the women, smiling, all of them knowing what was coming. That what their shaman said the spirits requested because it was good for them, was the same thing that was good for people.

Who could deny it? Who would throw away the chance for plenty?

Elik folded her hands, watched the way her fingers sat in her lap. A year ago she had danced the story of Eagle's Gift. And what did the Eagles teach but that spirits were pleased when people rejoiced? That people were meant to come together, not apart. Like the caribou, and the wolf, and the great flocks of birds, paired and nesting. Not alone. Not a woman without man. A man without a woman.

She lifted her eyes. Seal Talker had taken a drink of water; his sweat and the dripping bladder caused the paint to run down his chest. He wiped his mouth. Naked as he was, he started dancing in front of the men. One after the other he began marking them with soot and then the women, pairing them off. The way the spirits had requested . . .

The names went by. Elik wasn't surprised not to hear hers. Girls, whenever possible, to their father's sister's sons; boys to their mother's brother's daughters. For the one night they would call each other "dear little husband," and "little wife."

She felt angry, as if she'd been betrayed. He had not tranced for the caribou. He had tranced for himself. For his appetites, his greed.

There was laughter and shuffling, and directions being given, but nowhere was there a protest. Tomorrow, the couples would go back where they belonged, to their husbands and their wives, their own sleeping places. This was for one night, and not for themselves, but for the good of all.

A few couples made their way to the comfort of their own houses. Others unrolled their skins along the platform, beneath it in the corners, in the cooler entry tunnel, wherever there was room.

Naiya and Whale Fin. Sipsip and Iluperaq. Ema had disappeared. Again, Elik wasn't surprised. Her father's name was called with Salmonberry's. Gull without complaint to Saami's son. No names held surprises—no brothers called to sisters, no fathers to daughters. Only those who were already hunting partners, or the right kind of cousins. Only where the joining was welcome and allowed.

Finally, Seal Talker spoke her name. He had moved from the center floor near the entry tunnel, to a place beside the hearth. Someone had already laid out skins for their bed. Who? Ema? It didn't matter. "Elik." He called again.

Slowly, she edged toward the floor. She didn't dare complain, not aloud. She might have run earlier, when she first guessed. But who would understand?

When the spirits were pleased, the animals would come. When they spoke their wishes through a shaman, women as well as men were expected to comply. Would she want to be the cause of hunger, of disease? Wasn't the winter harsh enough already?

A hand touched her ankle and she jumped, then heard Naiya's giggle. Her sister's naked shoulder and breast peered like an eye from beneath the platform. "Go with him," Naiya whispered. "What's the matter, you walk so slow?"

Elik squatted down. "His will is too strong—"

"Too strong?" Naiya laughed. "Or else too hard?" Naiya rolled toward Whale Fin, whispered something, then turned back around. Elik tried to say something, but Naiya shook her head. "It's enough, sister. You're a woman, not a child. There are stories of what happens to women too haughty to marry. Pick up your needle—it's time."

Elik stopped listening. She crossed the small distance to where Seal Talker waited, patting the thick furs at his side. He smiled; a line of painted sweat dripped down his neck. "Sit," he said. "I have gone where others never go."

Elik pulled off the low boots she still wore—and the amulet bag from around her neck—she took that off, tucked it inside the foot of one of her boots.

There was nothing left to do. She had denied him once, pretended she was *kongak*. He wouldn't allow it again.

He leaned her down on the furs, moved above her. She looked up. Behind his face, a dim light outlined the sky of the *qasgi* roof. Men sighing and the sounds of women's rhythmic noises filled the air, everywhere. Seal Talker cupped her breast, tasted it with his tongue. He fitted himself closer to her side. "This will be good now," he whispered, "and even better later. Already I dream of how your hands will knead my legs at night."

Elik closed her eyes. She could shut out the sight of him, but not his words. She still could hear. And feel . . .

He moved to climb on her belly, to slip between her legs.

She stiffened—she couldn't help herself.

"What is this?" he demanded. He said it instantly, so sharply her eyes flew open. He stared down at her, his face so close, she couldn't breathe.

Her throat shut. What could she do? Seal Talker was a shaman, not an anxious boy to grab her, the way Naiya said Whale Fin did, his hand shooting up the loose hem of her parka whenever she walked near. . . .

"If you disobey," he warned, "who will hear you? The spirit who stole your grandmother's soul. That one is gone. . . ."

*Gone?* Elik sucked in her voice, not to cry. *What did he mean—gone? Grandmother—did he make you die? Did he . . . ?*

Seal Talker pulled back, watched her a moment and then, sensing his mistake, grew gentler, quieter. She was so young compared to him, a child really. He stroked her neck, touched her chin. More kindly, he said, "A woman's worth is in two places: the children she makes and in her hands that are never still."

He kept touching her, her hand, circling her wrist, stroking from her arm upward to her neck. "A woman's hands," he said, "must always remember the count of five. Five for the days of her bleeding time . . ."

Elik shiverered. Her muscles tightened, then released. She tried not to pull away. If she insulted him, if she did anything to offend him, or acted improperly . . . Who knows what power he had . . . ?

From her neck, he drew a line to her breast, to her belly. "Five for the days of a child's birth," he said.

Elik hid her protest. A sick taste filled her mouth. He had worked on Iluperaq, and cut away his finger. He had worked on Alu. And Alu now was gone.

"Five for the days of death," he whispered, and he flattened his palm on the mound of her dark hair, tucked his fingers between her legs. He lifted himself better, settled his knees between hers.

Elik flattened her cheek against the fur bedding, trying to breathe. Like the otter, who had come to her. Like the amulet it had given her—she too must learn to breathe in two worlds. She would shut her breath on Seal Talker and go inside, to an ocean of her devising. Air and water; she must live in both. . . .

Seal Talker moved: something grazed her face and she opened her eyes.

From a thong around his neck, a single amulet dangled in front of her. Smooth and white: the figure of a walrus. Etched with skeletal life lines. With ribs and tusks and eyes a walrus spirit could surely use to see . . .

To see her.

And the younger man whose hand she suddenly recognized in the shape of the amulet—did he see her too? Through the eyes of a walrus? Did he remember her?

She let out the breath she'd been holding. She understood now why the otter had shown itself—it was to help her breathe, to protect her so she wouldn't drown for lack of air.

Elik closed her eyes and while the hands that held her by the hips, and the face that hovered over her belonged to one man, it was a younger man, with slender hands and different eyes that she saw.

It was past the fifth day, as custom dictated—five for the death of a woman. Five in seclusion for the birth of a child.

Kimik's baby seemed to be thriving with Alu for his name. She had left the birth hut smiling and proud and returned to her mother's house, where Iluperaq waited. She had stitched him his first suit of clothes from birdskins, and then a second from the head of a hare.

She would have been content to stay with her mother, passing the child around to be admired, nursed, then shared. But that in spite of Seal Talker's trancing, the caribou had not yet come. Her mother's house was too crowded and the small size of their cache was beginning to show.

There was Kimik and the baby on one side of the platform. Iluperaq, because it was not yet permitted for him to sleep beside his wife, shared his blanket with Kimik's youngest brother, Olah, on the floor behind the hearth. Kimik's parents, Blue-Shadow and Sila, kept the warmest sleeping place, opposite the door. Along the third wall, or sometimes in the alcove off the entryway, slept Kimik's older brother, Singmiut with his wife, Salmonberry, and their son.

Five more nights they slept in that house until, from the men's gossiping in the *qasgi*, Iluperaq learned that Chevak planned on leaving Saami's house, where he and Gull and Elik had been sleeping since Alu's death, and returning to their own house.

At Kimik's insistence—before there was a misunderstanding—Iluperaq went to speak to his father. He found Chevak in his uncle Saami's house, sorting through his baskets.

"I am going to the Bent Point village," he announced.

Chevak kept his gaze on his baskets, figuring. He leaned toward Gull, whispered a question, then figured some more. When he was done he looked up and nodded. "Don't bring them any of our fish," he said.

Iluperaq looked to his mother, but Gull kept her gaze lowered. Her shoulders stiffened as if expecting an argument. "Only what I caught myself," Iluperaq said.

"Last summer, your uncle's catch was larger than ours."

"I'll carry only what we need—"

This time, Gull looked up. "We?" she repeated. "Kimik is going also?"

"Yes, and the baby, of course. He's young enough we'll have no trouble with him in her parka."

"It's best." Chevak looked more agreeable than usual. "With the winter here so harsh, not to have to feed a nursing mother . . . "

"My sister has also asked to come."

This time Gull nodded while Chevak showed surprise.

"Naiya? Naiya would leave her new husband?"

"No. Elik."

Chevak grunted. "Did anyone ask your mother, with no hands to help her?"

Gull kept her eyes lowered as she answered. "She already asked. I agreed."

Chevak stared at his wife. "You spoke with Seal Talker?"

Iluperaq knotted his four-fingered hand into a fist, hid it behind his back. "There isn't time," he answered before Gull had a chance. "I mean to leave while the weather's open. Tomorrow morning by the latest. My sister will be in Seal Talker's house by the spring anyway, so why not let her come? I'll hunt with Weyowin"—Iluperaq turned to leave—"or else that new cousin, Allanaq. We'll see what there is. It may be they have better luck there. Who knows?"

"Who knows?" Chevak repeated, and he went back to figuring the count of food, the cost of the shaman's gifts he still needed to gather in payment for his mother's burial.

The double line of fox tracks crossed the snow so often that the pattern looked like the mesh of a torn net, wind-blown strands, circles looping across the snow. Grey Owl fixed the wooden snow goggles on the bridge of his nose so the slits fit better, then scanned the glaring flats, waiting for Allanaq to join him.

This would be a good place to set their traps, with so many tracks crossing and the way the land opened to one side, with a covering of brush on the other.

Fox liked it this way; they liked to dig their dens near wide open places, grassy areas where ground squirrels lived, where a vixen could steal carrion from a wolf's kill-site, then run home to feed her spring-born kits.

Allanaq came up behind Grey Owl, lowered his goggles to his chest, then knelt on his snowshoes beside the tracks. He puffed his cheeks, blew the powder snow from the harder crust below, looking to see whether the tracks were fresh or old.

Grey Owl held quiet, giving him time. For more days than he cared to remember they had sat in the *qasgi* and grown moody, waiting out the weather—bad weather, filled with too many signs. This most recent storm had been the worst, not the snow that it dropped—that came only above the ankles—but thick, thick gales, visibility like a mask covering a man's face.

Alllanaq had worked on his chipped flint side blades,

the kind no one else had even seen hafted into a lance head. And his carvings of animals with put-together parts, head and rear like something out of a dream. Sometimes Grey Owl practiced in his head the words he would choose if things grew worse. How he would ask if, maybe, the best way to stay alive would be to put away his blades, his explanations of how they spread the wound wider, deeper. Put away his carvings with the skeletal lines that brought him nothing but troubled glances.

What use was there in so much skill if all it brought a man was enemies? If it made others so jealous, so foolish they went about finding demons in everything Allanaq touched?

He had hoped things would be better by now, a full turn of the seasons since Allanaq had come to him. And perhaps it would have been—if winter hadn't come on so angry and quick. If Squirrel had come to his bed a few times more. Who knows but Allanaq might have started a grandchild for Bear Hand? At least, then, the man might have quit his whispering.

Or if Allanaq had brought back more trade goods from the Bent Point village. But no—that wouldn't have helped. People might just as easily resent his wealth as they did his carvings.

And this weather, surely it wasn't a good sign for a wind to bring so many storms? So many that the last catch of salmon never happened, and the caribou . . . Who knew which way the caribou had gone? Certainly not the men inside the *qasgi*, waiting, singing, looking for whom to blame.

Allanaq signaled to Grey Owl: the fox tracks were new, better than the cold piles of scat they'd found earlier. True, they'd have preferred finding caribou, but without any signs—no broken willow, trampled snow, or piled droppings, they'd hunt where they could.

Everything depended on the weather, on what tracks they found, or if other men had come the same way earlier, hunting out the land.

"We'll start a line of deadfall traps here," Grey Owl said, and he turned to point out the snowblown pass between the nearest hills. "A day that way, maybe less. Then a day back, checking the traps, from the Lake Where Cattails Freeze to the Creek Between Two Hills."

"And then?" Allanaq followed where Grey Owl pointed.

"From there to another place we call Where Two Families Died Together. I'll show you. It would be good for you to know."

They spoke little as they worked, keeping their faces deep inside the shelter of their hoods. Grey Owl showed Allanaq the way he built something like a small house from upright sticks and brush, then found a trigger-stick and pushed it in, so one end was raised for a fox to reach the bit of fat, but only by bringing the heavier killer-log down on his back.

At the next site, Allanaq set a pit trap, which was good for a fox, but might also find a wolverine with its better-tasting meat, its heftier bones.

And another kind of trap, with a tunnel and a slab of stone set in front. Support the roof piece with a trigger line, Grey Owl said, hide it in the snow, and then, when the animal comes out, the roof shakes and it falls.

They talked about how the same kind of trap a person set for a fox could also be used for a lynx, or maybe a wolf. How it was a good time of year for the pelts now, because later the coats thinned out with hunger.

Grey Owl said that no fox he'd ever heard of came to a trap if a person was careless and left his scent. But every animal grew hungry and the fox, when it did, ate anything: rabbit or squirrel, ptarmigan or vole, and berries—even berries like a human or a bear.

Only the lemming and the ground squirrel were more plentiful than fox, and either would feed a man and clothe him, except the season was wrong. It was spring they needed for ground squirrels, not winter. And besides, Allanaq kept insisting that if a man set his snare right, the way he'd been taught, if he baited it and kept his thoughts on the animals, then later, when he came back to check, a fox would surely have come.

That was their first day after the storms. If either man had different thoughts, he kept them to himself. A man didn't talk about hunger unless he wanted to invite it into his house.

With luck, they would have meat to bring home. Without it, they might at least keep themselves alive, with ptarmigan, a few hare. So long as this weather held they wouldn't starve. And Nua, back home, needed less food alone than the three of them together.

When dark came, they dug a shelter into the ground, square like a house, except smaller, and only temporary. They cut down into the snow with a long knife, not deep, removed the blocks and piled them in a low line along one side. Against one end of the wall they set their sledge, tied it off to a break of willows. Above them, for a partial roof, they stretched a caribou skin and another below them, layered with willows to hold their backs from the colder ground.

They slept warm, though they were hungry. They filled their stomachs with water, and ate only a portion of the frozen fish Nua had packed.

The next day they started again, this time checking their traps before deciding whether to set anything new or try a different place.

It was in their second set they found a silver vixen, with a long white tail. She was dead, though she hadn't been for long—which was a good thing, else a wolverine might have found her first. The rear leg was cinched in the snare, but she was smart—there were her tracks, circling the bait a long while before she risked coming near.

"This one was eating well," Grey Owl said.

"It's a good sign—someone, at least, had food."

Allanaq loosened the snare from the frozen leg. The fur was as good as a man could hope, caught early, before the winter coat was rubbed thin. He smoothed the fur, then, before tying the stiffened body to their sledge, fixed a small ivory thimble to the carcass—a woman's gift, because it was female. So it would tell others there were good people here.

By dusk, they counted two fox and, in their pitfalls, three of the loping, long-eared arctic rabbits. Not a bad catch for their work. And they were done earlier than they'd hoped, the distance spent checking traps going quicker than breaking trail the day before.

The light was still strong enough to work by when they returned to their camp. Grey Owl rubbed seal fat on the fox's black nose—for food on the other side—and also on the rabbits they would bring back to Nua. On the vixen, he started with a cut up from its anus, then a knife prick to open the bag of its stomach. The contents unfolded in a mat. "It's been eating a vole," he said, and he showed it to Allanaq.

While Grey Owl worked on the fox, Allanaq built a fire on the snow. He used the black firestones he carried in a pouch, and pieces of dry willow cotton that he'd rubbed with charcoal before they'd left. The instant a spark caught, he added a bit of dry moss, willow shavings, grass he'd picked along the way. The flame caught and held, then grew.

It was after the meat was done boiling that Grey Owl laid his hand on Allanaq's knee. "Turn slowly," he said. "Toward the river."

There were two men on snowshoes, each dragging a sledge, walking along the wide path of the frozen river. Allanaq looked once, then quickly back. "Who are they?" he whispered.

Grey Owl bit into his meat, sliced off the larger portion near his mouth. He chewed, stole a glance, swallowed, looked again. They were still coming. "I don't know these," he said. "They're tall, and there are fringes on their clothing. It's best they see you smile. They already know we have food."

Allanaq reached for a water bladder, using the motion to peer beneath his arm. He took a drink, went back to chewing, so the two men would know they weren't afraid, that they weren't starving or weak, or interested in a fight.

Grey Owl was right. They were tall and they weren't Real People; their clothing wasn't right for that. But they weren't Seal People either. Allanaq's stomach twisted—not so much in disappointment, as at the realization that for one moment he had wondered if it might be. It was that close still, the hope of his own people. It hadn't left him yet.

If he ever did meet Seal People, they would come by sea, proudly, in their umiaks and kayaks. Not like these two men, with heads held down against the wind, as if they were lost. And their hoods weren't stitched to their parkas but separate, as if their heads had been severed.

"We could greet them and then break camp," Grey Owl suggested.

"In the dark? They'd see our fear and then grow bold."

"In the dark they wouldn't follow."

Allanaq pulled his pack closer, against his leg, where he could reach. He had his short knife for eating—they would know that already. And two more tucked inside the pack. And one that he slipped carefully inside his boot. Grey Owl did the same, then pushed aside the haunch of meat they'd been about to eat, so they'd have something to offer.

The men were close enough now for Allanaq to see that their sledges were built longer than Grey Owl's, with higher sides that were better for a place where the snow fell deeper—inland. Forest People.

Grey Owl said, "See the rolled skins on the sledge? They've had some luck, though it might be old; they could be hungry again. Maybe they'll want to trade—their skins for our oil. Let them talk first."

The two strangers stopped a short distance away. No dogs were with them. No women to share the work. But that didn't mean there weren't more men somewhere, behind a snow-blind, on the far side of the river. They could have seen the fire and planned.

They didn't have the look of hungry men, but definitely they were cold. Allanaq wondered if the caribou skins piled on the sledges meant there was food below, or if

Grey Owl was right and the meat was gone, and only the heavy load of skins remained.

They unloaded their gear, but only a little, set up a shelter, but not very strong. Allanaq whittled on a length of willow. Grey Owl rolled the fox pelt.

Finally, they heard the crisp sound of boots breaking through snow. Grey Owl stood, smiled as the two men approached. With hand signs, he showed there was meat to share, that the only weapons they had were the bows any man would carry on a hunt, not lances for war. The other men showed him the insides of their sleeves: empty. They too had brought no weapons except to hunt.

"*Waqaa*." Grey Owl kept a smile on his face. "Greetings."

The older of the two men said something. Grey Owl looked to Allanaq, but neither of them understood. Grey Owl motioned for them to share the food.

The two men bore little resemblance. Perhaps, Allanaq wondered, the older man was an uncle, not a father. That would make sense. It was the older one who was taller, while the younger man had a nose that stuck out from a too-long face, teeth missing, skin like gravel. *Ugly*, Allanaq found himself thinking. And their chins without labrets— even to his eye they looked naked.

"Did you see the weather last night? There was a ring around the moon?" Grey Owl lifted his chin toward the sky, pointing. "*Weather*," he said, more slowly, trying to help them understand.

*Weather*, the older man repeated, nodding, returning the same smile Grey Owl wore—tight, controlled. Worried.

Grey Owl and Allanaq sat back down. The two strangers sat down. Grey Owl pulled off a mitten. With his knife, he sliced a length of fox meat from the lower section of rib, passed it to the older man sitting near him now. The man laughed appreciatively. Grey Owl leaned toward Allanaq. "I don't think they understand."

Allanaq nodded. He waited till their faces were buried

in their meat, then looked again. Both men were long-limbed, with dark hair pulled back in a tie behind narrow faces, not round, their eyes straight, not slanted. They ate carelessly, like animals, not people, biting off huge chunks instead of cutting it near their mouths. They scooped snow by the handful—large hands, heavy and muscled. They sucked the water from the snow, drank, then spit the rest toward the fire. A coal spit back—the older man followed the flare, pointing with the meat in his hand and laughing as if he'd done something brave. Few teeth were left in his mouth and those he had were pointed, like dog teeth, all of them.

They finished the meat in silence, the two men exchanging only a few odd-sounding words. Grey Owl waited politely till they had sucked the marrow from the bones, chewed them, and spit the splintered ends in the fire before he tried talking.

He pointed vaguely toward the south, not to the Long Coast village, that would have been a foolish thing to tell, but toward the sea. "*Tapqaaq*," he tried, calling it the Straight Sandy Beach. The men didn't answer. "*Igiguq*," he tried, for the name they called a nearby hill.

The younger man stood up. Grey Owl tapped Allanaq's knee. "Maybe he knows something? *Igiguq*." He smiled excitedly and repeated the name again.

"*Igiguq*," the younger man repeated, and he started away.

"They know who they are," Grey Owl said.

Allanaq watched a moment. "He's only going to piss."

Grey Owl narrowed his eyes into the settling light. The man had walked off, not toward their shelter but in the other direction, and only as far as the edge of reddish snow outlined in the fire's light.

Grey Owl leaned over and whispered, "You could go see how he pisses. Maybe that will tell us something?"

Allanaq shrugged, then followed to where the younger man now stood. He planted his feet in the snow as the other man had done, drew up the front of his parka, pushed down his trouser top.

Two streams went out, two lines cut through the snow: a smell no different than he already knew.

Allanaq glanced sideways for a better look at the man's clothes: they were made of caribou, with the hair removed so only the leather was left. Plain leather, and soft, but why any woman would scrape the warming fur from winter garments, he couldn't guess. From the bottom of the hem walking upward toward the chest there was a dotted line and then a print, the track a raven leaves behind on snow.

The man kept his eyes mildly ahead, but Allanaq peered again, trying to see something. But no—it was dark and there were hands and belts and pouches hanging from the belt and maybe too much pubic hair in the way.

Sitting back next to Grey Owl, he shrugged. "He pissed yellow but, then, so does a dog." The other men also leaned together, made sounds that never quite turned into words. Allanaq nodded and smiled and watched their hands. "Do you think they'll trade?" he asked.

"Try."

Allanaq reached inside his parka. He hadn't brought baskets full of ivory and points as he had when he traveled to the Bent Point village, but he did have one amulet, an antler-carved wolf with pointed ears and teeth. He had gouged out a hole in the hump of its neck and set in real guard hairs from a wolf. It was his newest amulet and he wasn't sure of it yet—whether it was strong or dependable, where the speed of a wolf would come into any man who wore it, or only for him.

The men watched closely as he slid the cord over his head, held the amulet out to show. There was a long silence. Too long—Allanaq didn't know which way to read their faces or the quick, pointed gestures they made with their hands. He turned the wolf over, showed where he'd cut in the fourth lines to show the inner life, the strength and blood and speed.

He thought back to the family he'd traded with on his summer journey. Were these people related? He couldn't tell. The family had been interested in his map. He wouldn't object if these men took his ivory and gave him a map of the inland passes in exchange.

Finally, the younger man rose and walked to his sledge. When he returned he was carrying a pouch cinched with a drawstring and a small pelt. He unrolled the pelt on the wet snow in front of the fire: it was muskrat, dark and well furred. He emptied the pouch on top. There was a clanking sound. Stone falling against stone. Antler. Bone.

The older man motioned and Grey Owl reached to sample the blades. There were slate blades and barbed dart heads made of antler and bone, a few small grey scrapers, two fishhooks set in bone. A graving tool. Grey Owl picked out one of the blades: a stone that would have been hard to find in the Long Coast, thinned for lashing to a grooved handle.

When the older man nodded toward Allanaq's wolf, he passed it respectfully, holding it in two hands, showing how prized he thought the work. But all the while he held it, Allanaq kept a careful watch on the younger man's hand, the way he tried shielding something he'd kept back in the sack, something tapered, long and thin. And the way something poked its head from his boot top while he sat on his heels: another blade, another knife. Watching Allanaq's blade, watching his.

They traded quickly with little talk and, it seemed to Allanaq, less pleasure. In the end, the man traded Allanaq's wolf for three stone blades that Grey Owl's hand had lingered over.

The blades were flaked from a core, retouched on one side only—the kind of tool that was useful for more than one sort of work.

For himself Allanaq took a length of dense straight-grained wood that he hadn't been able to scratch with his fingernail. Not the map he had hoped for, but as he and Grey Owl went to their beds, it didn't seem a loss.

Allanaq tucked the caribou skins closer around his neck for warmth. Blocked by the wall of snow, the wind had quieted. He rolled to his side.

The men hadn't come looking to trade. If they had, they

would have brought more, and bargained harder, and taken not only for themselves, but with an eye to another trade, and the next.

More likely they had seen Grey Owl's fire while they were hunting. There were no nearby villages of Forest People, none that he had ever heard of. But anything was possible if the same storms that troubled the coast plagued their villages too. After all, they had to eat. These were men, not demons pretending to piss as humans did.

It was no use trying to sleep.

The fire had sunk into the snow. The only light came from the half-moon hiding behind a layer of thickening clouds.

Something in the wind reminded him of the hollow sound inside his father's house, those last breaths before Red Fox's men attacked. The way he and his father had stood, motionless, listening toward the roof, the door, listening through the walls.

He rolled to his other side; the willow branches he'd cut for matting creaked beneath him. He sat up, trying to hear.

The two men had set their sleeping furs near the sheltering willow. Not far, but far enough that Allanaq couldn't see or hear. And what he couldn't hear, he couldn't trust. He thought of something his father used to say—how any weapon used for hunting could also be used against a man.

Fully dressed, Allanaq slipped from his bedding, stepped back, and listened to the wind move through willow brush, the way the few dried leaves shook on their branches. But no sleeping sounds—snoring, a wheeze. Most men near Grey Owl's age breathed heavily in their sleep. He would have worried less if he heard them more.

He turned: Grey Owl was asleep in his mound of skins—he wouldn't wake him, not without more reason than his own tingling memories. He thought of taking his birding lance, but who would believe he was hunting ptarmigan in the dark? His ice pick then? He could say there was ice glaciating up from the river, that he was going for water. No one could fault him for watching where he walked. He brought it, checked the end: he'd changed the tip recently, lashing on an antler point. He'd say he was going to relieve himself. That he didn't want to fall through ice he couldn't see.

He started toward the bright snow on the river but circled wider, farther out than he had to, and carefully—so they wouldn't hear. If the men were sleeping, he didn't want to wake them. If they were talking, he would hear, and then skirt wider around.

It grew darker away from the fire. The clouds that had blown in covered the moon, blocked its light. He was close enough he should have heard them by now, if they were awake.

The line of river-brush was on his right. The beds and the gear the men had set against their upturned sledge ahead. There were shadows just strong enough to make out the hump of their blankets. He straightened and relaxed, let out his breath.

And then he heard it: not the fire, but something snapped. Not the wind, but voices. Human voices—to the side: Where? Not from their beds. The skins—they were in a roll, lengthwise—ready to throw atop the sledge, empty.

He started running. Toward Grey Owl. That was all he could think of. Grey Owl. In the dark. Asleep. Alone.

They didn't hear him—they were too intent on their own plan. On stealth and quiet and the bulge of the man asleep in the dugout snow. Knives in their hands. Allanaq saw them—creeping, one arm lifting over his father . . .

*Grey Owl. His father. Red Fox. The memory kicked against his gut, in his bowels. Not his father—Not again!*

He screamed. And they reeled to face him—both at the same time. He leaped for the one nearest Grey Owl, lifted the sharpened point of his ice pick, stomach high, then vaulted—over the fire and with all his strength flying toward them, toward the man rearing like a bear, facing him with his knife like a claw.

With the force of his leap behind him, Allanaq aimed the point for the man's heart. There was a moment where their blades met; the longer shaft of Allanaq's ice pick hitting first, before the blade. The blade cutting through Allanaq's parka while the point of his ice pick struck hard and deep and loud.

Allanaq's grip shuddered with the impact; his shoulder flared and burned. The man toppled backward and Allanaq fell with him, fell, then tore himself away, rolling away from the pain that seared his shoulder as the man's knees went up, as his hands struggled to tear the shaft from his chest, from his heart.

Allanaq was on his feet again, crouched and circling in front of Grey Owl, who was standing now, his own knife lifted, pointing.

He was alive, they both were—though something had happened to Allanaq's shoulder; a wet, sticking feeling, and pain: tight and throbbing. He was bleeding, but he hoped that was all. And alive—while the other man? Where was he? Allanaq peered into the shadows.

Grey Owl circled till his back was against Allanaq's, the two of them watching in every direction. There was a sound . . . Opposite the river . . . They swung round and both saw him at the same time, the only straight outline in the dark, lumbering through snow, fading. Allanaq looked to Grey Owl.

"I'm all right," Grey Owl said. He looked worriedly toward Allanaq's shoulder. "And you? What happened?"

Allanaq pressed his hand against the parka's torn fur. The underside stuck, held by blood. Allanaq took a long breath, let it out. There was pain, but not so much he couldn't fight. Or run. "This will heal," he said. "But that one—?" He stepped toward where the man had disappeared. "I can run him down—"

"Let him go." Grey Owl held Allanaq back. "He'll spread the word of what you've done. He'll tell his people we're men to fear. They won't come again. What about this one?" Grey Owl stood over the fallen man, tapped a lance point against the exposed neck, ready in case it was needed.

It wasn't. The man lay where he had fallen, arms to the

side, legs crumpled after. The shaft of Allanaq's ice pick angled above his chest.

"He's dead." Grey Owl knelt, twisted the knife from the man's closed fist. He listened near his mouth. "Dead," he said again.

"It isn't something we looked for, is it?"

"No. Yet it's done."

They stood there, peering toward the dim trail, down at the Forest Man's body, then out again, listening into the night.

Finally, Grey Owl said, "We need to leave this place."

Allanaq winced. "First the body," he said. "We need to burn it. His voice was low, almost a whisper. "They say . . . They say the body of a dead man must be buried properly, or the soul will never find the other world. If it's not—if the death taboos are broken—the ghost grows angry. It waits . . . It . . . If it's not buried . . ."

Allanaq stared into the air. The dark was full, the stars not so distant as he would have liked them to be. He took a breath, collected himself, then said, "We should burn this body. It could follow us . . ."

Grey Owl looked to his son, to the way his face knotted, with more thoughts than he realized he had shown. "We'll wait out the night," he said. "In case the other one returns. In the morning we'll break camp. We'll do as you say, then leave."

"What will we tell them?" Allanaq asked.

Grey Owl held quiet, thinking. A moment later he surprised Allanaq with a smile. "We'll say the truth. We'll bring food for your mother to share out. And two new sledges. And the story of how one man saved his father's life and chased an enemy from their home."

Ani's Wife's small house had grown too hot, overheated by the wood fire that cooked their thin, meatless soup to a boil, by the crowding of women and younger girls seated so close their needles nearly poked each other as they worked.

Their talk had turned to a droning in Elik's ears. She felt exhausted from the heat, from battling the wind for the three days it had taken to cross from the Bent Point village to her aunt Nua's empty house, to here, where now, with the women's voices fading one into the other, she wanted nothing more than a chance to sleep.

Tonight she would, she promised herself. She and Kimik and Kimik's baby would curl up together, while Iluperaq slept with the men in the *qasgi* and Nua hoped for the meat Grey Owl and Allanaq would bring back from their hunt.

She would sleep and sleep again and when she woke there would be the lighthearted company of her uncle Grey Owl. Perhaps he would have caribou for Nua to butcher and share. And Allanaq, his son, would visit. It was getting harder to remember his face: all she could see anymore was the sadness of the paint he'd rubbed on his cheeks. And the smooth ivory of his carvings—that she didn't have to remember.

She looked up. Squirrel, the girl at her side, leaned closer, stopping her own work to admire Elik's basket. Nua had given her the grass yesterday, shortly after they arrived. "Make your hands busy," she had said. "So the animals who are pulled into the beauty of your stitches will also be pulled toward your uncle's blade."

Already the sides of her basket were rising to a curve. She held the coil in her left hand, her largest-holed needle with its leading grass thread in her right. Her stitches were neat. She straightened each loop of grass before pulling it tight against the coil, but it was the pattern growing up the sides that Squirrel complimented: not a typical pattern of interlaced lines and triangles, but a shape of ravens Elik had seen in Malluar's house and copied.

Kimik's baby had finished his noisy sucking and fallen asleep; where his head rested on his mother's arm there was a sheen of sweat.

"I never saw that on a basket," Squirrel said.

"They're tracks. A raven here"—politely, Elik turned the basket to show—"and here."

Squirrel followed the design of red, berry-dyed grass. "Did you eat ravens along the way?" She wrinkled her nose in concern. "Were there no ptarmigan signs? Or caribou? My father says . . . "

"Hush," Meqo, Squirrel's mother, touched her knee. "Don't speak so," she warned, except—she already had.

The house grew suddenly quiet. The women took hurried stitches, to show the spirits how content they were, not to complain of hunger or invite in trouble.

Kimik stretched her back, adjusting the baby's weight to free her arm. She cupped her right breast—the one her new son had not yet nursed, and showed the stream of bluish milk that arced as she pinched the nipple. "As long as there's milk," she said, "the baby will be fine. As long as there's a baby in a village, what hunter wouldn't share his catch?"

No one answered.

Kimik glanced questioningly toward Elik. "We found tracks in the snow behind a willow brake." She tried to sound hopeful—they'd eaten better along the trip than they had at home: two hares one day, ptarmigan another. Not a great deal, but enough they hadn't been afraid.

"Only a few," Elik added, "but it was more than nothing."

The only answer was the airy breath of the women's needles, pushing in, pulling out. She would have felt more sure of herself if Nua had been able to join them, to guide the women's talk. But her aunt's bleeding had come on heavy. For three days, Nua said, there had been pains, like childbirth, but different. She had shrugged and made light of it, but she also said she didn't think it safe to leave the house, not even to sit with the women.

Elik missed her grandmother. She worried about her mother, left alone in their house. She hoped Gull was with Naiya, or Sipsip, or someone.

It was Ani's Wife who broke the silence. "In the Bent Point village," she asked, "is it also hard?"

Kimik smoothed a few of the fine dark hairs on her baby's head. "The winds are rough," she admitted.

"But the animals have only taken off their skin." Elik tried to sound hopeful. "Their spirit souls will find a new body. They'll come again—"

"Maybe in the Bent Point village," Long Feather said. "Except some of the men are saying *not here*. They say there may be ghosts here, demons chasing away the game."

"Ghosts?" Elik pulled in her chin. "How?"

A few faces turned, exchanged wary glances. Long Feather nodded as if everything was perfectly plain and clear. She was a gentle-looking woman with a nose that was flat between her eyes, broad above her mouth. Elik tried to remember her better. Long Feather was Meqo's sister, the two of them married to brothers, men her father's age: Kahkik and Bear Hand. She had known them all since she was a child, but with a child's memory.

Would her mother or grandmother have spoken so loudly of evil? She didn't think so. She remembered Squirrel from the runner's feast last winter, that she had giggled too much and listened too little. She had always known Two Ravens of course; not only from the runner's feast, but because they were near the same age, and related through her husband, Weyowin.

"We have done everything Olanna said," Long Feather continued. "We stored our cups upside down, so no evil would get in. And we made certain no women sat on bear hides; only men. We sucked no marrow from caribou bones, lest they felt our teeth, and hid."

Squirrel leaned forward. Her round eyes seemed more excited than afraid. "There's a man here," she whispered, and suddenly, Elik stopped, turned, and listened. Squirrel hadn't noticed. She went on. "He calls himself Allanaq, but it's not his real name. We don't know the real name of his father who is dead. But my father says it is because his father's bones have been kept so close to our houses that the *inuas* are angered. My father says if that man's father was a great shaman, as he claims, and if he was killed by a giant man with a face like a fox, as he claims, then the dead man's bones should be burned.

"The only way we can hope to chase away the ghost of the dead man who came in the umiak is to send away his bones, which hold him here."

Elik set down her basket, moved her hands to her knees to stop their shaking. All around the square of the house, the women nodded their heads in agreement. There was fear in their faces, the kind of fear that hunger puts there when it goes stalking, searching where to strike.

"This man," Elik made herself ask, "this Allanaq—he's the same one who danced at our Bent Point feast?"

"The same."

"And you say he is the one responsible for this hunger?"

Someone giggled, one of the younger girls. Elik looked up. There was another giggle, this time from Squirrel. "What is it?" Elik asked. There was a joke here, something everyone knew but her.

Squirrel said, "This Allanaq—he has a penis like a dog man and he gets stuck whenever he's with a woman. He gets stuck inside—" She started to laugh and covered her mouth, while the younger girl urged her to go on. More seriously, she said, "His hands are so rough, when he tries to push a woman back off his penis his hands slip, like fish scales going the wrong way—"

Elik looked to Kimik. Were they being teased? She couldn't tell. "But why are his hands rough?"

Meqo answered for her daughter. "Because of his carving, all day long, carving ivory."

"But Grey Owl trusted him?" Elik asked. "And there's no reason not to trust Grey Owl, so how can this man be bad?"

"He can be bad—" Meqo answered, "the way a spirit who has confused Grey Owl is bad, so that Grey Owl no longer recognizes truth."

Elik shifted her weight and the amulet pouch beneath her parka shifted with her, leaning against one breast. She had never thought of it that way. What if they were right and Grey Owl, whom she would have trusted with her soul, had been lied to by a demon?

She pushed her needle through the lower row of the grass coil, trying to appear unconcerned. "But are you sure it's this man and not something else? Perhaps it isn't that

Grey Owl is tricked, but that he's seen enough of the man's deeds to trust him, for the sake of his deeds?" Elik raised her eyes.

"Even so," Meqo said, "a man can mean well, he can sing his tales and mean well. But if he keeps making the same mistake—if he waits for walrus in the season when there are fish, or dreams of whales when there are only seals—he will be dead. He and his family will starve. The animals will not come. The people all will die."

No one spoke. The small sounds of needlework resumed. The fire sputtered. Above them on the roof of the house, the wind took hold of the gut window, tugged it free of the rocks that held its corners, and set it flapping against the frozen snow.

The brittle stalks of smoke-grass Nua had set upright in the ash layer of her hearth had long since burned to stubs. The smell of the acrid trail faded, too thin to find.

Elik had slept late, as she had hoped. Later than Kimik who, with Iluperaq in the *qasgi*, dozed on and off, suiting no one but her nursing baby. Nua also slept a good deal, slept and stayed inside the house these few days since they'd arrived. She had done no sewing while her husband was out hunting, waiting as was proper, so her stitches wouldn't scare the animals away.

From outside, the light of an early-winter morning reached down through the skyhole, into the house. It was too dim to see without a lamp yet, but the day seemed clear enough to hope that at least one of the men who had gone out on the ice would find a seal.

Elik sat up. She caught the excited barking of a dog, perhaps being outfitted with a pack. Behind the first bark came the high-pitched whining of another dog, worried at being left behind.

Kimik tapped her shoulder. "What's that sound?" Elik listened again.

Nua heard it also. She slipped from the platform to the floor. "Perhaps it's Grey Owl?" Hopefully, she brushed a coal out of the ashes in the hearth. With a pair of wooden tongs she lifted it, carried it to her seal oil lamp.

The talking was just outside, not on the roof, the way a visitor would call in, but at the entry. Loud. Men's voices. More than just Grey Owl's or his son's. And footsteps now, clamoring through the winter tunnel, loud enough that Kimik edged her way to Elik's side of the sleeping bench.

The first man to appear through the floor well was Grey Owl, Olanna climbing in more slowly behind him. And then another man—brushing snow from his parka to the floor—Lake, the cousin Naiya had poked fun at a year earlier—except that he'd grown. Not a man yet, but taller. Kimik relaxed as Iluperaq climbed through next. And then Bear Hand, with his shoulders hunched, his sternness barely contained.

Nua raised the light from her lamp. She stayed standing—bravely, Elik thought. Gull would never have been so calm with a houseful of men.

They straighted without glancing to the women, then crowded in around the hearth. Two more climbed in: the first was Kahkik, Bear Hand's brother, his hood already down, black hair standing out from his forehead. Last of all, a younger man straightened through the tunnel. It was he, of course, Allanaq—taller than she remembered but less strange, with his hair cut shorter, his chin carrying handsome labrets.

He and Grey Owl must have waited for first light outside the village. Or else they'd spent the night inside the *qasgi*. Had he seen their trail, she wondered? The wind might have hardened it, enough to find. Or someone might have told. She felt suddenly conscious of her unbrushed hair, her hands that were empty of work.

Allanaq squinted toward the lamp. With his sleeve, he wiped the frost from his eyelashes. He smiled when he found Nua but his gaze moved past her, circling the crowded house. Would he recognize her? Something was wrong—an anger had flowed with the men into the house, noise and anger—she didn't know why.

The men shuffled, opening her view. Nua stood beside Allanaq. He was holding the stiff carcass of a fox in one hand, a hare in the other. Bear Hand eyed the meat, raised his eyes to Nua's face. "My wife thought maybe you were in your woman's time?" he asked. "That you watched the count of days . . ."

"I was, but it's done." Nua pulled the fox against her chest. It was important for hunters to know if a woman bled—her flow was like a lamp the animals could hear, strong enough it could change the luck a man carved into his blades. It was a woman's duty to tell, and Bear Hand's right to ask. But not to beg.

"You are certain?" he asked again.

"It's done," she shrugged him away. "Whatever happened, it has nothing to do with me."

"It's food." Grey Owl defended her. "Little as it may be. There was no wrong bringing it home."

"If that was all he brought home, and nothing more—"

"You don't know." Grey Owl nearly shouted. "You can't see . . ."

Elik narrowed her eyes to see her uncle. What if Squirrel was right and he was deceived by a spirit? She'd loved her uncle since she was a child—with his eyes that danced and a mouth that had as many jokes as it had teeth. But sometimes, wasn't it the gentlest people who were most easily fooled?

She looked to the shaman. Olanna didn't seem to be an angry man, the way Seal Talker was, or her father. He was more like Grey Owl or Iluperaq in that way, serious but also filled with laughter. Except he wasn't laughing now. None of them were. Not the men. Not Nua.

Olanna stepped around toward Allanaq, purposely standing between Grey Owl and Bear Hand. "Show me this wound," he said, and Elik leaned with him, trying to see.

"His shoulder—?" Kimik winced and covered the baby. "What are they saying?"

"I don't know." Elik crept forward, away from the safety of the piled blankets.

Olanna stood with his back toward her. She could see his arms lifted to Allanaq's shoulder, pushing aside torn stitches, an open seam, but she couldn't see Allanaq's face, or this wound he had supposedly taken: whether it was deep, or dangerous, or something worse.

The men's circle widened, allowing the shaman space. The talking slowed. Olanna probed with his hands inside the torn sleeve. Elik watched: she had never seen Seal Talker work this way, with so many people standing about, with the lamps fully lit, without drums or spirit helpers whispering in a trance.

She found her brother, followed the line of his shoulder to his hand, to the finger he had lost. She remembered how Seal Talker said that because of the swelling, because of the strange color mottling the skin, the finger must come off.

Seal Talker had done the cutting himself: she hadn't been allowed to watch. Her brother had lived through that. What if Allanaq had to lose his arm? What kind of hunter could live with nothing but a shoulder?

"You did well." Nua spoke softly, reassuring him. "These are fat. Good meat for our guests."

Guests? Allanaq stopped at the word. As if a cord had tightened, he turned, lifted his head to see above Olanna's, and he looked at Elik. Directly at her. A moment passed. Olanna pressed harder; Allanaq winced, remembered himself, and turned away.

"But what if something got in the wound?" Bear Hand asked. "Something that followed the trail of his blood?"

"This is not that kind of hurt," Olanna said.

"Maybe there was a wind? A cloud? Did you see any sign?"

"Nothing," Grey Owl said. "We told you, we were there first. We set camp before them."

Kahkik stepped closer to Bear Hand. "You also said you weren't familiar with the land. . . ."

"Not the exact spot, but I knew the river. . . ."

"It could have been a place that belonged to a demon. Just because you didn't see one, doesn't mean it wasn't there. . . ."

"We saw the fox tracks. We told you that."

"These?" Bear Hand indicated the fox. Allanaq nodded. "And the men?"

Elik's hands tightened on the platform edge. His face was windburned, the tip of his nose, his cheeks and chin—couldn't they see he had been out in the weather? Hunting? There was a shadow line beneath his eyes where his snow goggles would have sat. He had been hunting for his household. What were they talking about? What had he done?

"The men?" Bear Hand repeated, but Allanaq hadn't heard—he was looking at her. His gaze stealing from her face to her chin, her shoulders, breasts . . .

Elik blushed deeply. She kept her eyes down. He couldn't possibly know she was wearing the loon he'd carved, could he? She wanted to reach up and hide it—but even that would seem too forward. If he was a demon . . . he would know . . .

"We told you—" Grey Owl answered for Allanaq. "The men were human. They bled. They died."

"One died, you said. One ran away."

"And it was a good thing, that running," Grey Owl said. "That man will go back to his people and warn them how dangerous we are. They won't come here troubling us. They won't dare."

"You saw no other weapons? Nothing like armor?"

"Nothing." Grey Owl's voice shook. "This was nothing like the stories we hear, of men who cover their chests in tree bark, so an arrow falls aside. No. These people had not come looking for a war."

"What then?"

"To trade," Allanaq said.

"You burned the body of a man who'd come only to trade?"

"It was the best thing we could do," Grey Owl said. "We severed the head, the hands, the elbow joints, and at the knees. If we only buried him, the man who ran away could have returned and found the bones. If we left them, then what was to stop the ghost from coming after us?"

"So you didn't leave at once, though the man who ran away could have doubled back and watched you?" Bear Hand spoke slowly now, accusing, but considering also. "You destroyed the bones because you thought that would keep you safest, away from the anger of the dead?"

Allanaq's blood pounded in his ears. To discuss the dead with this man who raged against his father—it wasn't right. It wasn't safe.

Grey Owl sensed the danger, though he couldn't see exactly its direction. He looked to Olanna for help. "We thought it best—"

Olanna tried to reason. "What is good and what is allowed for one man, may not be the same for another."

Bear Hand shook his head. "But you don't know. What if, though you meant no wrong, you bring revenge down on us? Either the living man comes back and attacks us, because you murdered his father, or uncle. Or the dead man's spirit comes here, following you. And maybe he doesn't find you, but he finds one of us. A spirit may not care where its anger strikes, so long as it's satisfied. And what do you do? You come here and carve your charms with their demon-faces. You say they make your harpoons powerful. But what else is true? What else don't we know?"

Olanna set his arm on Bear Hand's, trying to calm him. "It was the right thing," he said. "Did the fox not come to him? Is there not food here, for us to share?"

Bear Hand wasn't done. "Tell us again," he said. "The men followed the smell of your fire?"

"We invited them to share our food," Grey Owl said. "We showed them what we had to trade. By then night was full. We went to sleep. They attacked. There isn't any more."

Olanna patted Bear Hand's shoulder. "Then we need not worry—"

Bear Hand ignored him. "You traded with them?"

"Yes. This . . ." Grey Owl reached into a pouch.

Bear Hand nodded, but he didn't touch the blade. "And did they take something of yours?"

"For the blade, yes. A carving."

"A carving? Was it yours?" Bear Hand looked to Allanaq. "Or yours?"

Allanaq didn't answer.

"Then all that man has to do is show your carving around until it's recognized. A piece like yours—someone will know it."

"No—" Grey Owl protested. "It isn't that way. We were two days from home. The man turned inland, to the pass between two hills. He couldn't know which way we came. He—"

"He doesn't have to know. He only has to show it—anything this man has carved. It speaks. It tells our name. Ours as much as his." A murmured fear whispered through the room. "It was the act of a fool—trading with them. Letting one man go . . ."

Allanaq had had enough. He refused to answer, but he refused to stand there like a coward. With his back stiff, he made his way to the far wall where his tools and gear leaned beside Grey Owl's. He chose an ice-testing pole from the floor near the bench, a pouch made from a seal flipper for carrying meltwater.

"Where is my son going?" Nua called, and this time her voice showed fear.

"To hunt seal," Allanaq answered and somehow, the words calmed him. "To hunt seal," he said again. "So a man's catch will fill his mother's bowl."

Nua pulled her back up straighter, nodded.

Allanaq turned to leave. There was fear in the house. He could feel it surrounding him, so much fear and anger, like heat rising with the fire.

More than anything, he wanted to turn and look at the girl again, but he didn't dare. Not yet. The air was wavering, too thick with its layers of hunger and death. And the girl, with the fire's shadow glowing in her eyes . . .

10

*I am not the enemy,* Allanaq told himself as he walked over the rough ice nearest the shore, out onto the smoother windblown surface of the open fields.

He slowed only once, looking to the wind to study the weather. The air was sharply cold and still. Overhead, no stretching clouds showed where a wind might rise and move the ice. No haze, no snow. There was a water sky away in the distance, hovering, with a line of dark to show a lead reflecting open water, then another lighter line, where there would be ice again, and the moving edge of the ice pack somewhere beyond.

At home, in the Seal People's place, it would have been different. There would have been a north and a south side to the jutting land. And the wind—it would have moved in ways he understood. More dangerous as it blew from the north, shifting the ice, more trustworthy from the south. Closer to shore, he would have known how to tell whether the ice was safely grounded. Not like here, where people sometimes woke to find huge fields had broken off and floated free.

He kept on walking.

*I am not the enemy, and I have brought no evil into the Long Coast village.*

He reached the first ridge of towering pressure ice, the landfast piles that heaved upward in different patterns every year, built by storms, by currents, by the wind and sky itself. Even in this place, where the pack moved differently once winter settled, a man could generally trust this near-shore ice.

He climbed the boulders on knees and hands, feet and elbows, scrambling till he was over. Only when the ridge was behind him, blocking sight of the shore, did he slow and try to think.

He should have allowed his thoughts to guide him, instead of his anger. Anger made him careless, starting out on the ice like a child with daylight already fading, erasing the shadows a man needed to see by. He'd taken less gear than he should have, though with luck, what he had would suffice. And he'd been walking quickly, not even willing to use his ice tester, the long-handled *unaaq* that was fitted with his toggling harpoon head on one end, an antler ice-testing pick on the other.

Bear Hand had called him "foolish." And the girl, Elik, she had heard. How could she not have heard?

In the *qasgi* last night, just after he and Grey Owl returned, before their news brought arguing—her brother, Iluperaq, had told how he'd come to the Long Coast for hunting. The wife didn't need to invent reasons to travel with him, but Elik?—why had she come? Could they have hoped that food would be more plentiful here than in their own Bent Point village?

He couldn't know and it might not matter. For now he had other worries: Grey Owl, the Forest man who'd run away.

What if, even after burning the stranger's bones, the murdered spirit found its way to the Long Coast village? What if it brought sickness? Or what if the other man came back, hungry for revenge? What if, unwitting though it would have been, Bear Hand was right and he'd committed a terrible wrong?

Perhaps he would stay out, let the ice decide his fate? It would be a test: no seal would come if it sensed evil. Either he would die, or a seal would come.

He would only return when his hands had something to carry, a way to show the girl he was neither a boy nor a fool. He would go home with food, and the People would welcome him, and he would find a way to speak to her.

Allanaq stopped walking. He turned. Had he heard something? The wind had sharpened. It was more deceptive now and haunting. He had made good time, but only because he'd walked carelessly. There was no chance anyone in the village could see him out here, and yet . . . He listened again. What if someone had rushed ahead, hid behind the ice ridge, or flat on his belly behind a fractured hump?

Bear Hand could have done that. Or that Forest man. What if he hadn't returned to his people at all? What if he'd sneaked along behind them, waiting to find Allanaq alone?

The thoughts rippled through his legs, weakening him. He was alone again and worried. Alone when most men hunted in pairs, separating only when each had found a breathing hole worth waiting at. He was alone on the ice, and Bear Hand hated him. No—worse than that—Bear Hand feared him.

He made himself walk, not in a straight line, but veering wide to avoid the drifts and darker, waterlogged snow. He had brought no dog to help sniff out a seal's breathing hole, only his own nose and his anger that kept driving him, making him take risks. Foolish risks.

Bear Hand was a proud man, for all his fears. Not the kind of man to murder another without cause. Not alone, in secret. But then again, he was the kind of man to take it upon himself, without counsel, to go dig up and burn a dead man's bones, destroy them. Send them away. Whatever was necessary, so long as he believed it was right.

Allanaq shook his head. He had to stop thinking this way. Fretting, reliving each scene, each memory. No seal would come to a man with hate in his thoughts. It would be as loud as a drum to them, warning them away. He let out his breath, tried to think only of the ragged plain of ice stretching ahead, the signs at his feet.

He would never have seen the first breathing hole if he hadn't stopped to urinate. Even in the wind, in the dark places and alone, a man didn't stop living. He forced the muscles in his bladder to open against the cold; sent out a spray of yellow, watched it arc—the way a wolf would, marking its territory.

He slipped his penis back into the warmth of his trousers, then turned, looked down, and looked again at the slight hint of a shadow that had caught his eye. He knelt down to see.

It was a seal's breathing hole. He laughed. "This man says you're a male, my friend." And he checked to learn if the hole was new.

It was there: the tiny dome rising above the flattened snow, the blue tint of moisture that built up as the seal splashed from below, hungry for a breath of air to fill its lungs.

Allanaq's anger fled, replacing itself with a hunter's calm. He studied the dome. The color was a little different from the snow surrounding it, the texture also.

If the seal came up for a breath now, before his harpoon was ready, he would miss it. It would smell him and dive and hurry to another breathing hole—there'd be no hope of learning where, or how far away. Without a dog to help, he'd have to start again, watching for the shadow that marked another dome.

Using his blade, he picked through the layer of ice that had formed over the hole—it was thin; it cracked easily.

For the first time since he and Grey Owl had bitten into the fox's flesh, Allanaq smiled. The signs were good. Open water or a thin layer of ice covering a breathing hole meant it was being used. Thicker ice would have meant it was abandoned.

He checked which way the hole broadened beneath the ice. Then quietly filled the widened hole back over with snow. He made sure no hair fell from his clothing, that nowhere did he leave his scent.

He dropped a white feather he'd brought down in the center, to signal when the seal began to rise. And he marked where his harpoon should strike, and then he readied himself for the long wait.

Using his long-bladed knife, he cut blocks of hard-packed snow and lined them in a row to stop the wind. Close to the hole he set a single block down, for a seat. On this he spread a skin for warmth. Then he set out his weapons: his snow knife to the one side, his harpoon in its resting piece to the other.

Last of all, he tied his legs together, for without help against the long watch, a man's strength would fail. He would move, at the one moment when the seal finally decided to trust the world above the sea—a man would move and warn the seal away. He'd done it. Others had.

He wrapped the thong under his knees, looped it up and firm inside the buckle. He fixed the coil of his harpoon line in his lap then drew his arms inside his sleeves, against the cold.

The ice cracked and talked to itself, to the wind. He drew his hood forward to stop the biting outer cold, then sat to wait. It was the best way he knew to catch a seal in the winter: waiting at a breathing hole until it came for air. Guarding his thoughts.

The round house of the moon was full above his head, the white-and-silver light reflecting off the snow was bright enough to see by. When the seal came, it would taste the air first, a nibble, before it drank.

He would have time. Time to aim. To flex his arm. To thank the seal, who knew, for all it pretended otherwise, that a hunter stood above.

The stars turned, and he told himself stories to help stay awake. And he remembered—too many things. He remembered the laughter of his summers as a boy. The way the sun never left the sky and the boys played through one day into the next. As long as there was light they played out, and then slept where they fell, curled in a ball of arms and legs, carried by neighbors into houses, into furs. It was the way he had been taught: stay awake now and when you become a hunter you'll be strong. You'll do without sleep. Without food. Race through the cold. Bathe in the ice. Learn to hunt, for your people, learn to hunt.

He had almost decided to leave.

Bear Hand's taunting had rekindled the thought, if it had ever left. He could still do it: follow the coast north as far as he was able. Pray that it led somewhere he knew, eventually. Grey Owl, for all his loss, would live an easier life without him. And Nua . . . Well, perhaps Nua was different. Women mourned in ways a man couldn't always understand. But then again, so did a man.

And as a man, he had decided that he could not leave his father's bones untended. Not with that look that crossed Bear Hand's face when he spoke of burning an enemy's bones.

Allanaq didn't know how long he had been sitting, except that dawn came and he was still there. A bluish tint had spread across the ice when he finally heard it: a sound. Not the wind. Not his heart. It was a water sound, air bubbling and then scratching. A seal was scratching nearby, on the ice beneath him.

His blood leaped, but he didn't strike . . . Not yet. Not until after the seal's first breath. He slipped his arms back in his sleeves, lifted his harpoon, the line of sinew. And then he held . . .

Still. Forcing himself to wait. The seal that came for its first breath always came for a second, for a third. He raised his arm, pulled back, slowly—watching.

And then it came, water spilling away from the tip of its black nose, the triangle of head. He lifted the blade and struck.

Heavily, he drove the harpoon into the center of the hole. Till the point struck flesh and he knew it, knew by the shock of weight, the line burning suddenly through his hands. He let out the line. Tossed the shaft aside while the seal dived and tried to get away. All in the same instant he had the line anchored around himself, using his weight to fight the thrashing seal, side to side, in and out. He braced his feet. Locked his knees. Wound the line tighter while the seal dived and thrashed, dived and fought . . . Till finally . . .

Finally, he felt the fight give over, resistance ebb.

Quickly now—he could easily lose it—Allanaq chipped the ice until the hole was large enough for the seal to fit through. He tugged: the head showed and he dropped to his knees, held the line in case the harpoon cut free. He cut a hole beneath the seal's thin lip and threaded a line through. Then, hand over hand, leaning for leverage, he hauled it from the dark water to the frozen ledge of snow.

Allanaq knelt beside the seal. He patted the slick dripping hair on its head. There was ice forming around the mouth already, where the breath had ended. He watched it, the droplets hardening, the clear water changing to white.

On his knees, with a hand on the seal's wet fur, he thanked it. "It is good that you have come," he said. "It is good." And he poured a drink of fresh water on its mouth, so it wouldn't be thirsty.

He finished settling his gear, fixed a new point to his harpoon, then rose and turned toward land. With the line tied over his shoulders and around his chest and the seal sliding on the ice behind him, he started to walk. More carefully this time, the way he had been taught, never to rest his weight on one foot only, but shifting, balancing between his legs in case the ice was thin. Step and shift.

He stopped once to check the wind's direction. He squinted toward the distant rise of east–west pressure ice, wondering whether there would be a fog to think about, and when he could eat. He tightened the knot that held the dragline from the seal to his chest and started walking, when a shadow caught his eye, no more than a few steps from his boot tips.

Allanaq blinked against the bright snow, almost as if he didn't understand. A second breathing hole? Another seal? He held his breath, listened to the scratching—almost directly beneath his feet.

Quickly, he dropped to his knees, pulled his harpoon from his shoulder, just in time to hear the hissing sound of the seal's second breath.

He slipped the coiled line to his arm, raised his harpoon.

He waited only the space of a single heartbeat until again, a surge of water welled up, outlined the tiny, open hole. Into its center he shot his harpoon. Never thinking, only moving. Hard and sharp with a single driving motion for the center. Only the center . . .

And it struck, the point disappeared below the ice.

Down! Something was taking it down. The line uncoiled in his hands. He dropped it, let it out. Jumped to anchor his feet over the ice while the seal fought below, threw itself about, trying to escape the pain, the line, the shadow that wouldn't leave. Fighting, until it was over.

With his arms straining tightly, he tugged the line until the second seal was up, out of the hidden water and up on the solid ice. Its flippers moved and then lay still.

From a small pouch, Allanaq took out the ivory plugs that were used to close off wound holes. He forced one in, under the layer of skin and blubber, where his harpoon had bitten the seal's neck, just back from its head. He cinched the plug, not to lose any of the precious blood.

He would have liked to eat from it, to drink its strength-giving blood. To slow the cold that was seeping again into his feet, his hands. He wouldn't though. It was more important to have the People see how the seals had honored him. He would bring these to the shore. And someone would call Nua to fill her water pot with fresh water, and bring it down to soothe the dying soul.

He pulled his mitten from one hand, ran a finger over the wet fur between the seal's eyes, to its nose.

He would go home now. He was alive. The seal was dead, but that was the way the world had to be. Nor could it ever be different.

He felt humble, awed by the gift of two seals.

From the roof of Grey Owl's house, where she sat, Elik watched the shadow shift, then change. She waited. The winds that had kept the men from hunting were calm now, the fog of snow settled to the ground. Even so, in the distance, with the light so dim, it was hard to be certain.

The shadow was too wide in the hips for one man. It could have been a polar bear, that was possible. Or a cloud of condensation rising on the ice.

She straightened her back, unfolded her feet. The moving dot grew larger. Disappeared behind a whiter glare of ice. Emerged again in the shape of a man dragging something behind his back. Two somethings.

She didn't wait to find out what. "Aunt," she called down through the skylight—and inside the nearby houses, others heard as well.

She scrambled from the rooftop to the hide-covered entry, into the tunnel, then up into the house to tell her aunt. By the time she was outside again, hurrying toward the beach, the sun was showing a full two fingers above the horizon and a small crowd had already gathered, women to one line, men closer down, watching toward the ice.

Grey Owl was there already, standing beside Bear Hand. Olanna, Iluperaq, Kahkik, and the other men beside him.

Last night, after leaving Old Ani's house, the men had stood atop the *qasgi's* hard-packed roof and pointed to the sky, to the signs of haze flickering in the stars, to the direction the wind was rising. The signs all saying it was not a good time for a hunter to risk going out on the ice.

Even with their caches so low, they had agreed, it was safer to wait another day. When this newest storm blew past, they would see whether any leads had opened for the seals to climb out. Or if they should hunt farther, or inland, or anywhere else they might. They had gone inside and planned, then slept. And then, sometime during the night, the wind had shifted, a sudden settling of the skies. Clearing off. They hadn't seen when.

There was an awkward silence as the dark hump of Allanaq's two seals came into view. The silence changed, turned to a muttered remark from one man first, than another. Grey Owl caught a whisper, then laughed—loud and quick, to shame their anger. He hurried past them, onto the ice to help haul the heavy weight the last, long rise up the ice.

Bear Hand remained where he was, his mouth set, his eyebrows pulled together. Kahkik scraped a place for his feet in the snow. Behind them the empty drying racks held little more than a few lines of strung cod and herring, a wedge of seal ribs, black and dry from seasons past.

In the women's line, Squirrel raised herself to her toes to see the seals. "They're fat," she whispered tentatively.

Two Ravens nodded. "One would have been fat. Two will be a feast."

"They'll be eaten before they're cooked," Ani's Wife said.

Elik glanced at Squirrel, then quickly looked away. What had she meant when she called him a dog man? She held back, watching. Allanaq didn't walk like a dog, with his tail between his legs. He didn't stop to scratch himself, or raise his chin to howl.

On the trampled snow below the men, Allanaq dropped his drag handle. He pounded his hands to chase away the cold. Grey Owl laughed to break the tension. "I was sleeping," he said to Allanaq, loudly enough for the others to hear, "dreaming of my wife, while you went hunting. Which way did you go?"

Allanaq pointed out the path he'd taken over the ice. South and east into the rising wind the others hadn't dared.

Iluperaq first, then Kahkik, Weyowin, Lake, and the other men moved closer in to listen. Behind them, Olanna approached over the slippery ground. His chilled face was lit, smiling at the sight of two seals. "What have we found?" he called to Allanaq. Bear Hand moved reluctantly in behind him.

"Ringed seal, Grandfather," Allanaq said. "The wind was lighter farther out."

"And you sent your thoughts out properly, to lie with the seals while we slept with our legs around our wives."

Allanaq lowered his glance to his boot tips. He'd found the second breathing hole, but his thoughts had been with a woman, as much as with the seals. "I waited through the night—"

Bear Hand folded his arms.

With another thought, Allanaq added, "It was not the first time I set out at night, alone. Sometimes, I go walking. I plan my carvings. I was thinking of a Loon," he said loudly. "It must have been the Loon that brought me luck . . ."

Olanna laughed. "Luck enough to drag two seals across the ice. But—" He remembered—"Your shoulder? Is it well?"

Allanaq shrugged. "I slipped once and the cut started to bleed—"

"Wait—" Bear Hand interrupted. "You spilled blood on the seal?"

"No, I kept it away. I—"

The danger turned palpable, like heat from a fire. Olanna felt it and interrupted. "Listen," he said, and he pulled himself taller, shedding the years, taking control. "You men are too prideful. You forget—the seal or the fox, or any animal who gives itself to a hunter has first looked past the hunter to the woman sitting in her house. Allanaq—call your mother, the food is hers to butcher and share out."

Behind them the small line of women opened then closed again. Nua was not there.

Allanaq waited, and then grew concerned. "Where is Nua?" he asked.

Grey Owl hesitated. "Last night," he said, "her bleeding came on again. Too heavy to ignore. Iluperaq and I slept in the *qasgi* . . ."

"But—?" Allanaq stopped. The confusion was plain in his voice. "To whose house do I bring the seals?"

Elik shifted, waiting. Beneath her parka she clutched the bowl Nua had given her in the house, instructing her in a woman's duties. The bowl was Nua's most important ceremonial possession, made of a single piece of wood, painted with symbols of the sea mammals who would drink from it.

She listened to the talk, the women discussing the names of which house had the right to the meat. Which woman was closest. Olanna's sister Little Pot, they said, had been married to Nua's brother, and so she had a right to help. "Except for her hands," Ani's Wife said. "Her wrists give too much pain to hold a knife. Two Ravens could do the work."

Two Ravens busied herself with her baby—a lump, nearly invisible beneath her parka. "I have this little one to nurse. Perhaps Meqo?"

"She isn't related closely enough."

Squirrel shifted her feet. "Perhaps I might?"

Elik's glance shifted. Why to Squirrel when she was the one who had spoken loudest against Allanaq? She looked to Two Ravens, found no clues. To Ani's Wife, who was already squinting toward the drying racks, figuring each seal that had come during the season, to which house and when.

As was Squirrel. Elik could almost see the girl's thoughts turning, worrying less now about dog men and more about the count of pelts stretched on drying boards outside the house. The fox pelts and now the seals a certain man had caught when no other man brought any.

And now more clearly, Elik realized where the factions lay: Bear Hand whispered stories in the *qasgi* with the men. His daughter Squirrel spread gossip with the women in their houses.

As for her, she'd put her trust in her relatives, with Grey Owl and Nua.

Quickly, before someone spoke louder, she stepped from the women's line. With Nua's painted bowl held out for all to see, she stepped along the hard-packed path to where the men had gathered around the seals.

She knelt beside the larger seal, rolled it over so it would see upward, to the sky. From inside her parka, where her skin kept it from freezing, she pulled out the small bladder Nua had filled with water.

Carefully—she'd spill it if she thought about all the eyes watching her now—she undid the lashing that held the plug, poured a small amount into Nua's bowl, and held it to the seal's thin lips.

"For your thirst," she said. "So you will remember the people who thought of you."

Above her, Olanna's voice answered for the seal, "These people gave me water and I will tell my family that these things are here for them as well. I will tell them where to swim. . . ."

Elik tipped the bowl; a few drops spilled to the seal's mouth. "Come again," she said. "Forever, come again."

She brought out the *ulu* Nua had given her, lowered her hood. A few paces back from the seal, the soles of a man's boots came into her line of sight. She glanced at the boots, but no higher. Black crimped soles against the white of the snow. The pattern of caribou leggings stitched to the black soles of bearded seal. Nua's work. Nua's son.

Elik's knife hovered above the dark mound of the seal's belly and then dipped in. She felt the easing push of a well-sharpened knife: a good sign—the butchering wouldn't be painful for the seal. Upward she cut, through the skin, through the thick layer of fat into the choicest parts first: the ribs, the liver, the heart.

Her hands moved proudly as only a woman, an owner of meat, knew how.

Elik sat up. The lamp was about to burn itself out. A wisp of smoke coiled toward the ceiling, darkening the smudge that had long since dyed the roof poles a sooty grey. Her stomach was full but her thoughts felt empty. She was too restless to sleep. Beside her on the crowded platform, Nua wheezed and coughed. Kimik hummed to her baby, on and off again, never fully asleep.

Quietly, Elik lifted her boots from the floor below the sleeping platform, her parka and mittens from their drying place above the lamp. She didn't put them on until she was safely down in the cooler air of the entry tunnel. She pushed back the stiffly frozen bear hide flap, slipped out beneath the stars.

Instantly she felt the cold, the sharp night air biting her nose and chin. She pulled her hood closer, opened a tunnel to see.

Allanaq hadn't told her he would go walking—not in

words. Or that she could find him if she wanted. And yet something had been said. About the Loon. In the house, with his glances.

For a long time she leaned against an upright leg of a food cache, one that was nearest the house. If she saw anyone, she would squat down and pee. No one would stop to question.

One of the dogs woke—long enough to smell whether her hands were empty and then curl back to sleep. The wind settled. She listened toward the *qasgi*, where most of the men were asleep.

When the footsteps came they were from Weyowin's house, not from the *qasgi* after all. They moved through the dark, crunching on snow. Between Bear Hand's house and Old Ani's. Heavier than a woman's and quicker than an old man's. She started following, placing her steps between his, like an echo, so she could hear whether they stopped or turned. Or called.

It was Allanaq, of course. She knew it even before he'd passed the hump of the Long Coast's older, abandoned *qasgi*—a mound of indecipherable snow that marked the end of the houses.

The figure was taller than Iluperaq. Quicker than Bear Hand. In a parka that showed the alternating white and black caribou fur of Nua's stitching. But it wasn't until she had followed as far as the level flats beyond the village that she realized where she was going—toward the graveyard. Alone, in the hidden night. What was he doing? He'd brought a pack, an ice pick, and a wide-bladed adze. A rolled skin that he set down on the snow.

He would have seen her if he turned; there was no shelter or shrubs to hide behind. His back and raised hood were easily visible, a darkened line stretching along the ground, like an arrow toward the mounded rocks.

Not rocks. A burial.

She peered back toward the village. If anyone saw her, what would they say? There were stories of what people did. In the night. Jealous people stealing amulets from the dead. Stealing bones for the strength, the visions they hoped they'd bring.

And yet—she watched a moment longer—he wasn't doing anything more terrible than sitting. No. Not just sitting. He was scratching at the snow with a rock now. That was all. Squatting there, beside the mound of snow.

With the wind blowing, it was possible he hadn't heard her. She walked a few steps closer, close enough that she wondered why he didn't turn. She cleared her throat. "Who is it?" she asked.

"My father," he said. He stiffened, but he hadn't turned. His voice showed no surprise.

She remembered his grief more than anything else about him: the eyes of a man who had danced the story of his father's death. His fear that without proper burial his father's ghost would wander forever.

"You shouldn't be here," she said. "It isn't safe."

He stood, clapped the snow from his mittens, turned and faced her. He said, "It seems that whatever I do in this village, it isn't safe."

He took a step away from the mound; Elik stepped nearer. There was an awkward moment, each wanting to look at the other, neither wanting to stare. Allanaq's mouth was tight, his eyes narrow and sad. "There's too much arguing," he said. "Those people—they don't trust me."

Elik nodded. She wasn't frightened and it surprised her; it surprised her also that she wasn't too shy to speak to him, that there were words she wanted to say. "They have long memories. They wonder what it means for one man to bring home game, when no one else has luck."

"I'm sorry you had to hear them—"

"It's only talk," she shrugged. "It's better to laugh—"

"Except they don't." Allanaq looked at her. "They joke, until their joking grows too loud. And then they fight."

"It's difficult," she said, "to know what's right. Our elders speak and we should learn—"

"Which elders?" Allanaq asked. "Grey Owl is a good man. As is Nua. But Bear Hand speaks louder than both of them, and always first. Olanna grows quieter, even in the few seasons I've known him. And all of them tell me different things. Except my father—" He looked back to the burial. "His voice speaks inside my heart."

Elik watched him turn. She'd been wrong before to think he wasn't different from other men. He was. The way he spoke, with words traveling around his heart before they came out his mouth. She'd never heard any man speak that way before. And yet—she understood. Hadn't she also felt torn? Between her grandmother's words urging her to learn, and her mother urging her to be more careful? Between Malluar's words and Seal Talker's? Naiya's and her own?

Quietly, Allanaq said, "I've seen him, you know—my father. I haven't told anyone before. I've watched him walking, here and along the shore, beyond the village. He walks and he tries to hunt, but he has no tools. No harpoon, or knife or bow or anything that was his in life."

"Couldn't you leave a few gifts for him?" Elik suggested. "You could leave them—we do it here also, after a burial—"

"For Real People, not for a stranger. They wouldn't allow it. And if Bear Hand learned of it now, he'd grow angry. He says the weapons I offered my father would become too powerful in the hands of the dead. A curse, not a help. He fears my father will find the houses and strike in anger. He doesn't understand: I fear the same thing—that he'll be held here. Not as a harmful spirit, but as a prisoner himself." Allanaq turned to Elik. "I have the same questions as Bear Hand, but it isn't danger I find. It's my father's grief."

A breeze swept along the ground, carrying snow, swirling it at their feet. Elik shivered. She wanted to understand why it mattered so much to have the burial his way. They both agreed that it wasn't the body that mattered; the souls of the dead returned to the people. When a child was born to take the name, the name lived on. She'd seen it for herself—her grandmother in Kimik's new baby. In her uncle Saami's youngest son, who had the same lisp his namesake had.

"It matters so much," she asked, "to have him buried the way your own people would?"

"It matters."

"Is it so different? What will you do?"

A rock showed above the snow—Allanaq kicked it. It was smooth and rounded by the ocean, blue in the moon's light. He knelt down, brushed the snow away. "I think," he started, "I have to make amends. And I have to do it now. Tonight. Before Bear Hand decides I was right to burn the man I killed. That perhaps, that is exactly the same thing he should do with my father." He looked at her again. "You aren't afraid?"

"Some."

Allanaq hid his relief. Only a shaman would have bragged beside a grave. "That's probably best. If we're caught. If someone sees us. Or tries to follow—"

"Follow?"

"Yes."

Elik thoughts leaped ahead. She tightened her shoulders. "We won't be seen," she said, "not if we hurry."

It took him a moment to move, to look away from her. He started brushing the crusted snow off the rocks, pulling each overlapped layer from the rock below, catching it only when the tumbling threatened to grow too loud. Elik worked alongside, lifting and setting the rocks down, lowering one pile, raising another. Quickly, while the moon held in the sky.

The mound was not so high as she had guessed nor were there so many rocks. Before long there were bits of dark leather wrapping showing through the stones. Something near the size of a large dog. Or a seal. Or a man with his knees folded up, asleep.

She tried not to touch it, then told herself it didn't matter. The dead man who was inside that wrapping—he wouldn't come out. The body was what was left behind. The soul was elsewhere.

Only once did Allanaq turn his back on her; purposefully, while they pulled down the rocks. He felt for it with his hand—before she found it first—the burial amulet he had hidden for his father, the ivory open link chain with the loons' heads. He didn't want to see on her face the anger, the fear or disgust he'd seen on others'. He folded it in his hand, then away, inside his parka.

Then he signaled. Elik dug her heels into the snow, bent her knees. They pulled at a corner of the stitched hide that held his father. The last few rocks tumbled away; the hide shifted, scratched, and then broke free. With it a few arrowheads tumbled to the snow, a spoon and a miniature dagger. Allanaq scooped them up, laid them on the bottom hide. They slid his father the rest of the way on top.

Steadily, not to work up a sweat, but quickly as they were able, they set the rocks back in a hump, patted on snow so that, from a distance, it seemed no different than before. "We need a place now," Allanaq said. He said it quietly, so nothing could hear. "Someplace they won't find him. Someplace I can return."

They stood a moment. Elik surveyed the rising line of inland hills. Allanaq studied the shore. Most of the places he knew were from kayak trips with Grey Owl, the times they'd hunted caribou.

Elik thought about the places she knew—where the tundra was boggy and where, as a girl, she had picked berries with Nua and her mother. She tried to figure a place that would suit Allanaq's purpose, yet not so far they couldn't return safely before morning.

And then she remembered: a sod hut she had visited once. A place so long abandoned, no one went there, no one mentioned it anymore. She and her mother and Naiya had happened on it; they'd followed the north fork of a creek behind a berry bog, and she'd been stung by a bee. She remembered it suddenly: how she'd stumbled behind her mother: too old to be carried. Too young to do anything but cry and drop her berries. And remember.

They touched the hide only on its brittle folds, hoping they wouldn't feel his father deeper inside. They centered the burial hide atop the one Allanaq had brought for skidding. Carefully—he weighed so little Elik almost asked if it wasn't a child inside, instead of a man. Then folded the outer skin in half, fur side in, and tied draglines to the corners, then started.

The snow was crusted enough for the hide to slide though they worried about their own tracks and whether a wind would sweep them, or if they needed to brush the trail when they returned. They took a longer way around than they might have, choosing ground they hoped would hide their footprints. Constantly, they checked the moon's position, trying to figure how far they'd traveled, where the light would be when they returned. They talked little but they took turns, both of them, glancing to see if the other was truly there.

From the outside the house looked as much a beaver's den as a human habitation.

Snowdrifted and with a skin of hoarfrost, it was set on a wide bend beside the flats of a frozen creek. Nor was the place animal, though it could have been. It was human, or had been once: dug into the earth for warmth with rocks and sod and poles to hold the roof. The winter entrance was long since failed, the door a lopsided tunnel.

A fit place for the house of a dead man, Elik thought, and she wondered that Allanaq wasn't afraid. Only a shaman—or a girl foolish enough to want to be a shaman—would welcome a place like this. And yet—she watched as he quickened the last few paces—either it suited him, or else he was too foolish to know what a man ought to fear.

"It's facing the sea," he called. "And here—a bear hide would have covered the door—it's good—the way Seal People build their winterhouses, with the doors always open to the sea. Who lived here?"

Elik rubbed her palms where the skin had chafed. "I don't know. If there was a story, it would be old, an ancestor's story. I only happened on it once, with my mother, picking berries."

Allanaq set the dragline on the hump of his father's chest, left it as he brushed the overburden of snow from the door. He slipped in first, over the crest of windblown snow, onto hard packed earth. Elik followed after, both of them bending to fit through the frame, straightening where the fallen roof rose again. They stood aside to let the moonlight open a path along the floor.

There was no wind inside; the quiet reached their ears like a sigh. They let their hoods down. It was warmer than they'd expected, hollow more than cold. They would build no fire for fear the smoke might give them away, or the heat waken the body.

Opposite the entrance the roof had buckled and fallen to meet the floor, the house half the size it once had been. Clods of dirt pebbled the floor and there was a scent of musk and time. "It's so old—" Elik whispered. "A place even the dead would forget."

Allanaq winced. "Perhaps that's best," he said. "If no wandering spirits came—and no people."

"If he hears us—your father—he'll know we mean well."

Elik spoke so quietly, Allanaq turned to listen. He looked at her, looked again. Then abruptly turned, went out to drag his father in.

Elik let out her breath. She was nervous, no matter how she claimed she wasn't. This house. A dead man. And him. Sometimes she felt as if, for as long as she had carried his loon, she had carried him as well. Other times, she didn't understand him. Not the odd sound of his words—that, once she grew used to it, was not so difficult. It was the things he chose to say. The way he joked and then grew quiet.

Allanaq stepped backward inside; without snow to smooth the ground, his father's bundle was heavier and awkward. Allanaq tapped the hardened floor with his boot. "The ground's too frozen," he said. "We won't be able to dig until spring."

"Is that what you wanted, to bury him in the ground?"

"He should be inside a fine planked box. Like a house with sides like walls, and a floor."

She nodded, looked about. A few larger rocks lay in a pattern that must have been a hearth. Bits of broken clay pots, shards of stone pressed into the floor. Any large planks were frozen in place; they'd never be able to free them. It was odd, how she had been able to remember where this house was, but not the insides. It reminded her of the Long Coast village's older, abandoned *qasgi*; she didn't think anyone went there anymore. Perhaps his father would be safe here. Perhaps the entire house could be his burial.

"We could bring planks," she suggested. Her breath puffed clouds of condensation into the air.

Allanaq smiled. "We could," he said, and this time he didn't turn from watching her.

Elik's face grew warm. "Another time . . ." she said, and turned away, then knelt to brush a place beside the corner.

Behind her, Allanaq watched the way her hair lay against the back of her neck. The way the fur on her hood hung like a necklace around her shoulders. He said, "I brought salmon for my father's hunger."

She kept on brushing.

Allanaq shuffled his father toward the corner floor. From a pouch, he set out a bit of frozen salmon, a thumbful of oil from a small container. Whatever he gave, in the next world it would grow larger.

Except for the ivory chain. He didn't want that going any farther than here beside his father's body.

He glanced over his shoulder to see if she was looking, then quickly, with a blade, sliced the first stitch he could pull far enough from the hide wrapping not to chance cutting the hide itself. One stitch, then a second. He tugged the torn sinew from the needle holes. Then, holding the ivory chain so it wouldn't raise a sound, he slipped it through the hole, to lie beside his father.

All these months he'd never been certain whether something evil had climbed inside his father's corpse, through the eyes or the noseholes. He still didn't know. The sickness that spirits caused in people had a way of waiting, striking in its own season. His hope now was that with this burial chain, with the noise it made that reached to the other world, his father would have a way of fighting back.

Behind him, Elik began humming a song. Allanaq stiffened in surprise. Her voice was high, not loud, but the song—it was the kind of song his father might have sung, sure of itself, unafraid.

"Dead father," she sang. "We bring you something small to eat. You who are our Honored Dead, taste the oil we bring to quench your thirst. Below the sea. Above the sky. Like the Loon, You dive between two worlds, Yet still you have thirst . . ."

The song faded. It was beautiful, her voice, the words. He tried not to look up, yet he had to. She drew him and he wanted her. Yet how could he trust her, really?

Elik caught his expression; her stomach tightened. "What's wrong?"

"Nothing . . . I only wondered. Among my people, only elders, women past their time, they're the only people who . . ." He struggled after words. "Why aren't you more afraid? To touch . . . To sing to the dead?"

"It's an Offering song, that's all." Elik spoke quickly, defensively. Too many times, Naiya had spoken that way. "Anyone sings such a song. Everyone. It's nothing. But— you asked me that before, whether I was a shaman. The day you gave me the loon. Why?"

*Had she heard his thoughts? Why had she asked that question?* He didn't want to answer. He didn't want to hear her say that, yes, she was a shaman. That she tranced for people and took payment. Payment in skins and furs and blood. The way Red Fox had.

She said, "That morning, before the feast—I had gone walking along the shore. I heard a Loon call. Its *inua* showed itself to me . . . And then you held it out, a loon amulet. Why?"

Allanaq looked up. Had he done that? "When I first saw you in your *qasgi,* you sang How Eagle Taught the People to Feast."

"You remember that?"

"Yes. Because that was one of our songs also. It isn't something a person forgets. To hear your own song, when you're far from home. I wanted to thank you. That was all." Allanaq looked away, then back again. He didn't want to think about shamans. He didn't want to think about anything. Unless it was to be near her. To hear her voice that he had dreamed about. Touch her the way he had imagined.

He raised his hand to her cheek. If she said anything, anything at all, he would stop. He would go away and find another woman. He would leave. He would . . .

She didn't stop him. Elik pulled off her glove, set her hand over his, on her cheek. For one instant, the face coming near hers belonged to a different man. Older. Angrier. She shut her eyes, forced Seal Talker's face away.

A sound came from her mouth. Allanaq hushed her. "You mustn't make noise," he said, and he put his hand on the small of her back, pulling her in. "Even so far from the sea. A wife has to lure the seals closer."

Elik smiled. "Don't your fathers teach you never to raise your voice? You'll chase the animals away yourself."

"And a wife doesn't tell a husband how to hunt."

"And"—she pressed against him— "a husband doesn't think about his wife while he waits for the seal. . . ."

"Not any part of her?" He bent his knees, with a hand on both her hips, he brought her in.

Where he touched, a warmth moved inside her, spread up along her spine, down through her legs. Like nothing she had ever felt before; not from Seal Talker's hurried demands, not when she was younger. She closed her eyes. "What does the hunter say?" Her voice was husky.

"He says . . . " He buried his face in her neck, in the sweet smell of her hair. "He says . . . " He didn't finish.

Elik found his hands. She pulled him down with her, not slowly, but hurrying his weight onto hers. All of him. Over her, surrounding her, inside of her. His black hair, his dark eyes. His cheeks between her breasts. His hands warming her, everywhere. She wasn't cold anymore. And nothing mattered. Nothing else mattered but this.

∽

Elik had fallen asleep, there in the crook of his arm, beneath the shelter of their parkas. She had slept only little, but it was all they could risk. He would look at her one moment longer, then wake her.

He had lied to her before; he wondered if she guessed. Her eyes *were* like a shaman's. Dark and wild, darting, as if she was watching into another world.

And the Loon she mentioned—in his home, it was shamans who most often wore the feathered head and beak-pieces of a loon around their forehead. As the loon dives under the water, so the shaman dives, to the Land Below the Sea. He didn't understand the impulse that made him offer the loon. He had known the Eagle story, that part was true. But he also knew his manners had been poor, and he'd done it anyway. He didn't know why.

What he did know was that he was glad he hadn't asked, in words, whether she was a shaman. She was no more like Red Fox than he was. She wasn't arrogant or rude or greedy. She walked quietly, with respect. And she had wanted him . . . as much as he had wanted her.

He would marry with her, if she was willing. Besides, wasn't it true that most women who were shamans didn't practice, didn't trance until they were older, past their bleeding and their children grown?

If she was too shy to speak for herself, he would go to her brother. Iluperaq would speak for the father.

For now he was content to look at her, to memorize her face so that later he could take out the picture of her and hold it, the same as the way he held an idea for a carving, or the memory of a place he hunted: the curve of her chin beneath her lips, the way her hair drew a line across her face.

It was the one gift Red Fox would never be able to steal, the way, ever since he was young and he'd go walking, he would draw with a stick in the sand, or the snow. Faces. Torsos. Seals. Caribou. Fish or bird. The details of fur and muscle and wing.

There was power in carving; he'd always believed that. Not from his hands—he was no proud fool to think that, but that the animals gave themselves to his fingers, his hands, the same as they came to a harpoon, if it pleased them.

Elik lay sleeping. In her dream, she was out on the snowy flats of a bright winter landscape. Her hood was raised against a north wind and a wall stood behind her, a windblock built of snow and willow brush to shield the worst of the storm. Her head was bowed. There were tears on her cheeks, nearly frozen, though she didn't know why she had been crying. She was hungry, but it wasn't hunger that caused the worst pain. It was the loneliness, stalking so near.

Time must have passed. Enough so that finally, the hunger turned stronger than the loneliness. Elik rose and tried searching for a trail in the snowfields, for anything she might recognize. East and North, South and West, until finally, thankfully, she heard voices. "*Qamma!*" they called, using the word that people reserved for summoning shamans. "You are wanted."

Something moved—brown against the endless white. There were people. Different kinds of people. With her parka sleeve she wiped her eyes and, as if she'd been looking through a film of ice, her sight cleared.

It was a woman who reached her first, a Caribou Woman with pointing ears and a cap of small, newly sprouted antlers. With her hands—human hands, for she was in the shape of a person now—she held out a water pot, a small bentwood bowl, a *qattaq*, the same as a woman of the Real People used in ceremonies. "Take this," the Caribou Woman said. "It is for your own mouth to drink."

Elik tipped the bowl to her mouth and sipped.

"You must come down into our house," a Wolf Man with a long tail said. "You must fight us."

Elik laughed, though she felt uneasy. "How can I fight you? You are great and beautiful and strong."

"Not with your nails or your teeth, but with the amulets we have left in your path."

"I didn't find any amulets," she apologized.

"Look in your hand," the Loon said.

Elik looked. She was wearing no mittens. No mittens and on one hand—no skin. Her hand, her wrist, all the bones leading up her arm—they were visible on the inside now. The twin bones of her lower arm. The tiny bones of her fingers, separated yet attached. As if there was flesh, though there was none.

Elik opened her mouth in wonder. Wolf pointed his muzzle, telling her not to look away.

Beneath the bones of her hand, a few tiny amulets lay on the snow. A black feather given by a bird, a scrap of brown fur with the long hairs of a wolverine still on it. A single tooth, pointed and white. With the hand that was clothed in skin, she gathered them up.

Wolf said, "Gain these amulets, claim them and you'll gain their strength. You'll become fit enough, wise enough to speak with those of us who walk beside you."

"But first," Loon said, "you must use them to fight us. If you win we will agree to be your helping spirits. You will hear our voices and we will show you things you cannot see."

"What must I do to gain the amulets?"

"Test yourself," Caribou Woman said. "Test your strength and your courage—though there is no guarantee you will survive. And yet you must try. If you don't, you will die anyway. We will kill you."

Elik woke to the touch of cold against one leg, Allanaq's face above her. She smiled and he ran his hand along the curve of her shoulder. "You fell asleep," he said. "We have to go."

Reluctantly, she agreed. They moved against each other under the narrow blanket of clothes, slowing each time his foot slid against her leg, or her breast touched his chest, his arm, her hip. He laughed until, with a sigh, Elik pulled away, unraveled her parka, slipped it over her head.

The moon had changed and the house was darker. Allanaq's face was etched in shadow, too dark to see the details of his chest or stomach. He stood naked a moment longer than she had, breathing in the cold, steeling himself to it the way men did. Then he bent at the waist, pulled on a leg of his trousers and she laughed suddenly.

"You look as if you're trying to find the fish below the ice."

Allanaq looked up, saw her smile. "I'm stalking the seal," he said, playing to her and she slid back, pretending seriousness. Allanaq stepped one partially dressed leg forward. "The seal is suspicious." He leaned sideways, perilously far out on the pretend ice. "But I want to kill it in good salt water, so it won't sink quickly."

"Be careful." Elik covered her mouth, not to laugh.

"I am, but the wind is safe, from east to west today."

"Watch that lead"—she pointed toward the door—"so it doesn't widen over the pack ice."

"I will," he called, and he turned to watch her laughing as he lifted his hand behind his ear, thrusting toward the seal. He raised the joke to please her. "I have my line and sledge, and I can turn it into a raft if I have to paddle across a lead. And my best seal point harpoon, with lifelines and strength and a decent point, flaked on both sides. Not one of those flat slab blades of shale, but something real that knows how to cut. And . . ." he stopped.

Elik's face had fallen. Their joking had come full circle, pulling her back to the night, this house, his father. There was nothing funny in his words. Nothing. "Why do they hate you so?" she asked.

Allanaq straightened. The smile fled from his face. "They don't hate me," he said. "They fear me."

"Both are dangerous."

"Yes."

"Are we so different, you and I?"

Allanaq looked away. "I don't know. Perhaps."

"How?" she asked.

Allanaq shrugged, kicked his foot at something on the floor. "There." He pointed his boot. "Your clay pots, for one thing. Our women don't make those."

"Why? Don't they know how?"

"It's not that."

"I don't understand. Young people don't know things. They have to watch and learn. If your women watched, couldn't they learn?"

Allanaq didn't answer.

"Perhaps your clay is different? Or your people younger than we are?"

"No. It's not young or old like a child. It's what works and what you have. We don't have clay like this. You have more salmon. We have more walrus. We both hunt inland for caribou. What can anyone know? Why is there sickness? Why hunger, when no one does wrong?"

"But the salmon do come to you. And even here people say that one river may be better than another."

"Still, there are never so many. Why do more walrus come to my Seal Point People? Because we are better? One man can be a better hunter than another. Because he hears what his elders teach, because he is patient. Two brothers can be different."

Elik smiled. She had never thought to hear a man ask as many questions as she did. She looked to his father, to the sharp angles his body poked against the brown hide. "I had a dream," she started to say. "I was all alone and—"

"Wait," he put a finger to her mouth, hushing her. He said it kindly, outlining her lips, almost a caress. He sighed. When he stepped away, he was calm again. "Tell me later," he whispered. "Dreams—sometimes when we speak them, they grow to mean too much."

"We should go," she agreed. "Before light."

Allanaq nodded. "What is given away comes back," he said, "like the light, and the seasons, like birds in the nesting moon. What is shared comes back." He tried to laugh. "We sing that when the seals give birth. Do you know it?"

"Something like it. Did I share something?"

Allanaq brightened. "This night. Yourself."

Elik looked at him. "You're a strange man, Allanaq. Uncle's son."

"You are a strange woman. Mother's niece. Cousin. My newest relation."

"Relation?"

"Wife," he whispered. "A cousin who is a wife."

"Husband," she answered, and she turned toward the door. *Husband,* she repeated, to herself this time. She had never thought of it as a good word before, and yet it was, almost as if it were one of the amulets her dream had promised, only a different kind. Both were needed. Both were good.

Allanaq gave a last glance to his father, then turned and followed quickly out the door.

Allanaq climbed in through the central tunnel entrance of the *qasgi*, waited for his eyes to adjust to the dimmer light. He and Elik had returned in better time than he'd dared to hope. Trusting the wind to hide their path, they'd brushed their trail in only a few places. They stayed together until just outside the village, then separated, she to Nua's house—his house. He to Old Ani's house first, looking for Grey Owl: he wasn't there, but he had sat and visited awhile and told the story he intended to tell again in the *qasgi*, how the dogs had woken him and he'd gone outside to check, then found an owl circling and followed it to hunt.

He couldn't remember the last time he had had a full night's sleep, but he didn't feel tired. He felt exhilarated, as if he'd been hunting. And strong, as if already knowing there was a wife made him feel wise and respected and older.

There were fewer men inside the *qasgi* than Allanaq thought to find. He felt disoriented a moment, till he remembered that most of the men would be hunting. The wind had cleared. Weather signs were good. He wasn't acting wisely, he laughed, more like a boy with his first woman.

Not wanting to attract attention, he made his way quietly along the bench, took a seat in the rear. He folded his legs in, left his parka on, then realized the men were preparing the *qasgi* for a sweat bath.

Weyowin was piling an armload of driftwood near the hearth. And Iluperaq, also with his clothes on, while Weyowin was naked. Which meant that Iluperaq had just come in, or was leaving. Most likely, they were planning on hunting together as partners, which would make sense, given that Weyowin would be Iluperaq's closest relation, not counting him.

Olanna looked to be sleeping in the corner, with a caribou skin drawn over his shoulders. And Old Ani was there, spreading dry moss on the fire. Not Bear Hand, though, for the first time in a long time, it didn't matter whether Bear Hand was there or not. Allanaq would have a wife soon, and a family.

A man who went out every morning to bring home food was a man who was needed. Not scoffed at. He would have relatives to hold him in a circle that even Bear Hand would no longer break.

Allanaq set his chin on his raised knees, closed his eyes, rested a moment. But he winced and looked up suddenly. He thought he heard his name, and the words, *Forest People,* and *night raids.* Who had said that?

Weyowin and Iluperaq were nearest the fire. And now Bear Hand's brother, Kahkik, had joined them. With the folds of wrinkled skin covering the outside corner of one eye, Kahkik's face looked cold and masklike.

He turned to watch Iluperaq, moved closer. What little talking there had been quieted suddenly, he didn't know why. He fixed himself a place again, not on the bench this time but on the floor nearer the fire. Lake put a bowl in his hand and he smiled his thanks. He hadn't realized how hungry he was. This wasn't the bland fox meat that had been boiled into soup. That was gone already. Was this one of his seals? He searched with his fingers for a bite of meat, found some, scooped it into his mouth.

As soon as the time was right he would talk to Iluperaq. Iluperaq himself had a new wife, Kimik, and the new baby who had come with Elik.

If Allanaq spoke too shyly, or said the wrong thing, Iluperaq would understand. They were already cousins. Now they would be brothers as well.

Weyowin sat beside Iluperaq, the two of them with their voices low, but intent. "Two seals, for four households," he heard Iluperaq say. "It isn't enough."

"And even if we have to send the women away, or hide them somewhere, it never will be." That from Kahkik behind them.

Allanaq leaned closer to hear. What were they talking about? Him again? About the man he had killed?

"My wife worries," Iluperaq said.

"She's a woman."

"With a new child at her breast, she knows she can't run fast. That a baby cries, sometimes too loud. If there were trouble . . ." Iluperaq opened his hands in question.

"We'll leave," he said after a moment. "The hunting may be poor, but at least at the Bent Point village, I know the land as well as the sea."

Allanaq felt confused. When could that have been decided? He and Elik had just separated. He had sat and visited with Old Ani, but it had only been a short while. "You're leaving?" he asked, too loudly.

"My wife—" Iluperaq didn't meet his eyes.

"But we talked of hunting together—" Allanaq offered. "If it's food that worries you, I could show you where Grey Owl has luck, at the Place Where Two Hills Come Together. . . ."

Iluperaq sent a glance toward Weyowin that Allanaq couldn't see. He rose quickly, almost awkwardly. "It's my wife," he said, as if to show how helpless he was against a woman's will. "The child is colicky and Kimik looks for her own mother to help." He stepped to the entrance tunnel, then down.

Allanaq rose and hurried after him. It would be better anyway, he decided, to say what he had to outside, without others listening. "Wait," he called as soon as he was past the entry tunnel. Iluperaq didn't hear. "What about your sister?" he called again. *There! It is out,* he thought. *Now Iluperaq will have to speak.*

Iluperaq stopped, waited for Allanaq to reach him. For a

moment they stood face-to-face, the two of them equally tall, the same dark hair in a line along their foreheads. But then, before Allanaq had a chance to speak, Iluperaq said, "There's too much fighting in this place. Every house I stop in, every man who comes home empty-handed. My uncle says you're his son. But to some of these people, you're invisible. To others, you're blamed for every wrong."

The sun glared in Allanaq's eyes. "My fault?" he repeated. "I'm the one who should be afraid. I'm the one alone."

Iluperaq started walking; Allanaq had to follow. "I came here," Iluperaq said, "because there was too much arguing in my own house, but my wife is too afraid to stay. If we go back to our Bent Point place, at least one of us will be content."

"One of you? Your sister will stay with Grey Owl and Nua then?"

Iluperaq stopped and looked curiously at him. His voice was short, his patience gone. He said, "My sister will have a pot full of food wherever she goes."

"What do you mean?"

"Seal Talker will feed her."

"Seal Talker?" Allanaq's legs felt suddenly weak. "Seal Talker in the Bent Point village? The shaman?"

"Unless you know another?"

"Why would Seal Talker give her food?"

"Does no one speak to anyone here? What else should a husband do?"

"Husband? They are married?"

"They will be. He's visited with her. With both our parents. In the spring, she'll have a place in his house, and my father will have a new umiak to keep him quiet."

Iluperaq started walking, faster now, across the narrow path between the houses, toward where Allanaq saw a woman had been waiting. It was Kimik, lashing their gear on the sledge. Behind her stood another figure. Elik. Elik who would be another man's wife.

Allanaq couldn't move.

A shaman again. Bringing trouble. The way they always

did. How could he not have known? Not only Red Fox but Seal Talker. Even his own father, he realized now—even his father would have backed down if he'd been an ordinary man. Red Fox would have had his woman and they would have lived in peace.

Which is what he would do now.

Whether Elik was a shaman—and she hadn't answered him, had she? Or even if she was married to one.

Her greed would grow, merely being around him. It always did. Power twisted people. What did it matter if shamans had more strength to deal with spirits than other people, if all it did was twist them inside?

Nor was he the kind of man to steal a woman against her will. Some men did—he'd heard stories, but what would be the use always fighting to keep a woman that way? Waiting till she ran from him, back to her shaman-husband.

They were talking. Loudly. Elik was gesticulating, pointing, grabbing hold of Kimik's sledge.

He didn't care. She was married to a shaman.

She had seen him. Allanaq watched her expression change, turn to . . . To what?

How could he know? How could a man know anything? She called, but he didn't want to hear. He turned back along the hardened path. Anywhere, it didn't matter so long as it was away. He refused to hear her.

Whatever happened between them didn't matter. He would put it out of his thoughts. He would not cross Seal Talker. Not because he was a coward, but because there was no end possible without grief.

He veered quickly away from the path, away from the houses. He refused to look back, to show interest. Let the brother take her home to her husband. He would stay away from shamans and the women they wanted.

# 11

There might have been game: seals arching in the water below the ice, fish lying quiet on frozen lake bottoms. There might have been oil left to burn in the lamps. Firewood found beneath forgotten drifts, and fresh water—it might have been easier to find. Something. Anything. If it hadn't been for the storms. Not the cold alone but the wind blowing through it, blurring the skies, the land, even the houses that stood but a few lengths away.

Elik lowered her head against the wind, slowly made her way along the narrow path from her parents' house to Sipsip's drying rack, to Nagi's food cache, to the small sod house that Naiya and Whale Fin now shared.

Her father had sent her out of the house—again. This newest storm, the one that blew in from the southwest just after she and Iluperaq and Kimik returned from the Long Coast, only made Chevak more surly, irritable where he should have held quiet.

He had sat there, that first day after they returned, listening as they drank the thin blood soup Gull heated, complaining about the food they had not brought back. His food that they were eating when they should have seen how small were the portions Gull passed.

They talked about the trail and how the hunting had gone, about Kimik's fear that the Forest strangers would return. About Saami, who sat with him less since their mother had died than he ever had before. About how Kimik's father, Blue-Shadow, said the weather would change by two days time though Seal Talker said no, he'd had a dream, and the dream told him there would be caribou even sooner.

That was the first day.

The first night, after Chevak left to sleep with the men in the *qasgi*, Kimik quietly moved her and Iluperaq's belongings to a storage alcove dug out along the length of the winter entry.

While Gull slept heavily beneath her blankets, Kimik separated the two pots she had brought from her mother's house, the lamp she had suspended near her side of the sleeping bench. In the passageway, she sorted through sealskin containers of meat—mostly hare and ptarmigan they had hunted along the way. She separated it into piles, two for Iluperaq to take while he hunted, one for herself, while she stayed behind. A third for Chevak, in the hopes he wouldn't complain.

If Chevak noticed that the blankets had been moved, he didn't say. The first thing he did when he returned from the *qasgi* was to go directly to his sleeping platform, burrow into the warmth of Gull's furs, and start telling stories, long, twisting stories that Gull, Kimik, and Elik had no choice but to hear.

The first was about a boy whose hand had hunting power—a hole in his hand that could kill any animal he pointed at. Just like that, they would fall down dead. The second story was about a man who went crazy and never left his house from the time when slush ice formed on the sea, till the season when birds came again. And all the man ate was the leather of his blankets and his boots and clothing. Until he was naked, and then a skeleton. And then the kind of skeleton who killed anyone who came near the house, ever again.

Chevak's eyes were wide when he finished, almost surprised. He sighed, seemed to notice the women sitting around, and then grew more annoyed. He was frustrated with the storm, with the waiting it forced on the men. The faces of so many hungry people in his house. The voices reminding him that he was talked about, that his own brother hunted with other men, seldom with him.

His gaze lit on Elik and he wrinkled his nose. "Go and smell if there's any food in your sister's pot," he said.

Elik glanced to her mother. *Go* Gull shaped the word, to Kimik first, then to her, signing that it was safer to visit around and eat, than to sit inside their cold, angry walls. Elik didn't wait to be told again.

At Naiya's house, Elik coughed into the entrance, waited, heard nothing, then climbed around to the entry tunnel.

"Naiya?" she called again. No one answered. She lowered her hood, peered inside. Snow had blown over the skylight and the house was dark, but warm still. Elik took two measured steps, from the entry tunnel to the sidewall drying rack, knelt and felt for the lamp. From a pouch tied to the belt around her leggings, she took out her firestones, felt around the floor for the pile of dry wild cotton, and used that to draw the spark.

The lamp, she noticed, was not the one their mother had given Naiya for a present. This one was larger, its shallow bowl smoothly pecked from the center of a river rock. She thought of the saying people had, that a woman with a lamp could never be poor. Someone must have carried it here, or traded it, perhaps passed it down—except—No— If a lamp such as this had been in the village, she'd have recognized it. This one was new. A lamp that only someone in Seal Talker's family might have the wealth to own.

Oil to spare for warmth, not food, and a lamp to burn it in. She stood beside the lamp, surveying the house. It was small, but tidy. Their sleeping furs were neatly rolled and pushed to the wall. A nearly finished pair of dress boots with tops of patterned caribou belly-skins lay nearby. Everywhere she looked there were more than enough skins for one wife, more grass mats than even her sister's quick fingers could have woven.

Elik backed away from the lamp. If Naiya found her, she would smile in that new way she had, wise and patient with Elik's younger ways. Naiya would guess she had been touching her things, wanting her lamps, her food, perhaps even a little of what she shared with her husband.

There was an offer she'd already had, more than once: Naiya lifting her disheveled head with a laugh, Whale Fin craning his neck to ask if his little sister was cold and wanted warming in their bed.

Quickly, Elik drowned the wick in the rendered fat, kicked aside the clumps of snow she'd brought in on her boots.

Outside, she looked toward the direction of Malluar's house, north and over the slight hump of a ridge. The house was difficult to see in the best of weather, invisible with this wind and blowing snow.

Elik pictured her so clearly, she could almost feel the shaman, burrowed beneath her sod- and snow-covered roof, deep inside the ground. Did she know Elik had returned? Was she waiting?

Even if she did find a chance between her father's moody requests and Naiya's happiness, Elik wasn't certain she would go.

Malluar had told her to bring a gift, but what beside the parka, the pot, or knife that she'd already offered did she own? Her newest memory of Allanaq turning his back, refusing to see her, even as she called and cried and made a fool of herself in front of Kimik and Iluperaq?

Perhaps it was just as well she hadn't seen Malluar yet.

Kimik's mother Sila had passed on a story when they returned, that the reason Malluar had taken to staying in her house was not because she was ill, but because the two shamans were arguing over a bear that Seal Talker had seen in a trance.

Seal Talker had bragged, and Malluar had been offended. It was her own spirit helper, Malluar said, Black Bear, whom Seal Talker had seen. But Seal Talker said that in the trance, he had killed the Bear, and so Malluar had gone in her house and blamed the storm on him, and refused to come out. Like a woman in mourning she would not work, or sew, or go outside, certainly not until Seal Talker had taken the smile he went about wearing, and put it away.

Whether the story was true or not, Elik didn't know. It had come to Sila through Ema, to Ema from Seal Talker, not Malluar.

In the end, Elik decided it was better to wait before speaking to Malluar, rather than face being sent away.

Elik started toward the *qasgi*, stopped, then turned toward her own house, stopped again. She didn't know which way to go, where she wanted to be.

As she stood there, a figure emerged out of the fog of blowing snow. Elik shielded her eyes as Sipsip neared, then stood facing her, the fur of their hoods a tunnel against the wind.

"I thought my sister might be home." Elik's throat felt dry, as if she were lying.

"They went this morning to Whale Fin's family—"

"Ema's?" she asked, not used to having Sipsip know her sister's whereabouts before her.

"To Ema's, and then to the *qasgi*. Seal Talker called for people to come. Were you going? We could walk together—"

"No . . . I . . . My mother asked for seal meat, for a soup."

Sipsip offered a smile, mistaking Elik's reluctance. "You don't have to be proud," she said. "We're all hungry together."

Elik stepped back, looked at Sipsip. She was a good woman, always generous. Had her mother known to raise her that way, shushing her each time she spoke too loudly or showed any childish anger? Or was it that any stranger living among Real People eventually learned what was right?

Though her eyes were just as dark as another woman's and her hair the same kind of black, Dzan—Sipsip's mother—had always been called a stranger. She'd been tall for a woman, narrow in the hips. Grandmother Alu used to say how the woman couldn't do anything right, couldn't even learn. Others laughed at the way she shaped her words. Sipsip didn't speak in any odd way. She had been born among Real People, fished and ate with them, married her father's brother.

If it had taken Sipsip's mother more than a lifetime to be accepted, how long would it take Allanaq? Would people always laugh, call him dog man, talk behind his back?

Why hadn't he come after her? What had he and Iluperaq said while she stood there begging Kimik to wait, to let her speak with him?

"I'll come later," Elik stalled, "My brother had luck on the way home; the hare we caught decided our snares didn't taste so good—they didn't eat through. And now my father's going hunting. He asked me to stay with my mother."

"Where's Kimik?"

"With her mother."

"She could come for a while, sit with your mother?"

"And she does, she will, but I should go bring this—" Elik jingled her hand inside her parka, pretending something was there. Then quickly, unwilling to admit that Kimik, too, would rather sit in any other house but theirs, she turned, started to leave.

Sipsip also left, back to Marmot's house, where she had left her baby in the care of the older girls, and then to the *qasgi*. Elik turned the other way. She had no intention of visiting her sister in Seal Talker's house. Or in the *qasgi*, or anywhere the shaman might be.

Naiya was married, she had choices. And Kimik was free to sleep in her mother's house or with them. Only Elik wasn't married—and that was how she intended to stay— safely away from Seal Talker.

Still, she might have been happier if Kimik hadn't begged Iluperaq to take them home so soon. If Iluperaq hadn't listened to a new mother's fears.

She had dreamed of him again last night, of Allanaq. And not only last night. And not only of him. She had had many dreams lately. Sometimes Allanaq brought a gift of meat to her house. And sometimes she sang songs that brought the game to him. Some of the dreams she understood. Others she forgot before she woke.

Their house, when she returned, held a sour, rancid air. Again. Still.

Iluperaq and Chevak took turns going out to check the weather, but no matter how often they went, there was nothing they could see. No break in the clouds, no gentler air. It was as if the Wind was purposely hiding the sky from them, spitting up snow to make their eyes go blind.

For women there was always work. For men the waiting was difficult, watching the food supplies dwindle, watching the women watching them.

Iluperaq checked the rocks that held the gut window in place on their roof. Chevak carved new antler fishhooks. Iluperaq retied the knots on a torn ptarmigan net. When he climbed back inside the house with the sinew he'd brought from the *qasgi*, Chevak grew sour. When Chevak returned from outside, Iluperaq spit bitter, sideways comments, words that hung in the smoke, clouding their house.

Elik tried not to think about the caribou her father had killed. He never mentioned it, of course. Why, after Seal Talker found out that Kimik had broken a taboo, would he need to? He never spoke about their fishing season at all, except to ridicule Iluperaq's shortened hand.

She pitied her brother. And yet—he wasn't the only man to lose a finger. Would he be less angry if it had been frostbitten? Or lost in a hunting accident? Seal Talker had said he would grow used to it, and in this at least, Elik thought the shaman might be right.

Iluperaq could have chosen to leave the house if he wished; other sons disagreeing with their fathers did. For Real People, a man shamed himself by arguing, not by walking away. And yet Iluperaq stayed, partly because Gull kept him there, her quiet need filling his ears even more loudly than his own wife's wishes. Partly because his stubbornness toward Chevak continued to grow.

Gull never spoke about it, not exactly. A mother didn't use the same kind of words with a son as with a daughter, or a husband. And that was another thing Elik noticed: her mother had grown quieter since they returned. Tense, watching the way Kimik hid her ears when there was arguing. Nervous, wiping bowls that were already clean, rubbing and rubbing again on the hardened edges of caribou skins. Nor did she sing the way she used to when Grandmother Alu had been in the house. Instead, she let her eyes speak for her, sending quick glances to Iluperaq whenever she set food down in his place, the way she offered, almost too quickly, to beat the snow from his parka or chew his mittens soft while Kimik nursed the baby.

Gull's words were loud; no matter that they hadn't been spoken: *Stay with me,* her eyes said. *Keep a mother's light soul from wandering.*

Elik counted five days on her hand, from the time she and Iluperaq and Kimik returned home and the storms began, until the day the weather broke. They were long days, filled with too many ears listening to each other's complaints, and too little food to give them something else to talk about.

Even on the morning they left, Chevak and Iluperaq watched each other closely, each worrying that the other would forget some needed weapon, some part of their hunting ritual that surely, being left out, would bring bad luck.

They woke before sunrise. Without a word between them they bathed and decorated their parkas with the thick black nose-skins of seals they had caught earlier that year.

Iluperaq tied the foot of a peregrine falcon to his belt, to make him as gifted a slayer as that bird. Chevak stitched chips of dried fox pellets into the seams of his parka to give him cunning, so the animals would not make themselves invisible. And then, separately, where before they would have sat together, they practiced their hunting songs,

Chevak guarding his from Iluperaq and Iluperaq, in turn, singing his only in the entry alcove, away from his father.

When the men were ready they took up the gear they had laid out the night before: ice-testing sticks and retrieval line, an extra skin to stand on at the breathing hole, harpoon, draglines. Chevak stepped through the entry first, then Iluperaq, and then the women.

Outside the pale morning sky was laced with orange, yellows, and red. The winds had calmed to a steady hum. Because she was not married, Elik had no part in the hunting ceremony. She drew her face in behind her ruff and leaned against the empty driftwood food racks, wondering if this was the way her father's greed had begun as a young man, with an angry stomach. With Saami bringing home more meat, while he caught none. With a mother wringing her hands in fear.

Gull and Kimik lifted their bowls to the sky, asked the Moon to come and drop a seal inside their husbands' bowls. One for this season, and another for the next. Elik crossed her arms over her stomach, hiding the loud noises inside. She had gone hungry before, everyone did, but never for more than a few days at the same time. The worst she remembered was as a little girl when she and Naiya weren't permitted to eat all the while that the men were out on the ice, hunting down a polar bear that had hunted, and killed, one of the people.

Iluperaq took up the handle on the sledge, dragged it on its iced runners the short distance from the house to the shore. Along the snow-drifted shore ice, other hunting partners were doing the same. Except that out of their houses the bulky figures of the men walked shoulder to shoulder, not apart, while the women trailed behind and children played where they would.

Nearest to the shore, the ice was smoothed under a layer of newblown snow. Farther out, paralleling their beaches, a line of towering ice rose skyward, no longer in the same place it had sat before. Chevak's first step sank through drifted snow before reaching firm ice. Iluperaq followed after, testing in a few places with his ice-point, then smiling to show Kimik it was safe.

Carefully, then, Iluperaq fell in behind Chevak. Elik could see he was already watching for where the ice was firm and solid, or if it was *sikuliaq*—young ice that shifted dangerously, hiding beneath layers of fresh, windblown snow.

Gull turned immediately back for the house. Elik and Kimik remained awhile longer, watching as the men shrank to the size of two-legged caribou, then to two lines, two dots, till finally they were gone.

In the quiet left behind, Elik felt thick and drowsy, undecided whether to sleep first or find food. If she stayed, she might see Malluar or Seal Talker or even Ema. If she went home, the walls would echo.

Kimik, standing beside her, shifted the baby to a better position inside her parka. She seemed quiet—or maybe they both did. A year ago, Elik would have plied her with questions; what was the talk in her mother's house? And had she seen Malluar? What had Iluperaq told Allanaq?

There were other women along the shore and up, nearer the houses. A few were gathering their own jigging gear for ice fishing, reluctant to wait on the men's luck. A child cried and Kimik turned: it was her brother's wife Salmonberry with her little boy, wanting to be held.

Elik thought Kimik would go with her, that without Iluperaq, she would prefer the noisy chatter of an afternoon with relatives. But no, Kimik merely listened, compared the cries of an older boy to the way a younger one sounded, then motioned to Elik that she was ready.

Earlier in the house, Gull had lit a fire, brightening the walls and ceiling for the men. It was dim now and cool. Her mother knelt near a lamp, chewed a mouthful of seal fat, then spit in the pool of melted oil. "With fewer eyes," she said, "we don't need to waste light."

Kimik agreed. She hung her outer parka to dry, then carried the furs she'd moved out to the alcove back to the sleeping bench, rolled them once out on the side of the platform that had always been Iluperaq's, and lay down. The baby fidgeted, nursing then not nursing, his chin quivering with tears, until finally Gull asked if she could try to quiet him.

Kimik passed him over. "He needs to unload his stomach," Gull said. "You see, look here." He was naked, but for the short trousers holding the moss diaper in place. His skinny legs were long and dangling, his knees like the knees of a hare. Gull held him in the air, under his armpits, letting him squall and kick. "You see," she said again, and she set him in her lap. "His stomach hurts, on the inside; it makes him cry. Take his legs like this." She flipped him so his bottom was pointing in the air, then pumped his legs, heels to his tiny rump.

"He'll cry," Kimik worried, reaching to take him back. "Wait—"

The baby complained, then spit up a puddle of curdled milk from one end, a thin birdsong of gas from his other. Gull laughed. "You see?" She looked to Kimik. "Here, you take him. Or wait—he's nursed, yes?" Kimik nodded. "Then let him sleep with me. He's tired, as am I. The young and the old together."

Gull looked up just as Elik fit her hand to a caribou skin to measure out a mitten. Gull wrinkled her nose. "Put that away," she said. "It's forbidden, you know that. A sister or a daughter, or a mother—you aren't supposed to stitch while the men are away. It brings bad luck."

Kimik's expression was flat. "There's enough bad luck already in this house—"

"Hush," Gull said quickly. "You think the world isn't listening?"

Kimik shook her head. "In my mother's house, when two men hunt together, and share food together, they don't try to hide their luck from each other."

Gull opened her mouth, closed it. She turned on Elik. "What are you doing," she asked. "What are you working on there?"

"Mittens."

"Mittens?" Gull's voice flared, then just as suddenly grew tired. "A girl sews mittens. A child learning to sew tries mittens. But you—you're a woman. Why don't you sew like a wife."

Elik's face whitened. She stared at her lap.

Gull sighed heavily. "Maybe it doesn't matter," she said. "Maybe Seal Talker can get mittens from Ema, from any house. He doesn't want you in his bed for the sake of your mittens.

"I'm tired," Gull said again. "All night, your father—he doesn't let me sleep. He's a man, and men are like that. Husbands. They're good, but they're hungrier than women. For food. For a woman's heat. They make more trouble. Maybe it will be different for you, taking a husband who's already old, never without food. I don't know. I never did. Why don't you come—fix these furs for me. I never seem to sleep anymore. My legs feel as if I've been walking naked on the ice."

Kimik sent a troubled look to Elik, motioning her to hurry. But when Elik did, when she leaned forward to push the rough edge of the caribou skin from her mother's face, Gull stopped her. "What is that smell?"

Elik pulled away.

"You have a smell on your breath. Something sour. What did you eat?"

"Nothing," Elik said, but Gull was frightening her. She looked to Kimik for help. Kimik set the baby down—he was sleeping now—then crawled along the platform, trying to see.

"Only the same fish you ate," Elik said quietly, but by then, Gull had lowered her head back down, closed her eyes.

Elik waited a moment, then slid back to sit with Kimik. But for the circle of light surrounding the one lamp, the house was dark, nearly black. There were sounds from Gull's mouth, not like Alu when she had been ill—these were different. Thick and deep inside her throat. And—now that Elik thought about it—there was a smell. But it wasn't coming from her. It was from her mother. And not from her mother alone, but from the entire house.

Elik pushed aside the stitchwork she hadn't even begun, slipped on her outer clothes, and went outside.

The moment the cold air touched her face, she vomited into the snow, between the houses, on the ground. When she was done and she'd wiped her mouth, the specks of food were already freezing into the pocked, yellow snow. She kicked them toward the two nearest dogs. Let them eat the food she could not. That way, at least, her mother wouldn't smell it on her again.

Gull told her daughters to let the next night go by and then a day before they started looking for the men. It was on the second day after, when Saami, Whale Fin, and Blue-Shadow had all come back—with only one seal between them—that they began to worry. Not enough to speak a name aloud, that would have been unlucky, but enough so they began to listen more closely, raise their eyes toward the skyhole more often than before.

Morning came. The low winter sun crossed the horizon, started to set. Gull had already been careful not to do stitchwork. Now she made certain no water was boiled, no voices spoke too loudly. Till finally, just as night began to close, they heard a noise, a man's hoarse coughing.

It was Chevak, clattering, shuffling outside. The women sat in a row, eyes on the dark hole of the floor as he climbed through the entry tunnel into the house. Iluperaq wasn't there, but then, he could have easily stopped in the *qasgi* first. That would have made sense.

Chevak was still wearing his white caribou skin, the same clothing he'd worn when he left—for camouflage, so the seals would not find him. Except now, there was a dark gash around the shoulder, where the seam should have held the sleeve in place.

Elik looked behind him for Iluperaq but he hadn't come. With luck, she hoped, he'd be down in their ice-pit storing away a newly caught seal. She slipped from the platform to the floor, waited to help her father with his parka.

Most days he would have taken it off, handed it to one of the women to dry, to check for tears. This time, he didn't move. His face looked pale, almost grey.

With a troubled glance, Elik looked to where her mother sat on the platform, then to Kimik, holding the baby to her shoulder. Something in Chevak's eyes had stopped them. "Where is Iluperaq?" Kimik asked.

Chevak shuddered. "On the ice," he said. "We traveled upwind as we left, thinking it would be easier that way for the trip home, if we were hauling seal. But with the wind, we couldn't see. It came up that fast. Did you feel it here?"

"Nothing," Elik said. "We felt nothing."

"Out where?" Kimik asked.

Chevak pointed southward, and then west. "It was clear that first day and we took one seal. We decided to stay out a second day. We left that first seal with a marker, so we would find it again, in the snow. It was after that. The wind came up . . ." He looked to his torn shoulder seam, as if that explained it all.

"We had to find old ice, heavy enough it wouldn't drift away, take us with it." He turned to Kimik. "It's too soon to worry. Even for a wife—"

"Worry?" Kimik repeated the word.

"A man isn't lost until a year . . . If the ice takes him out, he might land somewhere again, find his way back. It could take as long as a year. Everyone knows it's happened before . . ."

"What are you saying?" Elik asked.

"We were separated."

Kimik shook her head, no. "How?" she asked, then again: "How?"

"I'm trying to say—"

"You waited for him?" Gull stood looking at her husband. Her eyes were hollow; her hands opened and closed on empty air.

"Of course." Chevak wrinkled his face in annoyance. "Why else would I have been gone so long, except that I did everything. Everything a man could do."

"A dog—did he have a dog," Gull asked, "to find the way home?"

"You were there. You know we took no dog."

Elik looked behind him. "Where is the seal you caught?"

"The seal—ah. Yes. I lost it. I never found the marker again. Why do you ask that?" He reeled toward Gull. "What's the matter with you, you teach a daughter to question a father? Why is she even here? Without a husband? Wasting our food? Can't you see, a man comes home—"

He would have said more, started shouting and throwing his anger around, but that Kimik slid from the platform, circled as wide away from him as the walls allowed.

She had the child in one arm, against her shoulder. With her free hand she pulled her parka from its peg, held it to her chest, not even bothering to put it on.

"You didn't . . ." she whispered and the words came out like a curse. "You didn't help him. You didn't do anything, did you?" With her foot, she felt for the floor opening behind her, reached it, then turned. A moment later and she was gone.

Elik stared at the empty floor. Chevak threw off his outside clothing. "It's too dark in here," he said. "A man comes home and he likes a warm lamp."

Elik couldn't look at him, not even pretending grief, talking about his stomach before he talked about his son. What she did remember was the way he'd looked that day with the rain dripping down his hair, lifting his knife to a caribou, the sight of her father mutilating a caribou.

Had he searched for her brother at all? Had he stood there watching as a lead widened? Or tried to throw a line?

"A man is tired," Chevak said, his voice at last beginning to show it. "A man is tired and there should be a woman somewhere to feed him broth and meat." He looked to Elik. "Why are you here?" He made a motion as if to shoo her away. "Eating, when I've been near to death from the cold? I told him not to go. Not to walk so fast, so far. But he had to prove himself stronger. Better. Harder. I tried to offer wisdom. That it was wiser to sit out the weather and build a shelter and wait to learn where we were. But young men—they are like that."

Gull hadn't said a word. She cocked her head at an odd angle, upward, poked at the mesh drying rack hanging against the rear wall. It was empty. She glanced to the walls, the sleeping platform, the storage places underneath. "What is it?" Elik asked. "What do you need?"

"Your brother's boots—where are they?"

"Wearing them," Chevak said, as if it were a joke.

Gull didn't seem to hear. "His old ones. Hang them up from the rafter, there—" She pointed. "If the boots move, my son is alive. They know him. They'll tell us what he's doing, if he's walking or if he's dead. We have to listen."

Under the yellow light of the oil lamp Gull's color had turned sallow. The skin on her face, on her cheeks as she lay on the platform seemed empty, as if there were no muscle inside to hold it up. And her sleep—it seemed too deep to mean anything good.

Elik watched her brother's boots. They had swayed—two times. She was certain. The first time after she'd pulled a stick of dry herring out from the ice-pit and brought it into the entry tunnel, so she wouldn't have to go outside so often. She had pulled off a flake of the pale meat, looked up, and caught a motion, a swaying, as if her brother was hungry somewhere, as if he smelled her food and was hoping for a share.

"Mother?" she called, hoping the news would reach Gull's soul, wherever it had gone, and lure it back inside her mother's body.

The first time she'd seen the boots move was yesterday. She'd woken from a dream and opened her eyes. That was all Elik did lately, sleep and wake and sleep again. She sang sometimes, and told stories she hoped would please her mother. And she stayed inside, peeing in the men's urine-tub, defecating in the entryway, then kicking the frozen turds outside for the dogs to eat. She helped her mother off the platform whenever she needed to relieve herself, which was less often each day.

And dreaming, that was the other thing Elik did.

She had been dreaming when her father climbed in through the entry. In her dream, a pine marten had allowed her to bury her fingers in the thick yellow hairs on his chest, and sit with him, which was odd because in the daytime, she had never known a marten to sit still so long. But that was what they were doing in the dream: sitting, talking together. Out on a bog lowland, near a lake that was small and round and glassy. When she looked down, in the dream, she could see through the water. There was land below, dry land, and people building tiny houses, far away. "*Qamma*," one of them looked up and called to her from the roof of their house. "*You are wanted.*"

Her father was leaning against the bench when she woke, filling his mouth with herring. "Your mother—" He shrugged toward the platform, chewed then swallowed. "She's sleeping still?"

Elik rubbed her face. Her father had not slept in their house since returning without Iluperaq. It smelled too much like women, he said, and he spent his nights in the *qasgi*, coming back only when he realized the women weren't bringing his food, the way other wives and daughters did, the way they used to.

"My mother is ill," Elik said, and she sat up, rubbed her eyes. The lake was gone. In place of the marten, her father had come.

Chevak glanced to the boots, watched a moment, then stepped sideways out of their shadow. "Did she say anything?"

"She sleeps. She only talks a little—"

"That woman? That woman never talked a lot." Chevak turned so Gull, if she woke, wouldn't see his face. "She was sitting up yesterday, with sinew in her hands and sewing. Was that yesterday?"

Elik shrugged.

"So. Something is wrong. I thought so—No. Don't answer," he stopped her before she tried. "I know what it is." He tipped the cook-pot that hung above the coals, peered over the rim. "I can see where there should have been a fire, food boiling for a father. You know, you have a gentle mother. She's a good woman, I never said different. But she loves her children too much, as if they were babies still. She does all their work herself. It isn't good. It hurts me to say this, and she wouldn't. But with your brother gone—"

"He's not dead."

"Gone. With your brother gone, I can't be the only man to hunt for so many women. You think I'm not grieving? I needed him—a father needs a son. And you—you're not a child—this is what I'm saying. It's you who'll soon be taking care of me. You and a husband. You need to be someone's wife, someone's mother. It isn't enough only to be a daughter—You hear?" He showed her the empty pot, as if it proved him right.

"An old man can't hunt so much alone. It's time you learned to work as hard as your mother, as hard as your grandmother did. You bring the food to me. I'll be in the *qasgi*." Chevak turned and left.

Elik climbed to the platform, leaned against the wall at Gull's side, hoping her mother hadn't heard.

Their house had grown quiet when it shouldn't have. It should have been filled with people visiting, with the sounds of her mother cooking and a fire being struck, and Naiya's stitches turning fur back into skin. It should have been filled with her grandmother's singing, and the sound of Kimik's baby's little cry.

A year ago, she remembered, the house had been filled with noises. It was empty now. A house should not be empty.

The day passed into night, then day again. Naiya came once but, seeing her mother ill, grew worried for the baby she hoped she might be carrying. She left, not to return. And Kimik also, but then, without Iluperaq, Elik wouldn't have expected Kimik to stay.

Elik was sitting near Gull, watching in case she woke, when her father's voice startled her. There was another man with him, a second voice, raspy and shrill: Seal Talker—it had to be. No other man spoke with a voice that rose and fell the way his did. She heard their voices, their footsteps crunching on the roof, then climbing through the entry.

Quickly, she set aside the unfinished skin she had been scraping on her knees. She glanced to her mother. Gull's shoulders rose and fell more heavily today than yesterday. And her breathing—it was also heavy. Elik smiled. It was a good sign: the air coming out her lips with a huffing, almost a snore. She would wake soon. Elik wouldn't have to worry. Chevak entered just as she twisted the lamp wick brighter. When she turned, she found Seal Talker smiling at her bent-over rump.

"Chevak," Seal Talker said, not to her but her father. "Your daughter Naiya, she's a good wife to my nephew. Did I tell you how thankful he is?"

Chevak bobbed his head in gratitude.

"She sews with a fine hand. Even my old wife has spoken of it. She is quiet, and well mannered, and the clothing she sews would rival a bird for its beauty. You raise good women," he chuckled, "but you keep them too long for yourself."

Elik climbed to the sleeping platform, lowered her eyes. She would feel safer if she didn't look at him. He frightened her. He had when she was a girl and now, even more. Why did he keep after her? Any woman could sew for him, push his baby out her vagina for him, say what he wanted to hear.

Seal Talker crossed to Gull's side of the platform. Lightly, he touched her shoulder, waited. He seemed almost surprised when she didn't move. All her noisy, straining breaths—he must have thought she was awake. He threw a glance at Chevak. "How long?" he asked.

Chevak shrugged, then lied. "Just since today," he said. Elik's eyes flickered in surprise, then quickly, she looked away. "She went to sleep last night, and now she's like this."

Seal Talker touched Gull's hand, watched the fingers— there was no response. He set her hand down on her chest, then seemed to weigh Chevak's word against what he saw.

"This is both good," he said, "and not good. It is not good because we cannot question her, and ask if she has broken any taboos—it is harder to find something which is not confessed. And yet, if her soul is wandering, because of some angry spirit, we may yet find it, and bring it home. If it has not wandered too far." Seal Talker stood quiet, watching Gull, glancing sideways toward Elik. Finally, he made his pronouncement.

"She should have a new name," he said, "something she won't be recognized by. Something that will invite strength back in—Ema. We will call her by my own wife's name. Also, I need to have an amulet brought. Chevak, you must go and ask Ema. Tell her the squirrel's skin. She'll know. Your daughter will stay here with me."

"A squirrel skin?" Chevak shrugged. He looked to Elik, wondering why he should go and not her.

"Go on," Seal Talker urged him. "My wife was butchering meat when I left."

This time Chevak smiled. He made a motion toward Elik, signing something. She was glad she didn't see. Then he left and, but for the sound of Gull's rippled breathing, the house grew still.

Seal Talker continued to sit with his back toward Elik. She sat, trying not to look at him. Finally, the shaman turned. "Is there water?" he asked, and Elik started, till she realized how calm he sounded. There was no threat in his voice, no anger.

She rose, crossed the floor to the bladder of water that hung above the hearth, found a dipper, filled it. She brought it back and held it out, reaching, so she wouldn't be near.

Seal Talker turned to take the dipper and she looked past him, to her mother. He opened his hand; he couldn't reach. She lifted the water closer.

This time, he grabbed her by the wrist.

She screamed, then choked the sound. The water flew, but no one noticed. She tried to pull away, but he tightened, held her fast. "Sit down," he said. "That's all I want." His voice was surprisingly calm.

Elik swallowed. With his hand circling her wrist, she climbed awkwardly to the bench, as far from the touch of his leg as his grip allowed.

She tried to sound calm. "My mother—she'll be well?"

"Perhaps. It's possible, if I'm able to find where her soul has wandered." His hand was sweaty and cold, and oddly soft. He loosened his grip enough to stroke her hand.

Elik forced herself to hold still, not to pull away or anger him. More than anything, not to anger him. She needed to tell herself that this was what she wanted, for Seal Talker to help her mother. Find her soul if he could. Whatever he could, so long as Gull didn't die.

"You see," he said, "I will not hurt you. A man who hurts his woman is a fool. A woman has power. But a woman can also be childish, and sometimes . . . Sometimes if she has not been raised properly, she must be taught . . ." He brought his hand lower, forcing her closer, his legs brushing hers.

"What—" she asked. "What should I do?"

"Sit here, nothing more. I will sing for your mother. And you will listen. Later, you will bring your things and come with me to my house."

"My father said . . . He asked if I would . . ."

"Don't lie. You see? Didn't I just tell you, you haven't been brought up properly? A new wife mustn't lie. Your father said nothing, unless it was the name of the gift he asked in trade for you."

Elik bit hard against her lip. She would have shouted, or cried—except she was afraid of what it would do to her mother.

"Now." Seal Talker sounded satisfied. "I will sing for your mother. Bring me my—" He stopped, looked around. "My drum? Where is it?" Elik glanced sideways, to the floor, the platform. "Did I bring it? I must have left it with Ema. Your father will . . . No. He wouldn't think to bring anything."

"Do you want me to go?" Elik hardly dared hope.

"No, but—thank you." He looked almost warmly at her.

"The drum is my strongest. You wouldn't be allowed to touch it. Wait here, I'll bring it myself."

Without daring to breathe, Elik watched him climb from the platform. Listened as his booted feet moved unevenly across the floor, through the entry, out the house . . .

He was gone! Her shoulders heaved in relief. She needed to think clearly. Quickly. Her father would return, or Seal Talker first. One of them. She had to think . . .

She hadn't fought; she was proud of that much. It would have shamed her mother to see a daughter fighting like a child.

Nor would she fight when he returned. How could she, with her mother's soul wandering, watching and ill? With Iluperaq somewhere, not dead—she refused to think of him as dead.

Whatever she did, if she fought the shaman, if she screamed—there were spirits who would see. Whatever she tried—it would be known . . .

"Mother?" Elik whispered. There was no answer. "Gull?" she tried again, but nothing. No movement. No sign of having heard.

She leaned over to offer her mother a sip of water. Her lips were colorless. She waited to see her shoulders rise, to hear the labored breaths that had filled the house.

They were gone. There was her face, but no movement. Her mouth, but no air. No breath. "Mother?"

Elik felt her mother's hand, lifted it. Then dropped it. There was no movement in the blankets. No answer. No pulsebeat in the wrist. No answer.

Elik backed away. She put out her hand, clutched air.

Her mother was dead. And yet . . . She had known this was coming. Somehow, inevitably, this had been coming.

She kept her eyes on her mother as she climbed from the platform, all the while praying this wasn't her fault, that nothing she'd done had made this happen.

Iluperaq. And now her mother. And who next? *Live with me, or she'll be dead.* Seal Talker might as well have said the words out loud. He could have found the cause, couldn't he? Couldn't he have done something? Or had he wanted Gull to die?

She would run away. That was what she would do. There was only the smallest window of a chance, but she might be able to do it. Leave this house where nothing happened the way it was supposed to, where the walls never laughed and fathers were jealous of their sons and daughters held silent rather than speak against either parent.

She grabbed for her sealskin boots, her best pair, for the deepest snow, the coldest weather. Frantically, she yanked a fistful of dry grass, stuffed it in the toes for warmth. She would need to stay warm.

She tore through the storage baskets, below the sleeping platform, in the entry. Caribou skin and lashing cord—sinew, it could always be used, snow goggles to save her eyes. Another knife—her brother's. That was good—Iluperaq would smile and say it was good.

She tried calming herself, but it wasn't working. There were too many stories falling into truth: the legend of a house where the dead never left. Where spirits waited to catch someone, waited with their stomachs crying for food . . .

She gulped for air, swallowed shallow too-quick mouthfuls of air, the smell of seal oil, of the urine tub, of sweat, and fevers and sickness all around—too much sickness.

She stayed only long enough to pull her brother's boots down from their peg. It would be better if they hung in his wife's house. Kimik would wait: one year for the ice to carry a hunter to land. A second year for him to build a kayak, find his way home.

Outside, the cold slap of wind brought her thoughts around. She had to run quickly, but where? Seal Talker's hand reached into any house he named. Her father didn't care. Naiya was too busy with her own happiness. Kimik with her sadness. She would have run to Malluar gladly, if only she had given Elik one sign, any sign she would be taken in. But Elik had found no gift; in truth, she had less to offer now than at the start.

She turned to see the weather: the clouds had opened a hole for the light to shine through. Ravens called from above the hills.

*Good-bye, Mother,* she whispered. *Good-bye.*

She would go to Kimik's house. She would beg her sister-in-law for a bit of food. A carry-pack. Already she realized how foolish she was, taking so little for such a trip. Except, she must leave quickly, before Seal Talker thought to search. She would go to her uncle Grey Owl's village again. There was no place else to go.

# 12

Allanaq had caught no seals. It was time to turn back. He needed to sleep someplace where the wind didn't prick his skin. Where there was food to quiet the hunger, not only in his stomach but in his hands that were almost shaking, in his vision that had blurred to a narrow slit.

He pulled together his sledge, strapped on his ice scoop, harpoon, and lances. He tried not to think about how Nua would look when he returned, the way she would raise a small fire and offer him warm, weak tea and hide her disappointment and ask him nothing of what he'd seen.

The winds had been strong these last few days. He'd have been wiser to turn back earlier, and safer. Twice today, he'd been lulled into sleep at the breathing hole. Both times the ice had woken him, noisily cracking, rubbing. He was lucky he hadn't woken to find the sea ice shifted, taking him out.

Walking back, he kept as close to the path he'd taken coming out as he could manage, toward safer landfast ice and the distant ridge that paralleled the shore. The walking was rough; over ridges of weathered, piled ice. Along the jagged fields he thought he remembered, but somehow wasn't sure.

He stopped several times, took his bearings. The sky had changed; it was heavy with clouds now, grey and low to the ground. And something else. What? Was it in the air? A wind? He looked for the sun, for a sign to tell him whether the wind had turned. Over his shoulder in the distance, not far, he followed the uneven shadow of a low ridge of jumbled ice he didn't think had been there before. And a smell. Like water, but something else as well.

He started toward it, tugging at his sledge, knowing it was foolish to climb a ridge of freshly piled ice. That whatever forces had built it, could be working still. Sliding, shifting the ice. He knew that, but he was curious just the same.

At the height of the ridge he looked down on an open lead of water, nothing so wide as a river, but more than a crack, certainly nothing he could cross without a boat. The edges were smooth; impossible to say how long it had been there. He started away from the lead, along the ridge, then stopped. He'd heard something. Loud and heavy as a wind. But not a wind. A breath. Unmistakable.

With his sledge bumping behind, he climbed down the other side. A moment later he was standing at the edge of an open lead looking into darkly moving water. He cocked his head, studied the surface. Scarcely a moment passed when the water opened. The long black curve of a whale skimmed the surface. The hump of a head, a blowhole. Allanaq's heart leaped, realizing what he'd found. A whale! A whale was trapped in a lead. And not just a whale, but a bowhead, smaller than the one he'd seen in the spring. But a bowhead. Arveq had come, to him!

Allanaq's thoughts darted and flew. The whale plaque he had traded with the Forest People, it was buried now, in his umiak, beneath a mound of snow. It wasn't the plaque that had brought this whale. Had the current shifted? Is that what happened? Or was it the wind and current together? In the Seal People's place, it was a wind from the north and east that brought the worst storms. But he wasn't at home. And this was a north–south lead, not paralleling the shore.

How long could the whale have been there? He couldn't say. The crack didn't appear fresh. Perhaps the whale had followed what began as open water, then the wind shifted and the ice closed in behind?

He didn't understand, but then—maybe understanding didn't matter.

The whale swam slowly past. He could hear it sucking in a breath of air, then blowing it out with a whooshing sound. The spray wasn't heavy, Allanaq didn't know why, but a cloud of frost rose with it. The whale dipped under the surface.

So quiet he hardly dared breathe, he unstrapped his harpoon with the toggling head, the lance that, he rejoiced now, hadn't been used on a seal. Slowly, because the whale would be annoyed if he grew loud, he walked to the ice edge where it first surfaced. *Stay, please,* he sang. "*You whale. You come again . . .*

He checked the bone wedge that held the point into his lance shaft, then dipped the tip down in the water, so it would know where to go.

He counted out the moments till the whale grew hungry again for air. Till the water rippled: there! He raised his lance. The water opened. The whale's huge head grew to an island. With a sudden thrust, with all his strength gathered to his arm, he heaved the lance. Aiming for its organs, its heart. He threw the lance and then the toggling harpoon to bleed it, help it die.

He stayed only long enough to repeat the song: *You whale, You come to me. Come, and your soul will again wear bones.* And then he started walking—not running, it wouldn't be good for the whale if he ran—back to the Long Coast houses. For help. For hands.

With the tip of her long-handled antler knife, Elik sliced a line into the snow, marking a dugout shelter where she could sleep.

She had covered a great distance. The first day especially, with the threat of Seal Talker driving her like a whip, she had walked—no, she had run—from the Bent Point village, following the winter trail, first around the bluff, past a small creek they called Jumps Across, to a place she knew with an abandoned cache.

Seal Talker was stronger than she was, in his arms, his legs. But she could run farther before giving out. If he wrestled her, he would win, but he would have to catch her first.

The second day she slowed her pace until, by midday, she reached a trail she knew even in the snow, a pass that funneled down between two hills to a frozen lake behind the shore. She felt safe enough to stop and rest and listen. The world was hilly beyond the bluff, the sky pale and, with the wind and the hushing sounds of birds' wings, never quiet.

She remembered how she'd traveled through many of these places as a young girl. Over there, the exact rise where her mother had once set their tent.

Her mother. So many things reminded her of her mother.

It had been spring. She remembered how wide the days had seemed, never hungry. She remembered her father and the other men paddling out in kayaks, directly in among a herd of beluga whales—the long white ones that came to their shores early in the spring. The men had seemed so brave, unafraid and quiet, herding them toward the narrows where she and Naiya stood with her mother and grandmother and the other women, waiting with their lances near the shore.

Memories. They seemed almost dangerous. She rose, put them away, started walking again.

With nightfall she built a camp, but no fire—she wouldn't risk the smoke. She fell asleep quickly, long and deep, then woke before sunrise, the hunger a knot inside her. She drank her fill of water she'd kept thawed against her side, then ate from the small packet of whitefish Kimik had pushed into her hands. She didn't eat it all, there was no knowing when there'd be more. Instead, she buried it in the deepest part of her pack, not to be tempted.

Sometime during the morning the wind picked up. Snow swirled high as her knees. Like mosquitoes in summer, it found every needle hole in her clothes. It struck her face, her eyes, forcing her to walk more slowly, to mark the distant hills by her right shoulder, the blue piled ice by her left. She wore snow goggles and kept her hood raised continuously. She walked till dusk—not a long day, nor far as she had hoped. She stopped to make camp at a site Iluperaq had also chosen on their return trip. *Ikniituq* it was called, a spring sealing camp, though no one was there now. Not there, and not in any of the places she passed.

Had it been summer, she might have found people to take her in, feed her, hide her. They would have been fishing along the mouths of rivers and creeks, following the salmon runs, the pike and herring. Food. She dreamed about food as she walked. Smelling it, tasting it.

She made up songs about how she would never get lost so long as she knew the way the snowdrifts pointed, and whether the buried grass bent east or west. How even this slow, tedious walking was easier now than it would be in the summer, because now she had the snow to smooth the uneven hummocks and the lakes and frozen creeks could be walked over, instead of around.

On the third night she again sought out the kind of crusted, deeper snow that was good for building a shelter. With her knife, she cut a series of snow blocks, lifted them to raise a wall for a windbreak, a hole going down for a shelter. She'd brought two caribou furs; one she angled for a roof, from the snow wall to the ground. The second fur she used for the ground, unrolled it over a layer of willow she'd picked along the way. She went to sleep hungry and feeling terribly alone, wondering whether the land knew she was there. And if it knew, would it leave a trail for Seal Talker to follow? Would it alert her relatives ahead? Tell them she was coming?

Her stomach woke her the next morning, hungry, nearly nauseous with the hollowness inside. She opened her eyes, tried turning her thoughts to something other than herself. But all she could see was Allanaq standing with his hands like flippers, laughing as he showed how he soothed a seal as he stalked it by the method called *utoq*, crawling sideways over the ice, pretending he was nothing but one seal approaching another.

Her smile faded. She was too much alone to laugh, and hungry, her muscles already tense, her lips dry. She pushed aside thoughts of men and the meat they caught, climbed to her knees and peered outside. There was no warmth in the sun, only a fish-scale sky of blue, and light glaring so strongly she couldn't make out the huge rock not far from where she'd slept.

She squinted, shielded her eyes against the snow. What had been a rock turned into something else. An animal, small-sized and round, waddling in front of her.

A porcupine—a porcupine had come! It must not have caught her scent, hiding in the ground the way she was. Porcupine meat was sweet and rich with fat, more so when a person was lucky enough to find one so far from the forest rim. She kneaded the strength back in her hands, grabbed the long-handled knife she'd used to cut the snow blocks, stepped up, away from the shelter.

The porcupine sat quiet, offering itself, a gift from the warmer months when it sometimes wandered the beaches. She raised her knife, clublike, overhead. Squeezed to stop her arms from shaking, then swung down, a hard blow to the side of its head. The porcupine skittered on its side, rolled, then stopped. Her hand shook with the impact and she lifted again, swung for the head, the same spot. Again the blow landed.

The porcupine lay dead, its eyes open, motionless. A dark trickle of blood against matting hair and stiff quills, bright red on the snow.

For a moment she felt weak, dizzy with the thought of food. She thanked the animal for its gift, then quickly yanked up a handful of dry grass, a few short sticks of willow she was lucky enough to find. With her mittened hands, she held the animal tightly, pierced it on a willow spit, then set it down to strike a fire. She wanted the heat and, surely, Seal Talker hadn't come—he would have found her by now if he'd followed. More likely, he had decided to wait till spring. . . .

The brush was dry and the wind small enough for the fire to catch quickly, grow into a flame. She squatted close, burning the quills off in the hottest part of the fire, singeing the hair and fur, hurrying it with a stick. She'd gut it quickly, she decided. With all the bark and willow porcupine liked to eat, their meat often turned bitter too quickly.

The fire sputtered with the dripping fat and she looked up, watched as the light wind took hold of the smoke and turned it. Not upward, where it would have melted into clouds but westward, in the same direction she was traveling. A second wisp of smoke turned downward again, pointed to the ground.

Her eye followed, watching the white smoke take on color. Something was moving. She gripped the porcupine spit, squinted and stared. It wasn't a cloud. Not a cloud at all. It was a campfire. People. She was looking at people. Three men, possibly another—it could be someone. Anyone.

She dropped to the snow, knocked her fist purposefully to the spit, toppling the porcupine, forcing it to tumble. And then lunging, catching it before a sound could be heard. Before the smoke changed or any fat sputtered— Dogs? Did they have dogs? She hadn't seen . . . She scooped snow in the crook of her arm, threw it on the fire, more snow, dousing the smoke before it rose.

She lay with her face to the snow, waiting to hear a shout, footsteps or dogs barking. If not Seal Talker, then they could be from Grey Owl's village, in which case they would laugh and have done with it. Or they could be someone else. Strangers. She didn't know who.

As soon as she listened, she heard them—eating, not shouting—talking, enough to be certain she couldn't understand the words. Which meant they were enemies. With weapons. Men without women.

She tried to think clearly. They hadn't seen her yet, but

they would, with her tail in the air, and the smell of meat
for any man to find. Sipsip's mother had been lucky. Not
every stolen woman was kept for a wife. She thought of
Allanaq, the emptiness on his face when they first met.

What if these were the people Allanaq spoke of? The
same as the man he had killed? Which meant that Allanaq
and Grey Owl were wrong and Bear Hand was right. The
man had been a relative, and he had tracked his carvings.
Maybe he showed Allanaq's carving around. Maybe someone remembered.

With tiny, shuffling motions, Elik crawled backward,
dragging the porcupine with one hand, burying the bloodstained snow with her other. Inside her shelter, she moved
more quickly, rolled the skins she'd slept in. Her snowshoes—she didn't dare stand now, but later? What if the
snow turned deeper? Bulky as they were, she had to take
them. If they had dogs, they'd sniff the sinew lacings, or
the porcupine, or her furs. Nothing would save her.

She peeked above her dugout: they were tall men, three
that she could see. Young—which meant they would be
full of themselves, not wise, and hot-blooded, too quick to
act. Their hair was long, showing out from under hats that
were separate from their parkas, as if their women didn't
know how to stitch a hood together.

Crawling backward out of the hole, she started moving—away, toward a line of dwarf willow.

If they saw the trampled snow, or the roof, or her tracks . . .

They had no real tent. Only a windbreak of skins tied to
the willows, as hastily built as hers. Packs with gear leaned
this way and that. No dogs that she could see. No sledge.
Four men, not three. And nearby, ravens waiting for their
shares. Perhaps they'd stopped to snare a few ptarmigan or
maybe a hare.

She turned about, started crawling on hands and knees,
so low to the ground the snow licked against her chin. If
they saw her, maybe they would mistake her for a strange
animal, snowshoes across her back. Maybe she could
frighten them, scream and chase them away. . . .

The one thing she knew was that she had to reach the Long Coast village before they did. Warn them. Give them time to prepare. If they were Allanaq's strangers—and who else would they be?—they would plan an attack at night. Shooting arrows into their houses, flaming arrows that killed whomever they touched. It didn't matter who.

The news she brought—it would be no help to Allanaq. Bear Hand would blame him for allowing that second man to escape. For trading his carvings. For everything . . .

But what if they had already been to her uncle's village? What if they were returning the way they had come? She was far enough away with the willow between them to stand. She stole one glance backward, only one, then started running, harder than she had ever run before.

It was the village dogs who saw her first, staked near the houses as they were. They growled and whined as soon as they sensed Elik's hurried steps, not like a woman going for water or to a food cache, but running, smelling of fear and meat—meat she might yet have to share.

She stopped as soon as she heard them, then stood there, doubled over with her hands on her knees, pushing back the pain that stabbed beneath her sides. The dogs were nearly starving—she saw it at once—the bleak line of their ribs, worn coats, confusion in their stance.

And yet—they were alive. Starving people chewed the leather of their blankets, their clothes, before they died. Before that, they ate their dogs.

She looked to the *qasgi*. No fire flew from the smoke hole. No one was outside. How many days had passed since she was here last? She couldn't remember. She hadn't thought past this moment, what she would do or say. The dogs had quieted and she could hear something now: was someone crying? A woman's voice, high, carried on the wind? Was that singing?

She counted out the humpbacked shape of snowed-in houses. Smoke came from the skyhole of one: Olanna's house. It was a wood fire—not animal fat. Wood that couldn't be eaten. And no smoke from Grey Owl's house. Not from Weyowin's or the *qasgi*. But from Bear Hand's— there, a sign of smoke.

She started walking, then faster, pulled by fear. Something had happened. She was too late. Someone was dead and those men had already found them, and she was too late.

She followed the singing to Olanna's house, not even thinking to call through the skyhole first. She pushed aside the door hide, felt the rise of heat inside her lungs. She felt cold for the first time all day.

Inside the large single room of the house, the singing abruptly quit. Shoulder to shoulder, people crowded on the sleeping platform, on the floor. They stared as if they didn't know what she was. As if they were ghosts already, and it didn't matter what her name had been or who she was.

Ani's Wife sat nearest the entry. Old Ani hunched opposite. She found Grey Owl, squinting as if he didn't trust his eyes. She searched for Nua, found her huddled on the platform with the women. Olanna's elder sister, Little Pot. Bear Hand's wife, Meqo. Squirrel. Not Allanaq. Where was Allanaq? Two Ravens sat with her arms tightly wrapped around her chest. Bear Hand opposite where she stood with a drum in his hand. Why Bear Hand? Where was Olanna?

It was Little Pot who spoke first. "You came alone?" she asked. Her voice sounded thin as a bird's bone. Elik nodded.

Ani's Wife reached up and felt her hand. Elik jumped. Her leathered fingers were startling, almost sharp, as if she'd changed from a woman to a stick. "You brought no man to hunt?" Ani's Wife asked.

"No, Grandmother. I came alone."

"Alone?" Bear Hand sounded afraid.

"Where is Olanna?" Elik asked.

"Gone. Him. Two Ravens' baby." Bear Hand made a vague motion with his chin. "Inside the *qasgi*. That's why we're here."

Elik looked to the women again, saw what she had

missed before: Two Ravens' arms were empty; her breasts were swollen with the milk she had to drain by hand. Olanna's sister sat on her haunches, chin resting on too-large knees, legs thin as beach grass. Had she been gone that long for people to change so quickly? "Where is Allanaq—?" Her voice was a whisper.

"Gone since before the storm."

"Gone? You mean dead? Were you attacked? What are you saying?"

"Not dead." Grey Owl opened his hands. "A young man hunts. An old man dies. Someone else grows ill because their soul has wandered. And some of us starve."

Bear Hand raised the flat shaman's drum he'd been holding. He spit on the tight face, rubbed saliva round the brittle skin. The motion set up an eerie windlike sound. "All winter," he said, "I warned you. Since the day he brought his father's bones to our land, I warned you. Now the animals turn away. Our oldest and our youngest die. As long as that dead shaman lies near our village, he'll bring us grief. We should dig them out. Burn them. Throw them to the sea."

A chill rose through Elik's back. Every face she saw was skewed and tight-lipped with grief. Grief and fear and something she hadn't seen before: hunger and the change it works on people.

"If Olanna's death is not proof of evil," Bear Hand continued, "then we have all gone blind. The storms grow worse. We searched our hearts. Has any of us done wrong that grief should come? That the animals who feed us, should turn their backs? No. It was none of our doing. It was . . ."

Elik couldn't listen. She couldn't allow him to go on. "I came along the winter trail," she said loudly, not caring that she interrupted. "Out of the Bent Point village. After five days of storms. My brother was lost on the ice. My mother died in her house—" she stopped, looked to Grey Owl, made herself continue.

"I came to tell my Long Coast relatives that the same storms that touch their shores touch ours. I left alone, but I arrive with a shadow at my back. Four men—I saw four men along the trail . . ."

The air was empty a moment, then, "What are you saying?" Weyowin asked first.

"I am saying I saw strangers. Men in clothes I've never seen, unless it was at a trading place."

"Did you see weapons? Or skins?"

"Did they see you?"

"Which way were they going?"

Someone set a bowl of broth in Elik's hands. The thin soup smelled more of water than meat. She sipped it, but couldn't eat.

"You see?" Bear Hand said. "Is this not what I said? Olanna dies from a spirit's anger. The same spirit sends enemies—"

"Olanna died the same as any man," Elik called back. "Fighting too long against hunger. He wasn't murdered. His soul walked away."

"Olanna was my hunting partner."

Elik turned to see who spoke. It was Old Ani, his small eyes covered by hair the color of dirty snow. "If your words are true," he said to Bear Hand, "then touching those bones, digging them up—it might bring harm. If our shaman didn't fear them in the ground, perhaps they should stay?"

Elik waited. *They don't know where the bones are. They haven't guessed.*

"Touch them or not," Two Ravens' voice cracked. "I don't care. What matters is that someone go into my house and bring the dead back out." She looked to her husband, but Weyowin's thoughts were on his weapons, not the child who was already gone.

"The baby must wait," he said quietly. "If there are raiders, we have to act."

Kahkik looked away from his brother. "Tell us again what you saw."

Elik squatted at the hearth. With a charred stick, she drew a map to her shelter showing where the willow break ran, where she had passed the sea cliffs where people gathered eggs. "If they had had dogs," she said, "they would have found me. What I don't know is which way they came from or—" she stopped.

There were footsteps outside, someone running past the houses. Heavier than a woman. Rushing. Hurrying past Olanna and Little Pot's house. Elik climbed to her feet. *"Forest People,"* she mouthed the words.

With quiet, almost helpless motions, the men reached for their knives. Tools. Anything that could be used for a weapon. The footsteps ran past. Past again. Kahkik slid closer to the skyhole. Weyowin moved in behind the entry.

The next sound came from the roof, above them. Footsteps, and then a voice, muffled yet familiar. Bear Hand snorted. Grey Owl lifted his chin.

"There is game!" a man's voice called through the skyhole. "A whale has come. On the ice . . . A whale . . . "

Elik stepped backward, away from the entry. She listened as the thump of hurried steps moved up through the tunnel, turned into the sight of mittened hands showing first, and then the fur of a trimmed hood. Allanaq.

He breathed heavily as he climbed in. Blinked his frosted eyelashes against the surprise of so many faces, the tension so strong it wrapped the house inside its fist. Except it didn't matter. It couldn't hurt him anymore. He had news, a message. He glanced to Grey Owl, nodded respectfully to Bear Hand. "There is an open lead," he started, "west and beyond the ridge of pressure ice. Following in a line from where the river comes down . . . " He raised his arm to show the direction, then stopped.

He was pointing directly at Elik, directly between Nua and Two Ravens. Elik lowered her gaze but she had been watching him, closely enough that anyone with eyes would have known it wasn't the way a married woman watched a man. "Elik?" She didn't move. Allanaq searched for another face. "Where is Seal Talker?"

Her voice came out a whisper. "In the Bent Point village."

"Where is your husband?" he asked again, louder with a sudden anger.

"I have no husband."

Allanaq stiffened. He studied her face, searching for the truth.

"I never had," she added, wanting him to believe.

Bear Hand grew impatient. "What whales did you see? Beluga?"

Allanaq pulled his gaze from Elik. "Not beluga. There is a great thing I've seen," he said, and again his smile broadened. "A gift . . ."

"How could there be beluga?" Bear Hand demanded. "With the ice still in, and no open water for another moon at least?"

"Because ice moves in its own season," Allanaq answered plainly. "Because while I stood beside a narrow lead hoping for seals, night came and with it, the wind. The wind shifted, blowing from the north, opening and widening a different lead with the sound of ice grating on ice, like thunder, like the moving of rocks. Because this is not a herd of the white beluga we see in the spring, but Arveq, the bowhead."

Kahkik snorted. "What's the use of a whale we cannot reach?"

"I didn't say in open water. It's trapped in a pinched-off lead surrounded by ice."

"I've never seen bowhead," Weyowin said, "except in ice-free water, farther out."

"Yet it's possible—" Old Ani pulled on his chin. "In the open sea, we couldn't hunt one. But if the ice opened, then forced it in toward shore. Or trapped it somehow . . . It's possible."

"It's more than possible," Grey Owl said.

"It's true."

"How do you know it didn't swim away, under the ice?" Kahkik asked.

"I don't know—we have to hurry," Allanaq said.

"It also happens," Bear Hand interrupted, "that rotten meat brings rotten stomachs. How do we know it isn't poisoned?"

Kahkik looked to his brother. "Poisoned? Perhaps, but what if it isn't? Can we dare waste it without knowing?"

Bear Hand snorted. He didn't like what he was hearing, his brother wavering. The thought of food so near, it clouded his thoughts. "In the old days, perhaps," he said, "or west and north of here, people speak of whaling places. But what use is it for us, unless the whale is beached and already dead?"

Lake agreed with Bear Hand. "Our sealing points could never kill a whale."

"And even if they did," Bear Hand asked, "how could we hope to bring it in? No. The whale swam in. It will just as easily swim out."

"With my larger walrus points . . . " Allanaq started.

"Toys." Bear Hand threw back his head, but the men weren't listening. Their thoughts were turning at the possibility of food.

"It's a chance," Old Ani said. "A gift. If the lead is right . . . "

"But the men—?" Elik started.

Allanaq turned on her. "What men?" he asked, and the story was quickly repeated, not by Elik but by Weyowin, Kahkik, Grey Owl, filling in as she sat quiet, repeating the locations she'd given, adding what they knew.

Allanaq's face fell as he listened. "How fast could that man have run, to return so quick?"

"We don't know if they came from a village," Kahkik said. "Or how many more there are."

"They're here," Bear Hand said. "That's what matters."

"But also who they are," Allanaq insisted, "and what they want."

"They're the same men," Grey Owl said sadly. "Allanaq—they are the same."

Allanaq held quiet. Had everything Bear Hand said come to pass? That his foolishness brought only trouble? If anyone died, it was his fault, as surely as if he and his father had cursed this place. "And yet—" he couldn't help but say, "if they see our weapons, fine enough to take a whale—a whale that is out there even now, offering itself"—he looked at each man in turn—"it will be strength they see, not fear."

Weyowin nodded. "How much harm can four men bring against all of us?"

"You're young. You don't know," Grey Owl said. "Unless we've food in our stomachs, how can we have strength in our arms?"

Ani's Wife leaned forward, her face lined with hunger. "What are our choices? To hide in the hills, in a cave perhaps?"

"And what's to stop them from following us onto the ice?" Bear Hand asked.

Little Pot agreed. "Perhaps wherever my brother's spirit has gone, he and the whale's *inua* will sit and talk? Perhaps they've decided to help? With a whale, these enemies will see a strong people, with weapons and food. Let them see how favored we are. Allanaq, you have more of your large walrus points?"

Allanaq nodded.

"They can be shared out?" Old Ani asked.

"Yes." Allanaq quickly nodded. "Yes."

Bear Hand pulled in his chin. "That many, when you worked so slow?"

"That many, when no one would take them."

The talk rose, voices speaking all at once. They would take Allanaq's harpoon heads with their skeletal markings and spurs, but they would also carry their own killing lances with the sleek ivory foreshafts and thin, slate blades. There were stories, everyone knew them, not only of enemies coming from inland, but from the sea also, great fleets of umiaks, of men wearing armor of slatted bones, bark, and wood. They spoke about how Arveq sometimes swam near points of land, in leads ahead of the open ice. And they remembered other seasons when a bowhead had died on their shore—the great gifts of meat and oil, the black sheets of baleen that hung inside its mouth.

The talk turned to plans. Bear Hand listened without speaking. He stared at the fire, watching into memories, stories he had always been taught: do nothing and the Long Coast People would be dead. Wait till the spring moon brought food, and they might survive on the leather of their boots and their blankets, but not if they also had to fight. Or what if it was possible, that the great whale had come for the sake of Allanaq's strange carvings? What if it meant that, perhaps, his father's ghost was satisfied? The harm was gone?

He looked up. "They'll wait until night to attack," he said, "not in the day. But perhaps, if they see us feasting with a whale on our shore, and weapons in our hands, perhaps they won't come at all."

Allanaq held his mouth tight, not to show surprise. Had he heard correctly? He looked to Bear Hand, saw eyes that were filled with thoughts of whale meat, of a new and different enemy. Not him. Allanaq said, "In my home, we sometimes feared attack, when we were gathered in the *qasgi*. We built tunnels, escape tunnels, so there would be a secret way to climb out—"

Kahkik shook his head. "We can't tunnel in the winter. Even if we could, we haven't time."

"Yet it's wise," Grey Owl said, "not to gather inside at night. Not to be trapped . . ."

Elik leaned past the men. She found Allanaq, glanced at him, a motion so small no one else would have found it, except he did. He returned it: a nod, a warmth in his eyes, lingering a moment longer than was needed. He turned back to the men, but Elik kept watching as he talked, his hands moving, explaining. But his eyes—there was a sadness that hadn't been there when he first ran in the house. She didn't understand. A downward slant to his mouth, just when she would have expected joy.

The moment passed; there was no time for words. Elik was pulled into the work ahead of them. She rose and left with Nua, with Two Ravens, Ani's Wife, and the others. There was work—for the women to call the whale, to lure it toward the men's harpoons. To start wood fires in every hearth so it looked as if their village was large.

They draped whole caribou furs over the outside racks, as if they were newly caught and drying in the wind. Two of the women carried heavy white polar bear hides, to stretch over their tallest racks, to show the luck of their men. They looped long lengths of finger-wide seal lines over the drying racks so that—from a distance—it looked as if they had newly cleaned seal intestines, as if they were the richest of villages.

Lake and Drummer were chosen as runners, sent to scout inland behind the village, to learn if Elik had been followed.

And Squirrel and Two Ravens set rows of sharpened stakes in the ground, hidden beneath the snow, in the likeliest places the Forest People might come.

In Grey Owl's house, Allanaq pulled his storage baskets from under the sleeping platforms, set them open on the floor. The best of his harpoon heads were kept in a hollow, whale-shaped box; he fanned them out on the floor.

Grey Owl and Weyowin, Old Ani then Kahkik and finally Bear Hand sorted through the pile, selecting from the awl-shaped antler pieces, some with side blades set into slots, others with end blades—the same that Bear Hand once ridiculed.

They set aside the small barbed harpoon heads they would have used for taking seals, then while Allanaq leaned back and watched, they picked through his largest chipped flint points, the heads all made of antler, all decorated with the four long lines that, this time, no one seemed to notice. The spurs on the head were made to twist and hold, deep beneath the skin. And though the line was knotted into the hole and the head was made to separate from the shaft, the drag of a weight that size would never be enough to slow the whale. But if enough points struck and hit, and if the ice didn't open a lead for the whale to swim away. Or under. If the whale didn't sink. If it didn't use the hard bones of its skull to crack a path back to ice-free water. And if the Forest People didn't follow them—they might yet bring it in.

With the harpoons they added amulets, eagle feathers

pinned to their parkas, fox tails, seal carvings, anything they thought might please the whale.

By the time they had iced the runners on the sledges and were ready, Lake and Drummer had returned. They had run as far as the Place Where Three Streams Come Together and then farther.

Crouching behind a drift, looking inland and to the larger hills, they had seen smoke, a grey line too sure of itself to be anything but a campfire.

Not yet close, unless the fire meant something else. There was still time, they thought. Men sneaking in to fight would not want to run as fast as they had. They wouldn't want to wear themselves out, or risk coming in so loud, they lost the advantage of surprise. By morning—unless they traveled in the dark—they would be there.

That night, late—would be the earliest they might attack.

It was past midday when Allanaq led them along the path he'd returned on earlier, out on the shore ice into a calm wind, toward the wall of pressure ice that blocked their view beyond.

The cold was steady, the sky bright. Carefully, they marked the position of the sun. It would be best if they were able to strike the whale and send the first sledge home while the sun was still in the sky. Best, but not likely.

If the whale was there at all, it would be possible to strike it quickly. But it could take longer to die. Longer still for them to slide a full-grown bowhead up onto the ice pack without losing it. And then to butcher it. And haul the bulky meat homeward over the uneven ice; not along the same trail they took now, climbing the near-shore ridge, but circling wide, searching for a level, safer path around. And not once, but twenty times twenty, if the whale was large.

Elik walked with the women, a short distance behind the men. She tried not to worry about Two Ravens, who had not been allowed to come, nor Little Pot, because of the death blood on their hands. Nua and Meqo had come because they were past the age for menstruation, and Squirrel and Elik were both between their times. Ani's Wife had also stayed behind, too old to make the trip.

Of the men, Grey Owl, Bear Hand, and Weyowin walked with Allanaq. The others stayed so the village would seem busy and active, so the women would not be unprotected if there was trouble. By night, if the whale had not been struck, they would think about who should return.

The men picked their way over uprooted blocks of pressure ice, stopping only to survey the ice ahead or steal a worried glance behind. They carried sealskin lines coiled over their shoulders, the long shafts of extra lances sideways on their backs, and their bows and folded skin quivers filled with arrows. With their ice-testing sticks they tapped for rotten ice whenever they thought it might be hiding under the light fall of snow.

The had brought two dogs, one of Grey Owl's and one of Old Ani's heaviest pullers, quiet dogs, not young. If they barked, they'd scare the whale. The dogs were harnessed, one to each of the sledges.

Nua and Meqo took the front, tugging the dogs, leading them on, while Squirrel and Elik walked behind, righting the sledges when they flipped, pushing whenever the narrow, extended runners caught. They brought caribou skins, in case they needed a shelter and water to drink, because the ice at that time of the year was salt. Over the pressure ridge, then down onto smoother ice, they walked and pushed and hurried toward the dark line of the water sky, marking the lead they prayed would still be open.

Elik heard the whale before she saw it. A frantic sound, high-pitched, carried on the wind. She looked up, startled to see they had walked so far. Behind them, the pressure ridge was a blue line catching light, barely showing on the horizon.

Nearly at her feet now, the channel of open water split the ice. The lead ran straight for a distance, then jagged. The wind had done this, rafting the ice to one side, separating it from its roots on the other. Exactly as Allanaq had described, the lead was too wide for a man to jump across, not so far a well-thrown harpoon couldn't reach.

Grey Owl and Bear Hand set down their gear first, the younger men following, watching for a place to stand. Squirrel and Meqo staked the anxious dogs a distance back, squeezing their muzzles, warning them to behave. The women formed a line, quieter than the men, resting from their heavier loads. They watched, but only for a moment, then quickly began unlashing the extra harpoon shafts and lances.

Grey Owl paced the ice edge, searching for a sign of where the whale's flukes might have drenched the rougher ice. He found it; not far. He raised his arm, signaling them to come see where water had soaked into ice, turning it slick, smoothing the snow on top. The whale had swum here, recently perhaps.

Allanaq spread his feet and stood carefully at the splintered edge. Behind him the ice was flecked with tufts of snow. Ahead, the lead stretched diagonally away from land in one direction, out to sea in the other. Close enough to the way he remembered, he didn't think the winds had changed. He saw what might be the lead's end: a tapering point where the water ended, too far, too deceptive to be sure.

The open water rippled slightly with the tide and hidden current. Using the pick end of his harpoon, Allanaq chipped off a few fragments of ice, let them fall into the water, then watched to see which way they floated. Left, it told him. It would be the same way the whale moved, if they struck it, if it tried to swim away.

Elik had been watching Allanaq when the water suddenly opened. She jumped back, then saw it: the huge world of the bowhead's back rising from the dark. Quietly—not a one of the people made a sound—she counted its size as it swam past. Two, three, four—the length of four men. Five. It was a young one, *ingutuk*, exactly as Allanaq had described, but graceful, almost at peace.

It must have been scouting for a trail. Somewhere beyond the pack ice lay open water and other bowheads, waiting for the wind to turn, the seas to open. How far away? She didn't know. She only knew she was grateful, awed beyond measure, that a whale had come to this place, shown itself.

Its rounded back slipped beneath the surface. A moment later . . . There! The flip of its broad black tail arched, then hit the flat of the water. So huge and graceful, even the spray of water seemed to dance, to sing.

Nua touched Elik's arm but she hardly felt it. She started walking, following the wake along the lead. This wasn't the first bowhead she had seen, but the others had only been sighted from shore and never this close, not alive. And not in this season, before the first snowbirds appeared. And yet, it wasn't early or late that mattered. The whale had come. It had come and shown itself for Allanaq . . .

The whale rolled, near enough below the surface so that she caught another glimpse of its huge head, its reaching flukes. There was the marked curve of its baleen-filled jaws, the hump of its head and white patch of skin on its chin and underside.

The next time it surfaced it was on the opposite side of the lead, not swimming this time but holding still, breathing heavily. They could hear the sound of it, like a great exhalation. The men moved as they listened, gathering their gear, following to stay in line. She picked up her pace, walked faster. It was too difficult to be proper and slow with the other women.

Each time they sighted it, they watched for a pattern: how often it surfaced, how fast it swam, where in the lead it would rise again, and how long it could go without a breath.

Except that, as they waited with their harpoons and watched, they saw the whale was doing something—holding at the surface. Not asleep, but not swimming. Rubbing itself back and forth against the ice edge while water swirled away. It was scratching, but so hard, it was tearing its own black skin. There were patches, Elik could see them: mottled and torn, blisterlike. And something else they hadn't noticed before: a sheen of blood skimming the water's surface. More blood seeping from a wound. Two wounds.

And where the wound opened, protruding from the flesh, the broken-off ends of two lances hung on. Cuts so deep, they would have long since killed a person. Where the shattered lance ends scraped the ice, the skin kept tearing, the gashes widening.

With its eye, the whale looked directly at them.

Elik shook herself from the sight, looked for Allanaq. He was walking ahead of the others, along the lead, a flint-tipped shaft in each of his hands.

The next time she looked, the whale had submerged. Water sloshed across the ice, almost to her feet. Grey Owl and Bear Hand looked to the sky: it was streaked with red, thin clouds high enough above the horizon they'd have light, but not for long, and only a thin wind, no sign of storms. A hope of moonlight after.

They signaled, then paced themselves along the lead. Their exhaustion had fled, replaced with tension, sharp-pitched and tight. Allanaq knelt and readied his coiled lines, watched to see the others doing the same: his etched antler harpoon heads fitted on their longest, heaviest shafts, his walrus points atop their lances.

A few lengths from Allanaq, Bear Hand held a harpoon foreshaft in his hand. He fitted his thumbnail to one of the grooves Allanaq had etched in with a burin. He turned it over, studied its other side. Bear Hand looked up and found Allanaq watching him. Their glances met.

Bear Hand lifted the piece, then held it out—not to pass, but to show. "It's beautiful," he said.

Allanaq allowed a smile. It wasn't necessary to answer, but he wanted to. He dipped his head. "The charms are for the whale, so it will want to come. The whale sees from afar. It appreciates the work."

"I never said it wasn't beautiful, only that it was slow work. And you were looking for walrus in the fishing time."

"And you were right," Allanaq said. "In these waters, a man has to hunt in different places for walrus, and for fish. So many fish you have—I never knew . . . "

"In the end," Bear Hand said, "the animals come to the blade that pleases them. They do come—" he stopped.

The whale's high back had broken the surface, not far from where they stood. They quieted, stopped, and marked it by the spume of water, not so heavy, nor as high as they expected. The whale clung just below the water, its blowhole clearing the surface repeatedly, catching after air. It never seemed to fill its lungs, but labored, taking shallow breaths.

The whale swam slowly, down the opposite side of the lead, skimming the surface. Slower than when Allanaq had first seen it. He rested the butt end of his harpoon on the ice, lifted it just as the whale submerged, its body turning into a shadow of green and black. He felt the other men watching him, their eyes like weights dragging at his arm.

The whale slowly turned, started toward them.

Allanaq shifted his grip up the length of the shaft to the balancing point. His eye held on the dark water, on the shadow skimming toward him.

Behind him, though he wouldn't look with the whale so near—Nua, Meqo, and Squirrel squatted back from the ice edge, quiet lest the whale find them and take fright. Elik left the women, walked nearer the edge.

She felt the cool spray off the water, lifting to her face. She had dreamed of a whale and a whale had come. She had heard a Loon speak and someday, she prayed, it would speak again. She had dreamed of a husband who was like no other and the husband was here.

The whale swam nearer.

Her throat caught at its size, its beauty.

Allanaq raised his harpoon, marking the whale's position. He waited . . .

Elik wondered how her world looked to the whale, if it saw colors dancing inside the ice, the way she did, or if it knew only fear of the world above water.

She tried to think in the same way the whale might, so

that if it heard her, if it found her thoughts, it would know that humans also try to understand what is right and what is true.

She thought of the way her mother taught her to greet the incoming birds in the spring. Each time the girls wakened in the morning, with the snow melting back and the sun warming their heads, they would look to find what new bird had returned to their coast, and they would greet it and sing to it by name.

Allanaq steadied his breathing. The wind had stilled. The whale was swimming nearer . . . Nearer. He waited . . .

Behind him, Elik sang:

*Welcome and great thanks.*
*Beautiful in the sea*
*Returning to our shores.*

*Anxious in my fears*
*In my hunger,*
*I nearly forgot the look of*
*Your face, your eyes.*
*Drink now, and come again.*

*There is wind, and there is you.*
*Ya yai, ya yaiya Ya yai, ya yaiya*

Allanaq listened: the whale drew breath. Its thin, sucking sounds matched Elik's for a moment, then filled the air as her voice faded.

Her words released Allanaq's grip. He gathered his strength, pulled his arm back, behind his ear. He aimed . . . High, near its blowhole. Where the rise of its head lifted above the water. The harpoon burst from his arm. It struck and then held, high in its neck. Immediately a second lance followed, piercing near the blowhole.

Behind Allanaq's hit, a volley of harpoons followed: Grey Owl, Bear Hand, each one striking, landing, helping after his.

The air rang with the whale's cry. In the water, a draining reddish color mingled with the wake. Lance shafts shook, embedded in its flanks. There was blood in its spout; a spray of red the color of sunset.

The whale rolled to its side; like an empty kayak in the shallows, it listed. Its dark eyes clouded. With the few lances they had left, they aimed near the base of its skull, its ear.

They sang for a quick death, and at the same time they sang, they threw their grappling hooks into the whale, in among the lines and shafts. They hung on to the lines, so the whale—it seemed weak already, as if it had no desire to fight—wouldn't sink.

Behind the men, Elik and the women grabbed the lines, holding tight, bracing their feet, while the men started to pull, to float the whale closer to their side.

As soon as it was near, Grey Owl went for the tendon in its flipper, severing it with his blade, so it wouldn't dive. He leaned so far, Weyowin put a hand to his parka, holding back. Bear Hand hauled in on his line, bringing the whale around, headfirst, flukes coming around after.

Grey Owl caught its tail with a snag hook while Bear Hand tied a line through a wound. If the whale sank, they would, perhaps, have something to grab onto.

It would be impossible to raise it out of the water onto the shelf. Even with slabs of ice for skidders, angled to slide the whale to higher pack, they could never lift it without flensing it first, in the water, where it floated.

Weyowin anchored their harpoons into the ice, steep at a diagonal, back from the edge, where the ice was less slick. Nua, Meqo and Squirrel helped lash the extra lines, steadied the whale against the ice wall, the same as they might have with a walrus or a bearded seal, too heavy for one man alone. Grey Owl climbed onto the whale's midsection. Crouching for balance, he traced lines as if it were a walrus, by section and by shares. Then, angling his knife point deeper, he made the first cut, through the black skin into the rich blubber hiding below.

Sometime between when the whale was securely tied

and the first marked out shares laid back, Elik turned and looked for Allanaq. He wasn't there. She looked again, not at the backs of the men's parkas, but at their faces: Grey Owl. Bear Hand. Weyowin.

An uneasy thought loosed her grip on the line she'd been holding. The open water? What if he'd slipped on the blood, on the ice? Wouldn't he have shouted? She reeled about. Nua and Meqo, Squirrel and the men—all were bent over the whale, climbing on its back, checking their knots and lines. She opened her mouth to call, then stopped.

A single set of tracks etched the snow behind the water's edge. Plainly, they caught the moonlight's rising angle: the oval shape of a man's boot leading back toward land.

What was he doing?

She stood confused a moment but then, as silently as he had gone, she bowed her head toward the whale, murmured her grateful thanks, then hurried away, before someone noticed or the dogs gave a call.

She was halfway back toward the ridge of pressure ice before she saw him: a moving shadow slipping into the uncertain light dividing ice from sky. She kept on, holding the distance between them equal, warmed by her walking, trying not to call.

She remembered his eyes inside Old Ani's house: sad, when she would have expected joy. It was that look, she guessed now, that had something to do with his plans. He would be hurrying back to the houses, to help in case of a raid. And she would help also. She would fight. She wasn't afraid. She wanted to be with him.

She lost sight of him as she clambered over the pressure ridge, then found him again as she peered down from the heights of heaved-up snow blocks. He was hurrying toward land, but circling wide of the houses. Not going in, as she had thought.

Her stomach knotted, but there was nothing for it but to follow. His tracks remained clear, wider-paced with hurrying the closer he came to the Long Coast shore. He didn't want to be seen.

She veered with his tracks. The sounds of drumming and voices singing reached her clearly from the houses: a song of feasting, not mourning. Relief strengthened her steps. It was possible the Forest People were hiding behind cover of a snowdrift, even now. But they hadn't attacked. Whatever their reasoning, they hadn't attacked.

A dog whined and the light of a fire lit the sky above the houses with an orange sheen. By the time the near-shore ice changed to the deeper snows of land, the moon had circled around her shoulders.

She followed Allanaq's tracks up the west side of the beach ridge, then inland, toward the flats of open snow. Behind the houses, she found a path of muddled tracks: snowshoes. He'd changed to snowshoes. When had he carried those, she wondered?

His steps left the harder, well-trodden path, but the snow was compacted beneath his newer, paw-shaped tracks, enough so that her lighter weight could follow without breaking through.

Her gaze was lowered, close on the ground immediately ahead, when suddenly, Allanaq rose up in front of her. Her hands flew to her mouth, not to shout.

Not only was he wearing snowshoes, he'd carried lances from the whale site and a sinew-backed bow he hadn't had with him before. He whispered one word, "Quiet." She nodded, then with a thought added, "Don't send me back."

Allanaq peered behind her. "Were you followed?" No, she shook her head. "Were you loud?" Again no.

She watched him as he stood, not speaking, planning. His lips were cracked, his eyes darkly rimmed. She caught the smudge of a shadow near his mouth, upward along one cheek. They hadn't yet cut the whale's heartmeat when she'd left, but Allanaq had eaten, at least some of the *muktuk* from the first strips of meat. Whatever came next, he'd have strength from the whale. For that, she gave thanks.

Allanaq followed her gaze. He lifted his mittened hand to his cheek, knowing what she thought. They were alive, both of them. She was not married to a shaman, and he had brought a whale. When they started walking again, Elik followed carefully in his tracks. Neither of them raised a sound. Neither dared think past this moment.

The next time Allanaq stopped, they were facing a tangled willow break nearby the Place Where Three Streams Come Together. Nearer to the village than Drummer and Lake had described the spot, but whether the Forest men had seen the feasting and turned back, or were merely biding their time, they couldn't guess. The sky was dark, past midnight, not yet morning. Allanaq removed his snowshoes, left them where they were.

Keeping their heads and shoulders lowered, they moved to crouch behind a blind of snow-bent willows. Opposite them, a single large hide had been tightly stretched between the stream's tangled brush and an upright pole. From a more distant vantage, the camp would have been impossible to find. So close and with the moonlight, they could easily see the angled hide roof shielding the four shapes: three men lying down. The fourth with his forehead to his knees, asleep sitting up.

Allanaq fixed his lance in his fist, straightened. His gaze went back to Elik, motioning her to stay. He took a step away, came back, pressed her heavily on the shoulder: down. He forced her almost to her belly in the snow. *Stay here. Don't move.*

Again he stepped away, again returned. This time he pressed something in her hand, closed her fingers over it: a short-handled knife with two side blades embedded at the tip. If he died and she was found, at least there'd be a chance she could kill one of them. Or kill herself first, if she was lucky.

The whaling party would never make it back to the people in time; he had known that from the first. There was no meat in those houses, only hunger. Dry tongues and no strength to fight with. And all of it was his fault. If anyone died tonight, it needed to be him.

Again he stepped away, but this time it was Elik's hand on his parka hem pulling him back. He turned. Her gaze was steady, not on his face, but on his lance, the bow across his back.

Earlier, in the rush of activity, he had hidden weapons in the snow behind the houses. A sinew-backed bow, arrows, and more knives. The lance was one he had used against the whale. The retrieval line had been untied but there were still bloodstains, running along the shaft, showing how the whale had died for him. For all of them.

Elik held out the knife he'd given her, motioned toward the long-handled lance instead. They traded weapons.

Finally Allanaq stepped away, moved from the break to an open view. From the quiver he removed three arrows. He laid them crosswise, readied on the snow. He fixed them, practiced grabbing, till he was convinced his hand knew, even before his eye, which way they lay.

He took off his mittens, fitted the first arrow to the cord. He crouched on one knee, picked out the seated man. He couldn't see enough of his face to know if he was the one they'd let run away. Perhaps that man was one of the sleepers. Perhaps he had stayed behind.

He couldn't hate them; he understood too well why they'd come. Avenging a relative's death—it was what he should be doing. And he would. Someday, if he was alive when morning came.

He clenched his teeth. Aimed, not for the raised knees, but for his exposed side, below the shoulder. If he missed, that would be the man most likely to kill him first.

He pulled back and smoothly, loosed the arrow.

If the man screamed, Allanaq never heard it. Already he held the second arrow to the cord. Turned and aimed for the outermost figure in the row of sleepers. Three men now. His second arrow flew. Two men were up already. Fully clothed, knives in their fists and free of their furs, while the third hadn't risen but lay on the ground, legs doubled up, rolling onto snow.

The two men came running toward him, but the snow

stole their balance. Their heavy steps jerked them to the side. One of the men was lighter on his feet, the other, older, circled wide behind.

Allanaq met the younger one halfway between the willow break and their lean-to. Too close to nock an arrow; he threw it down. Raised his arm, bearlike, knife in hand. The man jumped, caught him by the arms, just below the elbows. He was taller, but lighter built. The impact sent Allanaq's knife flying from his hand, burying itself in snow. Arms still locked, Allanaq whirled the man around, reaching with his hand as they danced. His fingers stretched for his boot top, groped for his knife.

And then he had it: each of them had a knife now. Fists trembled, fighting for a hold. They circled, wrestled each other's weight to the snow. The stranger's lips curled back, his pointed teeth near to Allanaq's neck. They heaved to the side, fighting for a hold.

From her place behind the willow, Elik followed the fourth man. He had lost his balance and with it his weapon, but he was on his feet again. Wary as a wolf; if he had hackles, they'd have been raised. He circled, half-crouched. From somewhere he found a knife. Its faceted point caught the moonlight, shone with its spark.

His back was toward her, the willows between. He stepped in toward Allanaq and his own man, twisting as they wrestled. The older man fell back when he found no opening, then tried again, jabbing with his blade.

He didn't know anyone was there. If he had, certainly, he wouldn't have expected a woman. She lowered her hood, pushed her braids aside and came walking, tentatively at first, then quicker, out from her blind.

The man caught her shadow and reeled about. She saw his black hair circling his shoulders. The way he lifted his arm, then lowered it, confused, as he realized she was a woman. Confused again as he realized she held a lance, raised, its night black point aiming toward his face. He pulled back his arm, leaned on his rear leg, but his step came down sideways into loose snow, his weight miscalculating.

By then she was leaping. Letting her weight carry her with Allanaq's lance in her fist, aiming for his chest. No different than if he were a ptarmigan, a gull, a bird on the gravel and she a girl with a rock in her hand, aiming the way she had learned a hundred times and more to bring down her prey, hunt for her life. Kill in order to live.

Down she came, her own weight guiding the shaft, the point, as it reached for his neck, buried itself in flesh between shoulder blade and rib.

The sound that came from his throat was deep and grim and she fell with him, over him, then rolled away. Rolled as the other man fighting Allanaq heard the sound and turned also. Turned, giving Allanaq the leverage he needed to come in under his arm, his knife aimed for the opening between heart and lung. His weight pressing with the point, piercing through furs into flesh, between bones into muscle.

Allanaq didn't let go. He carried the man back, lifting him onto his knife handle, then down onto snow. With a frantic, sweeping glance he looked for Elik, found her on the ground, arms crablike behind her, pulling away.

In front of her the third man lay dead.

Three men, and now four. Allanaq leaned over the one below him. With both his hands, he grabbed hold of his knife handle. Fiercely, he gripped it, yanked till the man's chest lifted with the blade, hung a moment, and then tore loose.

Behind him, Elik had risen. She trembled heavily. "Is it over?" she asked. Allanaq stood facing her. His hands were streaked in red, his face also, but he was whole, unhurt.

Allanaq turned, watched for a sign of movement, a hand grasping, a breath reaching for air. There was nothing. But it wasn't over. Not yet.

He left her to watch as he walked up to each of the men. One by one he rolled them over, face downward so they saw nothing but the snow. He didn't want them remembering this place where they died. The long stretch of straight land fronting on the shore. These shores. These people. He didn't want them finding their way back when they were dead.

He severed their tendons, in through the ankles, the elbows, the wrists. He sliced through their clothes, searching for amulets, faster, deeper, enough to be certain the ghosts of his enemies could not linger, or seek revenge. Not now. Not ever. He kept cutting.

# 13

Elik hefted the two sets of seal flippers from the pile Nua had set aside on the wet spring ice. The flippers were heavy but not so awkward as they might have been. Nua had left a strap of skin for a handle and Elik slipped her hand through one set of clawed flippers then the other, balancing each side.

The small of her back ached from bending all morning, but she smiled as she stepped around the partially butchered seal. This one wasn't finished yet and with its skin pulled back it looked like a round blanket for its body to lie on.

She carried the flippers to the hole they had dug in the newly exposed sand above the beach.

The whaling season was over. It was *Takookut*, the season of the Seal Month, when the weather was dry and each day the ice changed and new birds arrived.

The landfast ice closest to shore was firm but puddling; leads widened and splintered into craggy ice floes. Daylight stretched to cover the night. Everywhere people smiled and laughed to hear the calls of the eider ducks, the first of the year, and the auklets and low-flying cormorants. There was whale meat secure in their dugout pits and the large bearded seal were easier to find now. The winterhouses were waterlogged, the walls moist and smelling of damp, and most everyone had moved outside, into the welcome air of spring.

These two bearded seal that she and Nua were skinning would be saved to cover a new umiak. If more came to her uncle and her husband, the edges of those would be used for boot soles. The oil would fill their lamps. The meat would feed them. The intestines would clothe them in waterproof parkas.

Sometimes she and Allanaq talked about this together; how one person alone would never be able to make all the weapons, the boats, the clothing, and still have time to perform the rituals necessary for success in the first place.

They understood this more fully now, she as a wife, he with his name that meant A Stranger Who Becomes A Friend: how important it was to cooperate, to share. No one could live alone or for themselves, not a single man, not even a village.

Elik added a layer of last year's brittle grass to the bottom of the hole. Over the grass she set a few strips of yellowish blubber sliced from the outer curve near the seal's shoulder. The flippers were laid in with the blubber, then covered and left to ferment. When the hair fell off easily they would be ready to eat, but that wouldn't be until the days were short again and the meat turned heady and thick.

She pounded a driftwood pole into the sand to mark the hole. On another pole, beside the racks where they would hang the intestines and slabs of ribs to dry, she fitted an old hood and part of a parka for a ghost to scare away the birds. Then she started down again to where Nua had already sliced the second seal's stomach and was pulling the long intestines into a braid.

It was hard work, and exhausting, but there was also joy in it, joy because the seals found them worthy. Because the whale had shown itself to Allanaq. Because no Forest People had come looking for their dead.

She shouldn't complain. If the seals heard her thoughts, they would swim away. They would not come to her husband's harpoon. And yet . . .

She sighed. It wasn't the work that troubled her; it was her own thoughts, confused as seaweed caught in an eddy.

Since the first night after the whale had been butchered and the strangers killed, she and Allanaq had been sharing a bed in Grey Owl and Nua's house.

Except that she didn't feel like a wife, not fully. Or perhaps—not only.

Perhaps it was because she was so busy. In this spring season especially, there was no time but for the work at hand. She didn't even have the pleasure of waking first in the house anymore, the way she used to, slipping outside to go walking along the shore, toward the hills.

As a wife, she needed to be concerned with her husband first. When a man spent his days on the ice waiting for seals, or inland in the summer tracking caribou, he needed the food and clothing a wife made so he could hunt and bring back the animal which would become clothing.

But if she didn't see herself as a wife, certainly she wasn't a girl anymore. Not with the way she waited so eagerly for night to come, for Allanaq to smile in that way he had, when no one else could see, signaling that he would not be sleeping in the *qasgi* that night, nor out hunting.

There at least was one thing she was certain of: the way she felt when she touched him. Took him into her, not once in a great while but night after night in their own bed, rushing the moments till she and Nua finished tending the lamps, closing the skyhole, turning any clothing that had soaked through, caring for the furs before they were ruined. Allanaq would have long since put his own work aside, his stone-flaking tools and antler pieces all nesting in their baskets. She would climb to the platform where he waited, smiling, holding the blankets open for her, and ready, long since ready.

With the toe of her boot against the laid-out sealskin, Elik moved to stand opposite Nua. Leaning over from the waist, Nua angled her curved woman's knife into the space between the skin and meat while Elik clamped her fingers like hooks into the dark of the seal's chest and pulled back, lifting the bulk of the meat higher for Nua's more skilled knife to slip inside, make the cut closer to the spine.

Along the beach in front of their houses, other women were doing the same. Two Ravens and Little Pot had water boiling already, for the lungs they planned on cooking first. Farther along Meqo and Squirrel and one of her aunts were hanging lengths of pink intestine from which they had already scraped the rings of outer skin, squeezed the bile from the inside, and rinsed them in the clean meltwater ponds.

Elik looked past the women, up from the beach to where the men stood nearer the houses. With Olanna gone, Old Ani was eldest now. Then Bear Hand and Grey Owl, sitting together atop the *qasgi* roof, two men looking to the weather. Neither voice spoke louder than the other. There was peace; hard won but holding, large enough to include her husband in its arms.

There would be singing when they were done with the seals. Awhile after and they would move out to fish camp. It was the way things were in the world. The young men hunted. The elders taught them respect, so the animals would come. The women stitched the world together. And she . . . ? She . . . ?

She had her spirit-dreams. Elik straightened her back while Nua sorted piles—the membrane outside the liver for dog food along with the gall bladder. The blubber that would be rendered for lamp oil separate from the pile for food, the ribs that were less fishlike than those of the ringed seal, would be air-dried, the meat nearest the flipper slivered and frozen raw.

She remembered the dream she'd had, just that morning. She'd woken too quickly to think about it till now. She had dreamed that she was following a voice to a snow shelter, or a tent—she couldn't tell which. But Malluar had been there, waving her thin, naked arm, beckoning her inside.

When she entered, Elik saw that Malluar wasn't alone. There were others with her, but they weren't people, or not people only. One man had a ptarmigan's wing instead of an arm. And there was a woman with pointed ears sticking out from brown hair and a long fox's tail swishing beneath her parka. The third man was a Wolf, with a thick brown coat and a grey snout. Wolf followed her after she went home. He found her house. While she stood to hang her parka to dry, he sniffed with his nose against her crotch to make sure it was she. Then he watched as she held Allanaq between her legs and he jumped to the platform to be near, and nuzzled her armpit for salt.

In the dream there had been no doubting who they were: Malluar's spirit helpers. Ptarmigan. Fox. And Wolf. What Elik didn't learn before she woke was what they wanted, why they called.

And yet, she told herself as she and Nua put grass into the second seal's mouth and offered it a drink of fresh water—the spirits still visited. They visited and they spoke to her.

Not so clearly as she might have wished and not so often. But she was a married woman now, busier than she used to be. It would have to be enough.

Nua straightened, pushed at the strands of hair that had come loose from her braid, then laughed when she realized she'd streaked her face with blood.

Elik laughed with her, then stopped, turned an ear. She'd heard something. Not behind them, where the open cracks of ice siphoned meltwater through their channels. Toward land?

"What is it?" Nua asked.

Farther along the beach, in both directions, the other women were standing as they were, watching. And the men also, on higher ground near the houses. They were looking eastward, along the shore, not the sea.

A line of black dots. She thought at first it was a flock of birds, eider ducks, with their legs set far back, catching a southerly tailwind as they followed the breaking ice. The men would be watching to see which way to hunt.

But no—these weren't birds: the dots kept dipping into land. And not caribou, to hold such a line. It was people. Out of the east. People were coming.

"Three sledges," Nua said. "They're hauling them over their shoulders. No dogs."

"Who would it be? Real People?"

Nua shielded her eyes from the sun. "There are women," she said, and Elik nodded, let out the breath she hadn't realized she was holding.

They watched as the lead sledge came closer, then stopped. A man was hauling it in front. Someone smaller—a woman with the tail of a woman's longer parka—helped from behind.

She recognized them at the same moment as her aunt: Bent Point People. Her uncle Nagi with the first group. Another woman—was it Kimik, or Sipsip behind? A second sledge pulled up alongside. A third was in the distance, too far to tell the clothes. Except for one. The single, gaunt-faced man walking separate from the others. Seal Talker.

Elik's stomach twisted as sharply as if she'd been punched. *Run*, a voice inside her whispered. *Hide. Before he finds you. Before someone tells him of the blankets you share with Allanaq, instead of him.*

Seal Talker raised his arm and the men came forward, clustered around him. He lowered his hood, leaned toward the houses as if he were a hawk, as if the long beak of his face were searching for prey.

Nua rested her hand on Elik's shoulder, sensing her fear. She didn't know what was wrong, but she knew enough to step in front of Elik, blocking any view the shaman might have had.

Behind the men, the Bent Point women hauled the two first sledges to a line, guiding them over the newly exposed rocks to a level place where it seemed they meant to camp.

Nua set a cutting knife in Elik's hand. "Take up your things," she said, and she motioned toward the wooden bowls, the scraps of hides they'd brought for rags. Elik bent to the ground, then, as if she'd already forgotten Nua's instructions, straightened, watched again.

"What is it?" Nua whispered.

"My father . . . My brother—he isn't there?"

Nua looked to Seal Talker, the only man standing still, surveying the land while others worked. "If they are, I can't see—"

"Why is he here?"

Nua misunderstood. "They're hungry," she said. "See how it's tent skins they're unloading first? They mustn't have food. And the men—they move slowly. The only reason to come now—when each day walking becomes harder as the sun eats into the snow, and without waiting for the ice to go out, when traveling in boats would be easier, is if there's been sickness. Perhaps something happened—besides the storms. Perhaps they heard about Allanaq's whale?"

Elik shielded her eyes. "Kimik is there, behind the second sledge. Her mother, most of their family. My mother's brother, Nagi, but not my father's brother." She watched a moment longer. "And Naiya—my sister is with them, but not my father."

"They are relatives who side with Seal Talker then? Not your father's side?"

Elik winced, then nodded when she realized Nua was right.

Nua spoke gently, wanting to help but not to pry. "You should tell me—there was more, wasn't there? When you came to us with the news of the Forest People, the strangers—something you didn't tell?"

Elik kept watching as the Bent Point men approached, walking almost in a row, like teeth in a hungry mouth, toward the heavily loaded racks of seal and whale meat. She looked to her aunt, but she couldn't make herself say the words, explain her fears of what Seal Talker could do, to her, to Allanaq, to any of them.

"Come," Nua said. "This is no place you want to be."

The Long Coast men walked forward to greet the visitors. Old Ani, Grey Owl, Bear Hand. His brothers. Not Allanaq. Elik didn't know whether to worry or feel relieved.

"Come," Nua said again. "We'll cook a feast; the men will want to talk."

"Talk?" Elik felt confused. "What will they talk about?"

"About food. About where they'll sleep."

Nua led Elik back to where they'd butchered the seals. Mechanically, Elik helped scoop up chips of icy snow and spread them on the remaining meat, to keep it cool till they were done.

They carried the two heads closer to the water, away from the carcass and facing toward the sea. Elik glanced again, looking for her sister. She picked her out, but Naiya's back was turned.

Tomorrow she and Nua would come and turn the seal heads the other way, so the animals would know which way to swim. They would tell other seals that good people lived here and this was a worthy place to die and let their souls be born again.

The *qasgi* smelled damp, moist with the rains that seeped in through the sod walls, the puddles that formed in the dirt layer below the planking. The men had decided to open it anyway; with so many guests who were relatives, it was best to have one place to sit, to tell of the winter past, to eat.

Old Ani had taken the elder's seat, on a caribou skin beside the hearth, where Olanna would have sat. Beside him sat Seal Talker, then his two nearest male relatives, Blue-Shadow and Whale Fin. No one had yet mentioned the names that weren't there, whether they were dead, or lost, or gone.

The Bent Point People eyed the bowls of food, the wealth that had come to the Long Coast village after a winter of hunger. The fact that here only two places were empty: one man old enough to die, a baby too young to keep its name.

They had eaten—the men first and then the women crowded in on the raised bench along the walls. It wouldn't have been proper to spoil good food with bad stories and so they had eaten first and eaten again, as much as their shrunken stomachs could hold. Frozen *muktuk*, the black whaleskin that Nua and Meqo and the older women proudly set out.

Chunks of tongue, part blubber, part meat and from the huge seals—boiled heart and ribs dipped in rendered seal oil.

From the moment they arrived Elik had been busy helping the women prepare the feast. She had tried to steal a few moments to speak to Allanaq, but he had been in the *qasgi* surrounded by the men, the gossip, and by Seal Talker. Much as she'd looked for it, there'd been no chance yet to speak to him alone, to explain.

She had never told Allanaq about Seal Talker, about why she'd run from the Bent Point village. That it had not been because of hunger, but because of the shaman. Because she had been afraid that a man who stole her mother's soul could do more. Would do more . . . Anything he wanted . . .

She would pull Allanaq aside as soon as the feast was over and there was a chance, the first chance. It was important that he know.

At long last the wooden trays lay empty on the floor and the men belched and leaned back. On the raised bench, Elik clung to the shadows beside Nua. She leaned out. Naiya was sitting too far along the bench, pressed in between too many other women for Elik to greet her. She would find her next, after she spoke to Allanaq. There was so much she wanted to hear, and tell.

Seal Talker pulled a drum from a sidewall. Naked to the waist, he wore a pair of thick white polar bear trousers. Elik leaned forward, curious. No one so thin with hunger as these people would have hauled a suit of clothes so heavy and useless in the summer. Which meant it was Olanna's. As was the shaman's belt Seal Talker tied his trousers with. And the cap with its string of amulets. Elik glanced toward Little Pot, wondering what Seal Talker said to make her lend her brother's clothes so quickly.

Seal Talker folded his legs, sat, then rapped on the rim of the drum to begin his tale. "It was illness that came to the Bent Point village," he said, "that was the reason we finally left. More than the hunger, which we might have survived. There were still a few dogs, and the spring birds were not so far. We could have waited. Except that one of the babies died first. It was Sipsip's youngest, the child she still carried in her hood."

The row of Long Coast women leaned forward. *Aja*, they shook their heads and sighed.

*Aja*, Elik sighed for the child she'd often held. She stole a glance to Kimik. She had seen her earlier with the baby in her hood, but there'd been no time to visit. She glanced two people down along the bench to her sister. Though she couldn't say why, Elik knew she'd been avoiding Naiya. Her sister's eyes were dark and shadowed but, she realized, the larger difference was Naiya's hair. It wasn't oiled. The braids were days old, uncombed. Uncertain.

The fire in the hearth sputtered. Seal Talker tossed in a handful of powder, waited till it crackled and grew. "The child held no water," he continued. "Not from its mouth and not from its anus. It weakened and then it shriveled. It cried and then was dead. But the spirit that stole its soul was not yet satisfied. It walked among us, making others ill. It walked in Saami's house and took his youngest son."

*Aja*, the women moaned again.

"It walked in Blue-Shadow's house and fought with the soul of his grandson but did not win. And then it walked in my own house, and it took my wife. My wife who had been with me always—and that I could not bear.

"We were too weak to hunt. Whatever game we found kept hiding from our arrows. I began to search. For three days I tranced, begging my spirit helpers to reveal the trouble. I begged the people to tell me—Had any of them done wrong to anger so strong a spirit? Confess, I begged. Confess, so it will go away."

The qasgi had darkened. Elik had lived through enough of Seal Talker's ceremonies to know what he was doing, that he worked through fear to gain the people's will. From outside, there was a shrill and distant cry. And a smell rising from the fire, foul, like the stink of someone sick. Elik put her hands to her mouth to shield her insides. But it was Seal Talker's eyes searching along the crowded women's bench that made her skin grow cold.

But then a thought came, sudden enough to make her dizzy. *She knew where Seal Talker's words were leading. She knew . . .*

The air tightened. She leaned out to see her sister. She'd been wrong. It had been Naiya who was avoiding her.

Her lowered gaze—that was shame hiding itself, shame to have been her father's daughter.

"In the end," Seal Talker continued, "it was my spirit helper who showed the face to me. The face of the man who refused to confess. A man, sitting there among us. Calling himself an elder, not a boy. It was Chevak, the husband of a woman who also died. The son of a grandmother who also died . . ."

Elik's heart pounded. *He wasn't telling the truth. He was twisting it . . .*

"This season. Only this year. Though we hadn't seen how the evil walked until that day. That trance when I finally saw . . ."

Elik searched for Allanaq, found only the back of his head. Nua slid her arm around Elik and drew her in. "Quiet," she whispered to calm her. "It's better if he doesn't hear you."

"He had slaughtered a caribou without respect." Seal Talker raised his voice. "He had eaten of food that was taboo, mixing sea animals with land. Walrus with caribou. He had told no one. Not once, but twice. Not twice, but more than that. He thought his own power greater. He did not die. Though we died for him. Because he would not confess his wrongs. We who were weak, we confronted him. And at least he grew ashamed. He confessed, but for many of us, too late. . . ."

Seal Talker hesitated, planning his words. "We argued," he continued in a lower voice. "And a rift grew between our houses, louder even than the hunger of the winter. Loud enough that our voices sank into the pits of our empty stomachs, and there was nothing to do but come to you, our relatives who ate because they had done no wrong."

Elik breathed deeply, trying for calm. Someone had lit a

lamp. Seal Talker sat back, but he was winded, older-looking than she remembered. He coughed, then coughed again into his hand. Whale Fin asked for water.

Old Ani, embarrassed at not offering first, called to the younger women to bring more food, water for the men.

Ani's Wife motioned to Elik first and then Long Feather, choosing the women to serve. Elik looked frantically to Nua. Someone pressed a dipper into her hand. She wanted to drop it, to pass it to someone, anyone, rather than have Seal Talker watching her.

Nua caught her stumbling. "Give me the dipper," she whispered. "Come behind me, but don't serve him. Don't sit behind his shoulder. Or where he has to look at you."

Elik followed to the floor. With her gaze carefully lowered, she walked behind her aunt to the waterskin, filled her dipper, then started toward the men. She kept almost at Nua's heels but the *qasgi* was crowded. She had to step carefully over knees, behind shoulders.

It was habit that brought her behind Allanaq, in the safety of his shadow.

He turned thoughtfully to help her. He reached for her dipper and she leaned forward, kneeling toward him. At the same time, she looked for Nua, to make sure her aunt hadn't called her back.

Seal Talker was there, watching her, taking it all in, his one good eye following the line of her hand, watching Allanaq lingering near.

Too late she saw her mistake. She pulled back the dipper, then tried to cover her actions with a laugh, as if she were a child mistaking two men in the dark. She lifted her dipper for the next man—any man, it wouldn't matter who.

Seal Talker watched, enjoying every bit of the girl. He had forgotten how pleasing it was to look at her. Her long braids shining and thick. The way her hips moved as she slid between the men's shoulders. He didn't remember any woman looking so young yet full-breasted, both at the same time. The way she leaned down, serving water to the tall man. The man reached for the bowl she carried . . .

Seal Talker stopped, watched closer.

Something wasn't right. The man moved as if he'd done this before. Touching her hand. Accepting water so familiarly. As if he had the right . . .

Seal Talker opened his mouth to object, then caught himself, waited instead. *Go carefully,* he warned himself. *The girl knows you're watching.* She's young, but not foolish. Wasn't that one of the reasons he'd noticed her at all?

One of the older women, he'd remember her name in a moment, set a new tray of food in front of him. He fished through the oil, pulled out a piece of meat. He couldn't stop noticing the size of their portions, generous with whale meat and seal. The faces of the Long Coast men around the benches, smiling, and satisfied. No one hungry. No one's stomachs bloated with pain. They had bested him before, these people, the last time they had come together, at the runner's feast. He hadn't liked it then. He didn't like it now.

He looked to the girl again. This time he caught a glance passing between the man and the girl—the girl he had come for. Who had promised herself to him. What was she doing? Trying to shame him here, in front of relatives? When he had already been forced to beg—? He wouldn't be made to beg. Not again. And not by that man.

He thought back to the last time they had sat together. He didn't remember what they had spoken about, other than that they traded. What he did remember was the soup Ema had served them, how after the man left, she had thrown away the pottery bowl he used, broken it right into their fire and let it crack. *Who knows what he truly is?* Ema said after he was gone. *Who knows what water a stranger spits in his cup?* And they had laughed together, worried and laughed at the same time. And now, here was the same man with the girl who should be his wife, with his toobright eyes and he, Seal Talker, a shaman with no woman in his bed.

And here was something he hadn't noticed before—the rosy blush to her cheeks. She'd put on weight also. Hadn't her features been sharp before? Her face was rounder now, blurred almost. And her skin, her skin was shining.

Seal Talker almost stood in surprise. It took more than one time for a man to start a baby in a woman. His semen had to build up, till there was enough. But there could have been . . .

He was a fool not to have thought of it. He counted back over the months. It was possible, he realized. The girl could be carrying his child. His! The shaman-child he'd been waiting for. She might be sharing her blankets with a man here, but she had been wife to him first. Wife! He almost laughed aloud—here was something for him to tell Malluar, with all her talk about women's ways of knowing and seeing what men never saw.

A lie sprang to his lips—exactly the words this girl would want to hear. He sought out her uncle, Grey Owl, spoke to him first, loudly and smiling. "Your sister's death came earlier than looked for," he said.

Grey Owl's eyes flicked up in cautious surprise.

"And we've spoken of sadness." He glanced to make sure Elik was listening. "But there are also good times. The Long Coast People have a whale. And before we left, we heard word of your nephew, your sister's son . . . "

"Iluperaq?" It was Elik who had spoken, louder than she realized. "My brother is home?"

"There's word." Courteously, Seal Talker dipped his head. "Word came that he was alive, that he'd climbed out on the ice and woken and found himself and his kayak free."

"My brother is alive?" Elik drew closer. "When did you hear?"

Seal Talker smiled. "Not long ago." He lowered his voice, pulling her closer. "It was . . . " She took another step. "Perhaps . . . " he said, and then suddenly he reached, surprising her, stretching till he grabbed her by the hand. The dipper flew, water splashed. Seal Talker pulled her down, forced her to his lap.

Elik allowed it—his hands, his breath near her ear. "My brother? Is he here?"

"Not here, no." Seal Talker spoke the way he would to a child, high and too sweet. "I'll tell you—" With his eyes half-closed, he let out a sigh. "This is good. A man remembers the feel of his wife against his side."

Grey Owl lifted one eye. "Wife?" he repeated. Nua held her breath.

With stiff, deliberate motions, Allanaq set his water bowl to one side, shifted his legs out from under him.

Elik tugged against Seal Talker's bracing hands. "Where is my brother?" she asked, demanding now. "Where?"

Whale Fin and Blue-Shadow edged protectively closer to Seal Talker.

Elik struggled, then yanked one hand free. His arms slipped down around her hips and he locked them, holding her tighter.

"I'm not your wife," she said, but her words came out thin, uncertain. *When had she last made blood?* Her thoughts stumbled. She couldn't remember. Could it mean she was his? Could he take her? "Where is my brother?" Her eyes leaped desperately to Allanaq.

Seal Talker's confidence sang—"Grey Owl," he called. "I'll trade with you. News of your nephew's life for the life I put inside my wife."

Allanaq climbed to his feet, but he hesitated. The two men flanking Seal Talker's shoulders rose with him. Most of these people hadn't been in the Bent Point village when he'd last been through. He couldn't recognize them, didn't remember their names. Behind him the wall pressed closer. As if it were a memory. Different walls. A different house. "Seal Talker—" Allanaq tried to reason, "She isn't yours—"

"Perhaps she told you that, but the child inside her is the one I started there. Unless you know better than I how to switch a human once it's inside a womb?"

"I am not a man to go stealing women."

Elik forced herself to be still, to think, not to panic. Seal

Talker's attention shifted from her to Allanaq. His grip loosened. Quietly, she quit her struggles. He let go one hand. She let her weight slump, let it carry her to the floor.

Seal Talker glanced briefly, then let her go. A woman carrying a man's child—why would she fight? He reached out to stroke her hair. Signaled Whale Fin and Blue-Shadow to sit . . .

Allanaq lunged.

He grabbed Elik by the shoulder, yanked her up and out of the way.

With a cry Elik spun toward the wall, hit, and went down. A spasm of pain flashed along her back, pressing and sharp. It moved to her middle, lower down. She gasped, sucked in her breath and held it, held back the pain. Someone turned her around. It was Grey Owl; his arms enclosed her and she looked up to see Allanaq with a knife in his hands.

She screamed and Allanaq jumped. In the small, dark space of the *qasgi*, his foot struck against a hearthstone. He veered, lost his balance.

Seal Talker's men were on him, grabbing for the wavering knife. Grey Owl let go of Elik, leaped for Blue-Shadow's back and rolled, his heavier weight dragging him to the floor. All around them, people were yelling, backing against walls, waving their arms. "Run!" Elik screamed. "Find Iluperaq!"

Allanaq hesitated, but only long enough to see that Nua had Elik now. She would be safe. If he ran . . . If he ran, she wouldn't be hurt. The woman Red Fox had stolen from his father—she had been safe. Grey Owl would keep Elik safe. . . .

The two men knotted their hands to fists. "Run!" Elik shouted, and this time his legs obeyed. He jumped for the hide-covered summer door. Pushed through groping hands and fists.

Behind him, Grey Owl put out his leg, tripped one of Seal Talker's men as the other pushed past the women blocking them, slowing their way as they followed out the door.

⌒

Elik stumbled behind them out of the *qasgi*, away from Seal Talker and after Allanaq. She ran in the footprints they left behind, trampling the soft, water-soaked ground. The pain in her back was sharp, as was the other pain, lower down than she wanted to think about.

She ran on, dizzy and crooked, as if she were a shorebird escaping the rocks of a bola. As if the rocks had caught her wing and were dragging, dragging her down.

The men were ahead, farther than she could see, and faster. She forced herself to keep running, following the heavy trail as it turned along the shore, through the fissured ice of a creek drainage, a ledge of graveled beach. She ran, heedless of the small rocks cutting the soles of her boots, the tussocky ground that reached up to catch her ankles, twisting them, bringing her down. Stumbling and falling, once, then again. Again.

In the end, it wasn't the stabbing breathlessness in her side that made her stop. It was the other pain, gripping down low, inside of her, the one she'd been holding back, refusing. It forced her slower, to a walk. Till even walking wasn't possible.

Elik fell to her knees finally, giving in to the pain. Down to her hands and knees and she hung there, shaking, sweating, while waves passed through her, again and again. Swells rising, like the sea, unstoppable.

She knew what it was. As soon as the first stabbing pain shook inside of her, she knew. And that it was dead now, finished before it had begun.

Was it over? She didn't know. She was young and not yet wise. She hadn't been a woman long enough to know what to do with a death that came this way. Whether the tiny spirit inside her knew where to go. Whether to gather its blood like an amulet, save it or use it, hide it away.

When the pain slacked enough and the tightness seemed to have changed, she rolled herself over—slowly—testing her strength. She let out a breath. Drew it in. She could move again.

She tugged off her boots, her leggings. The inside skins

were stained with blood, red almost brown. Between her thighs—so much blood. It had run and spread its fingers down her legs, drying already where the fur of her trousers pressed her skin. Beneath her, a dark clot of blood seeped into the ground. With her fingernails, she scraped dirt and snow over it, refusing to see the mass at the center, trying to bury it, trying to hide it.

Her legs wobbled when she rose from her knees, but she couldn't stay there. She'd fall asleep if she stayed. The blood scent on her—anyone could track it. Wolf or Wolverine, Black Bear or Grizzly. She sank back down, leaned over, and vomited. All the food from the *qasgi* came out her mouth into a yellowish puddle. Nothing felt better. She vomited again.

When she was done, she inched away from the yellowish stain, looked to the sky. It was white with clouds, the sun pale and high overhead.

She looked back to find Wolf sitting on his rear legs, watching her. She hadn't heard him approach, didn't remember crossing any tracks.

His forelegs were straight, his back upright, giving him a tall, lean look. He snarled when he saw she'd noticed him, pushed back the fur hood of his wolf face, revealing the man inside. Fox came and lay beside Wolf, curling herself to a ball. From somewhere, Wolf had found a pair of boots. Their white-striped pattern hung in shreds now, between his mouth and his paws. He was chewing on them, on both boots at once. Fox lifted her nose, followed a scent, then lay back again, watching Elik.

Elik crawled back to where she'd dropped her soiled leggings, forced herself to touch them. She balled them up, then crawled again, closer to the water's edge. She did her best to weight the leggings under a few stones so that, with luck, the incoming tide would take them before some animal did.

She was shivering, barefoot and naked below her parka. She found a patch of snow, heavy with water, and quickly scrubbed the caked blood from her legs. Her fingers were bright red, burning with the cold, but she didn't care. Standing, she felt calmer. There was no chance she could run, but she gave thanks she could walk at all, that the trail wasn't difficult to find.

Their tracks had veered inland, away from the beach. And there were more footprints than belonged to three men. She followed over a slight rise, then down, over nearly snow-free, wet mossy ground. The sun was in her eyes but she could see them now, not so far ahead, facing inland, so they didn't see her approach.

Allanaq had been caught. Somehow it didn't surprise her. His arms were tied behind his back. A knot of people clustered around him. Someone else was dragging brush up from a gully. Seal Talker was there. And Blue-Shadow and Naiya's husband, who had chased after him. And Malluar.

Malluar? Malluar was here?

Elik blinked against the sun, held back the tears of relief. She'd been too afraid to ask, to hear the name counted among the dead. Her sledge had been slower—that was all, not dead, only slower. Malluar was here!

Elik drew near enough to hear a few of their words— Seal Talker and Malluar hissing at each other. Malluar all angles, nothing round left on her bones. She used the word *enemies*. And Seal Talker said something about refusing to beg. "With Olanna gone"—she could hear him clearly now—"the need has changed."

"The one thing changed is the size of your ambition," Malluar said, and then she stopped, both of them did, then all of them, turning to stare at Elik.

Vaguely, she realized how much like a demon she must look, a woman with no trousers, blood on her legs more powerful than menstruation, dripping down her thighs. Brown stains on her fingers.

Allanaq had turned with the others. His face was tightly drawn with pain—or was it anger? She couldn't tell. Her thoughts were muddled. She would have grabbed one of the men's harpoons, thrown it and saved Allanaq if she could, if she had the strength.

Except she didn't. Raven had appeared, bobbing up and down on the ground between her and Allanaq. What did he want with his black tail feathers dancing as he strutted, his voice squawking? He pecked at something on the ground, picked it up in his long beak. It was one of her bootstraps.

She walked through him, ignoring his complaints as he disappeared.

Seal Talker backed away as she came nearer. As did Whale Fin, Blue-Shadow, all of the men but for Allanaq. And Malluar, who also held her ground.

Elik opened her mouth, prayed some sense would come out, then stopped, turned her face to see.

Raven had appeared again, there in the small space of open ground between Allanaq and Malluar. Noisily, he flapped his wings, made a show of walking back and forth between them. Bobbing his head, pecking empty air.

He had something shiny in his beak. It was a ball of light, but not a ball. A light. Silvery. More like the moon than the sun. "What are you giving me?" she asked. "Is that light for Malluar?"

"*No*," Raven replied. "*For you.*"

"For you?" she repeated, but by the time she realized he'd spoken—spoken clearly and to her, in words she understood—he had disappeared again.

A tremor moved inside her and then something else: resolve, a sense of conviction. The gift she'd been searching for. And the words, exactly the words she needed most to say.

She stepped around Allanaq without daring to look at him. *Please,* she silently cried, *Don't hate me for this. Try to understand* . . .

Elik dropped to her knees in front of Malluar, in front of every person there. She hugged her arms around the older woman's legs. "I come to you," she cried loudly. "I come to you because I need to see. Teach me in the ways a shaman is taught, to hear, to see. I give myself to you—I . . . ."

"What is she saying?" Seal Talker interrupted.

Allanaq turned aside, not to hear this . . . He didn't want to hear . . .

Malluar laid her hand atop Elik's head then stood there with the corners of her thin mouth raised, as if at a joke no one else could share.

Gruffly, Seal Talker said, "This girl is my wife." But he made no move to go near.

"Was," Malluar said. "Perhaps. But yours is not the only claim. She is mine now, not yours." Malluar moved her hands to Elik's arms, helped her rise. And then to Elik, louder, so there would be no mistake, she said, "I am going to take your ordinary life and give you the life and the ways of a shaman."

"Her? A shaman?" Seal Talker's face darkened. "What lineage? Whose bloodline does she share to be given secrets she hasn't inherited?"

"None, but that I say she will."

"Say? You would say this against me? Choose to initiate her without me?"

"She is already chosen, by Those Who Speak."

Elik glanced toward Allanaq. His mouth was drawn to a line, his face knotted as tight as if he'd been struck.

Seal Talker's anger showed in his shallow, ugly gasps. "I will not argue with you. Not today. Not in this place that's been stained with death. But soon. My spirit helpers will meet yours in the Land Beneath the Sea. They will fight and, in the end, only one of us will claim the girl."

"I've heard your threats," Malluar answered. "An old man ranting, shouting until he hears."

Seal Talker couldn't answer. His throat knotted as surely as if a stone had lodged itself inside, squeezing shut the air. Abruptly, he turned to Whale Fin and Blue-Shadow, signaled them to cut the cords that bound his captive's hands. "I don't want him. Not his life and not his death. Let him go."

Then, slowly, because to do otherwise would have shamed him more than pride could bear, he started away, toward the row of new tents being set beside the Long Coast shore.

Allanaq rubbed the chafed skin on his wrists.

Elik's shoulders slumped with exhaustion. "Thank you," she murmured to Malluar. "Thank you."

Malluar looked for a place to rest, saw the sledge that had not yet been unloaded. Elik sat, then Malluar also leaned back. Her age, the weakness in her legs, the too-long bouts of hunger showed inside her eyes. "I enjoyed that," she said. "My cousin grows old, and the thought of time makes him more frightened than he's willing to admit. He needs someone to remind him that he was wiser when he was younger, before he grew afraid."

Malluar looked to Allanaq. She had met him, but only once. What she did know had come only as talk, through others. "You owe this woman your life," she said. "It was Elik whom Seal Talker wanted, not you. If he can't have the woman, he doesn't care about the man."

"The woman—the woman is my wife."

Malluar's eyes widened. "This is true?" she asked, but she didn't have to hear the answer to see it in both their faces. She chuckled, more at herself than anything. "It seems that my cousin is not the only one to have grown less wise."

Allanaq stepped toward Elik.

"No!" Malluar's voice stopped him.

"But Seal Talker is gone?"

"And I said only that I was less wise than I might have been. Not that I would continue to be a fool." Malluar flipped back the topskin covering on the sledge, picked out the oldest caribou hide from the pile. She helped Elik wrap it over her legs, then turned to Allanaq again.

"She's won you your life, but she long since gave herself to me. Were she to lie with anyone now—anyone—it would wound her deeper than all of Seal Talker's knives. If you could see as I see the light that shines from her, the spirits hovering about, you would know enough to be afraid. They are angered even by your odor, your thoughts pretending to have a claim. They would flee from her and never return."

Elik's eyes widened. Allanaq started toward her, but

Malluar lifted her hand. "No," she called. "It mustn't be risked."

Allanaq looked from Elik to Malluar. "How long?" he asked.

"The full time of her initiation and then until I say. Until I am satisfied with what she's learned, with the spirit helpers she's gained."

Allanaq lifted his eyes from the worn edge of Elik's blanket to her face. "This is what you want?" he asked. His voice was very small.

"This is what I want," she answered slowly. "But it isn't the only thing. Allanaq . . . Long before I heard the sound of your voice there were others calling my name. I want them. But I want you also, for my husband. Except—they are so near—they will not wait."

Allanaq sighed. He turned his face away, to the sea, to the quick-moving clouds, to the tundra showing through the snow. "Then it seems I must," he whispered.

"So you must," Malluar said. "Go away. Take with you the smells of a husband, the odors a man leaves on a wife. They mustn't be felt, or sensed or found."

Allanaq looked doubtful. "The same is true for Seal Talker?"

"For any man," she reassured him.

Elik tried to smile. "Find my brother," she asked. "If there was any truth in Seal Talker's words, if he's alive— along the coast? He might be found?"

"One orphan searching for another?" Allanaq nearly laughed until another moment and his thoughts started turning. "I could go and trade," he said. "While I ask about your brother. It is possible. I could go and then come back. I will come back."

"Not till the season comes again When Water Freezes," Malluar warned.

"Till the moon When Water Freezes," Allanaq agreed. "But not after."

# 14

⤳

Malluar walked a circle around the flat, graveled house site she had selected for their summer tent.

She walked backward and then forward, singing in the deep, thick part at the back of her throat. It was a secret song, as most shaman things were, built of words and sounds that Elik could not understand. When she asked, Malluar explained that it was a shutting-out song, a song to keep Seal Talker and his spirit helpers blind and far away.

More than that Elik would learn later, she said, when the time was right.

The house site was set off a distance from the others, and small, much the way Malluar's house in the Bent Point village had been. The willow frame they bent to form the roof needed only three hand's count of caribou hides to cover it. Nua, Ani's Wife, and Meqo carried over the skins themselves, early the morning after Allanaq left, before Seal Talker had a chance to protest.

They stayed to help Malluar with the work her hands were too old to do themselves: lapping the skins together with a double, waterproof boat stitch, stretching them tightly over the framework of willow, securing the edges with rocks.

Elik's blood had continued to flow and, so long as it made her visible to the spirits—Malluar forbade her from any work. For her the women erected a second lean-to out of older, worn-out hides that Nua later offered to burn.

The following day Ani's Wife, with her arms full and her back stooped, brought two wooden bowls, and a stone lamp and chunks of whale meat stitched into bags of their own skin. While Elik sat outside the covering of her lean-to straining to hear, Ani's Wife and Malluar leaned their heads close together, speaking in earnest tones, but only for a little while.

Nua came shortly after Ani's Wife left. She brought a clay pot large enough for boiling water and knives set in Allanaq's antler handles that Malluar held and studied and seemed to admire. Each day when she visited, Nua stayed longer than Ani's Wife—because she was a relative, Malluar later explained. Because not even Seal Talker could say she didn't have the right.

When the bleeding was finally lighter, Elik was permitted to sit behind, but not next to, the other women. She could stay, so long as her hood was drawn over her head. "Hiding you from above," Malluar said. But as soon as Elik tried asking whether Allanaq had left or what Seal Talker was saying, Malluar tapped her on the knee. "Hush," was all she said. "Your voice should be small, unnoticed."

Frustrated, Elik sat back and listened. Even Nua's stories seemed unusually small. She talked about how the younger children played out all night then fell asleep wherever they lay. How a few of the men had already gone inland for caribou. How the mussels she picked from the tide pools were large and sweet that spring.

It took another day till Elik noticed that neither Nua nor Ani's Wife ever brought their sewing. How, even when she lifted her hand and drank or ate, Nua glanced sideways toward the beach, where two lines of summer tents had been set in separate, distinct groupings: one for the Long Coast People, a second for those who came with Seal Talker. And if Nua caught sight of anyone, anyone at all looking toward them from the beach or from the flats behind the tent, she rose and quickly left.

It wasn't till the fifth day, after what seemed an interminable amount of waiting, that Malluar finally brought her drum to the lean-to.

She carried a second packet also, something folded flat and square that she set down on the ground. Briskly, without explanations, Malluar began to drum.

Elik sat opposite, legs crossed, trying not to be impatient. She managed to hold quiet until the moment Malluar set down the beater-stick. Elik jumped up, waiting to hear that her confinement was done, that her initiation would begin. She was hopeful, eager, and filled with anticipation.

Malluar closed her eyes and sat without moving.

Elik shuffled her feet. Was she supposed to say something? Or wait? Had she done something wrong? She winced, then finally sat back down.

Malluar looked at her with hard eyes. "Remove your old clothes," she said.

Obediently, Elik tugged off the parka and stood there, trying not to shiver. She felt more like a prospective bride being examined under a mother-in-law's gaze than a woman who would be a shaman.

Malluar moved till she blocked a view of Elik from anyone walking along either the beach or the village path. "Bathe," she said next. That was all, not another word.

Elik hesitated. In the water? Or the sea? Malluar spoke so harshly; none of this was what she'd expected, what she'd hoped so often in her dreams.

Malluar nodded toward a bowl she'd set down earlier and Elik crouched, then shivered as she ladled the icy water over her shoulders, down her stomach, her thighs. *Be calm,* she told herself. *You've done nothing wrong. Five days, almost without talking. It's over now.*

Malluar passed the packet of new clothes she'd brought. Elik unfolded a feather parka of cormorant skins. She slipped it on, allowed herself a smile as the warmth quieted her chill. She started to braid her hair.

"No." Malluar slapped her hand aside.

Elik froze.

"No more that way." Malluar's voice was all hard edges. "Tie it with a thong if you like, but a person waiting to meet her spirit helpers doesn't braid her hair. You are a woman, but you are other things also."

Confused, Elik set down the comb. "When will I—?"

"Hush." Malluar stopped her. "You speak when I allow. You belong to me." Sternly, she met Elik's eyes, held them till the girl lowered her gaze.

With a smile Elik didn't see, Malluar gathered up her drum and the bowl, then motioned her to follow back to the dark-skinned tent. At the door she stepped aside for Elik to enter.

Inside, it was the darkness that surprised Elik first. After so many days in the light, it was difficult to see. The floor was bare with no grass coverings and only one lamp, unlit. A small waterskin hung from the willow frame. A single roll of bedding had been pushed against the hide wall. Elik thought of the circle of wolverine skulls that lived with Malluar in her Bent Point house. Somehow she had expected to see them here.

They weren't, of course. What woman Malluar's age would pack skulls on a sledge she had to haul herself? Elik felt foolish for almost asking, simpleminded.

But for the one small drum Malluar set beside the door, the tent was empty. No feathered, painted masks swinging from a *qasgi* roof. No carvings spinning in the air.

Elik looked questioningly back to where Malluar stood, blocking the small bit of light. The shaman's face, after a winter's harsh dealing, seemed more drained than angry, pale as driftwood. Perhaps Malluar was tired, Elik hoped, and nothing else was wrong. Respectfully, she lowered her voice. "When do we begin?"

"Begin?"

"I thought . . . That is . . ." Elik stopped.

Malluar opened her hand and the bear hide door fell heavily shut. The tent walls, the floor, the low curved roof all disappeared in a heavy, dizzying black.

Elik leaned, then started to fall. Her hand went out, struck the too-soft walls of the tent.

"You thought what?" Malluar stepped so close, her eyes seemed to float in the dark.

Elik tried to answer, but only the smallest sound came out.

"I will tell you what you thought, and why you are wrong. I will tell you everything you know, and anything that I do not tell you, you do not know."

Elik held her hands to her mouth, not to cry. Outside, the wind lifted the sides of the tent, making it buckle and drum.

"You have given yourself to me and your old life is done. You are like the foetus of a caribou—opaque and thin, waiting to be born. Except that you are the mother also, and before your can give birth to your new self, the old self must die. Your skin must shrivel, like meat, desiccated by wind on the tundra. You cannot be born again until your bones are exposed, bleached white by the wind. Until you see yourself a skeleton."

Malluar breathed deeply, then coughed and let herself down on the sleeping furs. "You may sit," she said, and she waited while Elik groped about the floor—frightened, the way she wanted her to be. "Do not speak," Malluar said, "unless I bid you. And go nowhere, unless I allow."

Elik pulled her knees against her chest, praying she wouldn't cry or moan, or do anything to anger Malluar.

"Sing no song, unless I teach it."

Elik nodded, wiped at a tear before it fell.

"And any Dream or Voice that speaks to you, you tell to me . . ."

Elik sat up taller. *These are instructions,* she realized.

". . . Do not comb your hair. And do not sew because any needle in your hand is strong enough now that the *inuas* will feel their own skins being pierced."

*Malluar was telling her things. Ways of living. Ways to see . . .*

"Do not sleep on your stomach, lest something evil

reach through the ground to steal the soul from your heart."

Elik moved her lips, repeating each word, nodding in the dark. . . .

"And do not eat outside with your head uncovered, lest some spirit enter your mouth."

"I will. I swear it," Elik whispered. "Only tell me, and I will. I swear. Anything."

"When the land again turns white and cold, you will seek your spirit helpers. Alone and in the barrenlands. Through exposure to the weather. While fasting and in dreams. Through the power of your song and with your drum. Not before I say you may go. And not after.

"And now . . ." Malluar sighed. "I'm tired, and I need to rest. These days have been long. That journey here, it was difficult, more than either my cousin or I would like to admit.

"As to you, what you need to remember, my impatient child, is that a shaman alone is nothing. Time makes a shaman, bravery and the power of the spirits standing behind you. It is they who will make a shaman out of you. Either that, or make you run and hide in fear.

"Now come, sit with me while I sleep." Malluar leaned over. Unceremoniously, she laid her head on Elik's legs.

Elik lifted her arms while Malluar settled into her lap, then shifted her weight to her hands and wrists, behind her on the ground. Then she sat there, waiting. She didn't touch Malluar, didn't move or sing or do anything that might be wrong.

She already knew that she was braver than she'd ever thought possible. She had to learn now to be brave about waiting. She had to try.

The days passed slowly. The Hawk Moon turned into the Moon When Birds Lay Eggs. Sharp new blades of grass pushed up in place of the old. On the ground meltwater ran everywhere, in gullies and in rivulets.

From the rocky cliffs and above the waves, the cry of

new birds grew louder every day. The last of the spring ice went out; the few remaining pans melted and changed with the breakers, with each new wind and current.

The first run of salmon began. Early chinooks, with their blue-green backs and black-spotted fins, the bright silver sockeyes, streaking through the ocean water, hurrying toward creeks and rivers.

For the first time in all the years she remembered, Elik did not go to fish camp but stayed near the summer tent with Malluar. A simple routine set in, not the lessons she waited to learn, but the everyday work of a human life.

Each morning she checked the willow fishnet they had been given. Afternoons she chipped away at the square of ground they needed for an ice cellar. For the single, large meal of the day they ate birds more than seal meat—murres and shore birds that Grey Owl sent over with one or another of the younger girls.

And the chores were divided, not the way a mother and daughter divided work, by ability, but by whether on a given morning, someone signaled to Malluar that Seal Talker was sleeping late, or was busy with his own work. Only then would she allow Elik to haul fresh water, or gather driftwood, or dig for clams without fear she would be followed.

What she did not permit Elik to do was visit in the other tents. Or speak too long with the women who came to sit with them. Or learn anything more about being a shaman—yet. "In time," Malluar kept saying. "When you are ready, I will tell you."

From the hump of the ridge where their tent stood, Elik looked out and watched her sister searching the tide pools. Some days Naiya walked alone with a loose-weave basket over her shoulders, a digging stick in her hand. Some days she walked with Kimik or Squirrel, catching crabs, digging for clams. And some days they looked to her tent, though the distance was too far to see what their faces told. If no one else was near, they waved to Elik; otherwise, they walked on.

With her chores in her lap, Elik felt as if she was the

one who had aged while her sisters and friends grew younger. Their feet seemed to step so lightly, more dancing than at work. Their hair was shining and sleek. And what did they have to worry about, she wondered, besides the one world in front of them?

She'd heard from Nua that Kimik had refused an offer of marriage from Bear Hand's youngest brother, Drummer. That Naiya was looking to have a child by the time the Moon of the Shortest Sun came round.

Watching them, Elik thought of Allanaq and how for one season, life had seemed simple. It was difficult to remember how that felt, or the seasons before that, before she had lost her grandmother and her mother, her brother who, she still believed, was somewhere far away, not dead.

Yet life went on. A person who would be a shaman still ate, still needed sleep and shelter and the small, ordinary things of life. Still had fears—not only of the spirits she could not see but of people, one person. One man in particular.

Elik was down at the water's edge below their tent one day, when Nua came to visit. She had been tying a line of small herring—gutted first, then slit, with a line passed through the gills till they were strung in ropes as long as a man.

The wind caught her hair and she moved, then turned to see Malluar and Nua sitting down by the fire ring outside the tent. Quickly, she tied off the last knot, then carried the heavy string of fish in a basket to the tripod of poles where earlier ropes of the small fish were drying in the wind.

Nua patted the ground, inviting Elik to sit. Then, fussing and shuffling, she unrolled a grass mat she'd brought to work on. With large, circling motions, she showed Elik the twisting weave she had used—two above, one below into the earlier row.

Malluar nodded and smiled and waited till she was sure no one walking up behind them could hear. "So," she asked. "Seal Talker is still in Kahkik's house?"

Nua flipped the mat over, opened a knot on the unfinished end with a tapered bone awl. "Yes. But only for as long as Kahkik's gone on this one hunting trip. When he returns, he says he won't be made to sleep alone while Seal Talker enjoys his wife."

"And Meqo? What does she say?"

"The same. That she's content to do Seal Talker's cooking and warm his bed until Kahkik returns. So long as there's no trouble."

"She's generous."

"She's cautious." Nua looked up, nodded at Elik. "She says it's better he should be with her, an older woman used to men, rather than making trouble for someone else."

"What else? Did you let it out, the way I asked?"

Elik looked to Malluar. She'd heard nothing, none of this. What was going on?

Nua glanced along the beach. No one was there. "That you have been training her, yes. People know that."

"And that the miscarriage left her weak, did you say that?"

Nua hesitated.

"What?" Malluar's voice grew worried. "There was more?"

"More, yes. He's been talking among the men. Grey Owl heard. About Elik. That part you said—that she remains ill— it may not have been so good." Nua watched a bird dive after a fish. The bird splashed into the water, missed, then flew off to circle again. "Seal Talker says that when the blood flowed out between her legs something else climbed in."

"Something evil? Did he say what kind?"

"What kind?" Elik lifted her voice, louder than she realized. "What does it matter what kind . . . What—"

"Hush," Malluar quieted her. "Be glad he wants you. If your mother had given birth to another girl, or if there was another girl sharing the same name as you, you would be dead now. You and the trouble you've made him. You would be dead and Seal Talker would have his shaman-child from someone else."

"Is that it still?" Nua asked. "He wants a child? Would that it were food would satisfy him."

"And soft skins and well-stitched clothes. For any other man, it would suffice. But not him. His greed isn't so simple to be filled by a full stomach, a warm bed."

"But he left the Bent Point village because of food?"

"That's true, there was need. But it was need that matched his desire." Malluar sighed, looked away. "All my life I've lived beside this man. And all his life, being younger, he feared he was living in my shadow. But he was strong. For a while." She looked back to Nua, then Elik. "You weren't there. You don't remember what he was, the way the spirits took hold of him. The way he could stand, naked against the storms, turning them—on his own word—away from the Long Coast shores. You don't remember him as I do, how he would run screaming, as if the spirits inside of him were too large, too terrible to contain. He would writhe on the floor and race around the houses, out on the ice, for all of us. So the *inuas* would come to him. They would help him. His strength was real. His power—" Malluar shook her head, almost sadly.

"Perhaps," Nua said, "perhaps it is harder for a man to age than a woman. A woman lives always with blood and pain and life and death."

"As does a man," Elik said. "Facing the ice, the winter storm. You told me that yourself, the day I became a woman."

Malluar chuckled. "I did. Yes. You remember. But a man expects to die quickly, taken by the sea, killed by a bear. Even so, thoughts of death change a person."

"Grey Owl is old," Nua said. "I am old. That doesn't turn our thoughts to hate."

"True," Malluar said. "But is he filled with hate? Or desire? My cousin's no fool. I let it out that the girl is ill, thinking to keep men away. He twists the words to say there's a demon between her thighs. My way, not a man comes near. His way, no one else can get a child off her before him. Who has won?"

❧

The long days without night began to change. The rainy season came and evening returned with its charcoal smudge across the lighter sky. By the time Grey Owl came to build a winterhouse for Malluar and Elik, full nights were in the sky. It was the season when Caribou Shed Their Velvet and the honking songs of geese and ducks had already grown fainter and now were gone.

With his long-handled antler pick, and with Elik working on her knees behind him, Grey Owl dug out the floor where the tent had stood, laying out an underground passage for a cold-trap. They built no side rooms for storage, and the single main room remained small as the tent had been.

The day their work was to start, even before Grey Owl appeared, Elik woke to find a heavy polar bear skin set high on a rack where no dog could reach it. And along midday, while the gradual slope of the tunnel began to take shape, Bear Hand and his youngest brother, Drummer, carried over a stout ridgepole they claimed was old and small and no use to anyone.

Ani's Wife's young granddaughter skipped her way to a visit, with enough strips of seal gut for Elik to sew into a window. And while the little girl was still there, playing with a pile of beach stones, another of the children ran up, this time with rawhide webbing already tied into the ladder shape needed for a drying rack above a hearth.

Elik counted three days of work until the house was done and she and Malluar slept beneath a roof of wood and sod. But even with walls to hide behind no one but Nua and Ani's Wife came to visit.

Ani's Wife brought gifts of food when she came, sometimes strips of seal meat slick with oil. This day, she carried a huge grey-white gull with its webbed feet in her fist, its head dangling, almost bobbing along the ground.

She stood outside the house, laughing in spite of the bird's weight as she mimed the story of how the gull was lured with a fish carcass tied to a string. How the bird must have found the fish fat and sweet enough it was willing to come, even for an old woman's rock, and give itself up to die.

She'd been laughing, holding the gull in one hand, her other hand against her chest, when suddenly she stopped. "The wind's too strong," she said. "And the mosquitoes make me thirsty. Surely, some good people will invite me in their house?"

Malluar had been leaning against the large driftwood log they had found one day, following a storm. She rose, motioned to Elik to take the gull, then led the way inside. The house felt crowded with the three of them, but even so, they closed the skyhole down, and lit a lamp for light, rather than risk being heard.

"I'm not a gossip," Ani's Wife said. "When I was young, a new mother, people spoke only about how strong I was. My aunts used to say I was born with an old head."

Elik had flipped the gull on its back to skin, but she slowed as she realized Ani's Wife had news, real news. She listened toward the roof, to make sure no one had followed, but Ani's Wife shook her head. "He's not coming. No one is. Seal Talker sent me."

"There's trouble?" Malluar asked.

Ani's Wife stretched her short legs straight in front of her. "Trouble?" she repeated. "Yes. It's Kahkik. He's ill. Seal Talker says he will call a trance. That his soul is lost and he must search for it."

Elik thought of Seal Talker searching for her mother's soul. Working over Alu. Trancing for Iluperaq.

"How long?" Malluar asked.

"Three days now. He tried to hide from Seal Talker. Kahkik came home ill from fishing. He slept in Bear Hand's house, not even in his own—for fear Seal Talker would get it out of Meqo. It didn't help. Seal Talker sits with his drum in his lap and his caribou cap on his head. His pointed ears hear everything." Ani's Wife pulled at her lips. "He wants me to bring the girl."

"Yes," Malluar hurried her. "But how? How does he say it?"

"Must I answer, with her all ears?"

Elik stiffened. "Tell me," she said. "I'm not a child to be protected."

Ani's Wife lifted an eyebrow. "Brave words," she said. "Now listen: Seal Talker says that the demon that killed his child in your womb is the same as the one your father invited into the Bent Point village. The same one that killed your mother. Your grandmother. Sipsip and Saami's son and Ema. That it was not satisfied with your father's meager confession and wants more. He says he's seen the demon prowling near our houses. Waiting for its chance. He makes wild faces, frightening the girls. He says that their children will die if Elik isn't brought to him."

Malluar leaned over, spit in her hands, then rubbed the saliva protectively on her cheeks. "So. He tries to shift the fear they heaped on Allanaq onto her. It's not so far to turn. Tell me this now. It's important. Have you a sense how many believe him?"

"Some perhaps. But however many do—and he's ugly enough to be convincing—there are just as many whispering that he goes too far."

"Ahh." Malluar nodded. "That's good. It's what I hoped."

"This demon—" Elik started, but her throat caught.

"What is it, child?" Ani's Wife asked.

"This demon . . . I've seen it. Before. I think. It was a caribou. My father, he . . . "

With a touch as gentle as she'd ever used, Malluar said, "This is not about your father. Whatever wrongs he may have done, he's paid for. He lives alone. His family gone. People speak against him. It's enough. This is about Seal Talker."

"But what if . . . " Elik forced herself to say the words. "What if that demon saw me? What if it knew me from the start?"

Malluar watched Elik more closely, then shook her head. "No. This is not what you think it is. Whatever may have happened . . . "

"But if I went to Seal Talker, would he leave Kahkik alone?"

Ani's Wife shrugged. "Why would he stop? He remembers the wealth he had when he was young, and wants it back again." She rose, started out the entry while Elik and Malluar followed.

Outside, the sky had changed. It was snowing. Large wet flakes angled downward, slipped against the tent skins, drifted at the corners. Malluar touched Elik's hand, then pointed toward the sky. "It won't be much longer," she said. "Not now."

Kahkik, the sick man, lay naked on the floor of the newly opened *qasgi*, a bank of furs beneath him, his amulet string removed from his waist. Two shallow lamps lit the hollows of his cheeks. To one side, Seal Talker had hung a grass mat. Behind it, his shaman's mask, drum, strings and ropes and rattles were hidden from view.

Malluar and Elik were among the last to arrive. The ceremonial house quieted as they entered and Elik had to reassure herself that Malluar was right. It wasn't her the people had grown afraid of, but Seal Talker and his stories and demands.

She scanned the room, relaxed only when she realized the shaman was nowhere in sight. She followed Malluar to the end of the platform, waited while Two Ravens and Squirrel moved from the wall to give her room.

On the floor near Kahkik, Bear Hand and Drummer sat with their knees to their chins, too worried for their brother's life to hide their fears. Meqo sat nearer to his feet, far enough his illness couldn't touch her if it tried.

But for the sick man's rattling breath, there was little noise now, only a sense of waiting, heavy and mistrustful. Kahkik's skin had broken out in a film of sweat and there was an odor—not the ordinary smells of fishskin or of urine, but something heavier and too close.

Elik tried to separate out the number of people who had come from the Bent Point village. How many with relatives who had died. How many remembered or cared that the food they ate had been found first by Allanaq? By her husband?

The next time she looked to Kahkik's pallet, Seal Talker was crouching at his side. The shaman sat with his elbows digging into his knees, pulling at the thin hairs above his lip. He looked smaller than Elik remembered, his angular face shadowed more with bitterness than strength, anger more than pride.

She started to look away, then realized he was watching her. She turned back. She wouldn't look away. She'd promised herself she would face him and hold his stare. She straightened her shoulders, but he'd already turned aside. Smiling, as if he was already satisfied. As if he'd won something just by having her seated there, playing his game.

Malluar touched Elik's knee and the girl relaxed. Seal Talker had power, sickness-bringing power, and he had spirit helpers, but so did Malluar. For that, she was grateful, very grateful.

Seal Talker motioned to Grey Owl and the row of drummers started. From behind the curtain he brought out his shaman's headband, slipped it on so that the loon's beak hung toward his nose, the tail and wings came together behind. He added paint: three red lines streaked across each cheek, under his eyes. He put on his long-armed shaman mittens, took up his flat drum, started his own beat moving across the others.

There wasn't a person in the darkened room who wasn't listening now, so intently, Seal Talker could feel it. It was a power he'd always prided himself on, sensing the weight of an audience's attention. Their fear.

So long as they watched him, he would never show emotion. Emotion was for weaker men, for different times.

It was one of the few things he and Malluar agreed upon, that shamans must not be weak. Not for their own sake, though a shaman's life was sometimes precarious. So often, they were blamed for other people's misfortunes. Yet who was it for, all their pain, their trancing, if not for the people?

Seal Talker remembered a time, long ago, when he and Malluar used to speak of things like this, how often to show strength; it was necessary to keep people in fear.

The darkened *qasgi*. The clattering sounds and calls. Her wolverine skulls at home. What were they for if not to teach respect through fear?

It was fear that made people listen. Fear that brought them to his door. Placated him with gifts and meat. Fear of what they couldn't know, but he did. Malluar did.

Even this girl, Elik. She was no fool. She knew what he was about. His little staring tricks just now—she caught on quickly. He would have to be forceful tonight. To pit his will against both Malluar and Elik together, he was going to need all the fear he could raise.

He waited while the drumming worked its long, seductive repetitions. As if it were a heartbeat, his heartbeat, calling to the *qasgi* from two worlds. He waited till he saw the first few sets of eyes begin to droop. A few heads nod with the droning beat. Finally then, half-squatting, half in a duck walk, he danced past Kahkik's head, around his shoulder, along his side.

When he stopped, his flat drum covered the full length of Kahkik's naked stomach, from his groin to his nipples. He nodded toward the drummers and the beating slowed.

"Someone," Seal Talker called above the drumming, "someone has put an illness inside this man. He is weak because of what someone has done. Someone evil and jealous. Someone inside this room . . ."

Seal Talker set down his drum, lifted his hand, and a hollowed bone sucking tube appeared. Thin and long, one end disappeared inside his mouth; the other ended in the face of a grotesque bear.

*Let them stare.* Seal Talker smiled to himself. He had copied one of the faces from Allanaq's own work, a bear face with curling jaw, inset eyes, and hair. Loudly, Seal

Talker inhaled, puffed himself up with air, then leaned over Kahkik.

Behind him the lamp fluttered, shadows wavered. No one moved. But for the one thin, wheezing sound of his lips on the tube, there wasn't a person who dared to speak. "There is something inside," Seal Talker moaned, as if already he'd been weakened. "I can feel it now. Trying to flee. To find its owner. I can feel it now. It's coming near. Inside, inside the tube . . ."

Malluar set her hand on Elik's, bearing down so the girl wouldn't jump.

Elik leaned to ask what she wanted, but there was a shout and she looked quickly to the floor. Meqo jumped to her feet, pointing, her mouth pulled back in a grimace.

Seal Talker had risen. He'd lifted his drum again, by the handle with the end of the rim on the floor and it was there, on the floor where Meqo was staring.

It was Kahkik's illness. Seal Talker's tube had sucked it out, then spit it on the floor. It was standing on his drum. It was small and dark in color. Nothing like the shape of a person, though it could have been a doll, the way it looked so hard and wooden and dead.

Seal Talker moved and the illness fell. He laughed, the way a mean boy laughed at a dog, and he shook and watched it roll around the frame of his drum. He had left the sucking tube on the floor and he leaned down, feeling with his hand until he lit on it. He straightened, lifted the tube, set it between his lips again.

He pointed the tube toward Elik. Directly at her. There was no mistake.

The corners of his mouth lifted to a hideous smile. The tube dangled. He nodded at Elik, met her eyes, then lowered the end of the tube to the illness again. It was lying on its side now, naked as the man it had come out of, only smaller, darker. Seal Talker sucked and the illness began moving toward his tube. Crying. Elik was certain she heard it cry. It rolled itself toward his sucking tube in fits and starts, rolled closer as he blew again.

And then all at once, it was gone. And there was the tube in Seal Talker's mouth tipped downward as if it were fatter, heavier, weighted with something evil.

Slowly at first, then faster, Seal Talker began to dance, to circle and spin. As if the tube had become a hunting bola, and the illness was the rocks attached by lines. As if he were the lines, spinning, readying to strike, and the illness would wrap itself around her wings and bring her down. . . .

"Come," Malluar closed her hand tightly over Elik's. "Quickly, before he sees . . ."

Elik blinked; it took a moment till she remembered where she was. Another moment to pull herself away. Malluar tugged her along, over Nua's legs—more quietly than Elik had ever heard her move. Not a sound, not a noise. None of the people around them lifted their eyes to watch or give them away as they opened a path to let them out.

Seal Talker dug his toes into the floor. He was dizzy, but it didn't matter. He knew how to aim and the sucking tube was pointed exactly at the women's bench. He planted his feet, steadied himself and blew. He blew fast and hard and true . . . And he should have hit. It did hit . . . It . . .

She was gone.

Seal Talker stared at the empty bench. He lowered his hand, trying to understand. Behind him, someone shuffled and he wheeled about: the few men closest to the entry shifted their seats, then again, closing a gap.

It took only a moment for him to realize he'd been tricked. Then he was after them, furious at being made to appear weak. Not just by his cousin, but by the girl. By all of them. . . . He tripped over someone's outstretched legs, stumbled for the door, through the dark.

Outside, the wind had risen. It pricked his skin; he'd brought no parka, but that didn't matter. He could stand it. He could stand much more.

It was dark outside, too clouded for the moonlight to brighten the snow. Seal Talker hurried away from the qasgi, then stopped, stood to listen.

Instantly, he heard them, their footsteps rushing between the houses, nearer than he'd guessed. Malluar's legs must have slowed them. He cupped his hands to his mouth. "You can't go anywhere," he shouted. "The girl is mine."

In the darkness ahead, Malluar stopped. "Wait." She touched Elik's hand. They listened, caught the light sound of Seal Talker's steps, sliding through fresh powder snow.

"We should go," Elik hurried her.

"No. We face him. This is the only way to win. Stand behind me, but don't show fear. Don't look in his eyes."

Malluar straightened and turned to wait for her cousin. He reached them a moment later, red-faced with anger. "She comes with me," he said. "I'm done with waiting."

Malluar lifted an eyebrow, answered with a calculated, disbelieving smile.

"I'll take her," Seal Talker said, looking only at Malluar, never to Elik. "Even if she is shaman. No—even better if she is. If she lives to bear a child, he will grow to be the son I wanted."

Seal Talker waited for Malluar to speak. She didn't and he grew confused, as if he hadn't planned further. "Is that what you want?" he demanded. "To keep her only to stop me?"

No answer.

"She let the husband go. How much did she care?"

Malluar didn't answer.

"But isn't it good for both of us? To have a child off her?"

Elik shut her eyes, desperate for a way to close herself off, every opening in her body. She didn't want his child in her, stealing her strength, born with his eyes . . .

"Us?" Malluar said.

"Are you so old, you've forgotten your own dead children?"

"Are you so blind all you see is your own face on anything you want?"

"D-Did you think," he stammered, "did you think I should have come and grown my child in *you*? All those years ago? When I already knew how dry your breasts were? When was the last time a man asked for the warmth inside your blanket?"

"When was the last time you looked to the basket where your soul was put to sleep?" Malluar didn't wait for the meaning of her threat to take hold. She took Elik's arm, pulled her away. Quickly, neither of them daring to look back.

Seal Talker stood there, quivering with rage. Had he heard what he thought he had? Was she threatening his soul? "What are you saying?" he called, then he stopped, swallowed his words. There were sounds, people behind him.

He reeled about: they'd followed out of the *qasgi*, the rest of them. Long Coast people. Bent Point people. All of them listening, looking at him. Knowing he'd been bested.

He lifted his arms, made a face. "The illness of the man slipped inside me," he shouted. "I spoke with it, made it go away. But not for long. From the family of the sick man, it demands respect. To others, it tells me to give its message. Beware. It has not gone away. It has not . . ."

# 15

Elik was asleep on the narrow platform, her head toward the hearth, the echo of Seal Talker's drum still in her ears.

She was dreaming that a seal had emerged alongside her kayak, up front against the bow. The seal climbed out of the water, set the kayak dangerously rocking as it lifted itself to the deck, pulled closer to the hatch. So close she could touch it—and she did. It let her, no . . . more than that: it *wanted* to be touched. With its cold, hard nose it lifted her hand, showed her where to rub the smooth fur on its forehead, the wet curve of its neck. But all along she kept worrying how the seal's claws might scratch through the deck skins, how its weight could roll the kayak, take her down with it, into the sea. . . .

She woke suddenly. The house was dark but there'd been a sound. Where? Not in the dream. She glanced up. Something was out there, on the roof. Elik eased her blankets to her waist. She looked to Malluar, seated in the corner with her forehead on her knees, robes pulled over her head. What was she doing? She hadn't moved since they'd entered the house. Quietly, Elik slipped to the floor.

With her eyes toward the roof, Elik found a bowl, filled it with coals and ashes from the fire. Then, balancing on the largest stone beneath the skyhole, she tossed the coals out the roof: if anyone was there, she would say the ashes had smothered the fire and she was cleaning it, that was all.

The coals melted into the growing layers of snow, burying themselves. The ash dotted the white in grey-black pitholes. Farther out the wind was blowing, not fierce, not strong enough she couldn't hear . . .

What? Was it Seal Talker? What was he planning? Was Kahkik still alive?

The cloud cover that had darkened the village earlier had cleared. The moon's face shone like a shaman watching from above.

Whatever had woken her was gone now, but something had been there. Something human, something alive.

The flesh on her arms rose and she shivered, then quickly weighted the gut window down with a rock, let herself back inside.

She turned to find Malluar kneeling on the floor. She had taken a chunk of frozen blubber from a sack, pounded it to soften, then added it to the lamp. The light caught, spread the length of the wick.

"I heard something," Elik started, but Malluar hushed her.

"It's time," the older woman said. "Now. You have to go. Seal Talker was out all day yesterday searching for the place you miscarried—for your clothes. I hadn't told you before. He doesn't know I already dug it up, your leggings and the gravel beneath it. That very night, I went back." Malluar smiled. "Ahead of him."

"How could you find my leggings? The tide took it out."

Malluar shook her head. "And the tide brought it back as well." She grew more serious. "You should have been more careful. You were lucky that time. He didn't find it. But there are other ways he can reach you. He, or his spirit helpers, who would gladly, easily steal your soul. Even here, with me. You're too alone."

"Alone?"

"Without spirit helpers—those who live inside the Wind. Those who are Power. Who must be questioned. To be a shaman not only must you be able to see the spirits; they must also see you. You must learn magical songs that summon the *inuas,* convince them to be your helpers."

With a calm that Elik would never, earlier, have thought possible, she looked about the house. "Do I take anything? Food? A knife?"

"No." Malluar shook her head. "Nothing more than a scrap of skin to sit on when you sleep, but only when you sleep. All the while you are awake, you must keep walking." Malluar motioned Elik to sit near her on the floor.

"There are things I must tell you," she whispered. "There is a place you must reach. On the outside you will be alone. On the inside you must find a deeper silence. And you must stay there, in that place inside of you. You must think and you must wait to find *qarrtsiluni,* the Place Where a Song Is Born. In that stillness you must search, in the darkness. As my uncle who was shaman taught me, so I will try to teach you."

Malluar looked at her hands, then up to Elik's face. "It can be difficult for a woman to practice as a shaman."

Elik narrowed her eyes, not understanding.

"I didn't say to be a shaman," Malluar repeated. "I said to practice. Not that she can't, but that a new wife, a mother, has little time when she is not burdened with a woman's taboos, when she is able to make her drums, practice her magical songs."

Malluar reached across, lifted Elik's loon amulet from where it hung, no longer hidden in a pouch but open, breathing air. "Your Allanaq carved this?"

Elik nodded.

"Most people are practical. What concerns them is staying alive, shaping the best tools they can. They don't ask: *What is this rock I carve?* They ask: *How can I use it?* But your Allanaq, he's had to think in different ways, new ways. He's had to be concerned where others are not. As have you. He's a good man."

Elik bit her lip, not to cry or smile or say something foolish.

Malluar went on. "Someday, not yet, I will teach you how there are two kinds of amulets: those that work best when touched with things having to do with birth, and those that are strengthened by things of the dead. You will learn this, but it is the work of a lifetime. As is being a shaman. One must practice. One must risk the ordeal of a trance, the pain of having a spirit helper enter inside you. Not once but again and again. You must go out now and gain two things—a song, and a spirit helper. But only as time passes will you prove to the people what kind of shaman you are. You understand?"

"I understand," Elik said. Her eyes were bright now, shining.

"Perhaps. But perhaps you are only sure because you're young, because you haven't learned yet how little we really know." Malluar leaned back, searching for words to explain. "Bear Hand mistrusted Allanaq. Yet Allanaq's song brought a whale. Seal Talker and I both believed that the power of our magical songs could only be passed from relative to relative. Yet here is my cousin grown bitter by his son's refusal to learn his songs. The truth is different. Seal Talker's son did not refuse. He left because he had never been called.

"A person must desire, with all their being, to see the places a shaman sees—the skeleton hidden inside flesh, the sea people living below water. Seal Talker's son had a hunter's eyes, sharp enough to see the speck that becomes a seal, the track a wolf leaves in the snow. But no farther.

"What you have taught me is that for all the blood inside a person's veins, blood alone does not make a shaman. Instead, as one girl is taught to make her stitches fine and strong, another learns the difference between a fox's small round track and a wolf's larger pad. Another girl finds a lamp inside her and it is that girl who may be taught to raise the flame, to speak with the *inuas* who draw near to see."

Malluar seemed weary now, drained, in contrast to Elik's heightened excitement. "You must take no weapons," Malluar said. "And no food from this house—from anyone's house. You must go carefully. What you do, what you say, affects us all."

"I understand."

"Do you? Do you also understand that there are consequences for your actions—to all of us?" Malluar shook her head, almost sadly. "You aren't afraid, are you?"

"You've asked me that before," Elik said. "Do you remember? I was a new woman then, and yes—I was afraid. I'm not now. I'm ready."

Malluar turned away, poked with a stick at the hearth, at a coal that had long since lost its heat. "Granddaughter," she said, turning back around. "You will be."

Elik stopped outside the house to check for weather signs. The night seemed huge. The moon was high overhead and nearly full, the sky black and clear enough to see the stars—a thousand thousand stars. And no northern lights—for that she gave thanks. It would have made her nervous thinking people were above, watching which way she went. Come sunrise, the hills would be clear. With luck, she'd see no people. Bears would be hibernating. That too was good. Southward, the ice held quiet.

She pulled the long-haired ruff on her hood forward, forming a tunnel against the cold. She turned, started inland. Malluar had said little but that she must find her way alone. She must gain a song, and a spirit helper. Without food. Without human aid. Alone.

Once away from the houses and out in the tundra, the snow cover was deeper but hard-packed, crusted by the wind. Without snowshoes, she needed to watch for brush and hills where snowdrifts would be a problem.

The clothes she wore were the warmest she owned: the inner caribou layer worn with the fur against her skin, the outer layer reversed. The one thing that felt strange was the belt around her waist: her amulets had been removed. Not even the loon around her neck had been allowed. *Alone,* Malluar had said. Without pyrites to start a fire, without snowshoes or goggles or tools of any kind.

By the time the next day's sun was five fingers above the horizon, Elik was sure Seal Talker had not followed. If he'd hunted near these hills, it was so long ago, she didn't think he'd remember which way the trails went. And Malluar had assured her he would not. But if he did, she would hide. She would find a den, the way a bear did, or dig a snowcave, hide behind a cutbank, behind a rock.

She found animal signs as she walked, but no people. And most of what she found was small: two kinds of fox, one heavier, the smaller one probably white fox. Or perhaps it was a female.

Tundra hares were out also in the windswept flats. Whenever she found willow brush, she found tracks. It looked to be a good season for hare and ground squirrel. Also for the larger animals who lived on them. Wolves, she didn't think would want her. Not so long as she kept walking. Bears, she prayed, would stay asleep. And wolverine, she'd sometimes heard, didn't really attack unless they were starving. Unless someone tried stealing its kill.

The first night out, she waited to camp till she found a stand of willow brush to use for a shelter. A few of the branches she bent down for bedding. The remainder she left for the backbone of a camp. She found a rock, kicked it loose, then used it for a shovel. The snow was too powdery to cut blocks, but heavy enough for her to tamp into shape. She slept out of the wind, in her clothes, on the bed of willow packed with snow, then more brush.

Both the sun and the moon were in the sky the morning of the second day. A glittering snow fell and the wind that had chilled her when she built her shelter was so gentle now that huge flakes fell almost in threads, straight to the ground. She drank snow water, walked a few paces to relieve herself, then stood listening.

Had she been inland of the Bent Point village, even so far as this, she would have known which streams froze earliest and thick. Where there were berries in the summer, or lakes.

Here, she was certain of nothing except the line of hills ahead and the direction she had come behind her.

She took off her mitten, held her hand flat. She pointed her thumb to show the way back to the sea. Her small finger was the range of hills, ahead and spreading toward her wrist.

If she got lost, she would remember this middle finger pointed to a creek that circled back to a wider river. The deepest line on her palm she marked for the outcropping of boulders she'd climbed last night. She pulled her mitten back on. Started walking.

She wondered when her first dream might come. Malluar had said five nights. Was that how long it would take, she wondered? Or how many nights she was allowed? And how would a spirit come? She wished she knew ahead. It would make the days less slow. . . .

She hadn't been born when Malluar and Seal Talker began to practice as shamans. And her grandmother used to tell stories, but none were about initiations, shaman secrets. "You will be naked," Malluar had said, but did that mean she was expected to take off her clothes? Without shelter? Malluar said she might hear things, but what? She wished she knew.

Had Malluar ever done this? When she was young and her legs were strong enough? Had she gone away and come back saying she was a shaman? Or was she a shaman first, because of her uncle?

Time passed. Elik walked: through a sloping drainage that in summer would be a bog. Around the base of a lone hill. She followed the elbow of a skinny river, closed in ice, but talking as the water moved below. The river wasn't solid enough to cross: there were open cracks where condensation rose like smoke, and yellow ice where silt water rose from below. What river was this? She should have known. If she lost one name, what else could she lose?

She walked slowly, her face drawn inside her hood to ward off wind and glare. She kept her head lowered, studying the snow to see who else was there: a scurrying of voles, the footprint of a hare. A little farther along she found a great upheaval of snow and a rock where an owl had fought with a ptarmigan and won.

There were feathers and bits of bone to mark the fight. She wiped the frost from her eyelashes, then rummaged through the heap of tiny bones, trying not to think of food.

Of thick, yellowed caribou fat mixed with berries, the sweet taste of duck.

Surrounding the bones, there was a set of overlapping tracks. Someone else had come in, after the owl. A pad with five long toes, the points of claws dug in: *qavcik*, the wolverine. Alone, the way it liked to travel. She wondered if this one stayed in the area or if its territory circled wide?

The third night came on slowly. Or was it the fourth? She wiggled her fingers inside her mittens, trying to figure the count. How far had she walked? Which way? And how many people at home were dead now? Her mother? Was her mother dead? Or was it her father? She couldn't remember. Couldn't remember anything right at all.

With a frantic carelessness, she built a narrow shelter dug into a stand of willow shrubs. Mountains stood in the distance, white-topped, grey-brown below. She didn't want to go there. The wind would be rougher. And wasn't there another place nearby, she couldn't remember where, a woman had died from starvation? It was inside a cave, and people still heard her and the baby she had eaten before she died, both of them screaming.

She slept sitting up, wondering what her brother felt, the moment he knew he was lost. Was it the same as the sick feeling in her stomach when she saw the Forest People's fire? The way those men felt when Allanaq's arrow woke them into death?

She thought of stories she'd heard of how some people turned wild when a spirit entered their body. They bled from their mouth or chest. And once she'd heard of a man who was a shaman and could vomit blood from his ears, anytime he wanted.

She didn't want to do those things, didn't want that happening to her. She remembered the way her mother used to warn: *Stay away from shamans. Don't listen to their songs.* She hadn't remembered that in a great while, her mother's fears.

∽

In the morning, with a pale light in the sky and a streak of red outlining the hills, Elik once again pushed her hands back through her sleeves, peered out through her hasty shelter.

Directly in front of her a lemming sat upright on its hind legs. Not more than an arm's length away. Its brown fluffed coat was touched with frost, its small eyes more curious than afraid. When it did move, its claws clicked on its hardened track as it disappeared into a hollow.

Its house, she wondered, or only one of its tunnels? The entry seemed larger than a lemming would need, and the claw marks also. She flicked away the loose snow at the entry, probed inside. She had to reach deeper than she'd have thought. Almost crawling in herself . . .

The lemming had gone in, but what she brought out was a small dead wolverine. A solitary kit, frozen, tiny—no larger than the lemming.

From the looks of its thick white coat, the kit had been born alive, then died before it grew. How long ago? She couldn't tell, but she doubted if the lidded eyes had ever opened on the sun. Its four pinkish legs were stiff as a circle of sticks someone had left in the ground after stretching a hide. The fur was soft, the body hard. She wondered if it was the child of the one whose tracks she'd seen earlier. She lifted the tail to examine its genitals, noticed its weight instead.

Light as it was, there was still meat to it. Only a mouthful, but she'd eaten birds smaller than this.

She raised it toward her mouth, then stopped suddenly, picturing the way she'd look with fur and dry bones clinging to her teeth. She dropped the kit, then turned, clutched at her stomach as it heaved and she started to vomit.

Down on her hands and knees she vomited into the snow. White strands of mucus with no food inside, nothing solid but the smell. When it was done, she wiped the spittle from her mouth. The vomit burned her swollen lips. She started to bury it, the vomit, not to have something coming here later, sniffing at her smell, then wanting more.

She stopped. A bit of color caught her eye, a drop of red

against the mottled snow. Blood. She looked closer, then quickly swiped at her face. There was a smear of blood on her mitten now. From her mouth, she told herself. That was all. Her lips were cracked with cold—she shouldn't be afraid. Lips always bled. That was all . . .

She backed away. Her heart was pounding. Malluar had said that when a person goes out alone to become a shaman they must fast, and then they faint. They dream and spit up blood. Is that what was happening to her? Or was she dying? Why hadn't Malluar taught her anything? Given her words, or weapons—anything, anything at all to help.

She ran until the snow grabbed her leg and she fell. And then she walked, not fast; she was too weak anymore for that. She remembered she was supposed to be calm. And something about a quiet she needed to find. She didn't know where. It was time to sit, though. Sit down. She was too tired to worry anymore.

She found a rock with the snow drifted up on one side, facing into the sun on the other. She set down the scrap of skin Malluar had allowed, leaned back against the rock. She pulled her hands inside her sleeves, closed her eyes, and tried not to hear the voice of her hunger, though she felt it, gnawing up and down the length of her bones.

She made a song about it, not aloud but to herself. A little song to make the hunger fade. How she was like the wolverine she'd almost eaten. Bones without flesh. Drysleeved. Sticks without strength.

She wondered if the colorless, white world surrounding her was the same as the world she had started from. Or was she a ghost? A ghost who had stopped shitting, but still kept spittle in its mouth?

By the time full darkness came, she knew that something was watching her. And not just something, but the wolverine. Not the dead one—those tracks would have been tiny. But something large and quick and alive.

Wolverine tracks. She forced herself to think about them: all day she'd been crossing wolverine tracks. But that wasn't all. Each time she'd come to a place, the wolverine had been there first, ahead of her. So fast, she didn't know how, except that every so often, she'd hear a sound. Or find the signs of a well-eaten meal. A few coarse hairs frozen with the prints. Pellets not yet hard.

She spent the night leaning against the rock, sheltered from the wind, more often awake than asleep.

At daybreak, with the sky a streak of mottled colors above the hills, she tried remembering what she and the wolverine had spoken of during the night. She had slept so little, and they had talked so much. Funny, how difficult it was to remember . . .

He had come and she had told him how surprised she was that his speech wasn't difficult to understand. Easier than Allanaq's, the first time she'd heard his voice. The Wolverine wasn't a woman, it turned out, not the mother of the kit as Elik had first thought, but a man. He had lifted the hood of his Wolverine skin and stood in front of her. His face was shadowed, but it wasn't so dark she couldn't see how tall he was, how beautiful.

He'd gone off for a while. To hunt, he said. When he returned and told her about the wolves whose kill he hoped to steal, she already realized how eagerly she'd waited for his visit. How she could hardly keep from looking at him.

His short ears were small, slightly pointed, just showing from thick brown hair that he wore combed back from his forehead. His angular nose was sharp, but properly flat between his dark eyes. And his clothing—it was the suit of the finest hunter, with sleek, matched pelts all taken in their prime, two golden stripes traveling from the back, up and over the shoulder. Where the stripes ended, there were tassels of sharp claws that clinked together whenever he moved.

He liked to talk, and he told her that he liked the way she listened. That among his people, a good wife was someone who knew how to hear and smell, because that way she could hunt and protect her children. She asked him once how he was able to find her, and he threw back his head and laughed. "Finding you was the easy part. It was you who needed to find me. And you did," he said. "You are able to see through the darkness because of the inner light that shines from you. You are visible."

She was asleep again when next he came, asleep in the daylight. He walked upright, the same as any man and he invited her into his house. When she asked where it was, he pointed toward the mouth of a tunnel, a hole showing in the snow. The opening was small, and she had to lie down and flatten her cheek against the cold to see inside. But it was no different, really, than a winter entry to a human house, except that this was smaller. He led the way and she followed, crawling in behind. Inside, far away, she saw people sitting around a lamp. Wolf and Loon and Caribou, all with their hoods pulled back, their human faces showing.

He stopped. They'd come to a place where the tunnel widened enough so that a bench had been cut out of the snow along one side. The bench was covered in a layer of willow branches, then furs, a smooth stone for a pillow. The furs were beautiful, with the same two stripes as those he wore. He sat down first, took her hand, pulled her to sit beside him.

"To me," he said, "you are almost transparent, so thin, you are shining. You draw me, like the lamp that draws a moth in summer." He grew more serious. "I want to be inside you," he said.

Elik didn't know if she should answer. Some of the things he said were odd, as if he were no older than a child, without sense. But there was another part to him also, something made of power, so strong she could feel it, dwarfing all else. She lowered her gaze. He was beautiful and warm, and she was so cold. . . .

"Don't be afraid," he said, but she was. She couldn't help it. Her stomach tightened at the way he seemed to hear her thoughts before she spoke. "You will be my wife," he said.

"Who . . . Who made your coat?"

"My sister, but she is dead."

She caught a hint of something dark below his armpit,

not skin. When she looked closer, she saw how one of his hands was still a wolverine's. His claws had torn the stitches holding the parka's sleeve to the shoulder, nearly all the way round.

He leaned her gently down onto the furs, then leaned over her. He was long and he fitted well against her, his legs between hers. His sharp nose caressed her neck. He licked her ear. His skin, for all that he was a man, was as soft as if his legs were made of fur.

She opened her eyes. The snow-ceiling above her was thin and lit with the sun shining through from the other side. She looked down along the length of his back. Far away, she saw her own body larger that it had ever looked before, lying on the snow. One of her hands was sticking out from her parka sleeve, like a skeleton. That was what she saw: the skeleton of her hand, clean and beautiful, with a light all its own spreading on the snow.

She was beautiful! The bones inside her hand—there were so many and yet she could have named them. Counted them. Known them all—they were that clear, even from so far along the tunnel. It was as if there were two of her, one lying on the snow, looking back at the one lying with the Wolverine who was a man.

"Am I dead?" she asked, and she was smiling, filled with wonder, not fear.

"Not dead. You are alive in my world."

He was right. She was alive, and the realization filled her with an ecstasy. Ecstasy first, but than a certain understanding: if she stayed and married with him, then the body in the snow would die for lack of care. It would freeze and die and her soul would not return. His love-making would kill her if she allowed it.

But she was a woman, not a Wolverine spirit. She wasn't ready to be dead. She couldn't be his wife.

He started to roll her over by the hips; he urged her to lie so her breasts pointed to the fur blankets and her rump lifted sweetly toward him. Eagerly, he tugged at her trousers, felt for the belt that held them to her hips.

But Elik had an idea. She shifted back to her side, gently so that he moved with her. "I want to see the face of my husband," she said. She said it coyly, as if she were shy. "In my village, that's the way it's done when a woman is to be a bride. The man gives her the choice which way they'll couple."

Eagerly, his eye shone. He moved his legs, allowing her back to arch.

"Wait," she said as he started again to push her parka upward, revealing her waist, her breasts. "I'll be cold if I take off all my clothes."

"I can bring more furs?" he offered.

"It will be enough if your own parka warms me," she said and she pulled him lower, so he couldn't see what she was doing. Then, pretending she was getting comfortable, she quickly bit the few remaining stitches holding his sleeve to the shoulder. The stitch tore, the sleeve slid easily off his short Wolverine arm. One end of the sleeve she wedged beneath the heavy rock pillow so it couldn't move. The other end she brought up and around and through her legs, as if the opening were a warm vagina.

With her hand, she took hold of him, helped him find his way inside.

He closed his eyes, rocked back and forth into the sleeve, pushing then releasing. He burrowed his face into the furs below her shoulder. With a woman's quick fingers, she easily looped the thread around the sleeve, a knuckle's length down from the opening. She knotted it around his penis. She moaned as she did this. Moaned as he rocked, as she twisted the thread to a knot, cinched the sleeve warmly, securely, around him.

And now came the difficult part, the part without which she didn't dare go home. She whispered in his ear, "In my village it is the custom for husbands to give their new wives a present. Is it the same in yours?"

"Whatever you want, yes," he sighed. "I have the power to send all the game you could ever desire. You will never want for furs or the shelter of clothing."

"I would like you to sing for me."

The Wolverine-man stopped his rocking. He pulled his lips back in surprise. His long teeth gleamed menacingly.

Elik steadied her voice. "Surely, this is a small thing. You are so powerful—what is one song to you?"

Flattered, he lifted his chin, considering the idea. He peered along the length of the tunnel, to the room where the others still sat, sharing food. When he was satisfied they weren't watching he said, "Very well then. If you promise never to repeat the song except when I allow, I will do as you ask."

Elik held her breath, waiting.

"This is the song I'll come for. Like this: *"Ya, ya yu, ya axa, yu. Animal, Strong Animal, you are coming to my Song. You come nearer to the entry of my house. You are coming to me, beautiful and strong. My Song brings you. Ya, ya yu, ya axa yu."*

Elik repeated the song quietly, so she would not forget, each word following immediately after his. Until he came to the last word, finished then heard her voice, suddenly alone.

"No—don't sing!" he snapped. He turned his nose sharply toward her. "Never sing that unless I permit . . . "

Desperately, Elik wiggled out from under him.

He raised his fingernails to strike her. But it wasn't till she had jumped from the platform and he swiped to grab her parka, her hair, that he realized he couldn't break free. He looked down at himself. Angrily he saw his sleeve, stuck beneath the rock, tied to his penis.

Elik backed away, out toward the entry. She scraped the walls with her hands as she ran, grabbed up fistfuls of icy snow. "*Ya, ya yu, ya axa, yu . . .* " She flung the words with the frozen shards, praying they would stop him, praying she would reach her body before it died. . . .

Someone was shaking her. Shaking her, when all she wanted was to sleep, nothing more . . .

The shaking grew rougher. Insistent.

Her eyelids fluttered. The sun's light glared—too bright:

a rim of silver with a center all in black. If she opened her eyes, maybe they would go away . . .

"Wake up, Elik, it's time . . ."

Whose voice was that? Her hand came up to block the sun. Odd, that it could move that way—her hand, all by itself, when she felt nothing, nothing at all . . .

"There's trouble with Seal Talker. Another man is ill."

"Trouble?" Elik repeated, but the voice was familiar now. There was a name attached: Malluar. She tried to say it, but her lips wouldn't move. Her jaw locked. She tried again. "Seal Talker?" she said, and the memory took on shape. "My mother. My mother is sick."

"No. Old Ani. We'll talk about it later. Can you sit?"

"Maybe. Yes."

"Your hands—Where are your mittens?"

Elik looked behind her. There were no mittens, only drifted snow, white fields broken by shadowed hummocks. She had no idea where she was, what had happened. "Show me," Malluar said. Elik lifted her arms. Malluar squeezed two of her fingers, on the tips, near the nail where the skin was grey. Elik felt nothing.

"Pull your hands inside your parka, against your armpits. Can you walk?"

Elik tried. She lifted one leg, one knee, leaned into Malluar to stand.

Someone else was there, a few short paces back. A man standing close beside a sledge. Elik wavered, started to fall. Malluar grabbed her arm, eased her down against the rock. "Allanaq?" her voice was weak.

The man's mouth seemed pinched with pain. He looked away.

Elik lifted her gaze in a questioning glance but Malluar wasn't watching. She was kneeling on the snow, brushing the upmost windblown layer from the lower crusted tracks. She circled behind the rock, walked a short distance along the scattered trail Elik had left, running and then falling, running, then falling again.

At last Malluar turned back around. Returning to Elik,

she cupped her chin in her hand, peered into the girl's eyes. "So," she said. "You are alive." If she saw anything else, she didn't say. She didn't ask. She turned to Allanaq, sent him the sign he must have been waiting for. Malluar stepped back, allowing him to come forward.

He stopped when he was still an arm's length from Elik. "A man promised," he said, but his throat closed and he had to start again. "A man promised that he would come home when snow covered the ground."

"That man, did he—" Elik's shoulders racked with a sudden, heavy shivering, a cough that tore itself through her lungs, her chest. She couldn't speak till it passed. "That man—did he find my brother?"

Allanaq lowered his eyes. "There was no sign," he said. "Not in Fish River, not in the summer camps where I stopped along the way. I'm sorry."

"Maybe near *Nachirvik*," Elik whispered, "the Place Where You See All Around . . . ?" But she faltered, then, suddenly, her knees and ankles buckled.

Allanaq was there in a moment, catching, lifting her up. He didn't dare look at Malluar; he was too worried she'd warn him away, tell him again, after all this time, that he couldn't stay near.

He carried Elik to the sledge—Malluar had been right to have him bring it, along with furs for warmth and fresh water. Had Elik always been so light, he wondered? She was like the seed of a cattail, light enough to fly, to disappear.

There was so much he wanted to tell her. About the Fish River People he'd met, how they'd heard his story and yet were willing to trade. And more important: about how he had buried his father, in secret, at summer's end, when the ground had thawed enough to dig: a proper shaman's grave with floor and walls like a house. With eyes of ivory in place of his that no longer saw. About how frightened he had been to come home and find her gone. . . .

He straightened Elik's legs, covered her as carefully as if she were a sleeping child. As if her soul was only slightly tied to her body and any careless hurrying would snap the line that kept her there, take her away again.

It was well into the first dark of night before they reached the village. Quietly, not to be heard, Allanaq slipped secretly into Kahkik's house. Malluar and Elik crawled inside their own. Once settled, Malluar speared a chunk of seal fat on a stick, held it over the lamp's heat until the oil began to render. Cupping one hand beneath, she held it for Elik to suck, to bring back her strength.

Elik's eyes closed on the thick taste of oil in her mouth. Time passed, she didn't know when. She woke once to find Malluar gone. Then woke again to realize she had slept through the night, then into day. The few times Malluar did return, she seemed distracted. She muttered to herself and sang songs that Elik, waking from her own stilted dreams, didn't understand. She brought in frozen fish and left it for Elik to pick at. The next time Malluar left, she took her drum with her and her shaman mittens and a small, lidded box, the one in which she kept her strongest amulets.

Elik's thoughts hovered constantly around the Wolverine. What had happened, really? Had she been made love to by a spirit? Or had she tricked him, run away? If they fought, who had won? If not she—then why was she here, alive, and how else could she remember the song? "*Ya, ya yu, ya axa, yu. Animal, strong Animal, you are coming to my Song.* She didn't dare sing it aloud. Not yet. If it was a song of power, it would perhaps bring game to her house, but it would first bring the Wolverine spirit who'd promised the game.

It was on the third day after she returned that Malluar hurried into the house. Without explanations, she told Elik to dress in her outside clothes, then to wait with her, till they heard the sign.

It didn't come until late. The hooked moon had risen to a point visible through the skylight above the hearth. The dogs outside had quit their begging and quieted for the night. There was a sound, a scattering of pebbles on the brittle gut window overhead. Malluar looked to the roof, then rose as quickly as a woman half her age. "We're going out," she said, without naming where. "Whatever you hear spoken tonight, you must never repeat. Never."

Outside, the village dogs lay curled into circles of fur. They lifted their noses to see who was about, then burrowed without curiosity inside their own warmer fur. No smoke rose from the rooftops of any house. Not even from the *qasgi* where—Bear Hand had checked before he threw the pebbles—Seal Talker was soundly asleep.

Elik followed Malluar into Bear Hand's unlit entry, then climbed through the floor well to find the house already filled with people. Grey Owl and Drummer. Kahkik looking stronger. On the women's bench sat Little Pot and Nua. Meqo and Long Feather and Ani's Wife—Old Ani himself was too ill with a stomach sickness to leave his bed. And Allanaq.

Her gaze lit on the shoulder wound he'd taken . . . How long ago? Nearly a year? She remembered tending that scar when it was still new. It was lighter now, with a thinner shape curving like a bird's wing. Like a loon, she decided. Like a man who has lived in two worlds.

She looked away, made herself pay attention to the house again.

There were elders only: that was what she noticed now, that she was the youngest present. Not Kimik, not Squirrel. Not even Weyowin, or any younger man, married or not. The tension was marked more by what wasn't there, than what was. Meqo, whose house this was, had set no bowls. No food. No signs of hospitality.

Allanaq sat with his legs cautiously folded, hands resting on his knees. Elik had not seen him since she returned, nor—she'd been told, had anyone but Kahkik. He'd walked into the village shrouded in a snowstorm, pushed into the first door he found; Kahkik's fortunately. If it had been Seal Talker's, he might have been dead with the ill-

ness that Seal Talker had used first against Kahkik and
now Old Ani.

What was it Squirrel had once called Allanaq? A dog
man? Elik didn't think teasing such as that would come
from Squirrel's mouth anymore—not from anyone's.

She glanced to the wall where Bear Hand's gear was
neatly stored, found what she guessed would be there: a
well-worn bow straightener next to arrows with heads
made of antler—the four parallel lines Allanaq carved for
power and for life clearly visible.

A man like Bear Hand would have made his weapons
for use first, worrying as much about where the caribou
were hiding, as whether they found his carvings beautiful.
And the harpoons: three that she could see with line holes
drilled through toggling heads. Foreshafts, socket pieces,
and carefully worked flint blades of a kind that would not
have hung there a year ago. The kind that had pleased the
whale.

Elik turned, caught Allanaq's gaze following hers. He'd
been watching her. She folded her hands, smiled. Malluar
had been right to keep them apart this summer. Hadn't
there been a time when even the eyes of a dead father
couldn't stop their hands from reaching? He would want
her that way again, as surely as she wanted him. She would
ask Malluar. Perhaps she could go to him tonight. How
much longer need they wait?

Elik put the thought aside and turned to listen. Ani's
Wife had been speaking. She'd missed something.

"It must be done by his nearest male-lineage relative,"
Ani's Wife said.

"This is true," Bear Hand said. "It must be agreed by all.
We don't want someone coming back later, taking
revenge."

What should be done? Elik leaned forward. The men
held quiet, passed a skin of water, drank and passed it on.

Ani's Wife's tapped her fingers restlessly. "My husband
will be dead soon," she said. "And after that—who next?
We've already agreed. Bear Hand?"

Bear Hand looked to where Meqo sat near the edge of the bench. She opened her hands, nodded once. Yes. Bear Hand swallowed hard. He said, "No one in my line or my wife's will be watching. No one will speak."

"Kahkik?"

Kahkik glanced to his wife. As with Meqo, Long Feather already knew her answer. She opened her small hands, shook her head for her husband to see: *The women all agree.* Kahkik turned to Ani's Wife. "The children of my family are married to the children of yours. No one disagrees."

Little Pot, the oldest of the women, leaned forward. "Then only Whale Fin might have made trouble?"

Might have made? What is "*might have made?*" Elik looked to Allanaq but his gaze seemed locked on his own thoughts now. He sat and rubbed his hand back and forth on his knee. Her stomach twisted. "Where is my sister? What happened?"

"Whale Fin is gone," Grey Owl said.

"Gone?"

"Gone. It was better, he said."

"Who said? Where is my sister—?" Elik started to rise. Her face suddenly ashen. "My sister—she's dead?"

Nua slid closer, held her back. "Quiet yourself. No one is dead. Naiya and Whale Fin left together for the Fish River village, five days ago. It was after Allanaq returned. We talked. All of us. Whale Fin could no longer live in his uncle's household . . . "

Elik felt for the wall behind her. An emptiness settled on her shoulders. She had almost felt safe again, for one small moment. . . .

Grey Owl spoke quietly, explaining, "Whale Fin could no longer live with his uncle's deeds. He let it out that Naiya was eager to hold her husband's baby son, his first child in Fish River. We spoke together, in secret. He agreed that he could live with his uncle's death. But it would be easier, he said, to forget something his eyes had never seen."

"What are we saying?" Elik asked.

"We are saying," Little Pot answered, "that a man has come among us consumed with his own greed. A man who thinks nothing of using sickness-bringing power against us."

"My husband's soul wanders," Ani's Wife said, "because of what this man does. His body lies empty. I found a hole cut in his parka, a piece stolen from the hem to be used against him. To make him ill. It was a parka Seal Talker had borrowed. I want my husband alive again."

"And from my own head," Kahkik said, "Seal Talker cut hair, when I was sick. My wife found the strands in the doorway of our house."

"Then why do we wait?" Ani's Wife turned to the men. "If we all agree, and Whale Fin, who had the only blood right to vengeance, has left? What do we fear?"

"We fear the same things all people fear—" Grey Owl glanced worriedly toward Allanaq. "It is no small deed to kill a shaman."

"Unless we stand together," Nua said, "as in all things . . ."

There was a skittering sound on the roof above them, a night animal, or the wind. Or perhaps a pebble someone kicked. When the sound did not return, Malluar whispered, "It is difficult, and yet it may be done."

Bear Hand said, "I've heard of Songs with power to weaken an enemy—" He stopped.

Allanaq had risen. "I'll do it," he said.

"No!" Elik protested, but her voice was tiny as a bird's. What was he saying? He would be killed. Allanaq feared shamans . . . He'd said as much.

No other person showed a hint of surprise.

"Isn't this why we're here?" Allanaq asked. "Why I returned and why I've stayed hidden? Everyone knows the story of how I first came. That I've lived through this already."

Elik stepped to the floor. "You can't," she said. "You've a hunter's skill. Not the kind of strength it takes to fight a shaman. Not his hands, but his Power. His—"

"Hush!" Malluar rose, moved to stand between them. "We know you are a wife—"

Elik stopped short.

"—And we know a wife does not lightly send a husband off to die. But, listen—It may be done. But not by one man alone. Sit down. Both of you."

Nua pulled Elik's arm, reminding her to sit. *Wife, I am his wife. He is my husband. . . .*

Malluar reached inside the neck of her parka, pulled out a cord, at the end of a cord a pouch. From the pouch, she emptied something onto the floor planking for all to see.

It was the desiccated skin of a caribou's ear. Only a few sparse hairs remained, the rest had long since rubbed bald. "My cousin's amulet that I borrowed," Malluar said. "I couldn't trust it not to hear us whispering. Not to warn him."

She turned to Allanaq. "This woman—" she nodded toward Elik—"may be right. Partway. You say you fought a shaman, but I understood that that man won. Nor did you ever see what Seal Talker once was—the way a power came into him when his spirit helpers drew near. But—" Malluar turned to Elik.

"This man is also part right. If Seal Talker's amulets were to be weakened, then my cousin's skin would be as soft as any man's. There are secrets which I have, which I have kept and saved since he was born. There is a way, if we all work together. There is a way."

# Epilogue

~

They began their attack in the twilight hours before another dawn had risen. Allanaq, sitting cross-legged on the platform in Grey Owl's house, laid out his tools: a grooved whetstone for sharpening. An antler-handled engraver with a ground squirrel's incisor for the finishing work in the two wooden masks he was carving. His end scraper on a handle. The large side scraper without. His adze with a wolf head worked into the handle, and flared sides to hold his widest blade. It was one of the tools that had first set Bear Hand to standing behind his shoulder, suspicious at the way his blades bit deeper into wood, faster and with cleaner lines than Bear Hand had ever seen.

The eyes of these two masks would open only once. They would blink, the spirits lending strength would look out, and then they would close.

By the time Allanaq was done, each mask would be divided into two halves, the same as the mask Red Fox had worn: one side human, one spirit. One side he would paint with black, another with ground hematite for red. And when they were finished, he prayed, they would carry the strengths of both the Seal People and the Long Coast, for in both places a village sometimes came together against greed.

Allanaq spit on the driftwood log Bear Hand had pulled out from his pit cache, where it was stored. Before making a cut, even a small one, Allanaq rubbed in his saliva, so that when the mask was done and set over his face, the spirits would recognize who he was. What he wanted.

In the *qasgi*, where Seal Talker now spent his days, Meqo served his food and Bear Hand and Grey Owl, Blue-Shadow and Nagi sat with him and traded stories. Filled his time. Quieted his anger. At night, Meqo lay beside him whenever he complained of cold. She warmed his feet and picked his scalp, and told admiring stories she hoped he liked to hear.

Purposefully, Elik entered and left the house she shared with Malluar, so that Seal Talker knew where she was. She stood near the boat racks, on the paths, or near the frozen pond with Kimik or Squirrel or Two Ravens, making sure he'd believe the story they put out: that Elik had begun menstruating again, for the first time since the baby had been lost. But now that she was well, it happened that Malluar had grown a little ill. Elik needed to stay close, to care for her.

Seal Talker smiled when he heard the tale. It was enough for him that Elik was in the same village. There was no need to battle his cousin while there was illness surrounding her. The illness would leave, or Malluar would die. Either way, Seal Talker could wait.

A man might wait a lifetime to have what he wanted: revenge against an insult. A certain woman. In the end, though, he would have it. He needed only a little more time to plan.

At night, while Seal Talker slept, it was Meqo who unpacked the flaked blade Malluar had hidden inside her basket. And it was Meqo who slit the stitches that held his amulets that brought him strength. And in the early evening while the light faded and Seal Talker drowsed, Meqo slipped out from the bedding, from his side.

"Where are you going?" Seal Talker murmured.

"Outside, to the snow." She made her voice sound husky and content. "Wait for me, I'll come right back."

Two steps down the entry well, along the passage, two steps up again to the outside door where her husband Bear Hand stood waiting. She pushed the shaman's amulets to his hand. "Take them," she said. "If he asks, I won't know where they are."

Seal Talker murmured as Meqo climbed back in bed. "You're warm still," he said, and he rested his hand on the smooth inside of her thigh. She sighed then shaped herself to fit his side. He rolled over in his sleep, and Meqo waited till his mouth relaxed, forgot its words. His eyes stayed closed. She didn't have to lie.

Bear Hand hurried the amulets to Malluar.

And it was Kahkik's wife, Long Feather, with her hands so small, Seal Talker never would suspect a woman could do such a thing as cut his food with death. But she did. And later that night, while Meqo sang and exchanged gossip with Seal Talker of the way things used to be, Long Feather thought only of her husband, and how Seal Talker, with his greed and his anger, had chased Kahkik's soul so far from his body, it almost hadn't returned.

Following Malluar's instructions, Long Feather selected a frozen trout from her cache. It was a beautiful fish, with its back curving to the tail, the entire body encased in a layer of ice so thin that the colors still showed, silver and spots of green. The kind of fish a man would gladly want to eat.

Quickly, she carried it along the path beyond the houses, to the humped, snow-covered mounds of the graveyard, where Malluar waited in the dark, beside Olanna's grave.

With her heart pounding, Long Feather handed the fish to Malluar, then turned her back and stood there, stiffly listening to the sound of Malluar's small digging stick shoveling into the snow.

Malluar buried the fish as far inside the rocks that covered Olanna's body as she could reach, then patted the snow back in place, and spit it shut. They walked back to the houses together, one old woman, one no longer young.

They made so many tracks, a man following would have to give up in confusion.

Until the next night when they returned. Malluar pulled out the trout, carefully—she would burn the mittens that touched the fish. On the outside, it appeared the same. That was good. But on the inside, it was touched with death. Death that had spread through the meat of the fish and would spread in the body of the man who swallowed it, ate it. Though he shit it out his other end, it would leave its trail first, before it was done.

And it was that morning that Meqo slipped outside the *qasgi*, so early only women and the most eager hunters would be awake. She waited anxiously, till she heard her cousin's footsteps crunching on the snow. Long Feather handed the sack across. "For Olanna," she whispered. "For Two Ravens' child. For what he did to Kahkik."

"And for our Bent Point cousins," Long Feather added. "Iluperaq and Ema. For Alu and for Gull. For Blue-Shadow's grandchild. For Old Ani. For us all."

With seawater for salt and a layer of choicest blubber to make it sweet, Meqo cooked the meal. And smiled as she served it to Seal Talker. Who took it and ate it. Without benefit of his amulets to chase away the death. He lifted a full half length of the fish to his mouth, bit down, and with his knife sliced it smoothly in front of his lips.

A wave of drifted snow hid the entry to the Long Coast's oldest, abandoned *qasgi*. Not the *qasgi* that had been their ceremonial house for all the years that Elik remembered, but the older one. The one that had already been abandoned when Malluar was a girl.

One behind the other, they bent through the collapsed door, then straightened to feel their feet on dry frozen gravel inside. Elik pulled the stone lamp from inside her parka, then unwrapped the burning coal she'd brought to start the wick.

A moment later and the light stretched to the rotted

roofboards overhead, the clumps of fallen sod, tiny piles of black droppings where voles had searched for food.

Malluar stood there, staring. More than half her lifetime had passed since last she breathed this air. Still, she remembered the place so clearly that she could almost see her shadow reaching from beneath the platform where she'd crouched.

She'd been hiding while her uncle set the lidded bowl down on the floor. He'd dug the hole—there. Exactly there, beneath the floorboard. It hadn't been easy; he was ancient even then, humpbacked and half-blind, as if all the time spent talking with spirits had cost far more than the price he knew.

Behind her, the platform was gone. No matter. Her uncle had never found her out. Malluar could almost hear herself breathing, the echo of stale air catching as the girl she'd been forced herself to lie still, to breathe only in rhythm with her uncle's digging stick.

"Take your shovel," Malluar said. Elik followed where she pointed. "I won't be able to touch it you know, the container. My uncle painted it with eyes and the eyes would see me. And seeing me, they would tell.

"But you—" Malluar pulled her glance away from the floor. "You weren't here. Not you, and not your name. The eyes of that container will not see what hadn't been born. When it's out, keep it hidden."

Malluar moved as far from Elik's corner as the frozen walls allowed. She sat, settled her legs, and started humming—the strongest songs she owned, those she had composed with only the wind and white snow as listeners. She took them out and sang them now, used them as a shield against the memories. *Ayaai, aya ay ai ayaai*, she sang, a magical tune, stronger than ordinary words.

Elik started to dig.

Down on her knees, her back to Malluar, she chipped and scratched at the frozen ground. The planking that had once been the floor of the ceremonial house was rotted. She easily tore the first layer out.

It had been rotted then, too, she remembered. Winter, but warm enough inside that the smell of damp had been everywhere. Elik turned, looked over her shoulder, through Malluar.

Kimik's shadow lay across the floor where she and Iluperaq had rolled into the corner together, laughing. She could hear them still, light and so young, the way her brother's voice used to sound.

There was another shadow. Not one: two of them. Hers and her cousin Allanaq's. Standing by the wall. There.

Elik watched the shadow turn, the same as the girl and boy had also turned. First in curiosity toward the sound of Kimik's and Iluperaq's laughter knocking against walls, floorboards, dirt. The new tastes of their young bodies like salt and sweat and sweet oils all mixed together on their tongues.

Except it wasn't like that for the other two. The curiosity faded. There were too many shadows inside the walls, shadows watching shadows. There were voices and eyes and powerful, powerful secrets buried in the floor, peering from the ceiling. They could feel them. The shadow-Elik cried in sudden fear: too much. Allanaq felt it also. While their friends laughed, they backed away toward the entry, ducked through the door, pulling each other away. . . .

Elik remembered the rest of it now: it hadn't been here that she and Allanaq had come together. Their fingers had touched: there beside the door, where Malluar was sitting now. But they'd panicked and run, terrified, not for anything they'd seen, but for what they felt hiding inside the walls.

The gravel floor chipped away in sheets and brittle clumps. A shallow layer, and then a sound. Elik hit something. Carefully, she chipped around. The dirt lifted in needles, in shards of frozen ground.

Finally, she pulled it out: a lidded clay bowl, cracked but whole. There'd been paint; it was faded now, all but the thickest lines. Behind her, Malluar's humming stopped.

Without turning to show her, Elik slipped the bowl into the sack they'd brought. Hurriedly, she spread back the dirt, tamped it down. She laid what remained of the flooring back in place, then, quietly, she and Malluar backed outside.

Ani's Wife pushed aside the frost-hardened door flap of her house and stepped cautiously outside. The night was clear, the stars a thousand windows through the sky. Slicing through them, in a band that moved from the sea toward the mountains, a green-and-red-tinged ribbon of northern lights whipped and danced.

Ani's Wife ducked her head, pulled her face inside her hood. There was power in the sky tonight, enough so she preferred to be inside, safe with her husband, who likewise preferred to be alive. Not dead.

With hurried steps, she crossed between the houses, marking upright boat racks, food caches, anything solid and familiar.

She was shaking as she climbed into Malluar's house, more with her own fears than from cold. "He's the same," she said, as soon as she'd climbed inside. "My husband. No worse, he says, but he said the same thing yesterday. And today—he hardly speaks at all."

Malluar took Ani's Wife's hand, calming her. "Not much longer now. Everything's in place. You remember what we said?"

Ani's Wife nodded.

"Good. You must tell Seal Talker that Ani is worse. Say it any way you like. That his hands and feet are swollen, his breathing loud and wrong. Say that you're afraid if Ani comes to the qasgi, the death-spirit near him might endanger others. He needs to go—alone."

"To my house," Ani's Wife repeated. She looked behind Malluar to where Elik sat, fastening tie lines to a large, hooped mask. Seeing her, recognizing the mask, Ani's Wife grew calmer. "I'll say he can't walk. That his eyes are open but he doesn't see."

"Good," Malluar said. "Remember—say anything, but don't go home. Come, I'll walk with you as far as Bear Hand's house."

Elik waited till she heard their footsteps disappear along the entry. She set down Allanaq's mask, then crossed to the platform, where the gut parka Malluar had sewn for her lay hidden beneath their sleeping furs.

She slipped it on. The winter-tanned intestine felt nearly weightless over her parka. It rustled as she straightened it. She'd have to be careful Seal Talker didn't hear. Still, it was worth the chance. Binding her life to the life that had once belonged to the gut would keep her safe, out of harm.

With her eyes closed, Elik lifted the large hooped mask in front of her face. She fitted her chin to the hollowed cup of the mask's chin, fastened the ties behind her head.

In the dark, behind closed eyes, she sang the song Wolverine had given. "*Ya, ya yu, ya axa, yu. Animal, Strong Animal, you are coming to my Song. You come nearer to the entry of my house. Ya, ya yu, ya axa yu.*"

Slowly, she opened her eyes, peered out through the slits.

Instantly, she saw herself high above the beach ridge on the Long Coast's shore, as if she were looking down through a thin layer of clouds to the snow-covered beaches, the houses below.

Farther inland, a single dark wolverine circled near the hump of a hidden burrow, scenting out its prey. She smiled, and the wolverine's ears flicked. It looked up, found her. The wolverine spent the next few moments leaving a spray of urine to mark the burrow, then quickly it raced after her, following the long line of shadow she cast on the snow.

The vision took her higher. She saw the way the land expanded from where she had begun: house then village, shore then sea. And not only along the snow-covered surface, but down, deeper. The vision took her below the ground, showed her the houses of the spirits living inside the earth. To the *inuas*. Their faces. The spirits who dwelt inside the rock, inside the hill. Visible now. Knowing her. Seeing her. Greeting her from within.

Farther away, she saw a place that might have been Allanaq's: a village on a long finger of land, houses like theirs, except the doors all pointed to the sea. It seemed a good place for seals to come, for walrus to haul out of the water onto the ice. For the great whales to pass, in line upon line, spouting, blowing, singing their high-pitched calls. It was a place where Real People might live, no matter that it was far from here.

She came back down.

She was ready now.


Allanaq crouched on the snow-covered mound of Old Ani's house, on the rear face, away from the cold northerly wind. His hands burned with cold from dragging the skins he'd piled for a blind, but his face felt warm beneath the mask. The wide hoops were safely hidden.

It was a strange thing, realizing he was the one on the rooftop this time.

The season was different, it was winter now, the Shortest Ice Moon. That other time, when Red Fox's men had been on the roof and he was the one inside, it had been late summer, the water open. A boat had been waiting at the shore.

Beneath himself, inside the house, if all had gone as planned, the lamps would be darkened. Only the one lamp closest to the rear platform should be lit, next to where Old Ani lay sick.

All of Ani's coverings but one had been rolled back. Ani's Wife had taken paint and rubbed his face and drawn lines darkening his jaw, hoping the strange features would pull Seal Talker's curiosity forward, to the man in the bed rather than the one on the roof, or the girl hiding in the corner, behind the grass mat they'd hung against the wall.

The wind swept briskly, nearly masking the sound of Seal Talker's steps. But Allanaq was too tense, too ready to miss the shuffling sound of boots approaching the house.

Allanaq paced himself. He crawled to the flattened rooftop exactly at the moment Seal Talker ducked into the passage. Positioned himself at the skyhole just as the shaman stepped up through the entry well into the house.

He slid aside the one remaining rock that held the gut window in place, peeled back the corner and watched.

In the house below, Seal Talker crossed the floor toward the sleeping bench.

Old Ani sounded sick indeed. He moaned, kicked at his blankets. And his face: he looked near dead. Ashes and bone. He raised himself painfully up on one arm. "Is that you, Seal Talker?" he asked.

The shaman took a half step back. "Old Ani? You're awake? Yes, I'm here . . ." The floorboards creaked. Seal Talker heard, but he didn't turn. His attention was drawn to the man in the bed. How ill he appeared.

There was a rustling sound. This time Seal Talker looked to the shadows. To the bed again. "Ani?" Something was behind him. No. On the roof . . .

Allanaq dropped through the opening, hit the floor and caught his balance. As if he'd done this before, as if he were reliving a memory, he lifted the tip of his blade, circled it near the shaman.

Seal Talker swerved toward the sound. Who was it? He couldn't tell. The face was hidden behind the mask—wood and willow, feather and bone. There was another sound. He spun again. Where was it? Who?

Out from the shadowed wall, a second figure appeared, this one also wearing a mask, a match, except that the first was carved with the upturned mouth of a man. The second was a woman.

They flanked him from two directions, both watching for a sign.

Their efforts—the amulets, the death-tinged food, their songs—had anything made a difference?

Seal Talker needed only a moment to collect himself, to realize what this was. Not demons. Not Forest People. Only a man and a woman wearing masks. And the masks themselves, they were no more nor less than any he'd carved before.

He set his arms to his hips, allowed the first hint of a smile to come to his mouth. "You cannot touch me," he said.

Allanaq prodded with his knife. "We don't have to. Not our hands, and not our weapons. You are already dead."

Seal Talker scoffed at the threat. He'd brought a knife. Somewhere, where was it? In his pouch, yes. He'd have time to reach it if he distracted them, kept talking . . .

He looked from the man to the other figure, the woman. She was holding something. He hadn't noticed it before. He cursed his eyes for giving so much trouble lately. In the dark it was difficult to see . . .

He stared a moment. Below the mask's carved mouth, there were human hands. In the hands, a pot. No—not a pot exactly. The shape was somehow different. He narrowed his gaze. A lidded bowl. He'd seen it somewhere. Where? The curved sides. The painting, it was faded now, but . . .

With a sting of fear, Seal Talker remembered. Two times in his life his shaman-uncle had shown him that lidded bowl. Once when he was a boy, on a winter night he was feasted for killing his first ermine. The second time he'd been hardly older. The ceremony had been private; the occasion of his first dream-vision. His uncle had shown him the bowl, then buried it again for safety. Not opening it, with Seal Talker's afterbirth inside, not even his uncle would have dared.

But his uncle was long dead, and no one else could have known. No one—in all those years . . .

Seal Talker stepped backward. His mouth hung open, his heart beat wildly against his chest.

Elik lifted the bowl slowly, so he would feel the pain, every speck and weight of pain. She removed the lid. Held it out—there was no mistaking her intent. Slowly, she tipped the open bowl toward the floor. It took a moment, the weight inside was so slight—and then a falling of dust settled toward the floor, lighter than ash. His soul spilled toward the floor.

Seal Talker stepped backward. Somehow he managed to find his blade, lift it toward the man. He hesitated. Which way to strike? Toward the woman? But the bowl was already empty. Empty . . .

His vision dimmed. The house, it was so dark. The man so close, and sad, even through the thick eyes of the mask he saw sadness coming after him.

Seal Talker's knife grew heavy. Too heavy for his arm to support. He lowered it. His hands had no strength to them. Like snow they felt, falling without wind, a weight like nothing. Nothing at all. The knife dropped through his fingers.

He turned to the woman-mask. Was there nothing left inside the bowl? He felt so light, as if he couldn't feel his feet against the floor. He started to fall, caught himself, and tottered again, backward.

Into the man. And the blade in the man's hand below the eyes. And the hand. The mask. The blade . . .

Allanaq gripped his knife in both hands. Heavily, with all his strength, he jabbed into the shaman's back.

Seal Talker's moan filled the house. His hands shot up, his legs gave out. His weight heaved down, dragging the blade, forcing it between his ribs, as he fell forward, face toward the floor.

Seal Talker's weight dragged the knife from Allanaq's hands. Allanaq stepped backward, letting go the handle, letting him fall, watching the pool of dark blood already spilling along the floor.

Allanaq turned to the platform to see Old Ani lift himself up and sit. He was alive, his narrow eyes staring at Seal Talker's back. For one shadowed moment, Allanaq thought it was his own father he saw. But no—the tattoo pattern changed, lip holes appeared. Not his father, no. But a different man, a good man, whole and alive.

"Is he dead?" Old Ani asked.

"Dying, yes," Allanaq whispered.

"We need to leave. Help me get down, please . . ."

"Leave, yes," Allanaq repeated, but he wasn't listening. He turned, glanced to where Elik had been standing against the wall. He couldn't see her. He untied the mask. It was heavy and awkward but it had served its purpose. He pulled it from his face.

The bowl was there, lying empty on the floor, but Elik was gone. Confused, Allanaq looked to the grass hanging where she'd hid. To the entry well.

Old Ani touched his arm. "She's gone," he said. "As we should be. It isn't safe here. We have to be out."

The five days of prescribed mourning were finished.

Four, being the man's number, would be sufficient for the village, Malluar explained. No sewing. No hunting. And for Allanaq—four also. For Elik and herself she called for five days, five being the woman's number.

In addition, because she preferred caution to chance, Malluar announced that the five days should be passed in confinement, in their house.

This second, more difficult requirement she accepted on advice because, as Little Pot said, Malluar herself was Seal Talker's nearest relative. Also because it might help prevent Seal Talker's spirit from coming along later and remembering that it was Elik who spilled his soul in the first place.

Gossip still reached them, of course. Even confined to the house, there were people kind enough to drop a few loud words as they chanced to walk near the skyhole. They heard, for instance, that before the first day was done, an old suit of eider-duck clothes had been found and Seal Talker's body had been dressed, then taken out through the skyhole. That the house had afterward been sealed and would be abandoned, since neither Old Ani nor Ani's Wife had any wish to return. They heard also that the body had been left out on the snow, a safe distance from the village. That Seal Talker, along with his favorite harpoon heads and a bowl, had been covered in rocks and that the men who carried him, flexed and wrapped in caribou skins, had walked backward when they were done, disguising their trail with urine and the pure smoke of burned grass.

At the end of the fifth day, when Elik was permitted to leave the house, she carried the urine pots and emptied them in the snow behind the house. On her second trip out she tossed the few scraps of bones they hadn't eaten to the long-legged dog who'd moved in beneath their food cache.

On the next trip, Malluar shuffled out beside Elik.

A bank of low clouds had filled the sky in above the sea ice. White-on-white. It was difficult to tell them apart. Horizon, sky, and ice blurred to a single landscape. No difference between what was above and what was below.

Except that, as they stood admiring the cool air, they found the shape of one dot moving along the ice. Someone walking in toward shore.

Malluar touched Elik's arm. The figure kept walking, not in a straight line but veering widely, the way any boy of the Real People must learn to walk if he wants to grow to be a man: poking with his ice-testing stick, careful of light-colored slush, of holes and rotten places, deceptive drifts. This man was dragging something behind.

It was only awhile more till Allanaq stood before them.

Elik hesitated, not quite certain if she was unmarried, in which case it would be unseemly to stand closer. Or if she was married. In which case the seal meat belonged to her.

The seal lay on its back, a gash cut through its lip, then looped with a thong to the drag handle. It looked fat, with its skin rippling and content, as if it recognized where it had come.

Malluar smiled above her tattooed chin, wide as a girl with her joking. "Go on, butcher it," she teased. "Who else does a man bring his catch to if not his wife?"

Elik stole a glance at Allanaq. "I brought no water for its thirst."

"Spit in its mouth. The seal knows."

Elik leaned over the dry, black face, then looked up. "I have no knife," she said, and this time, she let her gaze rest a moment longer on Allanaq's face.

With a smile he didn't try to hide, Allanaq fished for something inside his parka, handed it to Malluar.

Malluar opened her hand. "Ah, look at this blade," she said admiringly. "Here's a stone that knows the way to stay sharp. None of those flat slabs of slate the boys pick off the beach." She passed it to Elik. "I had a feeling someone might bring me a present today."

Elik leaned out to reach the seal. She made the first cut between the fore flippers. Then a line from its chin to the arms, deep into the skin, easing the blade when she touched bone.

Skin and fat together; she cut section by section, the way a wife knew to share out her husband's food. Allanaq stepped out of the way while Malluar crouched next to the seal. "That share—" she pointed.

"What, the hind flippers?"

"Yes, that's *aigga*. You cut that one for your husband's hunting partner." Elik glanced to Allanaq. "That could be Drummer," she said. "A man needs a partner beyond his own family's house." Allanaq smiled. She made the second cut.

"Kimik's father could be second partner; the shoulder. You call him Shoulder now, too. And *Pengraliq,* the left rib." Malluar nudged Elik's arm. "Make the cut wider, up there. That share's important."

Elik shifted the blade where Malluar pointed.

"And the neck: *Uyaquq.* Watch you get the spine with the meat attached, not the lower vertebrae." Malluar wrapped her arms around her knees, rocked back. "It's a good way to eat," she said. "Knowing who your relatives are."

# Author's Note

The names of Elik's Bent Point village, the village on the Long Coast shore and Allanaq's Seal People's place cannot be found on any current map of Alaska. While I did take the liberty of borrowing historic Native place-names for several minor locations, the goals of my research aimed not so much toward describing a specific locale as toward finding a way to balance *Summer Light* somewhere between the ethnographies I'd been reading and the archaeological record itself.

In the earliest stages—before any work on the story had begun—I knew only that the novel would be set in Alaska's northwest coast, and that I preferred writing about a people who lived earlier than the traditional Eskimo whale hunters, but not so far in the distant past that I couldn't feel comfortable leaning on the rich ethnographic sources available, work such as that done by Knud Rasmussen in his *Report on the Fifth Thule Expedition* (1921–24), and Edward Nelson's *The Eskimo About Bering Strait,* published by the Smithsonian in 1899.

But who did that mean I would be writing about, and which specific culture? The story needed to locate itself not only in a physical geography that determined the seasonal round (What food sources were they dependent on? Were there settled villages?), but also a geography of time. The choices mattered immensely as they would become the foundation for everything that followed.

After much browsing through the Alaska Collection of the Rasmuson Library at the University of Alaska, Fairbanks, I eventually settled on a reference from *Inua, the Spirit World of the Bering Sea Eskimo,* wherein authors William Fitzhugh and Susan Kaplan helped narrow my search: "Between 500 B.C. and A.D. 500, several distinct Paleo-Eskimo cultures existed in the coastal regions of western Alaska, including Ipiutak in the region north of the Seward Peninsula . . ." And then south of Bering Strait where, "the local early Paleo-Eskimo culture developed into a different culture known as Norton."

Ipiutak and Norton, the two cultures I decided on as models for *Summer Light,* offered fascinating, suggestive contrasts. Helge Larsen and Froelich Rainey, summarizing their original excavations in *Ipiutak and the Arctic Whale Hunting Culture,* wrote that: "The general impression is that of highly complex and elaborate burial customs . . . A ghost cult and shamanism were the two most conspicuous elements of the spiritual culture of the Ipiutak people."

And while the Ipiutak's openwork ivory artifacts and finely flaked tools are often called "spectacular," J. L. Giddings in *Ancient Men of the Arctic* described the Norton people as being, "more practical in their outlook, less burdened by the demands of religious and artistic excellence . . ." Writing in somewhat harsh terms, Giddings decided that, "Common to all Norton people was their almost haphazard work with soft slate. Roughly scratching it into shape and polishing only its edges, they produced but few types of blades."

With the archaeology for a backdrop—but recognizing, even before I had a first draft in hand, that there was never going to be such a thing as complete accuracy—it remained my hope to have the plot arise from events that might have been plausible. There are, for instance, many accounts of walrus stealing seals as they're towed behind boats. Justice in traditional Eskimo villages was often meted out by village consensus. And shamans did go into trances and speak with the spirits of the animals.

With those explanations behind, it becomes necessary to apologize for the vast simplifications I allowed for the sake of the story: the differences in seal-hunting techniques, for instance, or the use of labrets, or the question of whether there actually were *Qasgis* at this early date. And perhaps most of all, the postulation that the dates allowed contact between the Norton phases and Ipiutak peoples.

That Allanaq and Elik would have been able to understand each other is my own invention. The branch of the Eskimo-Aleut language with the largest number of speakers in Alaska today is the Central Yup'ik Eskimo of western Alaska. Sometime earlier than a thousand years ago, roughly in the area of the Bering Sea, Eskimo languages split into the Yup'ik and Inupiaq, now spoken in northern Alaska. The Yup'ik spellings I have used for Elik's Real People come from the *Yup'ik Eskimo Dictionary,* compiled by Steven A. Jacobson for the Alaska Native Language Center at the University of Alaska. The place-names used in chapter 7 are from the Koyukon Athapaskan Indian language. It isn't possible after two thousand years to know which languages were spoken exactly where. What we can know is that people have always traveled Alaska's coast, hunting, trading, and maintaining ties with distant relatives. For the sake of the narrative, I describe these languages as mutually intelligible.

*Summer Light* is a work of fiction. The errors, and there may be many, are mine alone. I had thought that the effort I put into writing this book was large; having finished I see now that what came back was far the greater gift, enriching my life many times over.

For a brief reading list, I would like to recommend the following works:

Fitzhugh, William W., and Aron Crowell, *Crossroads of Continents: Cultures of Siberia and Alaska,* Washington, D.C.: Smithsonian Institution Press, 1988.

Hall, Edwin S., Jr., *The Eskimo Storyteller: Folktales from Noatak, Alaska,* Knoxville: University of Tennessee Press, 1975.

Nelson, E. W., *The Eskimo About Bering Strait,* Washington, D.C.: U.S. Bureau of American Ethnology, 1899.

Rainey, Froelich, *The Whale Hunters of Tigara,* New York: Anthropological Papers of the American Museum of Natural History, 1947.

Nelson, Richard, *Hunters of the Northern Ice,* Chicago: University of Chicago Press, 1969.

Rasmussen, Knud, *The Alaskan Eskimos, as Described in the Posthumous Notes of Knud Rasmussen,* Report of the Fifth Thule Expedition, 1921–1924, vol.10, no. 3, Copenhagen, 1931.

To the people who have supported and contributed to my efforts, I would like to acknowledge first and always Luke, for his unfailing patience, Selena, for her clear-sighted editorial reassurances, and Grier, for the many turns he gave up at the keyboard while his mother worked through one more draft. To my father Joe Guttenberg, for his willingness to stand at the copy machine and help with the driving, and show up with lunch the many times I forgot to eat. Special thanks also to Gloria Fischer, for allowing me to tap into her encyclopedic background; and to Nancy and Nicholas, my first nephew.

I would also like to thank Karen Olanna, Kyan, Tonya, and Brons for so warmly opening their home in Shishmaref and making it possible for me to walk on the sea ice I'd been writing about; Loretta Sinnok and Rachel Stasenko, also of Shishmaref, for their generous laughter while allowing me to "help" butcher a bearded seal on the spring ice; Jim Stimpfle and Bernadette Alvanna-Stimpfle, for their hospitality in Nome; Craig Gerlach of the University of Alaska, Fairbanks, for the conversation on harpoon types and throwing boards; Larry Kaplan of the Alaska Native Language Center for his help (which I apologize for not always following) with spellings; and to the Elmer E. Rasmuson Library at the University of Alaska, Fairbanks, which mailed out more overdue notices to a certain armchair anthropologist than she'd like to admit.

Among the many friends who always cared to ask how the writing was going, I'd like to thank John Bartlett, for sharing his enthusiasm and childhood stories; Susan McInnis, whose encouragements have grown into a volume I've come to depend on, and Thom Hart, for sitting across the table at Hot Licks and listening to my earliest ramblings. To Charlie and Sheree, for sharing the kayaks and the angst. To Libby, William, and Sasha, for the pod of killer whales, the breeding grounds of jellyfish, and the rocking chairs we will someday find the time to share. To Naomi, for her impeccable taste in books. To the seal in Kachemak Bay, who really did climb up on Selena and Ashlyn's kayaks, allowing them to touch it. To Ann Scarborough, for the many phone calls sharing the writer's life. To Jerah Chadwick in Unalaska, whose early approval of the first three chapters came as a great relief. To Linda Schandelmeier, friend, poet, and editorial advisor at many an odd hour of the night. To Madge Clark, who always listened, and to my mother, who whispers from behind my shoulder.

Thanks especially to my editors Christopher Schelling, who kept asking when I was going to do an Alaskan story, and John Silbersack who brought that story to HarperCollins. And to my agent and friend, Jim Frenkel.

August 1994
Fairbanks, Alaska

# ☰ HarperPrism

**SMALL GODS by Terry Pratchett.** International bestseller Terry Pratchett brings magic to life in his latest romp through Discworld, a land where the unexpected always happens—usually to the nicest people, like Brutha, former melon farmer, now The Chosen One. His only question: Why?

**0-06-109217-7 — $4.99**

**MAGIC: THE GATHERING™—ARENA by William R. Forstchen.** Based on the wildly bestselling trading-card game, the first novel in the *MAGIC: THE GATHERING™* novel series features wizards and warriors clashing in deadly battles. The book also includes an offer for two free, unique MAGIC cards.

**0-06-105424-0 — $4.99**

**SEAROAD:Chronicles of Klatsand by Ursula K. Le Guin.** Here is the culmination of Le Guin's lifelong fascination with small island cultures. In a sense, the Klatsand of these stories is a modern day successor to her bestselling *ALWAYS COMING HOME*. A world apart from our own, but part of it as well.

**0-06-105400-3 — $4.99**

**CALIBAN'S HOUR by Tad Williams.** The bestselling author of *TO GREEN ANGEL TOWER* brings to life a rich and incandescent fantasy tale of passion, betrayal, and death. The beast Caliban has been searching for decades for Miranda, the woman he loved—the woman who was taken from him by her father Prospero. Now that Caliban has found her, he has an hour to tell his tale of unrequited love and dark vengeance. And when the hour is over, Miranda must die.... Tad Williams has reached a new level of magic and emotion with this breathtaking tapestry in which yearning and passion are entwined.

**Hardcover, 0-06-105204-3 — $14.99**

# and Tomorrow

**W**RATH OF GOD by Robert Gleason. An apocalyptic novel of a future America about to fall under the rule of a murderous savage. Only a small group of survivors are left to fight — but they are joined by powerful forces from history when they learn how to open a hole in time. Three legendary heroes answer the call to the ultimate battle: George S. Patton, Amelia Earhart, and Stonewall Jackson. Add to that lineup a killer dinosaur and you have the most sweeping battle since *THE STAND*.
**Trade paperback, 0-06-105311-2 — $14.99**

**T**HE X-FILES™ by Charles L. Grant. America's hottest new TV series launches as a book series with FBI agents Mulder and Scully investigating the cases no one else will touch — the cases in the file marked X. There is one thing they know: The truth is out there.
**0-06-105414-3 — $4.99**

**T**HE WORLD OF DARKNESS™: VAMPIRE— DARK PRINCE by Keith Herber. The ground-breaking White Wolf role-playing game Vampire: The Masquerade is now featured in a chilling dark fantasy novel of a man trying to control the Beast within.
**0-06-105422-4 — $4.99**

**T**HE UNAUTHORIZED TREKKERS' GUIDE TO *THE NEXT GENERATION* AND *DEEP SPACE NINE* by James Van Hise. This two-in-one guidebook contains all the information on the shows, the characters, the creators, the stories behind the episodes, and the voyages that landed on the cutting room floor.
**0-06-105417-8 — $5.99**

## HarperPrism
An Imprint of HarperPaperbacks

PR-001